Under the Torrid Caribbean Sun,

the island of Bimini Springs lay like a dream of paradise. But for those who came to this fabulous resort, the dream soon turned into a hellish Walpurgisnight of passion and perversity.

For on this island money could buy anything . . . every bizarre desire could be transformed into reality. The staff was always ready to serve the guests' pleasure, whatever that pleasure might be . . . and the guests themselves never ceased in their quest for the ultimate in sensation, in self-abandonment . . .

Yes, on Bimini Springs, money could buy anything . . . anything except the happiness that desperately driven men and women feverishly sought.

The Resort

by

CHARLES BEARDSLEY

THIRD PRINTING

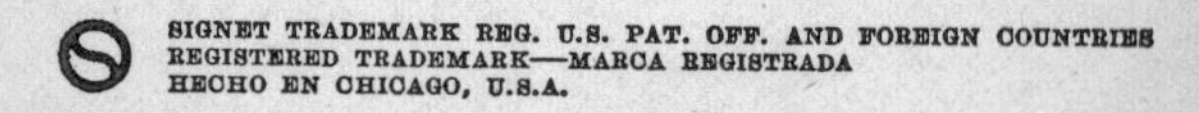

SIGNET, SIGNET CLASSICS, SIGNETTE, MENTOR AND PLUME BOOKS
are published by The New American Library, Inc.,
1301 Avenue of the Americas, New York, New York 10019

FIRST PRINTING, MARCH, 1972

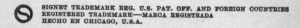

PRINTED IN THE UNITED STATES OF AMERICA

For Harry G. Frohman

Part

❁ ONE ❁

A few minutes before ten o'clock on a mid-January night, Terence P. Thompson walked into his spacious bedroom and stared for a moment at himself in the mirrored wall—a tall, bald, rather spare-framed man with an almost military bearing.

"You crafty old bastard!" he said aloud, and grinned conspiratorially at his image. "You're still one step ahead of them all!"

His plans were completed; after three years' virtual immobility he was going to move, and strike fast.

Thompson slid back the central mirror panel, took an old cashmere sweater from the clothes rack, and pulled it over his white, open-necked shirt. From a top shelf he selected a crumpled gray fedora and jammed it on his skull at a rakish angle, looking a bit like Paul Muni in *Scarface*, a resemblance he found amusing. Then, humming to himself, he strode briskly to the rear of his penthouse apartment atop the twelve-story office complex that served as his headquarters. The penthouse-capped edifice was the central feature of Thompson's sprawling 100,000-acre estate and sat on a massive bluff overlooking the rugged Big Sur coastline of California.

Avoiding the private patrolmen who had guarded his elevators around the clock for the past three years, Thompson eased his thin frame through a long-unused fire door and walked the twelve flights down an interior fire-escape route to the parking lot behind the office complex. Thompson was reasonably sure of leaving the building unrecognized, for no one except his very closest aides and his estranged wife had seen him face-to-face in more than a decade.

Thompson was in high spirits, enjoying his furtive getaway to the fullest.

In the parking lot two Cadillacs waited for him, and a retinue of employees, first among them his personal aide, Dan Francovich. Also Carl Winchester, his corporate attorney; John Moore, patents expert; and Abel Rose, his financial adviser. All good, able men, thought Thompson. And slightly apart stood the two male nurses who functioned as his personal servants and bodyguards. All were gathered to accompany Thompson to the jet airstrip he had built for himself some three miles from the penthouse office complex.

Thompson climbed into the rear seat of the lead Cadillac with Dan Francovich, his current favorite. The three advisers and two male nurses followed in the second Cadillac.

Thompson's mood was jovial as they drove off. "You ready for the big push, Danny boy?"

Dan Francovich smiled and nodded. "I'm ready for anything. You're going to be big news again, Terry. You really think you want it this way?"

"*They* want it this way, the dear fickle public. Once you start fighting *them* for your privacy, they won't ever leave you alone."

"This time they're due for a surprise," Francovich said. "A lot of them really think you're dead. You haven't shown your face anywhere for a long time."

"And more like ten since they've caught me for a photograph," Thompson boasted. "But why should I face the public? If I need a deal, you or the boys arrange everything for me. It's your job. And if I need a broad who'll keep her mouth shut and her legs open for the right price, the service has a long list of likely lovelies."

"Sure, of course," Francovich replied, for if that's the way his boss wanted it, that was the way it would have to be. Forgetting entirely about Marilyn Thompson. "I think we gave them the slip—" Francovich referred to the elevator guards back at the complex. More and more during the past six months, Francovich found himself lapsing all too easily into the big man's clichés. The twenty-five-year disparity in their ages was more apparent in speech than in point of view, he knew.

"Dumb, paid bastards," Thompson growled. "Dumb because I didn't hire them, and bastards because they'll report to Alexander as soon as they figure you and the boys aren't around." He laughed harshly. "Hey, I'll bet

Alexander's going to be mighty surprised when he finds out we've folded our tents and quietly stolen away."

"How soon do you think he'll know?"

Thompson stroked his chin. "Two, three days, maybe. But he'll have to use legal means to investigate. Even though he thinks he owns them, the guards won't let him in counter to my standing orders. They're heavily bonded against that contingency. I made special arrangements last month."

"Oh—?" said Francovich. His boss was always pulling little surprises out of thin air. He hadn't heard of the new bonding.

Ahead of them loomed the lights of the small airport station. Both men could see the silver silhouette of the Lockheed four-jet by the runway, its crew standing by.

"Paradise, here we come," said Thompson, his voice tense with excitement. "Never told you I hated flying, did I? Hell, I was scared shitless when I made that world speed record in the fighter, even more so that time I took the big bird up for a few minutes to satisfy the investors it would fly. My hands shook so goddam hard at the controls I thought for a second or two there I wasn't going to get it off the ground. . . ."

"You're always coming up with something," replied Francovich. Quite honestly, he felt that nothing Thompson ever told him would come as a surprise. He'd learned to expect the unique from this highly unpredictable man whose facets were endless. Miracles and cliff-hangers were everyday occurrences in Thompson's life. The only mystery was, how could Thompson settle down for three years' cloistered living atop his office complex, out there in the midst of a virtual wilderness? Especially when he'd once moved in the exalted ambiance of royalty and presidents, superstars and industrial giants—finally topping them all as his gross wealth and fame merged into tabloid myth. And then abruptly, America's richest tycoon since Howard Hughes—Getty didn't count; he was more or less an expatriate—he went into virtual seclusion, he became a living legend, a role in which the press had always fancied him.

The seclusion began with his second marriage: to Marilyn Mix, a Los Angeles heiress more than young enough to be his daughter. Speculation ran high as to why this society beauty had married Thompson at all. They seemed to have very little in common. Certainly she didn't need his money, the gossip columnists argued, for she was wealthy in her own right. Was it curiosity, the need to share the power and prestige of Thompson's vast domain? These and other questions were never satisfactorily answered during the time the couple lived together on Thompson's Big Sur estate. But when Marilyn departed of her own accord, actually disappearing from sight shortly afterward—from Thompson's organizational radar as well as the public's—the press had another field day in the face of Thompson's surly, stolid silence on the whole matter.

Now, suddenly, because Thompson's feud with Alexander had reached epic proportions and would inevitably make news, Thompson chose capriciously to focus the world press once more on his unphotographed features and make screaming, provocative headlines. For with his emergence from the period of anonymity, the inevitable clamor would start in all over again; he would be front-page news.

At sixty-two, one of the world's richest capitalists, Thompson's holdings covered the earth. Estimated at anywhere from $2 to $3 billion, his empire was privately owned and thus exempt from the laws that require public reports; he could do very much as he wished, exercising solitary control in the manner of an autocratic regent. His wealth was only exceeded by his arrogance. Having learned his lessons well when young through historical analysis, he moved empirically. All his orders to subordinates outside his immediate circle of aides were issued by telephone; he often wrote endless scribbled memoranda on large ruled sheets. He was above appearing personally among his subordinates, preferring by his inaccessibility to remain larger than life and generally feared. He acknowledged very few peers anywhere, and no superiors.

Thompson's obsession with privacy was well-known and all-devouring, Francovich learned early in his job. If you didn't respect it and circulated any stories to his subordinates that did not bear his stamp of approval, your days in the empire were definitely numbered. [Or even beyond it, for Thompson was famous for giving orders on down the line to outside business colleagues who feared him enough to do his blackballing.]

One of the reasons Francovich was moved from a high-salaried though relatively unimportant and powerless corporation attorney's duties on Thompson's busy legal staff to the number-one buddy spot in the empire was because he knew how to respect confidences. Hank Alexander, on the other hand, Thompson's present arch-enemy—there was always at least one—had become too powerful, too careless of his trusts, spread himself around too much, sought to build a personal fortune on the solid-rock base of Thompson's financial strength, and was long overdue for a disastrous fall. Alexander's personal holdings were about to be snatched from him and he'd be lucky, Francovich figured, if he managed to salvage a couple of hundred thousand from the several millions he'd built up. Alexander's ruin had been carefully scripted by Thompson over the past several months, and the nighttime exodus from the California citadel was Thompson's first overt move in a drama that had several ramifications. For Thompson never made a single move in any direction without several depending motives clearly in view.

So, step number one involved the professional demise of Hank Alexander. Step number two, known to Francovich, was a subplot, and of course Thompson had others up his sleeve, to be revealed whenever he was in the mood to act upon one of his carefully hoarded secrets. . . .

On the tarmac, Thompson paused a moment and surveyed the waiting Lockheed with obvious pride.

"Danny boy, this is what it's all about. When you've got it, you can do anything you want. You can change the world," he said, and stepped briskly up the gangway. Over his shoulder he added, "And if money can't buy it, it's not worth having. . . ."

Francovich suppressed a smile. Step number two in the latest corporate Thompson drama concerned the big man's never-ending search for a second headquarters site. It had to be slightly outside the continental United States, but not too far, and not controlled by Washington. Recent exhaustive considerations pointed either to the Caribbean or the South Atlantic, and they were on their way there for tentative exploration.

Step number three? Did this subplot concern Marilyn Mix Thompson, Francovich wondered? A woman for whom the gross bargaining power of money held no charms? Not even Thompson's private security force hounds had been able to track Marilyn beyond her mother's Beverly Hills mansion where that good woman had resolutely refused to answer any questions involving her daughter's whereabouts. Through her mother, Marilyn announced that she would not return to California and was holding out for a divorce. This Thompson adamantly refused to give her, his way of nursing wounded pride.

Quite recently a report had reached Thompson from a Florida security agency anxious to handle the Thompson Miami Medical Center's safety contract. Last glimpsed at a New York theater the previous autumn, the report claimed that Mrs. Thompson was now renting an apartment somewhere south of Coral Gables under an unspecified alias and was rumored to be considering a move to Nassau. She had visited travel agencies and obtained brochures.

If money can't buy it, it's not worth having. . . . This arrogant bigotry had a flip side, Francovich knew, which probably meant that the big man had already decided to go along with Marilyn and agree to the divorce, or pretend to, hoping she would return to him and he could then persuade her to stay. Thompson could certainly never hope to woo her back with anything like money. Or perhaps, buried somewhere in Thompson's peculiar psyche, too deep for it ever to surface in any other speech pattern, was the profound conviction that not even money could really buy what he coveted most: Marilyn's love and respect and devotion. But nevertheless, eschewing Thompson as well as his money, Marilyn meanwhile remained somewhere in hiding, expressing through her mother's attorney that she would stay hidden until she wished to identify herself again and that nothing Thompson did would have any influence on her actions. . . .

At the top of the gangway Captain Morris touched his visored cap with his index finger and said, "Good evening, sir!" to Thompson in reverent tones. Fifteen minutes later the Lockheed was airborne and soaring up into a cloudless, star-glittery California night, making a wide arc out over the Pacific, then heading toward Miami.

From his private forward cabin, Thompson got Captain Morris on the intercom and explained their altered course and destination. The captain started to protest.

"Just set her down like I say, Ed, and don't argue. . . ."

"But sir, the regulations require—"

"Fuck regulations!" bellowed Thompson. "Do as I say, goddamit! If Nassau wants to know what we're up to, tell them Terence P. Thompson's coming in for a landing. That ought to stir up their guts. And if they start to pussyfoot, just say that I'm planning maybe to buy the goddam islands and they'd all better watch their asses!"

"And why are *you* going to Bimini Springs?" asked Mrs. Tuttle, an old bird with bright plumage, of the portly gentleman across the aisle on the Bahama Airways flight from Nassau.

"We're both going," Phil Bernheim replied, "me and my wife. To dissolve some of the fine food we've eaten since news of my retirement."

"You don't look old enough to be retired," Mrs. Tuttle observed, always used to speaking her mind, whatever the results. "You look *preserved*. . . ."

"And then some," interjected Mrs. Bernheim from the window seat, across her husband's substantial stomach. "I'm light years ahead of him, and I ought to know."

"What my wife means," explained Mr. Bernheim, "is that she's sixty-two and I'm sixty. I've worked for a very liberal outfit for a long time. They're letting me retire with thirty years' service in."

"I wish my husband felt like that," said Mrs. Tuttle wistfully, "but Howard would never retire."

"What's your husband do?" inquired Mrs. Bernheim, squinting at Mrs. Tuttle. "Lean back, Phil, you're blocking my clear view."

"My husband is Howard Tuttle of Washington, D.C.," Mrs. Tuttle announced emphatically, in a very clear voice.

Mrs. Bernheim knew who he was, all right; so did Phil. Howard Tuttle had lobbied against practically everything the Bernheims believed in: aid for Israel, low-income housing for minority groups, black equality, even going as far back as the Rosenberg issue. Howard Tuttle was militantly against peace, pot, pills, and pornography.

"Ah yes," said Mrs. Bernheim, also in a very clear voice. "He's the well-known fascist."

Phil gave her a sharp but barely perceptible dig in the ribs. "For Christ's sake, Alice—"

Mrs. Tuttle turned a rare shade of violet and started fanning herself with a copy of *Reader's Digest* until her control returned. A moment later she said icily over the drone of the plane, "I don't believe that you're being fair to Howard. He's trying to uphold American traditions. . . ."

"Yes, but who for—?" demanded Mrs. Bernheim, whereupon Mrs. Tuttle, tight-lipped, merely glared at her and applied herself solely to *Reader's Digest*.

Under his breath Phil said to Alice, "Sometimes you piss me off, even if you are right."

Alice sent him the angry, sour look he knew so well that meant he wouldn't be off the hook for the rest of the day, maybe the rest of the week. "I'd never've come down here with you if I'd known it was going to be of those chauvinistic waterholes. You get me into the gruesomest messes, Phil. . . ."

"Bimini Springs is a high-class spa, nonsectarian and reputable, and you damn' well better shut up and not ruin everything for us."

"Yeah, I'll bet we're the only Jews in the place."

"Maybe, maybe not."

"Quite likely *maybe*, if I know you, you goy lover. And a lot of WASPs milling around like they thought they came with Columbus. You could've come alone. I'm sorry I didn't stay in Miami. To think I gave up that pinochle tournament for you. . . ."

"Oh, come on, you were dying to get here. You're the one who loved the brochures."

"I didn't have to come," Alice said darkly.

There was no argument here, just her irritation over Mrs. Tuttle, Phil knew.

"Oh, come on," he told her, "stop being foolish. Enjoy. . . ." He patted her hand, which she immediately snatched away, turning her head toward the window. "We don't have to pay any attention to her. She's nothing."

"She's hideous," said Alice. "So's that monster husband of hers."

"O.K., O.K. Relax. We're going to a perfect climate, with nice clear water all around, good weather, no hurricanes scheduled. We ought to have a great time. Warm days, cool nights. And best of all, one of the reasons we got to like it is I'll be shaving *this* off. . . ." He patted his paunch. "And you, yours—" He pinched his wife's waist roll.

"Stop it!" Alice said, dissolving into giggles, turning and squeezing Phil's hand. "I'm sorry, lover. But that schmuck she's married to gets to me. I didn't mean to lose my temper. But," and she giggled again, "I keep thinking of that story about the two fat bellies. Sure, I could use a little shaving myself."

Irene Tuttle could see the Bernheims out of the corner of her eye, mumbling to each other. How horrid Bimini Springs would be if there were many of *them* around. She fervently hoped there weren't. And as for blacks, well, they'd all be the help, and she wouldn't even notice them even if Howard had told her about the rumor that the Bahamas, along with Jamaica, was due for some possibly bloody riotings. After all, things had been in quite a state of local upheaval since Lyndon O. Pindling got into power, despite his good record. With ninety per cent of the population black and slave-descended, labor was so cheap the blacks had to behave, even at Bimini Springs. Run by southerners, too, who'd know how to handle them.

The captain's voice came over the public-address system, burry and patronizing: "Ladies and gentlemen, down there to your left is Bimini Springs Lodge on Devil Cay.

We'll be landing directly, so please fasten your seat belts and extinguish all cigarettes. We hope you've—"

"God, Phil, it's simply gorgeous!" Alice cried, clutching her husband's thigh.

And it was. Below them lay the small, verdant two-mile-long island with its miniature lake set in a cleft of low hills, its several wide pink beaches, its complex of Mediterranean-style buildings capped by a graceful bell-tower. Its large sheltered pool faced a maze of bright formal gardens. Shaped like a jagged triangle, Devil Cay's northern point rose into a rugged coralline limestone cliff face about sixty feet high that plunged abruptly into the sea. The island's southern curve was broken by a small, narrow-mouthed, reef-encircled harbor.

"So gorgeous it doesn't look hard to like," said Alice.

"So hold the thought for our tour of duty," Phil said.

"How about my lapsing? I'm determined to try that konked-out fish or whatever it is."

"You mean conch—it's pronounced *konk* out here. Why not? No rabbis are counting noses in the Bahamas."

"Will we lose the weight?" Alice asked seriously. "Have we got a chance?"

"That's only one of the projects," Phil said. "Just play your usual good game of pinochle, Alice, and everything's going to be O.K."

They bounced down to a smart little landing and taxied up to the airport waiting station. Several black porters in spotless white uniforms waited indolently for their bags in the shade of the station.

Subservient enough, Mrs. Tuttle decided, and stuffed her *Reader's Digest* into the large black alligator reticule she had placed on the window seat beside her, to ward off company.

"Welcome to Bimini Springs," the pretty brunette stewardess chirped as the plane braked to a complete standstill and its motors died. "On behalf of Captain Winston and the crew we hope you've had a very pleasant flight down. . . ."

And now for a substantial weight loss, prayed Mrs. Tuttle, wondering how long she'd be able to resist that box of chocolates buried deep under her finest lingerie.

If Bimini Springs happened to be something other than a reducing spa, thought Dr. Kevin Mack as he made his afternoon patient rounds, it would be a paradise. The tiny pink, green, and gold island, set in a sea of breathtaking beauty, ought to be given over to something less self-indulgent than weight reduction. The buildings could house amputees and a rehabilitation program, and the pool and sun ought to be healing cosmetic surgery cases. It was frustrating as hell to Kevin that the Maples had this marvelous place and didn't do anything with it besides make money.

And at money-making, the Maples were persuasive; money came easily and regularly to Devil Cay and Bimini Springs Lodge. The affluent guilty flocked to expatiate the sin of fat, and part of the lure was the setting, the rest good advertising.

He'd been attracted, too, by the ad the Maples sent him when he had first applied for the job of medical director: "BIMINI SPRINGS invites you to enjoy fabulous Bahama resort living at 10% Reduction All Room Rates! Overweight? Join the 'Springs' crowd now, men and women, singles and couples, at popular Bimini Springs on Devil Cay and enjoy tropical leisure while you reduce. M.D. supervision, average weight loss a pound a day. Activities include therapeutic pool, outdoor heated pool, social center, ACBL duplicate and rubber bridge, entertainments, games, beauty salon, massage, etc. Sunny and smog-free always; attractive modern air-conditioned accommodations. Weekly from $175. . . ."

No doubt about it, the Maples had done a remarkable job of parlaying a rather scrawny, undeveloped piece of land into a lucrative and going concern. The Maples' methods were another thing altogether; they were avarice-prone, often unjust, suspicious, and rumored given to bizarre sexual extremes, but Kevin didn't concern himself with these things since they never touched his operation. What he disliked, really, was the 24-hour-a-day, live-in job situation. He could never get away from it. That, plus the utter uselessness of his position. He felt wasted, for he knew there was more to medicine than buttering up patients who were obviously their own worst enemies and, if they did lose weight, would gain it right back again once they returned home. Bimini Springs was a posh madhouse, an asylum, and the types that had come and gone since his residence were just too crazy and boring to remember.

And here was another load, he thought, as he watched the Bahama Airways plane float down to a gentle landing and taxi up to the airstrip waiting station, then consulted his watch. One hour in which to make his rounds, hit the row of afternoon patients, and still have plenty of time to make the diet conference.

Kevin knocked at the door of Mr. and Mrs. Jack

Fleming's suite. Fleming was a Miami stockbroker who was never without a *Wall Street Journal,* and his smile was so pleasant Kevin wondered if the market had taken another sharp upward turn; he never followed it himself, having no stocks.

"How's everything today?" Kevin deposited his black bag on the table.

"I'm O.K., Doc." He lowered his voice. "It's Rose. In the john; she'll be there awhile. The fresh green salad got to her fast."

"Oh, I'm sorry. Has she been bothered before with this since you arrived? I don't recall hearing—"

"Don't worry about it, Doc. It's emotional with Rose. We have a little knockdown, you know, out of boredom, and she's all water suddenly. Likes to blame it on her diet, but her guts're her target area. . . ."

"That happens," Kevin said, and reached for Fleming's pulse, took it, and found it normal.

"I hope you're eating everything on the prescribed menu, Mr. Fleming," said Kevin. Patients never did, of course. If they'd possessed that kind of control, they wouldn't be here. "Take that brisk walk around the garden twice a day and the daily pool dip—as many laps as you can without overdoing it."

Fleming sighed. "I will, Doc, I will. And I'll get Rose into the pool, too, if it kills me. The old bathing suit she brought with her, the fat one, she's too self-conscious to wear. And the other one, the new size twelve, she can't get into it yet."

Common problems, happening every day. "Of course," said Kevin, "I understand." Enough time here; move on. "See that Mrs. Fleming eats lightly today, a bland soup at supper, maybe a packet of dry crackers. And be sure she stays away from salads and fruits until tomorrow. If she needs something to calm her stomach, call me. I'll instruct Mr. Street to give her something. . . ."

"Thanks, Doc. . . ." Fleming moved to the door with him. "You work too hard, Doc. Take it easy. Nothing wrong with any of us here, except we're all a bunch of spoiled brats."

Kevin grinned at him, already outside. "I know that, Mr. Fleming. Have a good afternoon. . . ."

Number two: another couple, the Jarvis pair from Wyoming. Elderly, mild-mannered people; he was a sheep rancher. Mrs. Jarvis complained of a constant, gnawing hunger that wouldn't go away. "It doesn't *hurt,*" she told Kevin, "but it's keeping me awake nights."

Kevin wrote out a prescription for her, since one was required for barbiturates, and handed it to her. "Take one each night. You'll sleep with this. . . ."

"But it says only three capsules," Mrs. Jarvis quavered.

"That's right, only three. Any more and you'd be an addict," he said, and grinned at her.

Mr. Jarvis guffawed. "We couldn't have that, could we, Thelma?"

As he came out into the sunshine again, he saw Eva Cassel waiting for him down the terrace. Eva Cassel, his second nurse, usually accompanied him when he made the rounds of single female patients. The Maples thought this redundant, Kevin didn't. There was nothing more embarrassing than being compromised by a female patient of any age wanting a little extra attention. Touch them and they screamed, ignore them and they report you for attempted rape. Eva Cassel's presence obviated such crises.

"Hi, Kevin. Ellison's first," Eva said, smiling brightly at him, her brown halo of hair gleaming in the bright sunlight. Eva, doll-like, trim, was the happiest creature around Bimini Springs. Kevin had never been able to fathom what made her so blithe, so completely detached from the whole scene of diet, therapy, and odd games, but since she generally performed efficiently, he never questioned her motives. Sometimes Eva got a distant glaze in her hazel eyes that made her seem as wistful as a ten-year-old regarding her first party dress, then at others the dark current of her thoughts clouded her clear brow. But the dazzling smile was always there, radiant as ever. The best way to deal successfully with Eva was to keep the relationship as formal as possible, something he'd always tried to do.

"Ellison has a problem," Eva told him, hugging a pile of patient charts to her breast. "Can't sleep, poor dear. Insists on sedation. She called us this morning."

"Mrs. Jarvis had the same problem, but not the same kind. Ellison's a hypochondriac. I'm not going to prescribe barbiturates. We've got Sominex and some other non-narcotic. She'll get that."

"I agree with you, Doctor, but she's noisy without a real sedative. After all," Eva's firm smile told him nothing, "she's a bit senile, and she won't exercise. She refuses to walk outside at all, says it's too hot."

"I wonder why they come here when they know it's not the Arctic," Kevin said. "Look, you've got a way with old ladies, Eva. Come back and visit with her after we've done the wing. See if you can persuade her to be a good child."

Eva's eyes did not change expression; the smile was still fixed, wide and bright. "What does that mean, Doctor?" she asked, her voice darkening.

"Just that you're good with them. Pomeroy soothes them, you tranquilize. Come on, don't read meanings into everything I say. We've got work to do. . . ." And he knocked briskly on Mrs. Ellison's door, wondering why he understood medicine so well and women so little. . . .

A few minutes later Kevin walked into the large white kitchen which was bustling with black help. His mission was to remind Joan Harrison, housekeeper and dietitian, about the afternoon diet-bulletin conference and to suggest to Kilroy Howard, headwaiter, that he should also come along, that there might be some information that would help to improve service for the new diet program now being put together.

Joan Harrison was a very dark Bahamian in her late twenties, tall and regal, and Kevin had long ago decided that she was remarkable. Joan made her way toward him between ranges and serving tables. The modified Afro coiffure she wore suited her, a strong contrast to her sleek white uniform. Stateside-educated, thoroughly cognizant of the reality gap between black and white in the States as well as in her islands, she was warm and friendly to most whites, but she liked him better than most, Kevin knew, and she approached him with an easy grin. He could trust her absolutely; she had already been an invaluable intermediary when general black staff problems arose. She was not happy with the Maples but was determined to make her point working within the island establishment, and she liked Kilroy Howard, as Kevin did, which gave them another bond.

"I know, I know," Joan said, "you're here about that bloody diet program, Dr. Mack."

Kevin laughed. "I just wanted to remind you of the meeting."

"Don't sweat it, I'll be there. Up half the night making final evaluations. You'll like what I've done. Maybe even *they* will," she said, meaning the Maples.

"Oh, *they* won't be at the conference, Joan. You, Kill, Tom, and the girls will, that's all."

Joan emitted a sigh of relief. "Bully! Hey, Doctor, I don't know about that Kill. He's been throwing his weight around something awful since yesterday. Giving the waiters hell and all that."

"You think *they* got to him?"

"I think maybe *she* did."

"Then that's where you come in."

Joan never batted an eye. "I'm not that friendly with him, Doctor," she said blandly.

"You ought to be," Kevin said. "The secret's to keep him guessing. Have a surprise up your sleeve."

Joan chuckled and slapped her bare arm. "No sleeves, Doctor. See you at two. . . ."

There was never any need to make a detailed physical inspection of the kitchen. Joan and Kill policed it rigidly, and it was always immaculate. As usual, Kevin merely walked through the room, saying hello to various helpers, stopping to chat briefly with the chef. The Maples required a daily token visit, but it wasn't necessary. With an all-white kitchen staff, the Maples wouldn't have worried about a dirty neck, Kevin was certain, and nobody would get chewed no matter how it looked. But when it came to the blacks. . . .

Yes, the blacks. Kill and Joan were as dependable as any two people could be. Kill had served in Vietnam when Kevin was there, and although Kevin had eaten at the mess club where Kill worked, he'd never seen him. He liked to think of Joan and Kill as a team, Kill totally American, Joan typically Bahamian. Or maybe that was the reason they clashed so frequently over mindless issues. Well, the contest was their problem, not his. Love, hate, or merely friendship—let them do what they wished. In any case, they appeared freer and less pressured than almost anyone else on the island. The other blacks were mostly married, all here without their familes, and the whites, other than the Maples and the medical staff, were all guests, single or married, dependent on the massage staff or other guests for extracurricular relief.

Joan's only real cross was Marge Maple; Kill's was Harry. As if the four had their own race war going, most of it subliminal. Only Joan and Kill had advantages; their race had fought harder and longer than the whites, and they knew everything there was to know about field tactics. A ruthless honesty was Joan's and Kill's prime tactical weapon. By virtue of this alone they came out superior to their employers.

As Kevin started out of the kitchen, the stores supply-room door opened, and Kill Howard emerged.

"Hey, Doc, I need some medication," Kill said, towering over Kevin Mack's near six feet.

"Medication? What kind?"

"Something to make that black filly humble," Kill explained, grinning. "She's in the air about something most of the time and won't admit to ever being wrong about anything. Yeah, medication. Something to turn her around and make her say yes to me once in a while."

"I'm afraid the prescription lies with you, Kill. You're the doctor in this case."

Kill said, resigned, "I oughtta get me some love medicine, Doc. Something to turn her eye in my direction and make it stay there."

"She's strong-willed," Kevin reminded Kill.

"Tell me some more, Doc."

"And cantharides won't help in this case."

"Oh, oh. You mean Spanish fly—?"

"That's right. You'll have to use charm."

"I'm short on that. I'll read it up somewhere."

"You do that. Meanwhile, don't forget the two o'clock meeting."

"With Mistah and Missus Wondahful, right?"

"The Maples aren't coming."

"In that case, I'll be there early," Kill said. "I gotta move some canned goods. See you. . . ."

As Kevin walked toward the pharmacy, he saw Linc Bailey, the black caretaker, supervising the preparation of a new garden area for bedding plants from his greenhouse. Linc was an industrious, quiet man, simple and uneducated, with a deep desire to make his work prideful. With his wife Lulu, he lived in a cottage removed from the main buildings.

"Afternoon, Dr. Mack," Linc said as Kevin passed.

"Good afternoon, Linc. I see you're busy as usual."

Linc grinned. "Only way to make it 'round here, Doctor." He nodded toward his two helpers working a dozen or so yards from them. "If I don't prod 'em by example, they ain't gonna do nothin'. . . ."

Learn by experience, thought Kevin, and said, "Well, don't overdo it. I might have you as a patient yet."

"Notta chance," Linc said. "Healthy folk, that's me, and my family."

"Stay that way. I don't need new business."

"Got some potted plants for your office, Doctor. I'll bring them 'round later."

"Thanks, that's thoughtful of you," Kevin told Linc. "But why always my office—?"

"You're not like *them*," he said, rolling his eyes toward the belltower and the Maples' apartment. "It's a pleasure to remember you."

"I'll try to deserve that compliment," Kevin said, and moved on.

As Kevin turned toward the pharmacy, that central core of the medical operation around which Ruth Severn's nursing depot revolved, he couldn't help but compare Kill, Joan, and Linc Bailey with Tom Street, the pharmacist. They always tried, but Tom never did more than was required, sometimes not quite that. Strange, introverted, Tom was one of those types that often cropped up in peripheral medicine at home and abroad. Tom's record was clear enough: Korean war duty, a couple of years in construction at Guam, several years in Morocco, contracts in Saudi Arabia, then back home to Florida for a year. Finally, bored with the States, he'd come down to Bimini Springs. The Maples liked him, said they trusted him implicitly because Kevin knew Tom gave them all the pills they wanted, and in turn they left him alone.

Kevin often wondered about Tom, what he was like really. Superficially he was a charming, rather boyish forty, with a large fund of off-color jokes, seemingly aimed at shocking people when he could, always laughing loudest at his own attempts. His tenure was Bimini's longest among the medical staff; all of them signed for two years. If they resigned at any time during that period, they forfeited their vacation pay and return travel expenses to point of hire. At the end of the first year all received a two-week paid vacation to the U.S., which somehow made the whole thing more bearable. Tom was luckier than most; he managed frequent flights to Nassau and Miami for medical purchases, also substituting as purchasing agent on those trips if Harry Maple couldn't get away himself.

Tom had arranged the front half of the pharmacy into a comfortable waiting room with divan, pictures, lounge chairs, lamps, and potted plants. A counter bisected the waiting room from the office area that lay behind a ceiling-high partition of shelves. Tom reached his office through a swinging louvered door behind the counter. His office contained the large hard-drugs safe. File cabinets were banked against one wall, a large desk and chair stood opposite. Beside Tom's desk sat the master control board for a closed-circuit TV operation that monitored all guest rooms, offices, and the pharmacy lounge. A viewing screen was angled into the pharmacy wall near the ceiling to give Tom easy viewing from his desk.

Tom really had it made, Kevin sometimes thought enviously. All he had to do was sit on his ass, smile once in a while at patients, and keep his shelves stocked. Like right now, as he walked into the pharmacy; Tom was leaning idly over the counter facing the waiting room, dressed in an immaculate white smock and reading a fresh copy of the *New York Times* that had come in by the afternoon plane.

"Hi there, Doc!" Tom said cheerily, laying down his newspaper. "What's the latest medical crisis in paradise?"

Kevin was not in the mood for small talk and frowned slightly. "Nothing, Tom. All quiet and normal."

"Normal is as normal does," Tom replied. "Dull Day at Dip Stick, isn't it?"

Kevin assumed that Tom was referring to the monitor on the closed-circuit TV system. A second emergency-control unit was installed in the Maples' executive office, but apparently Tom monitored most of the room action in his free time, over and above the call of duty. Anyway, he started the guest rumors. *Dip Stick?* What kind of sly fag drollery was that? Nobody, of course, had ever caught Tom in a homosexual situation, and he talked volubly about his past female conquests, but still, he was too perfect, too predictable in certain areas, thought Kevin. Groomed, affable, he had the look of an educated, middle-class homosexual, or was that just too easy? Well, whatever his true story was, Kevin suspected that Tom used the monitor system to his own private advantage.

"It's never dull for you around here, Tom," said Kevin. "You *read* a lot."

"Love books. And haven't missed a day's duty since I signed my contract," Tom replied.

"Your devotion's rare," Kevin said, and walked behind the counter, through the swinging door and into Tom's office, and sat down at Tom's desk. Tom followed. In front of Kevin lay the closed-circuit TV master-control unit, a field of white keys numbered to correspond with guest rooms and offices. Kevin thoroughly disliked this portion of the checkout procedure, but Harry Maple demanded that he perform it twice a day. Shortly before Kevin's arrival at Bimini Springs an elderly male guest, too religious about his diet, had stroked out and almost died in his room because no one thought to check his absence from lunch and dinner. They found him unconscious toward evening on the wall-to-wall carpeting of his suite. The Maples were fortunate that he was single and without heirs, for no one was able to sue them when he died two days later in a Miami hospital. It was a clear case of negligence, had anybody wished to press it, and the closed-circuit TV monitor was installed over a year ago to obviate another such incident. It was in operation only a week when Kevin arrived. Harry Maple wanted no more such incidents and demanded regular monitoring of all designated areas.

Kevin began to flip keys. As they passed the room of an elderly male guest who'd been having matinees with one of the black maids, Tom whistled, catching a flurry of movement on a bed. Kevin continued to flip switches, not trusting himself to speak until the job was done. Tom's unprofessional voyeurism made him boil. At last he swiveled the chair toward Tom and said in a steely voice, "What goes on in those rooms is no personal concern of yours, Tom. I'm not threatening you with dismissal, Tom, I like your work, but people do screw, Tom, even our guests, and whatever you see is confidential. I certainly don't want to hear about it. What you tell Mr. Maple is between you two, but when I'm monitoring, would you mind omitting the whistles, please?"

Tom looked crestfallen. "What the hell do I do around here to keep from going mad?"

It was on the tip of Kevin's tongue to tell him either to masturbate more often or find a partner, male or female, anything to bring his emotional blood pressure into focus.

"Keep your own counsel," Kevin said, and at that moment the phone on Tom's desk rang.

Tom picked it up. "Sure, Mr. Gordon, I'll send someone right over with the aspirin. If it persists, I suggest you call Dr. Mack. . . ."

When Tom hung up, Kevin Mack had gone; the pharmacy office door was still swinging. Tom had to smile. Kevin was actually a nice guy in some ways, kind of cute, but straight as a die, absolutely legit. He couldn't imagine Kevin's ever letting himself go, like blowing a stick of grass or soaring on pills. He bet Kevin even made it with Ruth via missionary position.

Well, whatever the good doctor told him, he was still going to have some wild fun with the dial-an-orgasm system by his desk. You sure saw some funny things, even between marrieds, by checking out the closed-circut TV monitor day or night. Sometimes. He sat down in the chair Kevin had just vacated and started flipping switches, one after another. No action at all so far today, just people doing ordinary things. Except that old fart Homer with the maid, and who cared about that?

Well, maybe he could give Loyal the signal to drop over tonight without anybody digging it. Blackville after taps, necessary once in a while. Old Loyal, stripped and tense, standing over him silently—no talking, ever—and running those long mahogany fingers across the back of his neck. But shit, thought Tom, sex is all in your mind. He'd done it a few times with Loyal, but nothing exceptional there. Better to watch than to perform. When you perform you're committed. . . .

The best he could ever remember had happened that winter years ago in the small, seedy Medina hotel in Tangier, not far from the Zokko Chico. His room was part of a suite from more spacious days, separated from the next room by heavy cedar-wood doors, intricately hand-carved. Peepholes had been cunningly worked into the knobby carved arabesques on the doors. Alone, Tom often enjoyed a variety of hour-by-hour action in the next room, for it was rented by the orgasm. One thing to have sex and try to lose yourself in the act, something he could never do, but much better to wallow in it by proxy, invisibly.

Sure, he'd try to see Loyal tonight, blow a couple of joints with him. And if Loyal wasn't in the mood, never mind, he'd come back to the office after dinner and fool around with the circuit, see what he could pick up. You had to get your kicks when and how you could, as quietly and uninvolved as possible, as invisibly. He walked out to the counter, picked up his *Times*, and brought it to his desk to read. Maybe there'd be some action later on, and in that case he couldn't be too far from the TV monitor. . . .

Tom was still skimming the *Times* columns when Eva Cassel strolled through the swinging door of his office. Tom glowered at her.

"I didn't think I had to knock," she said.

"I heard you." Tom considered Eva diverting; her mind

was something else, an X quotient. He was never able to isolate Eva's specific views on anything. She managed to render her opinions as though she were merely exploring tentative possibilities, pros and cons, preparatory to writing a thesis on them. She never said, "I think," "I feel," "I believe," or showed involvement in any significant way. Ruth Severn, on the other hand, was always extremely reserved, sometimes almost cold, often removed from the events around her; but she had definite warmth, a strong sense of righteous involvement, and positive views on almost everything. So, because he couldn't take Eva seriously, their relationship had become a continual jostling match.

Eva parked her trim behind on the edge of Tom's desk and stared at the TV monitor board. "So what's new on the networks today?" she inquired brightly. "Anything special I ought to know about?"

"There's nothing new about an empty bedroom."

"Maybe you ought to set up your own situations."

"Old man Homer was trying on one of the maids for size."

Eva made a face; Homer bored her, too. "I'm not interested in geriatrical erections," she said, "or anyone else's right now."

"Yeah," Tom observed, "not for some weeks," referring to a male guest about fifty who'd come to Bimini Springs a couple of months back. A recent widower, Eva reminded him of his deceased wife; he wouldn't leave her alone and stayed on after his weight reduction was accomplished. Not content with asking for her services at every trumped-up opportunity, he had gifts flown in from the States and Nassau for her: a pearl necklace, Mikimoto-matched; a gold wrist watch and strap; some fetching beachwear from Nieman-Marcus. The harder he tried to get Eva to respond to him, the more resistant she became. Whatever Eva did, she had to be the aggressor, and the widower wouldn't acknowledge this and leave the island until she walked into his room one day and dumped all his presents, neatly rewrapped, on his bed and walked out. The Maples weren't too pleased with Eva's conduct, for the guest had complained bitterly to them, but they said nothing to her, glad she hadn't run off with him and left them short a competent nurse.

"You know, baby," Eva told Tom, "for a boy of your advanced years you're a nasty-tongued bitch a good share of the time."

"And you're a transparent cunt," Tom replied good-naturedly. "Nothing nasty about me that a new scene wouldn't change to sweetness and light."

"Then why not leave? With the money you've got from all those foreign jobs, you could live in Mexico. I hear Guadalajara's a paradise for geronto gents. Practically no laws at all."

Tom accepted the jab gracefully. "You mean for gerontophiles, sweetie. You got it backwards. Youth likes them older there."

"But why stay here if you're bored most of the time?"

Tom grinned at her in a knowing way. "I could ask you the same question. Pretty girl, mature and capable, could work anywhere, but you stay at Bimini with all its hang-ups and bullshit. Why—?"

"Go ahead. Ask. I don't have to give answers."

"Fucking right you don't. You don't even give logical evasions."

"I'm leaving if you keep on talking that way!"

"Go ahead, leave. I don't need your version of why you're here. Got my own sources." He tapped his forehead. "Good old intuition. . . ."

"It would never hold up in court, Tom. You're too analytical in the wrong way, that's your trouble. Protective omniscience." She pointed to the TV master-control unit. "I'll bet that's how you rationalize staying on. You're guarding sacred human rights by bird-dogging the system for some interesting action."

"I put two and two together, like you couldn't imagine."

"You live in a dream world, Tom. I'd never believe your fantasies. We're at opposite ends of the earth. It's lucky we communicate at all. . . . So, what else is new?"

"Carter and Maple are close to a split."

"I said *new*. You're slipping. That twosome was never serious. Marge has a mind like a steel trap, and Harry's incapable of taking any other bait. If ever two people were meant for each other, it's the Maples. Carter never stood a chance, not Dickie boy."

"What about Anita and Harry?"

"Same imbalance," Eva declared. "You think too much, Tom, and you need new glasses. You've squinted through too many glory holes in your day."

Tom glared at her. "Glory holes? Why, you foul bitch!"

Eva smiled. "A few minutes ago it was cunt. You don't enlarge your vocabulary much with all those books, do you?" Eva said sweetly.

"What the hell did you come in here for, anyway?" Tom demanded.

"Merely on my way to the conference with Mack and Severn and Harrison and Howard and you, Tom."

"I thought you had some therapy sessions this afternoon."

"Sandhoff, but that's later, not till three-thirty."

"Crochety old bastard! He washes his own socks," Tom said, "and pees in the sink, I've seen him. His camera angles across the bed into the bathroom."

"You're disgusting, Tom!" Eva jumped off his desk and smoothed her uniform. "Maybe you ought to give him *my* treatments, you're so interested in what he does."

Tom wagged a finger at her. "Sometime you'll throw the first stone once too often, Eva."

"And what'll you do about it, darling?" Eva taunted as she flounced toward the swinging door. "Especially if I hit on target? And I always do—!"

"Keep your rotten filthy hands off me!" screamed Agnes Bird from the refuge of an overstuffed canary-yellow divan as Anita Pomeroy entered her cabana suite, trim in white nylon. "I don't want any goddam broads touching me, I want Dick Carter!"

So this wreck was the famous Agnes Bird, fallen Hollywood star trying to get her poor, raddled slob of a self into condition for a comeback! God preserve me, thought Anita, from ever becoming anything like this, and thanked her luck that she'd left the whole scene behind her long ago. . . .

Frostily statuesque, with just the faintest suggestion of a leer in her full-lipped smile, Anita advanced slowly on the cowering Aggie Bird. Given a commitment, Anita could be as firm as her clients.

"Mr. Carter's busy right now, Miss Bird, and Mr. Maple sent me along instead. I can do just about everything Mr. Carter does. . . ." Except stick it in you, you fat-assed, quivering old ruin, thought Anita, for when the chips are down, that's all Bird had left.

Anita smiled warmly. "Come, come, Miss Bird. Let's relax. . . ." And I could even stick it in you, if that's what you want, Anita mused. All the equipment's right down there in the massage center. It wouldn't be the first time she'd played the role of Myra.

Aggie puckered up her famous features, her past and her future. The tousled salt-and-pepper close crop, which her agent Wayne insisted was the only way to go now, framed her face perfectly, Anita observed. If she could just slim down, she'd be almost stunning, better-looking than she'd been in a decade. Aging had given her a kind of distinctive arrogance that Anita found compelling.

"I'm relaxed," said Aggie, "but I'm used to Mr. Carter. He's got the touch."

And that ain't all, thought Anita. Hung like a bull, will screw anything around, no conscience, self-centered, lazy. Should have been a P.I., but too gutless.

"I'm gentle, too, Miss Bird. . . ." Anita closed in on her reluctant quarry. "Let me help you into the bedroom. . . ."

"Don't touch me!" Aggie screamed, folding herself into a corner of the divan. "Don't you dare lay a hand on me!"

Anita was quite used to difficult patients. If they didn't try to ravish you, men and women alike, then they repulsed you. Rare was the day when more than one of the guests behaved in what she wistfully referred to as a normal manner. . . . Try another tack.

"My dear Miss Bird," Anita's softest tone was mellow with wheedle and promises of glory, "you've made a considerable trip to come to Bimini Springs. I've a special responsibility to you since I respect you as an artist. You're a person of great talent and reputation. You're training to extend that reputation, and the Maples have instructed all staff to do everything possible to help you effect the program you've requested. No sedatives, no alcohol, strict diet, massage, and some exercise. I'm not personally concerned with any part of your program except massage. And if you don't care to cooperate, I shall have to report to Mr. Maple that I've failed in my duty. . . ."

"Why don't you?" Aggie challenged. "Why don't you just lift up that phone and put him straight that I want Dick Carter and *nobody else*!"

Anita produced her most unctuous smile, ambled over to the table at Aggie's elbow, and picked up the coral phone. She detected the fumes of secondhand gin. The old ruin's been nipping, she thought, secreted a bottle somewhere probably, and could be well into what might prove a difficult tantrum. Anita welcomed the chance to dump the situation into Horny Harry's hands for a change; let the son of a bitch tackle a problem once in a while. He got the lion's share of loot.

"Mr. Maple? I'm in Miss Bird's suite. . . . Yes, she knows Mr. Carter's engaged, and she doesn't want my services. . . . That's right, she's refused to let me touch her. . . . Good, all right. . . . Thank you. . . ."

Anita cradled the phone, walked over to a canary chair and sat down, her knees locked together. Aggie regarded her mutely, only the eyes brilliantly vibrant and alive in the slack features. If this is what the limelight's like, thought Anita, I'm glad I missed it. What was Aggie's count? Married seven times to a parade of publicity hounds and not a few freaks, Aggie'd been even more lurid in her choice of lovers. Five foot three and one hundred and seventy pounds of raddled beef now. Once tough as nails, the director's dilemma. But still and all, Anita had to admit, a stunning talent when Bird had herself in control. But right smack up against her last chance at the moment, backed into a corner and fighting like a terrified tigress.

"I want Dick Carter," Aggie moaned, and sank on her pudgy knees into the deep divan. The silk robe she wore parted at the waist, revealing the rolls of slack flesh, the pancake paps. Christ, thought Anita, dying for a cigarette, I'd kill myself before I'd get that way. *And this creature still has another chance!*

"Mr. Maple will be here right away," Anita said with a soothing smile.

"He goddam well better be," Aggie growled, and stared at Anita's radiant flesh. "Christ, you're some looker," she observed, not ungenerously.

Anita kept her smile in place. "Oh, thank you, Miss Bird. I've always thought *you* were the greatest. . . ." Tempted to underscore the *were*, but this would be senseless. She didn't dislike Bimini Springs quite enough to get Harry after her again. Money wasn't too bad, most of the tricks weren't awful, they could be manipulated, and some were generous. And it was a lot better than those rotten, degrading years as a model. Model, my ass, she thought, I was on my back more than I was on my feet. For Joe. Then suddenly, as she'd begun that long slide almost into oblivion, she'd seen it all for what it was; she was rescued by the wise, kind elderly friend who made her take the massage course, even paid her school tuition. . . . But I'm still a handsome thing, she told herself, even if the first bloom's gone. I don't look like this one, and never will with a little care. And she could always get a parlor job almost anywhere. Chief madam, or something else. . . .

"Not bad at all," Aggie was saying, her strident mood gone. "You should have tried films. You remind me of Ekberg. . . ."

"Yes, the comparison's been made before, Miss Bird. I'm holding up. You know, Hollywood's my home town, I used to work there. I saw you walk into Grauman's Chinese once with Tom Ergo for the premiere of *New Orleans*. You wore jade-green satin, cut very low, and a black ankle-length mink. You were slimmer then, but—"

Aggie had to laugh. "Oh Christ, that silly fag Tom Ergo! How could you remember what I wore? That was fifteen years ago. . . ."

"You were one of my idols as a kid," Anita said honestly. "You still are."

"Yeah, well, you ought to know the truth. My first job was in a Grauman's Chinese Theatre prologue, for God's sake. I sang in the chorus with a bunch of kids. . . ." Remembering, Aggie's mottled face underwent a miracle of change; her flesh cleared, the lines eased out, a radiance suffused her, sparkled in her eyes, curled her lips. She almost became that earlier Agnes Bird at premiere time. Almost, not quite, but almost.

"And I still admire you," Anita said. Anyone who'd brought interpretation to the point of Aggie's high control was special.

"Child," said Aggie in a warm, throaty voice, "what's your name?"

"Anita Pomeroy, Miss Bird."

"Yes, child, you're a beauty, all right. Too bad you never tried pictures," Aggie said again.

"But I did. I made a test once—"

Aggie climbed off the divan, pulled her robe together and sat down, hunched forward with interest, elbows on her knees, bare feet on the carpet. "Tell me. What happened—?"

Anita shrugged her shoulders. "What always happens when you don't have the talent or the determination, all the things that *you* have. . . . I modeled, that's all."

Aggie's laugh was shrill. "*Had* is more like it, child. I've got no goddam confidence anymore."

"The papers say you're going to star in the film version of *The Bungalow*. You'll be great."

"Well, I've got the contract," Aggie admitted, a nagging bitterness clouding her features, "but there's just one teensy-weensy fly in the goddam ointment—"

"What's that?"

"You know fucking well what it is—it's this damned blob that's me! A hundred and seventy pounds and I've got to shuck forty just like that and be a dazzling success. Let me tell you something, child, there isn't a nastier word in the English language than *comeback*. Back from where,

I'd like to know? Back from hell, that's what, and the round trip shows!"

Anita visualized a flash of past headlines about Agnes Bird: Hours late to her set, sometimes not even showing up; shooting suspended, contracts broken. . . . Wild scenes in a London boutique, a Roman restaurant, a Paris couturier's. . . . Aggie, drunk, unkempt, battling waiters in a New York nightclub, photographed as they were throwing her out on her ear. The long succession of husbands and lovers, the legal controversies, the pills, the booze. There were even rumors of morphine addiction, Anita remembered, but it was plain enough to see now what was wrong with Agnes Bird. As she said, her self-confidence was gone; she bore the knowledge badly. Or perhaps she'd never had any in the first place, couldn't any longer rationalize the lack of it. Anita knew all about that.

"You've got to do it," said Anita firmly, rising to her feet, a rush of honest compassion crowding her own good common sense aside. "You've got to reduce, you owe it to yourself and your fans to shape up and be ready for the picture. No ifs or buts, Miss Bird, you *must*!"

Aggie smiled and showed her gorgeous caps. "Child," she murmured wistfully, "I'll try, God knows I'll try. But it's only one month off. I won't make any promises. . . ."

At that point Harry Maple knocked sharply on the suite door and, without waiting for a signal, barged in.

Harry Maple was what elderly women often call a fine figure of a man, meaning that he was tall, solidly built, neatly turned out, prepossessingly masculine. A distinguished business demeanor hovered around the tanned edges of his eyes. The full, genial mouth was glib with sexual promise, the thick chestnut hair wavy and without a strand of gray. His lavender silk jac shirt, wash-wear slims, and sandals did nothing to contradict the general impression of a man supremely confident of his ability and magnetism.

The professional exchange between Harry and Anita was automatic: Anita indicated her willingness to turn Agnes Bird over to Harry, although at this point she would have liked to credit herself with a completed job. Docile, she waited for Harry to decide whether he would stay and soothe their celebrity or she would.

"Miss Bird!" Anita caught the tone of awe in Harry's voice as he advanced on his most distinguished client of the season.

"Mr. Maple," replied Aggie, plainly impressed with the physical man.

"Shall I report back to the exercise deck, Mr. Maple?" Anita asked, no trace of inference in her tone.

"By all means, Anita," Harry told her. Aggie Bird was just about the largest shark they'd ever landed, and Harry was quite willing to perform almost any service demanded to keep her satisfied; the routine was already mapped out in his mind. "Everything's just fine, just fine. You run along, my dear. Thirty-two needs treatment. Check it out with Miss Severn, please, will you?"

And close the door after you, thought Anita. "Certainly, Mr. Maple, I'll do that. . . ." She swished past him, her back to Aggie, winking broadly as she went. She knew what he was up to, the prick. He couldn't wait to dent that sagging mound of famous flesh.

"Oh, and flick the lock on your way out, Miss Pomeroy. . . ."

As if she needed to be told, and emerged blinking into the dazzling outdoor light.

"Well, well," Harry murmured, "I'm very glad to see you so calmed down, Miss Bird."

"Aggie to *you*," she murmured right back, "all the way down the line."

Harry knew a thing or two about strategic female entry when all systems were go. As Aggie simpered at him from the canary divan, he peeled off his shirt, revealing the most evenly tanned pectorals in the Bahamas—twenty minutes a day nude, front and back, under the special sun lamp in his office. He loathed direct solar exposure but knew the social value of a good tan for a resort director.

Jesus, how could he keep it erect? He concentrated hard on the long, clean lines of Anita Pomeroy's beautiful body beneath him in the chaste and frosty air-conditioning of his private office on the slippery couch. Lately she'd been difficult, but Christ, what a bang she was! The best. Now she'd begun to use the pretext that Marge knew about them, which wasn't true, of course, thank God! Marge didn't object to his serving clients' needs in the line of duty; what Marge wouldn't countenance was staff lusts, including Anita. But she didn't know; he kept a tight ship, took his pleasures when and where he could. That day on the couch, for instance, Marge was elsewhere, socializing. He ran no risk. But that time in the boathouse, while Marge received some obese salesman's pitch in his cabana suite, Harry had humped one of the black maids. For

Marge that was considered blasphemy; she'd have had his balls had she known, so shortly afterward he'd fired the maid, rushed her off the island without notice on the mail boat. But Anita was something else, exactly his type. Sweet, soft Anita. . . .

Aggie was relishing the slow strip; her eyes glittered. "I had no idea you were so well equipped."

"Mmmmh," Harry smacked his lips, "Yeah, well, Aggie, right on down the line, all the way. We're a pair," he pointed out, and shucked his sandals and dacron slims, finally standing before her in his imported two-net knit cotton briefs, cut rate from Curaçao. He dropped them, and his erection, inspired by Anita, zinged up at her.

"Oh God," Aggie gulped, "you're too goddam much!"

Yeah, sure, too much, thought Harry, hoping the thing would stay up until he got it in.

"Come to daddy, sweetheart," Harry hissed urgently, stroking himself to make sure it was still there, "let's strike while the rod's hot!"

Aggie was out of her robe in a flash; for her mature years she could move fast in a crisis.

"Let's go into the bedroom where we can spread out on the king-size, honey," Aggie cooed throatily, holding out her arms.

"No!" Harry cried out, so sharply that Aggie took an involuntary step backward and stumbled against the canary divan.

"Why not? It's more comfortable in there. We can take our time. . . ."

"I—I don't have that much time, my dear," Harry lied, thinking of the TV eye monitoring the bedroom. "I'm on a tight schedule today," gathering her masterfully into his well-muscled arms, "and I can't spare the luxury. Once I get you *anywhere*, like on this couch right here, you won't worry about bedrooms or Dick Carter or anything, baby. . . ." He clutched her against him, speared her right ear with his tongue.

Aggie shrieked and squirmed in his solid embrace.

He chewed on her neck.

"O.K., O.K.," she said breathlessly, "standing up or sitting down or swinging from the chandeliers, it's all the same to me. Only don't stop, just do it, do it! Jesus—!"

"O.K. . . ." Harry dropped her to the divan. "Just so it's not in the bedroom. Gotta thing about bedrooms; they remind me of home. . . ." He spread himself expertly over her horizontal, undulating corpulence.

"Anything you say, lover. Aggie's all yours, yours. But hurry, hurry—!"

"Easy does it," mumbled Harry, and slipped in without resistance, except for the small token "No!" that escaped Aggie's lips.

As he began to service her with the famous Maple stroke known throughout the southern states and the West Indies, he began to wonder if he hadn't committed a fatal error. Maybe she'd like it so much she'd make a goddam pest of herself. Would she lose the required weight because of this extra attention? How much could he tell Marge? For Marge would be jealous of a celebrity. But at least they weren't doing it in the bedroom; Marge wouldn't be able to see him by flipping a switch in their suite, nor could Tom Street catch the act, or Dr. Mack, if they were making routine checks.

"Oh God," wailed Aggie as the Maple stroke gained its full, galloping stride. "Oh mother, oh dear, oooooooh!" and beat a wild tattoo with her heels on Harry's firm bronzed rump, urging him on to the finish line.

God or no God, thought Harry, beginning to perspire, it was hard work with the old ones. But never mind, years ago he and Marge had determined that anything done in the interests of business was permissible; money in the bank made all the difference in the world, made everything right as rain. Money in the bank, money in the bank, money in the bank. That was it, that was the right phrase. And, matching the chant to his rhythmic stroke, he sent Aggie screaming up the stairway toward an earthly paradise. . . .

Ruth Severn, head nurse at Bimini Springs, glanced up from her desk as Anita breezed into the office and began checking customer charts.

"Through with Bird so soon?" Ruth asked, and went on working.

"Yes, and she's no lark, to coin a phrase." Anita had reservations about Ruth, for although Severn was easy to work with, she wasn't anyone you ever got to know well. And you thought out the answers carefully when she made the questions. "Had to leave, Ruth. She wouldn't accept me. I called Hairless Harry, and he took over."

"Oh—" Ruth knew what that meant and made a cloudy face. "Our most celebrated client gets the star treatment. But then, that's how fat farms survive, pleasing their clients."

"As long as it wasn't me," Anita said. "This isn't my

season for girls." She pointed to the charts. "Is there any rush with these? Maple said something about thirty-two."

"No real rush. He wants a massage, but he's too shy to come to the treatment room."

"Oh God, another mouse!" Anita sighed and sat down in the chair beside Ruth's desk. "The shy ones are always the worst kind. When they lunge, they really lunge. They act like they own you. . . ."

"I should think you'd know how to handle anyone," Ruth said, scribbling away on a report.

Anita regarded her critically as she lighted a cigarette. "Not much bothers you, does it, Ruth? You've been here as long as I have and I've never seen anything get to you. Whereas I'm chock-full of trauma all the time."

Ruth stopped working, looked up with her serene, detached smile that went perfectly with her short dark hair and brown eyes. Slightly younger than Anita, she'd learned long ago to reserve her emotional extremes for the truly vital situation, should it come along. Consequently, anger, superficial bitchiness, daily irritation, all these rarely surfaced in her manner.

"How do you keep your eternal cool?" Anita asked. "It's phenomenal. I'm always so vulnerable."

Anita wasn't really looking for answers, Ruth knew, but for friendly clichés where she could hang a few moments' talk. Self-sufficient on the surface, Ruth had always known how lonely this beautiful creature really was. Although she had no tangible facts about Anita's emotional past, she knew that if Anita ever did react seriously, deeply, to something or someone, it would then be time to offer a shoulder and give her questions serious consideration.

"What should bother me, for heaven's sake?" said Ruth. "After two years in Vietnam very little gets to me. This factory's only a mild symptom of that. Here we carve them down, not up. . . ." She decided abruptly to change the subject. "By the way, Dr. Mack's making his rounds a bit early today. And since we've only got about two-thirds the usual number of guests this week, we're going to implement the new diet bulletin. It'll take some discussion in depth, so he wants us all here in this office for a briefing at two this afternoon. . . ."

"But I won't be administering it," said Anita; she hated conferences. "You and Cassel and the other staff do that."

"Yes, but you and Carter are going to be in on all the medical meetings from now on," Ruth told her. "We feel—the Maples do anyway, it was their idea—that you and Carter will be more interested in Bimini Springs if you're more involved with its problems."

"Mmmmh. Is that the Maples' or Dr. Mack's way of saying I'm not doing a good job?"

Ruth paused, thinking, God, that seductive perfume, that half-bra and the low-necked uniform, her walk, her look. No wonder the male clients vibrate to her, want her.

"If anything," said Ruth, "you're doing too good a job. Now don't get touchy and build inferences out of that remark. You are without a doubt the most satisfactory masseuse they've ever had here, and you're great in the exercise room, too. Conferences are vital to staff cohesiveness, unity. Everyone ought to be in on them whether the information's entirely pertinent or not."

Anita stubbed out her cigarette. "All right, Dick Carter can take the one in thirty-two."

"He doesn't want Dick Carter."

"It won't hurt him to sub for me once in a while. I sub for him."

"Maybe you're right," Ruth said. "I'll work it out. I'm inclined to agree that the old ones are the worst. Kevin does too."

"Some are," said Anita, wondering about the relationship between Ruth and Dr. Mack, for there was something mighty wrong with that picture. "Most of the old ones talk too much. Overcompensation. That's all right. But when they drag out mother's pearl necklace or a pair of ancient gold spike heels and want you to strip and go to work on their backs, it's a problem."

"That's never happened to you here!" Ruth said sharply, not at all sure it hadn't.

"No," Anita replied, "but lots of other things have. Weird things. Be glad you're a nurse."

"I've never regretted it. Forty-eight wants a massage. Are you ready for it?"

"Forty-eight. Franklin. No problem there—he goes to sleep and snores on me. I mean, on the table. . . ."

"However you mean it, I understand."

The two women exchanged impersonal smiles. Anita stood up. "Well, I'm off to the slaughter block."

"You never do like to play it straight, Anita, do you? We're all in the same unsavory mess together."

"Being flippant bolsters my ego, Ruth. I'm not trying to make you feel uncomfortable."

"You're not making me feel any which way, dear girl."

"I've got to feel superior to the situation. Otherwise, it's a gruesome business."

"Just as long as you stay uninvolved and the Maples authorize everything as official business," Ruth said. "Unwind, girl, it's not that bad."

Anita started to hum under her breath as she stepped toward the door. "I'm planning to unwind when I cut myself loose from this sordid spread, Ruth, and not before. See you at the seminar. . . ."

"Happy rubbing," Ruth called after her, and Anita turned and beamed her warm, meaningful violet gaze straight at Ruth, who fumbled it and turned to her paperwork. There was something overwhelmingly sensual in Anita that had nothing to do with her gaudy exterior; it went deep down. Anita exuded promise of fulfillment in the way that some women deny it. And to be honest, Ruth had to include herself in the denial group these days. Where she had retreated from using her body as a weapon, Anita apparently knew no other. And in searching for herself, some inner peace, Anita had merely offered body for body. Probably, Ruth couldn't know for sure, not knowing Anita's life. But using flesh as a weapon was a shame, a shame that anyone so beautiful couldn't coordinate her beauty with her sincere desires. Or perhaps the fault lay partly with Anita's contacts, so dazzled by the eternal façade they couldn't read what was written in fine print underneath. Yes, a crying shame. A terrible waste. Anita was really a kind, gentle creature, looking for love—and would probably never find it.

Well for God's sake, Ruth mused irritably, she had better things to do than to analyze Anita Pomeroy, who would either one day find her own level or else drift off into apathetic middle age, not too far ahead for her at that. Yes, an awful misuse of good woman power. And Anita was right, Bimini Springs was a sordid spread, a waste of good people. In an organization where six efficient medical personnel would be merely adequate, Ruth and Kevin Mack had to work with one registered nurse, several black untutored nurses' aides, willing enough but unspecialized, the massage staff of Pomeroy and Carter, the dietitian, Joan Harrison, who also doubled as housekeeper, and a very limited kitchen staff. Oh, and Tom Street, pharmacist, who was also trained as a male nurse but didn't function here in that capacity.

Paperwork was the biggest hassle; Ruth was never on top of it mainly because the Maples wanted exhaustive records in case they were sued. Kevin didn't have the time to assist much, and Eva and Anita weren't interested enough to assume more responsibility voluntarily. Tom could have helped, but that meant he would have access to confidential medical files, and with his well-known penchant for snooping, not always innocently, either, this was perilous. Bad enough that he knew everyone's daily temperature, what pills they took, and could see them via the monitor, for he could weave anyone's simple history into a very heavy pattern, Ruth knew, given half a chance.

Ruth stared in frustration at the mound of work on her desk, asking herself for perhaps the thousandth time why she didn't just pick up and take the next flight out, leave it all. Kevin Mack was the obvious reason—well, one of them. And the other was that she hated loose ends and unfinished business almost as much as she loved being passionately involved in her work, for involvement gave it shape and meaning. Without work life had no purpose, no goals, especially if you ran from work, so even though Bimini Springs was a deadly grind, she'd keep on for a while. Reducing spas were hardly her idea of a significant contribution to human welfare, not with bosses like the Maples, who were best left unjudged, unanalyzed, if you wanted to keep your temper and your sanity.

Straightening up in her chair, she began preparing charts for departing guests, to be carried home as souvenirs from the fat wars; trophies, conversation pieces attesting to the baptism of fire that weight loss meant for these creatures. So that they could show their friends, foes, and doctors. A useless duty, Ruth reminded herself, but all the same, part of the job. A pity that such a lovely place couldn't be used as the simple paradise nature intended it to be.

She sighed and dug into the forms, so engrossed after a few minutes that she wasn't aware of Kevin Mack's presence until he stood beside her desk and spoke to her.

Kevin Mack rapped his knuckles sharply on Ruth's desk top; she looked up, startled.

"Hey, you're really into it," Kevin said. "Doing some vital research?"

Ruth leaned back in her chair and smiled at him. "Mrs. Redfield's avoirdupois."

"More have than have not. If she's convinced herself she's thin when she's only lost half the weight her doctor advised, then she ought to get some kind of a citation. She's a living blimp. . . ."

There was always this light bantering in Kevin; Ruth had never known anyone who could be so amiable, especially when he wasn't doing what he really wanted to do.

Although under duress he could speak his mind and would stand firm. Mildly handsome, personable, clean-cut in a straight-out professional way, Kevin was just about everybody's TV image of the successful young medico, Ruth thought, knowing how this bugged him. Even in Vietnam where they'd met, Ruth could never see Kevin even in casual clothing without visualizing him in a white smock against a gleaming chrome office, testing, probing, giving sober advice to old ladies, telling the young husband his wife had terminal cancer, administering to the aches and pains of children. He had seemed totally out of place in the filthy, grim horror of Vietnam where death was a way of life and hardly any longer remarkable even in its abomination. Standing before her now, so neat and cheerful and bright-eyed, she wondered again what had happened to their once serious and slightly sentimental attachment, why they had come to mask their real feelings with this continual light subterfuge.

"Beneath that twinkle I sense a problem," Ruth said.

Kevin's grin faded. "It's the Kingsley girl. She's dropped the fifteen-pound maximum in two weeks, and the appetite curb's working; she's stopped sneaking into the kitchen and raiding the reefers."

"What do you see that you don't like?"

"She says she's not ready to go home yet. I suspect it's Carter; she's been taking massages."

"There's nothing you can do about that, not if she requests the service."

"I know," Kevin said angrily. "I wish to hell we were somewhere else. She's too nice, too young, to get involved with him."

"Agnes Bird has. . . ."

"That hardly counts in the same category."

"Maybe it isn't that bad. Maybe she has problems at home she doesn't want to go back to yet, and she's simply reached the end of her ability to rationalize them. The end of her patience, I really mean."

This frequently happened to guests when they were about to leave, both Kevin and Ruth knew. Adhering to a strict regimen for from one to three weeks, sometimes longer, gave many patients the courage to accept the deprivation of a continuing rigid diet; with others it often merely broke down the morale of will and habit, leaving them stranded at a point of no return. They could lose no more weight, if such were required, and they felt they could not hang onto the weight loss they'd already made. When this point was reached, it was better to send them home immediately than have them hang on and possibly undo the good they'd already achieved for themselves. The Bimini staff could handle the general weight-loss program for patients to a point, but they weren't equipped to deal with the individual emotional problems involved in projecting long-range diet regimens. Often when patients departed, Kevin wrote letters to their doctors suggesting possible psychiatric consultation as an adjunct to further dieting. It was one way of letting the doctor know that the patient had problems no amount of dieting could solve.

"Sending her home is the answer, not further sedation," Kevin replied. "I'm going to tell her tomorrow."

"You're probably right. She's not stable. She's been under drugs of one sort or another for years. I don't understand her G.P. The only issue is her will power in conflict with her emotions. Surely, since he's the family doctor, he ought to be aware of the source of her depression."

Kevin sighed. "Single childless women, virgins, emancipation. Quite a mess for today's female."

Ruth gave him her special wry smile that meant she was aware of the innuendo. "You mean Kingsley, of course."

"Who else—?"

"My God," Ruth said, "what we've come to, working here. We're getting really upset about some fat-assed, irritable creature who doesn't even know that there's suffering and misery in the world a lot more important than her bathroom scales. In some circles this would brand us as just as callous and unfeeling as our patients."

"We're not here for life, Ruthie. You know that as well as I do," Kevin said sternly.

"You'll excuse me for having reservations about that remark," Ruth replied.

"By the way, the Brown girl's about ready for the special fast."

Ruth checked a bank of charts on a side table, running her finger down them. "Yes, Brown. Something rather regal about her, can't put my finger on it. I would imagine that beneath that lump of lard lurks a lovely little thing. Or hadn't you noticed—?" She turned toward him with the Brown chart.

"I try not to miss anything."

"Could be that even the few pounds she's already lost have made her powerfully attractive—?"

"Come on, Ruthie. You know where my interests lie. I'm bound over to you."

"Hand and foot? Who needs long engagements? Maybe that's a big mistake, being bound over, as you put."

He stared at her sharply. "What kind of silly talk is this for business hours? You know how I feel." He glanced at his watch. "Hey, got to run. I'm seeing Marge about that new couple, the Bernheims, and some dowager named Irene Tuttle."

"You mean Mrs. Howard Tuttle, from Washington, D.C. I've heard. What do the Bernheims want?"

"They're asking about kosher food, and we're a far cry from it around here."

"They can pick and choose like everybody else," Ruth replied. "The Flemings make out. Why should the Bernheims be so special?"

"I can ask Marge. It'll soothe their nerves."

"You're not a doctor anymore, Kev, and I'm not a surgical nurse. We're pawns, blobs, ciphers. Any untrained person could do what we do. How much skill does it take to open a bottle of aspirin?"

"We're putting money in the bank," Kevin reminded her, "And one of these days we'll quit this sweathole and do what we have to do. Just you and me. . . ."

"I starve on promises," Ruth said, and batted her brown eyes at him. "Hadn't you better hurry? The Bernheims might decide on the lobster instead of the whitefish for dinner if you hang around here any longer. Go—!"

"I'll settle with you later," Kevin said playfully, squeezing her arm.

"As I said," Ruth called after him as he walked out, "I could starve on promises."

Posing further questions about what they meant to each other involved examining the remnants of their relationship in the light of their possible future. Pretty dim prospect, thought Ruth, too one-sided. All very well for her to hang around while Kevin saved for advanced medical studies, but it was turning her into a drifter, something she hated. Not that she had ever intended to pin him down to marriage, but she did worry about the future without it. She'd known quite a few single nurses who'd followed doctors with no ultimate success, for they'd finally married someone else. She also knew nurses who liked drifting, who did seasonal migrations: Florida in the winter at some rest home, California in the summer at another rest home. Wherever they liked, whenever they liked it, sampling men and seasons at will. An existence she deplored, thought pitiable. She was strong enough to go it alone, strong enough not to be like the others, so why was she sticking around when it was obvious that Kevin was letting her down slowly, easily, but still letting her down? Setting her adrift, making her deny her sense of place, of direction, leaving her more or less alone. How long had it been since they'd gone to bed? She didn't even want to count . . . Sighing, she buckled down to work, knowing she couldn't make any decisions right now and knowing, too, that work was the only way to sidestep the issue, to shake the black mood that occasionally closed in on her. . . .

Marge Maple entered the large, comfortable apartment that attached to the main structure of Bimini Springs and served as home and executive office for the Maples. The seaside portion was the office, with outside and interior entrances, while the spacious lounge in sea green and gold had entrances both poolside and gardenside looking toward the sea. The master bedroom in shocking pink, Marge's choice, had slide-back glass walls through which the Maples could view their garden and the aquamarine sea beyond, if they wished, as they lay snugly in their king-size bed.

Marge no sooner put down her notebooks when the telephone began to ring. The dial phone system the Maples had only recently installed at Bimini Springs was a source of constant pleasure to Marge. She adored giving commands by telephone, lying abed mornings after Harry arose, planning menus with the housekeeper, Joan Harrison, whose qualifications for the job should have struck some humility in Marge, and conferring with Dr. Mack about the new guests, the diet status of the old ones.

Marge glowered at the telephone for a moment, then scooped it up as if she knew exactly who would be on the line.

"Hullo—" she said in her most tentative tone.

"Marge—?" Dick Carter was calling from his room across the garden. "Is it O.K.?"

"You must be sitting by your window again."

"Yeah. . . . You're alone, aren't you?"

"More or less. . . ." Marge tried to keep the tension out of her voice. She had only to hear Carter on the phone to experience a tremor of excitement, and she hated her lack of control.

"What does 'more or less' mean?" Dick asked.

"More I'd like, less I should have," Marge retorted.

"Dammit, Marge! Don't start dripping guilt again!"

Marge sniffed. "I can't help it! You know where he is?" She meant Harry, her husband.

"Presently with Bird in her suite," Dick announced. "That ought to 'lay your guilt—or maybe overlay it."

"The bastard!" Marge rasped. "And you *love* telling me about it because you know I can't ever say anything about it unless he decides to tell me. He'd know right off where I got the info. . . . It would have to be you or Pomeroy. . . ."

"Pomeroy? You're inferring something—"

"Only that I don't think we ought to meet again, Dick. It's getting too risky."

"You're losing interest!"

"Christ, I wish I was. . . ." Marge was silent for a few moments.

"Marge—are you still there?"

"I'm here," she said, "I'm thinking. Maybe Pomeroy *does* have something to do with us. How do I know what you two are up to when I'm in bed nights with Harry?"

"Oh, for Christ's sake!"

"You could be banging up a storm every night. Who'd be the wiser?"

Dick sighed audibly into the mouthpiece. "It could never happen," he said truthfully. Anita had always refused to cooperate with him; now he didn't care that much. "Nobody mixes business and pleasure, is her motto. We're both in the same game, and what isn't paid for has got to be for pleasure. And she's not giving me any. . . ."

Although Anita offered him no favors, Dick wasn't above using Anita as an irritant in his running relationship with Marge—if you could call a few flimsy fucks during the past months with your clothes half on, nervous as hell you might get caught, a relationship. Marge was a harried, really cold and frightened broad, totally incapable of relaxing or making something nice and pleasant out of a sometime thing; she always had to define her attitudes by creating conflict.

"What's the matter, Dick? You must be slipping," she taunted him. "And by the way, I detect a bored and distant note in your voice. Don't you want to see me again?"

Now she was reversing the pattern, Christ almighty!

"It's not that, Marge. It's Harry. He said something very funny to me about an hour after you and I parted the last time, the other day. Something about its being all right for me to do anything I wanted in the line of work—hetero, homo, anything—but I'd better not try to take over. He was talking about guests, but the inference was *us*. I'm sure he knows—"

"Impossible," Marge said with conviction. "So, it's Anita

now, is it?" and her question was charged with venom. "That slut!"

"I told you I've never been with Anita, baby. Honest—"

"Since when has honesty been your best policy, Dick?"

"Well, jealousy's yours, you're green with it," he said, and chuckled so that Marge caught it. "I like you green, I'll be right over—"

"You will not!" Marge shrieked into the phone. "You'll go about your regular nasty business just like you always do. It's about time we looked at this thing realistically. We haven't a prayer, Dick, I'm calling it quits. And as for you ever taking over from Harry, that's the laugh of a lifetime."

"Marge, I never said anything like that to you, and you know it. The remark was Harry's." It was the moment to play one last card. "Hey, let's run off together."

Marge heehawed in his ear. "Oh, that's great, that's just dandy. Imagine me, at my age, turning tricks for *you*! How the hell else would we ever get any money?" she demanded caustically.

Dick ignored her thrust. "Where would we go, love?" he purred. "Acapulco, the Copacabana, the Riviera, Palm Springs, Hawaii—?"

"Oh, come off it, Dick. We don't have a chance. We never did."

"You mean you wouldn't ever really leave Harry?"

At one time Dick thought she might actually run off with him, bringing her share of Bimini Springs with her. But as he got to know her better, he realized that the escape fantasy was a requisite safety valve in her character, that she was almost as dependent on Harry as he was on her. Almost, not quite. But they were a welded unit, and nothing could change this. And so it was crystal clear that his continued tenure at Bimini was actually due to Marge, not Harry. If he stopped pleasing Marge, he'd get severance pay in a minute. But the fact was, he wasn't quite ready to move on, not this season.

"You might think about splitting if I dropped a few hints around—" he began in a joking voice, but Marge cut him short.

"You do that, you son of a bitch, and you're a real dead duck. I'll personally get you barred from the health-resort business forever. You won't even be able to get a job as towel boy in Nevada, and that would really frost you, wouldn't it?" Marge knew that whenever California failed to produce employment for Dick, he went to Reno to work for Harrah's. She had all his exits covered; she could call all the cards. He was already regretting his remark.

"Aw, come on, Marge, I was only kidding. I'm no blackmailer."

"No, you couldn't be," Marge replied. "Your mouth's too big, and you're not sharp enough. Anyway, love, I didn't say you were."

Ah, so she'd changed her mind again; he could tell by her tone. In a moment she'd be naming a future rendezvous.

"Be *sensible,* Dick. Bide your time. I'm a bundle of open wounds today. Maybe tomorrow—"

"Yeah, just go on doing what I've been doing and keep my big mouth shut, huh? You sure like the whole pie sliced your way, don't you?"

"No, only the largest piece, baby, which yours is," Marge abruptly confessed.

"I know when I'm appreciated."

"I hope you do, dear, because deep down inside me you are. Yum, yum!"

The shadow of a plane flitted across the sunny garden outside Marge's window. "I see the aircraft's just coming in. I'll talk to you later. . . ."

Dick grinned to himself; he'd won, she was still dangling.

"O.K.," he said mildly, "I understand. It stays status quo, huh?"

"Well, like temperature," Marge said, "love's unpredictable."

She calls it love now, he thought, and said, "I'm real good at it."

"Sometimes you are. Other times you're plain cocksure. We'll see—"

"Promises—" Dick commenced, but Marge hung up on him. It didn't bother him a bit. He closed his draperies, stepped out of his briefs and into the shower. Under the benison of warm water he began to daydream about better times, as he often did. When blissfully young, there were no hurdles; now life was beginning to be an obstacle race. He'd always had the equipment to fascinate people, the ability to enjoy himself with either sex and bring them satisfaction in every possible way. Doris, John, Evelyn, Carl, Louise, Joe. . . . All luscious variations, and good old Rex Bulfinch, the aging designer, old enough to be his great-aunt, wild for arena sex. Dick knew he was lucky that Rex's brutal murder in that Los Angeles park hadn't brought him into the police investigation, luckier still that

Rex had left him a respectable hunk of dough he'd promptly squandered, except for buying the massage studio.

But at twenty-six Dick couldn't go on being the professional stud forever. He'd lost the massage studio when he got mixed up with Louise, the director's wife, and the director had put his name in with the Jewish mafia. He'd had to flee L.A., losing all of his investment. For a while it was Las Vegas, Reno, then east. And finally, after a series of short jobs with various hotels he'd come to Florida. The jump to the Bahamas and Bimini Springs was inevitable.

But where did he go from here? he wondered as he toweled himself dry in front of the profile mirror. One possibility looked very hot: Agnes Bird. After one session with Maple, Aggie would want him more than ever; no worry there, Dick knew the range of his talents. Harry might be more jovial, but age was against him; he couldn't drive them crazy the way a younger man could. No real stamina.

And that's what Aggie Bird wanted, staying power. Maybe not the freshest, sweetest fruit on the tree, a little withered and overripe, but a helluva good meal ticket if he wanted out of this dump in a hurry and a quick, all-expenses-paid trip to the Coast. In a way, he was glad he'd kept in touch with Wayne, who'd clued him on Aggie Bird, Wayne's client. Fuck that silly bitch Marge Maple!

He reached for the new cologne and doused himself liberally with it. All the broads liked this one, it was French. He'd wear the new silk shirt, Pierre Cardin, with the green scarf. He turned and posed for himself in the mirror before he slipped into fresh briefs. Mighty goddam good equipment, he thought admiringly, flexing his biceps, his buttocks, and smiled a benevolent smile into the mirror that might have been genuine if he'd meant it for anyone other than himself.

The laundry-room lounge was the point of central focus for the housekeeping staff, Marge Maple knew only too well, for she'd arranged things that way. So whenever she was alerted to any difficulty, or anyone had a personal grievance to air, she headed directly for the lounge to involve herself in the action.

In the present case she was concerned with Joan Harrison as housekeeper and dietitian. Marge and Harry had killed two birds with one stone here, hiring Joan on as a dietitian, then dumping the additional house-maintenance duties in her lap, too, as soon as she arrived. Joan had never forgiven the Maples for this shaft; the maintenance job was the toughest part of her assignment. She could prepare fifty individual diets a day without working up an office sweat, but trying to keep the Bahamians in line as well as jumping through hoops and bowing and scraping to all the guest Charlies around wasn't the easiest of obligations.

On Joan's arrival, all staff responded warmly to her. The Maples thought her exceptional—for a black. Born in the Bahamas, Stateside-educated, Joan's exposure to race rights in a black southern college conditioned her to know her own mind quickly, to become fiercely defendant of black rights. A proud, strong woman, Joan was well aware of her potential and her limitations. She also knew how grossly unfair the Maples could be, and she was determined to do what she thought was right and honest at all times no matter how the Maples reacted, no matter if it meant her job. It was the least she could do, she felt, for her poor, benighted, and ignorant black countrymen who worked at Bimini Springs.

Joan was checking in a new shipment of cleaning supplies when Marge stormed into the lounge and slapped her hand down on the issue counter. Marge was still upset about Dick Carter, wanting him and simultaneously wishing she'd never become involved with him. No one appreciated Joan's efficiency more than Marge, but until she investigated the rumor about some trouble with the maids, she intended to maintain a brisk aggressiveness with Joan. Not hostile, not exactly friendly, more like firm.

"What's wrong now, Joan?" Marge asked curtly. "I've got a busy schedule this afternoon, but the grapevine tells me we've got a problem."

"I'm busy, too," Joan said in a honeyed voice, inventory board in hand. "It's the girls, Mrs. Maple." The "girls" were the maids. "They refuse to work those four extra hours you and Mr. Maple put in their contract. They say there's just no cause for it, and they demand the time off. We're not even all full up so far this season, and the four hours were to cover a maximum guest list, as I understand it."

Marge beetled her brow. "Joan," she said evenly, in control of her temper, "the maids are under standard contract to work forty-four hours a week, with no overtime. You know that as well as I do. Mr. Maple's issued orders they're to remain on standby for four more—forty-eight—*if* we request it. And that's also in the contract, no matter how they gripe about it. It's our prerogative to invoke the standby clause any time we want to. Now I hear that you say there's no need for the maids to work forty-eight hours, so if they're forced to, they'll go on strike. Joan, you and I know there's no such thing as strikes around Bimini Springs. . . ."

"That's right, Mrs. Maple, there never has been. . . ."

Joan stared across the counter at this strange white woman who was one of her bosses. All those cosmetics and garish clothes, that cloud of perfume. Good God, with all that righteous evil she was everything you learn to hate in whites, thought Joan, all the sins of the southland rolled into one tiny woman. There was no real need for the girls to work forty-eight hours a week, even if it was only to standby. If there had been, Joan would have argued the whole staff into it. After all, if the need arose, the obligation was in their contract. But at the same time, she couldn't stand by and let the Maples exercise their power at will this way, even if they were the owners. The girls weren't going on standby; she'd see to that.

"I didn't say 'strike,' Mrs. Maple," said Joan calmly. "I said they refuse to *work* the extra four hours as a form of *protest*."

"They'll work or quit," Marge said adamantly. "And if they don't conform, then it's your responsibility, Joan, you're in charge of them. That's the reason Mr. Maple and I decided to let you have a try at the job. We expected you to take care of all housekeeping labor troubles. We haven't the time to arbitrate these disputes."

"And I suppose my predecessor arbitrated—?" Joan said. She knew well enough that neither the Maples nor the housekeeper who preceded her had been able to handle the blacks half as well as she did.

"Mrs. Brecht was a hard case, Joan. She arbitrated nothing, but she didn't have any trouble with the help, either."

"Because they looked right through her. I'm not having trouble, Mrs. Maple. Besides, I handle the diet schedules *in addition* to watching over the girls." Joan put both elbows on the counter, feeling confident now that she had the situation well in hand. "You see, it's not just that they won't work those extra four hours under the present guest load, they're organizing—"

The word staggered Marge. "Organizing! My God, what kind of organizing?"

"Well, lectures. They're holding practical forums on various subjects. They aim to use those extra hours for evening study sessions, ma'am, not standby."

"What kind of—sessions?" Marge asked cautiously.

"Oh, basic subjects. Black female liberation, oppression of minority groups. There're also some less controversial subjects they want to explore, such as dressmaking and needlepoint, so they can eventually make things to sell to the Bay Street boutiques in Nassau. . . ."

Marge's complexion turned a pale puce. "Jesus," she muttered, "now I've heard everything! Don't they know that we whites are the minority group in the Bahamas?"

Joan began to twinkle. "Yes, Mrs. Maple, they know. I told them. Ninety per cent of the Bahamas is black, all right, but the girls say they're not talking about the whole archipelago, just right here at Devil Cay. And you got to admit they're being realistic statistically, Mrs. Maple. You whites here outnumber us blacks by a wide margin. It's an inescapable fact—like being truthful about where we're located geographically. Your brochures say the West Indies, the beautiful Caribbean. Truth is, we're in the Atlantic Ocean. . . ."

For a moment, hands on her hips, mouth set in a narrow straight line, Marge Maple stood her ground and glared stonily at Joan's wide, easy smile. You couldn't deal with Joan Harrison like any other bush nigger. She'd learned that the first day Joan walked on to the island. The woman was too smart, too poised and clever and subtle; she could twist things around until she always got her way. But they needed her for the rest of the season. Fire her and where would they find a replacement? It was even worse than that; fire her and all the blacks would walk out. Then where would they be? They couldn't get new help this time of year when everybody employable in the islands was already working.

"All right," said Marge, "I'll talk to Mr. Maple, I'll see how he feels about the angle you've presented. *If* the girls are doing something constructive with that standby time, maybe it's all for the best to let them go ahead and have their classes. But if I hear one loose word about Communism or see one copy of Marx or Mao circulating, there'll be trouble. . . ."

"I understand," said Joan, masking her elation. "They're good girls, Mrs. Maple. They were only demanding their rights."

"Rights, my ass!" Marge exploded, unable to control any longer. "You all got them a hundred years ago in my country!"

"Yes, supposedly in the U.S.A.," said Joan slowly, "but

this is *my* country. And some people don't feel like they've ever had them."

"That may be the case," Marge replied, thinking she'd better leave well enough alone. "How's the inventory coming?"

"Better than I expected. Would you believe it? I turned up a dusty old packing box with over three dozen brand-new contour sheets that Mrs. Brecht had either overlooked or tucked away for emergencies."

Marge snorted. "Tucked away to ship out privately, I imagine, and didn't have time. . . . Just keep on like this and you'll be captain of the ship someday," Marge said. "I've got to run."

"I intend to keep right on, ma'am," Joan purred. "I do indeed. . . ."

Keep right on until the end of the season, Joan mused, watching Marge walk out of the lounge and close the door carefully behind her. Then what? What had her education really done for her? Made her capable of teaching, mainly, but she didn't want to do that, couldn't get a decent post, anyway, in the islands. When she returned from college, she'd had to hire on as a housekeeper for the St. Martins in Nassau, and finally, just when she couldn't stand that any longer, she'd seen the advertisement about Bimini Springs and this thing, her job. It was a thing all right, but the good bit of it was that she could save some money. Kill Howard too, of course. If it was just herself and that Kilroy on Devil Cay, she'd have something to work toward. But with what went on—the venal Maples and all, the trick-turning massage department, the smuggled alcohol, all those coddled, physically sick white patients that drifted on and off the island—what was the point?

She finished checking off the last of the boxed supplies, thinking much of the time she felt like one of those blacks in that film by Tennessee Williams, *Baby Doll,* the ones who lolled around on the lawn outside the big house, lying smack up against tree trunks, feigning sleep, bottle in coveralls, laughing like hell under their breath at the outrageous antics of their idiot, white-faced overlords. Only in her case the antics weren't so funny; they just made her nauseated. Because she believed that something could and had to be done for the island blacks. Too many had been too servile for too long. Jamaica and other worlds were waking up. Why not hers?

Joan moved the stock-room ladder against the shelves next to the counter and began to shelve the supplies she'd checked out. She knew she ought to call one of Bailey's maintenance boys, that's what they were hired for, but by the time one would drag his lazy ass around, she could do the job herself.

She was regrouping some cans of enamel cleaner when Dick Carter walked into the lounge and up to the counter. He was wearing a jaunty silk shirt and a meat-hunting expression, Joan noted.

"Hi, girl!" Dick's joviality was the last thing Joan needed right now.

"You want something, Mr. Carter?" She didn't budge from her position on the ladder.

Dick stared at Joan's shapely calves, on his eye level. "I'm reminded of a corny old joke: 'You know what I *want*, lady. Unscrew it and toss it down,' as the guy said to the old maid in the window."

"I said, do you want something?"

"Yeah, sure. A couple of bottles of massage lotion."

"The stock was transferred to Mr. Street last week," said Joan, "if you recall. Mr. Maple decided it comes under medical supplies from now on."

"Oh sure, sure, I remember. . . ." Then, nimbly, he vaulted the counter, reached for Joan, and ran his hand up her skirt.

Surprised and outraged, Joan kicked out at him, catching him under the chin with the toe of her sandal. Dick backed against the counter, his face white with fury.

"What's wrong with you?" he growled.

Without stirring from her stance on the ladder, Joan said, "Get outta here, you son of a bitch, and leave me alone!"

"Don't be such a goddam stick," Dick said, trying to cover his embarrassment and shock with a weak grin. "I'm going—" and he jumped back over the counter into the lounge area.

"I'll *stick you* if you ever try that again," Joan raged quietly. "I'm not one of your table tricks, you rotten ofay."

"I was only trying to be friendly. You play rough."

"I play it like I see it! You whites think you can get away with anything, anytime—with anybody. Even now, after the warnings have gone up, blacks still don't have a chance."

"You do all right."

"With no thanks to honkies like you," Joan shot back. "In the future you keep away from me. I got friends around here."

"Kill Howard's possessive, is that it?"

Joan jumped from the ladder to the floor of the supply room and gripped the counter's edge, a fierce pride in her eyes. "Kill Howard's got nothing at all to do with my life, Mister Charlie! Anyway, he's at least a decent person. And we can turn our backs on the likes of you no matter what it costs."

"O.K., O.K.," Dick said, admitting defeat. "Next time I'll go to the pharmacy for my goodies. . . ."

"See that you do!"

Joan watched him leave, jaunty again, whistling. What in hell did an education mean, she thought, when people could still treat you like a piece of meat? If all the whites on this job were as decent as Ruth Severn and Dr. Mack, everything would be fine. But Bimini Springs was no paradise. It was a microcosm of the United States, the status world, with all its attendant decadence, disorder, and dishonesty.

The phone ringing jolted her out of her somber mood; it was Kill Howard.

"No," Joan said firmly, smiling to herself. "Can't make it tonight. . . . Sure, I'll tell you why: got a needlepoint class, that's why. And don't call *me* a liar, Kill Howard, or you'll never get me to meet you anywhere again!"

Part
❁ TWO ❁

For several weeks past at Thompson's California ranch headquarters and prior to the sudden Nassau exodus, Dan Francovich had noticed that his boss didn't seem to be too well. His features were drawn, his complexion pale. He tired easily, began to take short afternoon naps, and although Thompson was in touch with his doctors, his condition didn't seem to improve all that much.

When Francovich pressed him about this one day, Thompson simply warned him off the subject. The big man was one of the world's most ardent Mammon worshipers, relishing every aspect of his money power, and he wasn't at all ready yet to depart his earthly empire: nor did he normally neglect his health. There was some logical reason why Thompson evaded his question; he didn't discover it until they arrived at Nassau. The mystery about Thompson's health was finally cleared up aboard the *Sarcophagus*, early on the morning of their arrival, and before they started their cruise through the Bahamian archipelago.

Dan unpacked in his cabin, then went up on deck for a breath of fresh air before turning in. Passing an open hatch, he heard voices—Thompson's and another he thought he recognized—and paused to listen for some reason he couldn't explain to himself; it wasn't his nature to eavesdrop.

In a few moments he learned that the man with Thompson was Dr. John Becker and that he was briefing the big man on his physical condition. Dr. Becker, director of the Miami Medical Center and an old personal friend of Thompson's, had flown down the night before to be on hand for a consultation with Thompson. Becker, it seemed, had ordered certain tests made on Thompson when he'd come out to the Coast a couple of months earlier to settle some routine organizational details about the research program at the Miami institute.

What Francovich heard shocked him. Terence P. Thompson was ill, very ill. Unless he continued to follow a strict program of palliative medication for his condition, it could be terminal any time in the future. Francovich remained by the open hatch long enough to hear the vital details, then went to the lounge library, took down a medical manual, and returned to his cabin. A perusal of the manual prompted him to lock his cabin door and write a letter, a letter he never imagined he would ever write. Yet he could not restrain himself; it had to be done. His job wasn't to go poking into the sacrosanct private life of Terence P. Thompson, and if Thompson knew what he was doing, divulging highly classified personal information, Francovich knew he'd be out on his rump in a minute, fired on the spot. Thompson would consider this the grossest kind of betrayal. But even so, the other situation had gone on too long; it was too childish, unnecessary. Perhaps his letter would clear it up.

He wrote:

Dear Mrs. Thompson:

This is probably the most difficult letter I'll ever write, and I'm not at all sure I should involve myself. Your husband would take a very dim view of my action, anyway. But there's something I just found out and thought you ought to know since it concerns his life. I have no idea how this knowledge will affect your eventual decisions concerning Terry, and that's none of my business. Even though we've never met, my feeling for you is one of respect, and I felt very simply that you ought to know the facts as I've heard them.

A few minutes ago I inadvertently overheard a significant conversation between your husband and Dr. John Becker of the Miami Medical Center. We're in Nassau now, aboard the *Sarcophagus*, and there's a chance that you're also in this area, and by sending this letter to your mother it will hopefully reach you through forwarding before we return to the Coast.

When Dr. Becker was out at the Big Sur ranch on an organizational conference recently, Becker and your husband had some very long, sequestered talks together. After Becker's departure I noticed an air of worry about Terry which was anything but characteristic and a certain steady fatigue he hadn't manifested before. When I questioned him about it, for he was taking afternoon naps and retiring earlier than usual, he said not to be silly, he was perfectly O.K.

Well, now it seems that accidentally I've learned the real reason for the change in him. Terry has what appears to be a cryptogenic cirrhosis of the liver. I didn't hear all the fine details, but this is generally thought of as a classic female disease—and, incidentally, this seemed to bother him the most—although more and more men are being diagnosed with it every day. The disease is called systemic lupus erythematosus, or more simply, SLE. I checked this out five minutes ago with a current Swiss medical manual from ship's library. It's an auto-immune condition where the body produces powerful immunity against itself. And there's no known cure. . . .

But it's not quite that black, however, Becker said. At Big Sur he apparently prescribed a specific series of tests and treatment which were administered by staff without my being at all aware of it. Terry responded well, so Becker told him as I listened. He could die in a few months; he could live another twenty years. The disease is entirely unpredictable. Therapy consists of diuretics to control body fluids and carefully administered corticoids to suppress some of the more debilitating effects of the disease. But energy levels aren't normal, ever, so Becker said, and this is to be expected. You can check all this out with a physician if you want to, to get a clearer picture.

I'm going out now to mail this in care of your mother, whose address I have, feeling certain that she'll know exactly how to get it to you. I'll enclose a note for her along with this sealed envelope explaining its urgency, and I trust she'll forward it to you without delay. We'll be on a cruise for the next few days, but you can always leave a message for Terry at the Aquarius Tower, his Nassau property. We'll be staying in his apartment there on our return to Nassau for a brief but indefinite period.

I would appreciate your saying nothing to Terry about this letter and destroying it at once. I don't relish losing my job over this breach of confidence but felt that your knowing this information was even more important than my job as his personal aide. Although we have never met, I feel fairly certain that this knowledge may influence your future plans.

Sincerely,

Dan Francovich

As Dan Francovich returned the sentry's salute at the gangway and went ashore to drive into town to the Aquarius Tower and mail the letter to Mrs. Mix, Marilyn's mother in Beverly Hills, Thompson and Becker were still in conference. Dr. Becker was trying to persuade Thompson to retire from active business life, to conserve his energy in favor of his health and a prolonged life, and Thompson was telling him to go to hell, he'd do just as he'd always done—work.

Cindy Brown began to feel rotten the moment she walked into the Bimini Springs dining salon for her evening meal of a jumbo low-calorie salad, broiled grapefruit with saccharine sauce, and the perennial pot of unsugared tea. . . .

She wasn't sure whether it was the heady aroma of baked whitefish, the reeking perfume some dowager guest was wearing, or some other unidentifiable scent that gave her the vapors. Everything was upsetting to her today. She'd been thinking heavily about the two most important people in her life—her hammer-headed mother and her husband, and they were generally the sources of her current discontent. But even they couldn't account for the thick waves of nausea that suddenly swept over her as she threaded her way between the tables of noisy dieters, smiling sweetly at guests she knew, toward her single corner table.

Life was engaging her in the same old battle once again. She'd been at Bimini Springs a whole week so far and hadn't been able to shed more than a few miserable pounds, and the more she thought about the weight, the more she blamed her mother and her husband with the responsibility.

The black headwaiter, the handsome Fred Williamson type named Kilroy Howard, happened to be moving in the vicinity of her table when she arrived. He seated her courteously, for which she was grateful. The way she felt, she wasn't strong enough to pull out her own chair.

"Thank you," she murmured to Kilroy Howard as he bowed, smiling. Such a fantastically controlled person, she thought through her nausea, always soothing the ruffled features of some old biddy, seating people, arriving with some special surprise dish for a spoiled, disgruntled guest. And he knew the precise moment to disappear so he wouldn't be an easy target for some idiot's unreasonable rage. Diet never made anybody too happy, she knew all too well.

Howard was leaning over her solicitously, she realized. "You all right, Miss Brown? Something special you want—?"

"I—I'll just have some of those diet wafers and a pot of black tea," Cindy faltered, really too weak to pick up the menu and order her salad.

"Right, ma'am." She saw the faint reproof in his eyes, as if she ought to be eating something sensible and solid, something for strength, for she was worn out.

"Thank you. . . ." She leaned back against the stiff chair, hoping the room would quit whirling and dipping.

Fat, fat, fat, layers of it, acres of it, eddying around her all her life. It seemed sometimes that she'd been born overweight, that by some trick of fate her scales would continue to frustrate her indefinitely. When something exciting and attractive entered her life, she could get her weight under control, groom herself into a charming image. Then, if the least little thing went wrong, bang, crash, up went the weight again, back into the land of blubber. All through early childhood there was the burden of fat. And her mother, Patsy, hadn't helped any. An overcompensating, have-another-chocolate, sweetheart-type of parent who found her own security in her daughter's chubby, awkward confrontation with the world. And the money hadn't helped, either. The inheritance from her maternal grandmother made her a multimillionairess at eight. "Who cares what you weigh, darling," Patsy said when she broke the news of the inheritance, "as long as your pockets are full?" And that was the same week that the kids down the block called her slopfat and wouldn't invite her to their party; she was too gross. Fatso and slobass were common labels, she got used to them early; and before she was fourteen, there was another, ugly duckling. And this one had hurt terribly at the time, sending her weight up another twenty pounds. But she knew now that she'd never been as plain as her mother or her acquaintances said she was. She had good features, good bone structure, her figure wasn't bad when she was slimmed down. Nice skin, good teeth, pretty hair, nice eyes. But that imprisoning wall of fat had surrounded her, on and off, for so long that she'd come to think of herself as subnormal, torpid, caught in the grinding mesh of fate, unable to extricate herself.

A few times she'd willed away the fat and managed to get on top of her eating habits. Life had become lyrical in these short-lived periods; she was almost completely happy. Almost happy, not quite, because she knew from experience the periods couldn't last. Something always happened to burst the bubble. She was still a prisoner, even without the security-tight cell of flesh around her, for the minute some crisis hit her, she'd start eating again and revert to her former rotundity. She'd once managed to put on ten pounds over a weekend; twenty in a week was easy.

She'd married Poppy to find release, to stop thinking about herself all the time and concentrate on her husband, on friends. If Patsy hadn't fought the marriage so hard, she might have remained single. But of course there was the love part—she'd quite simply fallen in love with him. Maybe she was looking for the father who was dead before she could form memories of him, leaving all that money to her mother, for the Brown women were always wealthy, always outlived their spouses. God knows the attraction to Poppy was honest enough, mutual enough. She liked the power he represented, and he found her sexually attractive, not being interested in her money. So the insulation that money had always given her, the protective covering with which she insulated herself against the world, suddenly had no meaning. The idea of having to find other values stimulated her even before they were married. In their month of courtship she lost eighteen pounds; the rest was easy. And it appeared for a while as though the marriage would bring her into the full flower of her middle and late twenties, matching Poppy's sixties. But all the scope of marriage was denied her. Poppy intended to keep her in a far worse kind of prison than fat and loneliness and rejection had put her. Although he hadn't bought her, Cindy found out soon enough that he thought he had. He allowed her no status as a human being, all the while smothering her with jewels, clothes, electronics gadgets, expensive cars. She wasn't allowed to drive anywhere by herself, to take a solitary day's outing when she wished. She couldn't attend school again or even hire teachers for her instruction at the ranch. She wanted to paint, but Poppy laughed at her. "You want pictures, I'll buy you the best there are," he told her. "Don't go making amateur smears of your own." So the arguments over her freedom began almost at once, and she discovered very soon that she had gained nothing, merely exchanging one kind of restrictive confinement for another. What she was and what she felt simply did not matter to Poppy. She was his plaything, his amusement parlor. That she was there in his bed when he needed her—and he needed her, wanted her, every night—was her most important contribution to their strange, lopsided marriage, she knew. But then, their sexual climate was the one successful aspect of the union. Poppy was a good teacher. She was awakened from a long dormancy and was drawn gradually into the elaborate kinky games played under soft pink lights, in front of wide mirrors, to the soft purring of a hidden camera projecting color pornos on a sliding wall. There was a certain reluctance at first, but gradually she accepted all the props and paraphernalia, even to the delicate whips that were made of satin and suede in Mexico. She liked the costumes, sometimes she was delighted with them, and her delight was instantly communicable to Poppy who could only rise to an occasion when she responded. She did her best, and in really trying to cooperate, she found in herself an almost frighteningly avid capacity for varying her own moods, for although she was no virgin when she married Poppy, she came to his bed with the limited experience of several one-sided lunges by men her own age who hadn't bothered to bring her to orgasm. That was the one thing about Poppy she could totally accept—his enormous sexual vitality and creativity. She rather missed that, although she tried to turn it off completely when she ran away. For she'd had to run. When everything else in their relationship became meaningless, she found she couldn't function in bed. And when this stopped, Poppy stopped, the whole marriage stopped.

Her mother had planned the disappearance—engineered it, was more exact. Patsy disliked Poppy so much she was glad to have this control over his emotions, so she had kept Cindy's secret well. Patsy played the role of righteous, protective parent to the hilt, fighting off the hound dogs on her trail, the private eyes Poppy employed. Cindy managed to take off from her mother's Beverly Hills mansion and, to all intents and purposes, disappear forever from her husband's life.

Cindy followed a crazy, zigzag trail across the U.S., and after considerable running and backtracking, got the job in New York, which immediately dropped away the sheath of blubber the end of her marriage had returned to her. But then, Poppy's hounds had located her and she was off again, fat harpy fleeing to Coral Gables, Florida. With the imbalance in her life, the weight shot up again, alarmingly, about as high now as it had ever gone. So how could she not brood upon the shambles of her life? A marriage that was a separation, with neither party giving in to divorce in the same way, therefore deadlocked? How could she avoid thinking without emotion about Poppy, for whatever the son of a bitch was, he was the only man who'd ever loved her, in his own peculiar way, which may merely have been the hunger he saw in her eyes. Hunger after hunger, none of it ever appeased for long. Then the treadmill, the moving scenery. Christ, how long would it go on, she sometimes wondered, for they were both so rotten stubborn, neither willing to give in to the other, that the battle could rage forever. She certainly wasn't going to capitulate, nor was he. . . .

Abruptly the room began to sway before her eyes. She braced her feet flat on the floor, praying that the vertigo would pass quickly; she would hate to be sick in the dining room. And slowly, slowly, the thing subsided. But that terrible perfume, like taffy candy, lingered in her nostrils.

Well, if she hadn't lost much weight at Bimini, she'd certainly lost something else—her sense of proportion, her inner balance and direction. Her cool. For here, at long last, after swimming around like an aimless fat fish for endless months, in a limbo of fright wigs and other disguises, she'd found a point of focus: Dr. Kevin Mack. Never mind that it didn't make sense, that it was incredible—there it was; *he* was. All six feet two of him. Every time he swung that big body of his into the dining salon, crooked a smile at her across the pool, or took her pulse on his rounds, clamped her wrist in his cool fingers, such a delicious shivering sensation raced through her that she almost fountained into orgasm—gushed, oozed, groaned, and became totally undone. Even Dr. Mack's formal bedside amiability and his resonant, manly voice made her simply let go.

Her reaction was beyond analyzing, unless of course she had finally rejected Poppy deep down and this was the first external manifestation. It was nothing like the tidal wave that had tumbled her into Poppy's arms—that was a roaring holocaust, awe mingled with admiration, indignation, a layer of rage topped with the whipped cream of strong sexual curiosity, as if dildos and knives and whips and jingle bells were coming at her from all directions. Now once again something was happening to her. And not a rational kind of response, either, though not like that turbulent melodrama of her marriage. This time there was a gentle, almost sugary sentiment, a motherly urge to gather Kevin Mack to her soft, creamy breasts, stroke and soothe his little-boy charm, nurse and fondle him, cuddle, coddle, love, love love!

Ugh—! There it was again—that leaping nausea. She gritted her teeth and hung on until it passed.

And there was something else about Dr. Mack—his awareness of her; he wasn't indifferent, that she knew, even if he did have other interests. Like that antiseptic nurse, Ruth Severn, or was he having a wild thing with the masseuse, Anita Pomeroy? Or maybe he liked boys, men. Kilroy Howard, Tom Street, the pharmacist?

Oh, for God's sake, she thought irritably, what's *happening* to me? Yes, it had to be Ruth Severn and Dr. Mack, for there was more than just professional rapport between the good doctor and little Nurse Valiant. Maybe he was actually in love with her, Cindy allowed, admitting to herself that she was developing a definite hostility toward that calm, efficient woman who sat only a few tables away from her in profile, so hygienic and smiling, so self-contained. And the hostility was patently ridiculous, for Kevin Mack had never given her the slightest reason or right to be so persuaded by her own emotions. For that's all the infatuation was—pure simpering, drooling emotion, nothing more. Patients in TB sanitoriums always fell in love with their doctors, or so Thomas Mann had led her to believe. And why not at a reducing spa? With so damned little else to do to relieve the dread monotony of diet and routine on this tiny sunburned isle, she was examining her emotions too closely, building a situation. But this was more than fantasy. It was as real as the nausea, like the prison of fat in which she was cocooned, seemingly forever. . . .

Loyal, the waiter, brought her pot of tea and the wafers. She hoisted the heavy ceramic teapot jerkily, dreaming of an improbable situation—herself, gorgeous and unrecognizable after cosmetic surgery, reborn from the ugly chrysalis, irresistible to the good doctor who would walk right up to her, grab her with his powerful arms, press his throbbing masculinity against her, open mouth on her own, exploring her tongue and teeth, then ripping open her dress while throwing her on the bed, slithering his tongue down across her breasts, her nipples, down the curve of her belly to that shadowed secret place, licking into corners and crevices along the way, while she begged him frantically to wait, wait, for she was about to crest the giant wave, legs in the air. . . .

Good God, she thought, swimming up out of the deep trench of her hallucination, steadying the tilted teapot, begging for the strength to pour herself a simple cup of tea.

Cosmetic surgery: only the other day she'd discussed the matter with Dr. Mack. "Doctor, I'd like to do something about the basic me, something drastic."

Dr. Mack read her tone. "Miss Brown," his voice stern, "there's nothing wrong with the basic you. You're young and healthy. Fat isn't a social disorder or a lifetime handicap. You're simply blocking off self-control for reasons best known to yourself. Underneath what offends you is a lovely, pleasant, charming person. Let her emerge, give her a chance. But please stop thinking of yourself as the fat stand in a freakshow."

"I feel like one. I've been at it a long time."

"All the more reason to stop it now," Dr. Mack had replied sternly. "The drop in weight will come automatically and dramatically once you control your point of view. And one good way is to stop worrying."

"I need plastic surgery—"

Dr. Mack had smiled, shaken his head. "You're brainwashed with hogwash, young lady. Many are—"

"But if I had nose and chin corrections," hurrying brightly on, "and maybe an eyebrow lift. . . ." Cupping her breasts with both hands: "And these hang to my knees. . . ." Grabbing the pendulous fold of fat that dangled from the underside of one forearm: "Arm lifts, too—" She slapped her chunky thigh: "And lifts here, I think. And then maybe some take-up across the abdomen, and I'd be all set. . . ."

Dr. Mack's gentle tolerance was melting her. "My dear Miss Brown, you're developing gerontophobia, and you're not even thirty. Diet's the answer, not cosmetic surgery. I'm only here, of course, to supervise your reduction, but let me say this: I think I know what your problem is. You've allowed something, maybe one bad emotional peak, to throw your whole life out of gear, and that means your metabolic responses."

"My life's always been out of gear, Doctor. Not just one bad emotional peak, a whole range of them."

Here he'd patted her hand, sending a tiny shiver into her toes. "There's nothing wrong with you but self-indulgence. Forget about the surgery; it isn't required. No doctor worth his salt would allow you to have it. All you need is—"

Cindy sighed and cut in, "I know, I know. Diet and more diet."

"Right, right. And don't ever forget it," he said, leaving her to brood about her fat, to ponder the utter futility of life that couldn't be ordered so that Dr. Mack would regard her as something other than a specimen. . . .

The heavy teapot wavered in her hands, began to slip away, and thudded against the white tablecloth, sending a steamy wave of amber liquid racing across the table, narrowly missing her knees. A sharp, reactive movement of her right hand as she released the pot handle swept the cup and saucer onto the tile floor, smashing them to bits.

People were now staring at her. She made one enormous effort of will to rise, gulping air, fighting off the enveloping veil of nausea that closed in over her, then gave up and collapsed heavily onto her chair, hitting the seat hard and slowly sliding, limp as a water-filled balloon, from the chair onto the floor, out cold in a dead faint. . . .

Ruth Severn and Dr. Mack abandoned their dinner and rushed to her aid, all professional concern.

It was only natural that a pair of couples as gregarious and garrulous as the Flemings and Bernheims would eventually find each other's level at Bimini Springs. As Cindy Brown fainted, the Flemings and Bernheims were having their first dinner together—they'd joined tables by a large window and were expressing their pleasure with the Springs—the pool deck, the therapeutic waters, the cuisine, the climate. Their enthusiasm was excessive, but then, as Kill Howard observed to himself, they were excessive people: too corpulent, too loud, too hungry, they played pinochle too hard, and they took too much sun. In fact, they would have been standard caricature American tourists if abroad.

When Cindy slipped away, a few tables from the Flemings and Bernheims, Alice Bernheim became unreasonably hysterical. It took the other three to calm her.

"From trying to lose weight," she wailed, "I'm having as hard a time as that poor Brown girl. Maybe I'm going to be the next victim myself!" She clutched at her husband. "Phil, you're taking me back home tomorrow!"

"I'll take you to the room," Phil said, "and that's all."

"Or some place where everything I eat goes to water, not to fat. . . ."

"Speaking of water—" Rose Fleming forced a glass of ice water on Alice. "It's no good this cold for ulcers. You ever had them?" Up until now, the two couples had merely passed courtesy conversation back and forth without exploring one another's biographical data.

"I did," said Phil. "Mama's always wanted one, too. All she ever got was a rundown on mine."

"Well, I've had them," Rose said proudly, "and Jack hasn't."

"So give her a medal," said Jack. "The little woman's always one-upping me. . . . But there's one thing she's never gonna have." He winked at Phil. "And that's prostrate trouble!"

"Pros*trate*?" said Alice, sitting up straight, her hysterics gone. "Its pro*state*. You can't even spell it! My God, who'd want an exclusive on something like that?" she demanded.

"Because," said Phil dryly, "women don't have them."

"You're so full of news," Alice said.

"And you're so full of surprises," Phil rejoined.

Jack Fleming cleared his throat and said irrelevantly, "Christmas. We don't celebrate it at home, so that's when we travel. We just close the business and go. We deferred it this year. Business was that good. . . ."

"Ah," said Phil, more relaxed with Alice back to normal, "no family?"

"No kids," Jack explained. "Lousy with cousins, aunts, uncles. Plenty of those." He sighed.

Phil sighed in empathy. "Yeah, same with us. So we always go somewhere, too. . . . Well, I'll be damned. Last year we spent Christmas in Jerusalem, on the Israeli side, of course. Got friends there, the Rosenblatts. Fools went over from New York. He left a good dental practice. . . ."

"Well," said Jack, "it's all in the way you want to dedicate yourselves. You know, I thought you two looked familiar. Rose, we seen them in Tel-Aviv. . . ."

Rose snapped her fingers. "Oh God, I'm sure we did."

Alice Bernheim giggled, sipped on her ice water. "Cripes, the long arm of coincidentalness. I must say, for real *kosher* food you can't beat home products. Theirs was real *dreck*. Awful!"

"Right! Lord, how I'd love a bagel sandwich with lox and cream cheese. Mmmmmm!" Rose smacked her lips. "Hey, I wonder if we're going to lose enough here so's we can take another trip around Easter, Jack, like the Catskills, and put it all back on?"

Jack shrugged coldly. "You talking to me, I'm not listening. You're an expensive woman."

Phil chuckled. "Not put it back on, eh? Daydreamers, all of us. We'll put it back on. Hey, let's make a nice, safe bet, no money involved. We'll meet at some other Bimini Springs-type place this coming Passover. How's that?"

Jack regarded Phil and the two women without humor. "You're spineless fatsos, all three of you," he said severely. "Talking light like this about your will power. What would the Maples think if they heard you, doubting the success of their system? Or that Dr. Mack—?"

"That we're just like everybody else here," Rose declared sensibly. "Who knows? Maybe the Maples actually pray that the guests'll get gross after they leave so they'll all have to come back!"

"That's a revolting idea that could only come from my dear wife's tongue," Jack said, turning up his long nose. "Hey, Phil, I'll take the bet. We meet somewhere for Passover, all four of us, still all slimmed down and gorgeous. Why not Marrakesh—?"

"Morocco? A Moslem country—?" Alice said, genuinely horrified. "Not me!"

"Honey, we've always wanted to go to Marrakesh and stay at the La Mamounia," Rose said to Jack.

"It's on," Phil said, grasping Jack's outstretched hand and crushing it heartily in his own. "We'll take it."

The two women smiled conspiratorially at one another, a common bond established, over and above social games.

"Don't worry about the Arabs," said Rose. "They're really Moors. It would be pleasant, Alice. We'd sneak away and do some exotic shopping. And nobody eats pork—"

"Yeah," said Alice, reassured, "I'd forgotten. We could see the sights, maybe blow some grass. My nephew Sammy turns on. He was there. He said some of the best hash in the world comes from Marrakesh, also from Tel-Aviv. . . ."

Rose grinned, her eyes bright. "You wouldn't—" she challenged.

Alice flicked an oblique glance at Phil's grim jawline. "Yeah, I think I would. It'd be something different. . . ."

"*Oy vey*, wouldn't it!" exclaimed Rose.

"I'm surprised at both you ladies," Phil said stiffly, "and especially you, Alice. Under the circumstances. The other guests might overhear you. . . ."

"So it's a *crime*," said Alice defensively, "and pretty soon fifty million people are going to be doing it in the U.S.A. It sure isn't a *sin*—"

"Myself," Jack said, "I'll stick to French cognac. It's cheap as hell in North Africa."

"Poison's poison," said Alice, "bottled or smoked."

"So's herring," said Phil. "Tomorrow let's start that pinochle tournament. How about it?"

"Poolside," Rose agreed.

"Definitely poolside," Jack said. "In the morning—?"

"In the afternoon," said Alice, "I'm a slow waker. In the morning I intend to jog around the island on that cinder path."

"And *I'm* with *you*," Rose said, patting Alice's hand. "It's nice we're getting acquainted."

"It's as nice as anything," Alice responded warmly. "But I wish to God I had a great big gorgeous cold buffet in front of me right now. I'm slowly dying of malnutrition."

Phil lowered his voice and leaned forward. "Confidentially, it's not very good, is it?" he asked the Flemings.

"Nothing ever is *that* good in goy establishments," Jack replied solemnly. "And the *schvartze* help yet, too!"

"*If* we go to Marrakesh, I'm certainly going to try to get—" Alice began, but Phil silenced her with a heavy glance.

"Yeah, the *souks*—" Rose murmured dreamily. "I got to have a camel-skin pouf, gold-embossed, for our sundeck lounge. The best ones come from Morocco. . . ."

"Boy, am I glad we met," said Phil to Jack, and the two men exchanged private smiles.

"Sure, even if the food's fit for rabbits," Jack replied.

"Even if I'd give my happy marriage for some lox and cream cheese," Alice sighed.

"Stop torturing yourself!" Phil snapped.

"Yeah, *this* place," Rose said, "just isn't with it."

"Especially *this* place," Alice agreed.

"Everything all right, folks—?" Kill Howard was hovering over them solicitously, with his pleasant, fixed smile.

"Delicious," said Alice, "perfectly delicious—" and hefted a hunk of Romaine lettuce drenched in lemon juice.

"Fabulous," said Rose, fingering her glass of tepid tomato juice.

"Healthy," Phil conceded. "Isn't that right, Jack?"

"That's right, Phil," said Jack. "Healthy's the word. And that's why we're here, isn't it? Health!"

"Well, anything you need, folks, just ask for it," Kill Howard told them courteously, and turned away to another table, thinking that the bullshit people put up with at a place like Bimini Springs was equal to the bullshit they brought with them. . . .

At least, thought Kill Howard, the Flemings and Bernheims are enjoying themselves with their feeble corny jokes and their brittle Yiddish parrot chatter. They were going to be O.K., those Jews, among the easy ones to serve. Oh, they'd bitch and *kvetch* and outshout anybody else poolside while they played their pinochle, but they'd struggle to lose the weight they aspired to, and they'd tell all their friends what a deluxe place Bimini was, a place of tolerance where the races lived together harmoniously.

Well, maybe the white races, but blacks and whites didn't mix too well here. The same old story, Bimini was really the exclusive province of fat, rich white slobs. And speaking of slobs or blobs, that chubby Cindy Brown girl seemed to be a fool as well. Doing unauthorized fasting to the point where she passed out. at mealtime and they lugged her off to her room. Maybe she was grandstanding for the doc; women did. Severn didn't even seem to mind, or did she? Was indifference her way of staying close to him? Funny people around here—complex, involved, tense. Even Joan, among the blacks. When really the only good thing about life was that you didn't have to raise your temperature or your voice. Invisible, you could coast along and do as you liked. Some people never learned the knack of this, and Kill knew he wouldn't have either except for Vietnam; it taught him patience and tolerance through the worst lessons of all. From despair came a knowledge of self and a balance with the world.

A black waiter passed with a very sloppy serving tray. Kill grabbed him by the elbow.

"Loyal—" Kill's voice was low but firm. "The next time you rock through those swinging doors with a mess of garbage like this I'm going to fine you a day's pay, you hear? And since I'm blacker than you are, Sambo, nobody's gonna call it discrimination, are they—?"

Loyal grinned through his sweat and hurry. "O.K., Mr. Kilroy, I'll watch it. Rushed tonight. . . ."

"Rushed *every* night," said Kill. "Cool it. We can't have the guests up bitching to Mr. and Mrs. Whitey, can we, huh?"

"*Shee*itt, no!" said Loyal, and snaked around and back into the kitchen to restack his tray.

Kill entered the kitchen a few minutes later to check the evening service tables again. In his job he had to watch everything, all the time. The large kitchen was all steam and bustle. A big black matron with a white towel tied bandanna fashion around her head, her face glittery with sweat diamonds, was stacking some salad dishes onto shelves in an open standing reefer. Kill walked over to inspect the operation.

"Don't refrigerate those salads again, Lena. They've been at room temperature too long. Somebody'll get sick. There's fish in them."

"But Mr. Howard," Lena protested, "they ain't wilted. They fresh as anything."

"Maybe timewise, sure," Kill replied, "but they're gone, Lena. The tropics plus the kitchen does it. They won't come back. Chilled, they'll just turn at the edges. Better throw them out right now."

Lena sighed. "Wasteful, I calls it."

"Wasteful it is," Kill agreed, "but isn't it better than losing your job when somebody turns up with a roaring case of diarrhea, or worse, even ptomaine poisoning, and blames it on you—?"

"Yes, Mr. Howard, it is," said Lena obediently, and Kill moved on.

He was determined to bring them all around, the whole bumbling staff, in any way he could. Kindness, consideration, infinite patience—these were his tools. But if these didn't work, then he'd get as tough as the Maples were with everybody. His years as mess sergeant had drilled into him the indisputable reality that when you prepared food, somebody's ass was always at stake. Someone was going to bitch about something, however perfect it was, even if there was no need to, however much pains had gone into its preparation. The trick was not to let it be your ass that was chewed. So, on that premise, Kill exercised no leniency on laxity or poor judgment; he refused to tolerate it. Either his staff did the job they were required to do or suffered the consequences. So far he hadn't had to fire anybody, although they hadn't any of them yet come anywhere near to his standards, poor dumb bastards. But they'd better soon or some heads would roll.

Kill stopped beside the grill chef, a man named Hamilton from Nassau. "Take over, Ham. Got a lousy headache; I'm going to quarters. Call if you need me."

Ham grinned. "Sure thing, boss."

Kill returned Ham's grin. "And none of your blackass boss shit, Uncle Tom!"

"Yassuh, Massah Kill, suh," croaked Ham, winking broadly. "And you save a drag foah me, heah?"

Nodding, Kill walked out the rear entrance of the kitchen, heading for his staff quarters in the long, low wooden building some distance from the main lodge behind a palmetto screen. In Georgia they were cabbage palms; at places like Bimini the ofays called them palmettos, dig. After three months hustling things into fair shape around the kitchen and dining salon, ironing out production and service to coordinate with Joan's menus, he was on the verge of an easy time and could coast through the rest of the season, provided staff didn't get demoralized for some unforeseen reason. He was fond of Joan, fonder than he wanted to be; but she was a hothead, she caused trouble, no denying it. Always stirring up some kind of shit. But then, things could get too relaxed around Bimini, and life would pall, it might even become downright deadly. And that would never do.

In any case, his present life wasn't much like Vietnam, the tail end of fifteen years in the army: Germany, Casablanca, Stateside duty, Nam. Actually, Nam was the best. . . .

Because of Nguyen Van Tong—he called her Yen. Huge liquid black eyes and breasts like small pagoda turrets, a rarity among the mainly flat-chested VN chicks. Her loyalty, her gentleness, her devotion and quiet sense of humor, her way with food. . . . Born in Hanoi, a town of beautiful women, before the French sustained their defeat at Dien Bien Phu, she'd drifted to Saigon with an older brother after the rest of the family died in a bomb shelter. He met her as a bar girl before many GIs got to her. . . . And he had loved the muggy climate, too; it made him warm all over, relaxed, constantly horny. As Yen was, her appetite matched his; as they both were together in those languid nights. . . . He'd landed that cushy mess-club job after the accident, where he could do a bit of black marketing on the side with discreet VN merchants, and then he'd met Yen and made the big shack during his second year.

Soul Alley. . . . That's what the press called it, but it was just an ordinary ghetto street where he and his friends lived, eked out an existence. . . .

Kill entered his quarters and locked the door behind him, turned on his personal A/C unit, activated a Jimi Hendrix already on the turntable, and relaxed as the current of cool air began to fill the room. The Maples didn't furnish A/C to black help, using the specious argument that since most staff blacks were born in the tropics, they were already acclimated, dig.

From his closet Kill lifted out a locked handbag, keyed it open, and withdrew a large cardboard box of unmanicured grass—some loose stuff and two key bricks whose aroma tickled his nostrils as he lifted off the box lid.

Sweet, seductive dope, man! He sat down in an armchair and immediately rolled himself a big, fat joint. Headache? Shit! A joint and memories. . . . Saigon, Yen. . . .

Whites who ventured into Saigon's Soul Alley did so at their own risk. A black and brown world that excluded all others as enemies, as two military police learned shortly before the big raid, Kill recalled. Five minutes after the police drove their official jeep into the area at midmorning, they were hobbling back out—minus the vehicle, weapons, pants, even their shorts—bare butts and balls hanging out, hangdog shameful.

Although Kill wasn't a deserter, he'd done his AWOLs in the past; but Soul Alley was filled with career AWOLs. Some were his good friends. Easy enough to stash yourself there, being as it was as much Africa as Asia and everybody belonged to the same club, really. The army knew all about Soul Alley and its deserters—it had ever since the ghetto sprang up some three years before. MPs often staged minor raids and roundups and netted little. But MPs who came staggering out of the district balls-ass that day really triggered the big sweep.

Kill didn't like to think about it; he'd been working at the officers' mess when it happened. The raiding MPs were followed into the area by some ARVN MPs, Vietnamese forces who were attached to the Americans, and the ARVNs were uptight grim about the VN girls who shacked, bore children by, and served the black GIs. Treated them like shit when they got the chance.

Yen was at home when they raided the Alley, eight months pregnant with his child. The ARVN found Kill's stash of grass easy. It wasn't difficult to locate in the locked teakwood chest; they broke it open with their rifle butts. Then when they demanded to know whose it was—the Americans had moved on up the street by that time—Yen refused to tell them, so they beat her savagely. She was still lying bloody and unconscious on the polished floor when he returned in the evening, an old neighbor woman tending her as best she could, crooning and crying, too frightened to call a doctor if she could have found one who'd have come to Soul Alley.

Yen's face was unnaturally flushed from fever; she was almost delirious and having a miscarriage. Kill borrowed a jeep and rushed her to the nearest hospital, too late. Too late for the baby—a boy, stillborn. Yen died the following morning from massive internal injuries.

Kill had a new enemy; he lived up to his nickname. He and two buddies from Soul Alley accounted for three ARVN MPs a few nights later as the Vietnamese troops sauntered through Soul Alley. They stripped and dumped the bodies into the Saigon River at ebb tide so they'd float out to sea. No one ever pinned the disappearance on them. It wasn't much of a retribution, it didn't really ease his mind; he was only doing it for Yen. . . .

After that, he decided not to stay on. Without Yen there wasn't any reason. . . .

Back in Atlanta, out of the service at last, at the end of his rope, finding it difficult to adjust, he saw the ad the Maples placed in a newspaper for Bimini Springs help. Maître d'hôtel, they called it, but it turned out to be headwaiter, routine dish jockey. Harry had examined him like a side of questionable beef during their interview—he expected at any moment he'd have to show his teeth—and then hired him. . . .

High now, the grass buzzing pleasantly through him, he decided to clean some more of it. Nice to have his own sources, not having to make that perilous three-day run to Atlanta anymore. He'd been right to talk Linc into it, a system that just couldn't be beat. No narcs could detect the clever graft switch unless he was exceptionally hip, looking specifically for it.

Thanks to that little book with the section on how to grow cannabis plants that didn't look like marijuana. Shortly after World War II some enterprising cats tried to produce an improved hybrid by grafting pot plants onto the rootstocks of hops—cannabis's nearest relative. The experiment failed to produce a strong THC resin, but when the experiment was reversed—hops grafted onto cannabis plants—not only was the transfer successful, the matured hops leaves contained as much cannabis resin as the original marijuana plants would have produced. In plain words, what you came up with was a thirty-foot-long vegetable that *looked* like ordinary hops vines [you mixed them in with morning glories] but which contained the real stoned chemistry of high-quality pot. Their first harvest yielded seven kilo bricks and a lot of loose stuff. Some harvest!

Linc had been reluctant to embark on such an experiment, much as he savored grass. "No problem about growin' hops," he said. "Maples won't know or care. If somebody else sees them in that initial period when they both growin' . . ."

"All right then," Kill said, "build a greenhouse and grow flowers there, too. They won't object to that."

And that's what happened: Under carefully controlled conditions, they grew their greenhouse hops and grass, did the grafting by ground-level wedge in private. Later the plants were moved from the greenhouse to an arbor Linc built for them on which morning glories already bloomed. Nobody but Linc and Lulu and Joan knew anything about the operation besides Kill. Or if any others on the black staff did, nobody mentioned it; they were all too glad to be Kill's customers. Liquor was hard to come by on the island, the Maples prohibited it for all staff; even beer was rationed. Had to be some place to go, and up was as good a route as any.

A couple of whites were among Kill's customers: Tom Street came on for a lid now and then. Old Nellie Nosey had to have something to do besides jack off; nothing much for him to blow on the island but a little grass. And Dick Carter, Mister Muscles, stud extraordinaire, wow! Funny thing about ofays, though. Now these two smoked, but they never shared the confidence with each other, they were too cagey. Paranoid as hell. . . . And then, of course, there was Joan who loved her ration but sometimes denied it, and other soul brothers and sisters, long live the tribe. What Kill couldn't see was what the middle-aged establishment honkies put down grass so for. Far better for you than swilling booze, and much cooler.

As he worked, he thought about Joan and their relationship. Too easy that first night. They'd walked down to the moonlit beach, and she put out right there on the soft, warm sand, like frenzied, man, clawing and biting. Then, with those wild conflicts flying through her head, not crazy high like that first night, she'd later become tense with him, saying absolutely no, never again. All she'd do was talk that militant feminist bullshit and brandish books around like *Sexual Politics* and *The Female Eunuch*.

Shit, man, *sense*, he thought, as he winnnowed down the grass to a smooth consistency with his sieve and divided it into plastic-bagged lids, each an ounce by his pocket scales, for convenient vending. What kind of life was any place without some digging? If you can't screw the help and can't touch the guests, then what happened? At moments like this he felt cornered and looked for a way out. A wild hair hit him, flushed through his face, his limbs, settled in his gut. Why not re-enlist with the explicit request for VN duty? he mused. Back to Soul Alley and find himself another girl like Yen? Only you can't go back the same way, he knew, you go back some other road, man. And there were no other girls anywhere like Yen. . . . Well then, why not disappear into the Saigon ghetto for good, destroy his identity, desert? End up farming a hillside around Da Lat with some woman and raise scrawny kids? Or get out entirely through Cambodia to Thailand, or someplace, anyplace? Like the others who said fuck this fuckin' scene and the U.S. and went their own way with balls and determination.

It was really so easy. From an army of papa-san forgers he'd get a phony ID and ration cards. At the PX he'd buy a refrigerator for about $500 in MPCs, sell it in the black market. That would keep him for a while. And TV and stereo rigs went just as high. All kinds of money around if you put your shoulder to the problem.

Or sell grass and heavier things. Better living than here. But really not all that much; you got pissed on anywhere if you were black. Who got caught and hung for grass over there? Not the white GI motherfuckers who smoked it or dealt, just the blacks. A vicious circle that always came around to you in the end. Might as well stay right here at Bimini Springs, with your eyes on your boots. For a spell. Save enough bread in a couple of years to open a beer and hamburger joint somewhere in the U.S., maybe in some backwater spot removed from black/white prejudice alike. He chuckled aloud to himself. Yeah, good idea, but *where*, for Chris'sake? Revolution touched everywhere nowadays.

Having parceled several lids, he put the box aside, picked up the phone, and dialed Joan's room in quarters behind the laundry lounge and supply room. Joan answered immediately.

"Ma'am," he said gravely, "your order's ready."

"Clarify yourself. Which one you mean—?"

"Clarify it yourself. I got plenty of both."

"Not tonight, thanks." Joan sounded cold. "I just don't get you at all sometimes, Kill."

"I read you all right, baby. You fight yourself."

"I don't know what you're talking about."

"On-and-on-again moods. You gyrate all over the place. Or else you're neck-deep in some weighty book. . . ."

Joan laughed. "That's ambition, something you don't even want to understand. You could go to college, you could still *make* something of yourself, Kill, not just float. You aren't stupid, but you act like you want to play blackamoor in a food factory all your life to a bunch of white pigs."

"Hey, woman, please—no sermons, hear?" He could give her a few of his own, pointing out her inconsistencies, except it would turn her icy-cold. "It's a good night for pleasure, and I just called up to say I'd deliver—"

Joan cut him off. "No, not here at my place. Mrs. Charlie's been actin' up today. On me about that four-hour bit. Both of them're liable to be prowlin' tonight. I'll sneak up to the rock. Make it one hour from now. . . ."

Maybe, just maybe, Kill thought, his crotch swelling. "You come ready, don't bug me," he said softly.

The line was silent for a moment, then Joan said, "With money in my pocket, you mean? I like to pay you for an order."

"You know what I mean," said Kill, "and I'll see *you*. . . ."

In the bedroom of her cabana suite, Aggie Bird was playing hostess to Dick Carter, there on an official visit, although it was long past his available appointment hours. Dick was hard at work with a twofold purpose: an expert massage and some titillation to make his point once more. He had to cover the competition that prick Harry had given him the day before as best he could, although Aggie hadn't given any indication that Harry had done anything for her that he couldn't do, something fancier.

"Oh God," moaned Aggie from the depths of her comfort, relaxed under Dick's skilled fingers, "don't you dare stop. I could go on like this forever. Time's suspended. . . ."

Dick chuckled over her supine figure, gross and wattled, really beyond salvage. "Aw, come on," he said, pleased, "it's not that good."

"Never found anything better," said Aggie. "I don't know why I've resisted massage all my life. Fought it. Couldn't stand having any of them touch me. Didn't know what I was missing. Hey, how about chucking this joint and coming out to the Coast with me? I could use a good private operator like you. It would have to be exclusive, of course. I got a jealous disposition and a very low boiling point."

"Thanks, Miss Bird, but this is steady work, and I'm committed for a while. Like I enjoy eating regularly, owning some good threads, having a little money in the bank. You know. . . ."

Aggie pushed his hands away, plopped over on one

naked hip, her face awry with anger. "Why the hell that 'Miss Bird' shit all of a sudden, huh? Isn't 'Aggie' good enough for you? It certainly was yesterday and the day before. And while we're on the subject, why couldn't you come instead of sending that big dike?"

Dick chuckled. "Anita's no dike, take my word for it."

"Then maybe you are," Aggie retorted. "You remind me of some old-time stripper. All tease and no action. . . ."

"I'm trying to be professional—Aggie. That comes first. I've an obligation to you, and you've an obligation to *The Bungalow*."

Aggie sat bolt upright, not even bothering to cover her pendulous breasts. She glared at Dick, and he backed slightly away, still smiling, but wary.

"What the hell do you know about my work?" she demanded.

"You told me yourself," Dick reminded her. Christ, was she going to be difficult? he wondered.

Aggie recalled vaguely the details she may have given him, all juiced up on that smuggled bottle the day she'd arrived, figuring she must have told him a lot, maybe too much.

"Well, don't pay any attention to what I say when I'm in a state," she declared. "Gauge me by my actions. . . . Come here, baby. Do me again. . . ."

She flopped over on her stomach, her quivering buttocks in the air. Dick racked his list of responses to get her into conversation again that would keep her fairly quiet.

"You told me you'd give me the real focus on movies," he said, chancing at a safe generality.

Aggie grunted, cheek against forearm. "Movies are one fucking bore. Dullest business on earth."

"How'd you get into them?" Dick asked, manipulating her clammy flesh with gentle, even strokes. He knew the public story, of course. Everyone did. Little Aggie Bird, one half of a sister duo, stage mother in the background. Barnstorming around the western states, singing for everything from church socials to football rallies. Making a living but not much else. Then the nationwide search for a thirteen-year-old innocent to play a simple farm girl and horse lover in a film called *Kansas Cyclone*. It wasn't her figure, the fan magazines had said, that made her a star, or her voice, which was only fair. It was the piquant sadness in her eyes, the wraithlike smile that flitted across her face and gave promise of the woman to come. She didn't really act, they all said, she reacted. One picture was publicity, but the second, the little blind girl in *Rainbow,* gave her that special Academy Award, and she was on her way. . . .

That was the myth out of which the later legend grew. The truth was obviously something else. Aggie seldom faced it.

"How'd I get into movies—?" she echoed. "Good old Mom, rest her dead body and lively soul. Yeah, Mom did it all. There was this Hollywood agent, smalltime jerk, wretched little weirdo. I think he wanted me and my sister Betty all laid out nice for him, premenstrual hang-up, something like that. But he didn't have the guts to ask. Mom had real sense; she brought him to bed right in the other room, and we watched through the half-open door. I think that cinched it. She kind of blackmailed him after that, and the guilt-ridden old bastard gobbled her bait. He wangled both Betty and me tests for *Cyclone.* Betty worked in it as an extra, I got the big part."

"Then what happened?"

"To me or Mom?"

"You, naturally. . . ."

"Well, Betty deserted me at sixteen, got married, and blew show business, and Mom had that heart attack after my second picture, and I took care of her until she died a few years later. . . ." Aggie was silent a moment. "Then I got married for the first time, and the rest of it's a goddam bore. Why do you want to know about me? All you're ever going to learn is right up there in that thing I do on the screen. Nothing's real except that, nothing ever has been."

"I doubt that," said Dick.

"Doubt my ass if you want to, but it's true. You know what I am? Not what you see up there, but me, the *real* me, the messy old broad who's done too much and seen too little? I'm what's wrong with America, I'm all the mistakes everybody's made since World War Two. That's me! Jesus Christ," she groaned, "I wish I had a fucking dish of ice cream! *And* a vodka martini, *and* a whole chocolate cake piled high with whipped cream. I don't see what difference it makes if I'm fat or skinny. Mama Cass does it fat, Totie Fields and Gleason. Why the hell do *I* have to diet and wear my goddam nerves to a frazzle for one lousy part that's not going to make that much difference at this late date, anyway!"

"What kind of talk is that for a star?" Dick asked automatically.

"The kind that makes sense in this do-nothing, bullshit place! Hey, Dick, you know where there's some booze?"

Dick had two bottles of brandy stashed in his room, but he wasn't going to tell her about it. "I haven't the remotest," he said. He wasn't going to help her make a fool of herself—not that he gave a rat's ass if she did. He had a vague respect for her ability to become something quite different from what she was, her acting, he was aware, but otherwise she was just another customer and a broken-down old broad. He'd had better *and* worse. But it was part of his business to fake concern, which didn't interfere with his determination to hustle clients if he could. Only he hadn't figured out an angle here yet. Whatever it was, it would have to be something over which the Maples couldn't crucify him, for they'd sure try if they thought he was pulling something. They were ruthless when anybody went against their rules.

"You don't need the booze, Aggie."

Aggie grunted. "How do you know what I need? Shit, I been married seven times, I lost count of my lovers. Married to a real parade of publicity freaks. Tufty was a washed-up director when he talked me into marriage, and he kept right on being washed-up afterwards, and right on laying his leading ladies. . . . Harvey Bristol was more interested in what men said about him than women, although I never caught him in bed with either sex, just preening himself in the mirror. That newspaper gossip he had the hots for some fag designer wasn't true; he just wouldn't kiss the press's ass. . . . Noel Johnson wasn't a bad architect, but he couldn't engineer a good screw for the life of him. Not with me, anyway. Then he ran off with one of my secretaries, female. . . . When I married Alec Meadows, playboy-lush, I thought I was all set. Alec liked my name, I liked his, and besides, he had more money than I'd ever seen; I knew he didn't want mine. The trouble with him was, he'd wilt in the clinches. No staying power. And I got bored with all those crotch kisses. *You* know. . . ."

"Hey, you've been around," Dick said, trying to keep patronage from his voice.

"A fucking carousel," Aggie agreed from her relaxed position. "That's my life. And there's more you haven't heard. I never dug tennis, I thought it was a fruit game—until I met Laird Agrew, the champ. I still don't know why we got married, but he was on a health kick, and we didn't last six months. He couldn't take my pill-booze path, I couldn't take those six o'clock jump-out-of-the-sack-into-the-shower routines for very long, either. Christ, he didn't say one goddam word to me, not what the papers carried about a sensible agreed separation. Son of a bitch just hefted his tennis racket, and the last anybody saw of him was a fast week in Palm Springs at the Racquet Club. . . ."

"You got a divorce—?"

"Yeah, in Mexico, and married again right away to the King of Rock, Matty Hellman. I don't know why we bothered; one night was enough for both of us. But we had this talk thing going on uppers about old and new music, and he was weaned on me as a kid from Saturday matinees in his hick home town. All pretty goddam grim. . . . And then there was Chris Moxley, left end for the Eagles. We talked about football, a nice change from music. . . . Maybe I've overdone it along the line; there were plenty others in between. Like that Janis Joplin, I was available. . . ."

"But you had fun—?"

"Not much after the preview of my first picture. *Cyclone* was a glorious gas. Ever since it's been downhill."

"Nobody's ever made you happy?"

"Oh yeah, a couple of people. My mother, Betty, my present manager." Aggie giggled into her forearm. "Hey, you want to know something? Can I trust you—?"

"I know when to keep counsel, Aggie. You learn it in this business."

"O.K. I'll make a confession. It doesn't make good sense, but there was a good reason why I kept yelling for you instead of Anita. You—upset me."

"Upset *you*—?"

"Plenty. I've never been to the promised land before, Dick, if you know what I mean."

Dick was fairly sure of her meaning, but he wanted her to come out and state it openly. "Promised land? I guess I—"

"You brought me off, made me come, scream for the ceiling," said Aggie. "Christ, Dick, you're not that naïve, are you?"

"No, but it's hard to believe. I'll bet you tell that to all the kids. . . ."

His ego urged him to accredit her statement; his experience told him not to. During his long and active sexual maturity quite a few woman claimed he was their one true way to orgasm, but most of them were lying for private reasons. Aggie could be lying, too, and even if she happened to be truthful, where would the Bird orgasm get him? Somebody stood in his way, the one person to whom he owed a debt of allegiance: Wayne Winslow. And Wayne was Aggie's present manager, also Dick's oldest and probably closest friend. Dick didn't think Aggie knew the whole story, but she was here at Bimini due to Wayne's insistence and at Dick's recommendation. After Wayne had secured her contract for *The Bungalow*, he'd written to Dick: "The place you're in sounds like an ideal hideaway, one place where she won't be prey to any problems. . . . I trust you, Dick, I know you'll look after her. She's pretty gross sometimes, but she's goodhearted and sincere. I'll write and arrange the details through her doctor. Keep an eye on her for me. . . . I'm counting on your discretion and friendship. . . ."

"You're no goddam kid," Aggie told him. "You're a real stud."

"Sure, sure," he stalled, knowing it had to come out sooner or later. "But you don't understand what I mean. I'm trying to tell you I've got a responsibility."

"Oh shit!" exclaimed Aggie, "you want to play my disappearing father or something?"

"A responsibility I can't ignore," Dick continued. Better make it slow and good, he decided. Even if you knock the old bitch out of her skin, you've still got to honor your obligation to Wayne. . . .

"Don't con me, Dick. I won't have it!"

"I'm not," he said honestly. "Wayne's charged me with the responsibility of looking after you at Bimini Springs. . . ."

Aggie's response was a galvanic spasm that carried her to a crouching position on the massage table, a mad, glittering scowl on her face.

"*You know Wayne Winslow—?*" she gasped, stunned.

Dick nodded. "From a long time ago when we trained at the same gym in California. We've kept in touch."

Aggie clenched her fists. "Why you double-crossing, blackmailing, spying son of a bitch!" She started off the table, opening her hands into talons, her face screwed tight with rage.

Dick backed away from her, genuinely alarmed. She certainly had a low boiling point for anger, too.

"Now wait a minute, Aggie," he said. "I haven't lied to you, and I'm no spy or blackmailer, whatever else I've been in my life. . . ."

"Then how come you never told me right off about you and Wayne?" she demanded. "And more to the point, how come you wasted no time laying me? What kind of collusion tricks are you two working—?"

"There's no collusion," Dick said quietly. "Calm down. I sent Wayne a Christmas card and a letter at his mother's address. I told him about Bimini Springs, sent him a brochure, and said to him I'd be around awhile. I didn't even know he was associated with you at the time—"

"Associated," Aggie scoffed. "That's a rich one!"

"He shot a letter right back, asking for more information, saying he had a client he thought might need some time here."

"Specifically, what information—?"

"Private suites, rates, was the place really legit, that kind of thing. . . ."

Aggie laughed. "So you told him it was paradise, everything was on the up and up? Yeah, he conned me all about Bimini Springs, but he didn't say one fucking word about you."

"I shouldn't have told you. He said it was better if I didn't."

"Why? That's what I'd like to know."

"I guess he just thought it was best that way. . . ." Dick knew why: Wayne was fully aware of the famous Carter deep-probe treatments for middle-aged females and how emotional some of them got over him. "I didn't promise him anything. I just agreed it was probably better you didn't know. . . ."

"So why tell me now?" said Aggie.

"As I said, I got a responsibility to Wayne, and he's got your welfare at heart. He's a decent guy, a good friend. I wouldn't want to hurt him."

"What about *me*?"

"Just this. He said to get you in good shape for the big event, he was counting on me. . . ."

"He did, did he?" Aggie became suddenly aware that she was standing in the middle of the room, nude, her hair awry, her claws bared, and it made her laugh.

"Christ," she said, and turned and got back onto the table, "I don't know what to think. . . ." She propped herself up on one elbow and draped one end of the massage sheet across her pubes.

"Don't think," Dick advised, for he could see what was coming.

"Yeah, thinking makes problems. Hey, Dick, you got any problems?" she asked, the famous voice turning low and throaty, but very much under control. Some of the magnetic charm that registered on the screen was vibrating from her features.

"What do you mean?" Dick said, approaching her warily; she might reach out and wring his nuts without warning.

"Come here. . . ." She crooked a finger at him. "Come close to me. . . ." She reached out a pudgy hand in the general direction of his genitals.

He hesitated, wondering what idiot impulse had prompted him to mention Wayne Winslow to her when Wayne had specifically asked him not to.

"Come on, Dick, quit stalling. . . ."

Well, he rationalized, maybe he'd earned the right to have another go at her by being honest, or whatever you wanted to call it.

"I won't tell Wayne you told me," she bribed. "Not if you behave right. . . ."

"O.K.—" He grinned and moved closer.

Aggie's hand touched his white smock, moving down under it. Her smile was gamine, beguiling, the famous features were almost beautiful. He'd seen that look many times in her films; now it excited him, powerfully. Nothing else about her did, just that look. Monroe'd had it—Harlow, Hayworth. The look that sent blood pounding into the ducts that counted the most. A look of promise that caused itself to be fulfilled.

"My, my," Aggie said huskily, unzipping his fly, "aren't we the eager one. . . ."

Dick flashed a moment when his obligation to Wayne stirred guilt, but it was only a moment. "Please—" he said to her, as an afterthought, unaware of it.

"Please *what*—?" she asked, reaching her hand inside his trousers, flesh against flesh, caressing him.

"Don't stop!" he groaned, meaning it.

She pulled him slowly against the table and whispered, "I'm so hungry I'll eat *anything*!"—and vectored in with her lips. . . .

"Wow! That does it," Tom Street said aloud to himself in the quiet of the pharmacy office where he had been watching Aggie Bird and Dick Carter complete their ritual. He reached over and shut off the whirring video-tape reel, switched out the closed-circuit TV featuring Aggie's massage table, grateful that Aggie herself (so obligingly and unwittingly) had earlier wheeled that damned contraption right into the camera eye's line of fire. How considerate to put the action where he could record the whole aspirate act on his little VTR! Pleased with what he'd captured, he disconnected the VTR unit, stowed it gently in the large safe next to the exposed video-tape reels and other films, shut the ponderous door, and twirled the dial to lock it.

Yes, he had it made! Gradually he was building up a video-tape file that covered the entire range of human sexual response except bestiality; he didn't dig dogs, they repelled him. And now tonight he'd added a famous face to his collection. And what was so cool about this system was he could collect moving images right in his office with nobody the wiser. Anyone who started wondering why he hung around the pharmacy nights, he could show them his immaculate up-to-the-minute workbooks, his meticulously arranged shelves, his flawless inventory, his scrubbed and polished floors—and himself, always ready, always handy for any emergency until well after midnight. No, the late-night diligence was beyond suspicion. And the fun was groovy, watching people cohabit, then figuring the right opportunity to use the scenes. When he'd returned from his latest Stateside buying junket some five weeks ago, he'd brought along a complete home color video-tape recorder of Japanese make, and a TV color component. As a system these two instruments produced superb color-sound tapes, which Tom could either preserve or erase instantly as he wished, and from which he could print his own 35 mm. color slides, a touchy technique he had mastered without too much difficulty.

Nassau customs could have been a problem, but he'd had no trouble bringing in his equipment. The man ahead of him at customs, an obvious New York operator, didn't seem to realize that all customs officials have a sixth sense about smugglers. The idiot thought he could sneak in a load of expensive handmade jewelry in an innocent-looking attaché case. By the time the official was through with the man and turned to Tom, whom he knew from previous visits, he merely wiped his brow and waved Tom through with a "Hello, have a good trip?" and no inspection.

Once Tom had set up the unit and learned to photograph frozen TV frames, he was all set. Now, if he could only get into Harry Maple's locked photo lab in the office-apartment suite and develop his negatives, he could do the printing in his room. He was itching to get the VTR film frames into more permanent 35 mm. color negatives. For if anything happened to his tapes before he did, all his efforts would be wiped out.

Originally Tom hadn't expected to use the VTR for

more than self-amusement, but once he'd discovered the dynamic potential of the equipment, he started to speculate on its various uses. Why not collect other people's foibles on tape? Such a collection could be used later to definite monetary advantage. Not blackmail, of course, merely a technique of persuasion.

Tom's first view of house sex was purely accidental. Engrossed one night in his inventory, he'd switched on the closed-circuit TV to check on a guest who'd phoned in for some cough medicine at Dr. Mack's request but hadn't come for it nor sent one of the maids. Tom surprised the old man naked on his bed, happily engaged in humping one of the buxom black maids. Tom sat down at his desk to hear as well as see the entire arena match. It was hilarious. After that he was hooked; he created a game of boudoir roulette out of the master control unit, checking and choosing at whim. But of course, he had to be discreet. He could maybe kid around with someone like Eva Cassel, who was a witch, but Mack and the Maples and Ruth Severn were something else again.

The closed-circuit TV monitoring system was controlled at two points: from the pharmacy unit and from the Maples' executive suite. He wondered tonight if Harry and Marge had caught the Bird woman's act, and if so, what their reaction was. What the hell really went on with them anyway? Did they simply use the electronic voyeur for routine checkups on guests, or had they, too, discovered its erotic potential and were they sitting entwined in each other's flesh, eyes glued to the TV screen, really getting their jollies? Well, whatever they did, Tom was certain that the action he'd filmed tonight, plus the other clips he'd made, could bring him some very fine reactions later on. He would save them for another time, another place—get some kinky kids of both sexes together, start from there. A little grass, a few groans. Nothing like having your own personal collection of VTR pornos in living color to trigger an orgy.

But then, there was another face to the coin: extortion—a very sensitive area and not one to be dismissed entirely, especially if times grew lean. Tom didn't know quite how to go about this procedure, but if he could just get all the right scenes down about the right people, knowing beforehand what he needed on them, he might be in a favorable position to ask and receive.

Man oh man, he really had something succulent! It was one thing to have evidence on people, but another to make it pay off. He just wished to hell he could catch

Harry or Marge Maple with their respective bang buddies, Anita and Dick Carter. Now wouldn't that be something exclusive? Pitting a group of Harry-oriented color prints against a group of Marge-oriented color prints, he might possibly be able to squeeze comfortable sums of green from both of them without either one realizing that the other was being taken. . . .

Ho, ho! It was something to think about, he reflected, as he locked the lounge door to the pharmacy and headed through the balmy night air to his quarters, feeling safe and smug. The soft ripple of surf running in against the island shoreline brought a delicate breeze that caressed him gently as he walked. It would be nice to take a shallow shore skinny dip in the lagoon, he thought, but he had other things on his mind besides pleasuring his body. He wanted to think about the films in the safe; they got to him, they were comforting and predictable, better than friends, really. And inviolately secure; nobody could seize or confiscate them, for they were in hard-drug security, only accessible to qualified personnel. Even Kevin Mack didn't have the safe's new combination, which allowed Tom complete control. If Ruth Severn or Cassel wanted something at doctor's orders, then they had to come to him with a written prescription for morphine or Demerol, amphetamines and barbiturates. For Tom knew he was trusted, being an impeccable pharmacist.

Well, he smiled, with the drugs, anyway.

As he fitted his key into his door, he noticed that Kill Howard's light was still on. Too bad he couldn't show Kill the films, share the sensual excitement of them, watch Kill's reaction. It would be something, really something. Well, meanwhile there were those books he'd brought back with him, the stories, and every time he read one of them he found something new to stimulate him. They were just as good in their way as catching the room scenes, and so safe. One-handed literature took imagination and response, and Tom had plenty of both, enough to last him as long as he stayed at Bimini Springs. And he didn't intend to leave until he'd landed the biggest fisherman's prize on the island, both the Maples, screeching and clawing their way to the top. . . .

"Harry!" Marge yelled from the bedroom to Harry in the executive suite of their apartment. "Turn that goddam thing off and come to bed. . . ."

Marge knew what Harry was up to; he wasn't checking accounts, he was viewing some kind of action on that portable monitor in the office, taking care first to turn off the TV monitor screen in their bedroom.

"I'm coming!" Harry called to her, and a moment later he entered their bedroom, happily excited.

"Wow!" he exclaimed, "that was some show! Son of a bitch sure is pooped." A double inference there, he realized, for he himself had been the last but one to service Aggie Bird's needs in quite a different manner. For a broad who'd been married seven times with countless lovers in between and during probably, she sure as hell was sex-starved. Or maybe insatiable, he wasn't sure.

"You've got a dirty mind," Marge told him from her dressing table. "You're prurient as hell."

"What's prur—?"

"You'd know if you ever cracked a dictionary. Itchy," Marge told him, "and it fits you to a tee."

"So what'm I supposed to do now for a little excitement? Come to bed and chalk up another on the marital scoreboard?"

"You can damn' well please yourself with some nigger maid if you want to, for all I care!" Marge said in a nasty tone. "Only don't start going funky on me just when we've got three thousand brochures to send off if we want to get filled up for the rest of the winter season. You got distracted last year over that Chinese piece from Trinidad—and don't deny it, I know what happened. So now you're playing around with a celebrity caper and kidding yourself all over again it's in the line of duty."

"I am fond of interesting women," said Harry, "and this one sure is a celebrity. I'm always attracted to power."

In lounge shorts, bare-chested, Harry had a certain power of his own, Marge noted for the millionth time as she saw him reversed in her mirror. Whatever else he was, she couldn't deny he was sexy.

"What I need now is a good shower. . . ." He passed so close to her she could feel his body heat as he entered the bathroom, leaving the door open.

Aware of his familiar, sex-smug expression, Marge commented, "You look like you swallowed a secret."

"No, but Aggie did," he said. "I'm just thinking. We could make some glamour shots of our celebrity, and they might bring us a pretty penny in the right market."

"*Black* market, you mean," Marge scoffed. "Sometimes I think you're a plain damn' fool. The trouble we had with what's-his-name wasn't worth it. You don't have the nerve to be an extortionist. Anyway, who needs *that*? We're doing all right."

"Don't you want a little fun along with everything else?" Harry said. "But you got a point." He dropped his shorts on the bathroom floor and turned on the shower.

"Don't be too long," Marge said, as she climbed into bed, her night toilet completed.

"Patience, sweetheart," Harry replied from their bath, stepping into the shower and closing the frosted glass door behind him.

Marge pulled her bed jacket across her ample breasts to ward off the frosty air conditioning. Underneath the jacket she was nude, which was the way Harry always wanted to receive her. Teamwork, she thought, that's what counts in a marriage and the reason why so many of them sputter out like gutted candles. Realistic teamwork; you joined hands and bodies and buffed the world. With a partnership like that, most anything was possible; this was how they'd managed the Bahama property, with nothing more than the camera and a good eye for news. Marge dating the old codger, Ira Benton, whose one weakness was redheaded women with big breasts and creamy complexions, Marge's exact adornments. Then, Harry, as planned, photographing them through the window of that shoddy motel room, crashing in minutes later just as the old boy was about to let loose a load, finding them totally compromised. Shouting, bellowing, making a great scene, threatening Benton with exposure and ultimate embarrassments. And the cowering Ira Benton, a church pillar in his small Alabama county seat, horrified of scandal, only too willing to placate Harry for his abuse of Marge. . . .

Among the possessions of old Ira Benton was a ninety-nine-year lease on a Bahama cay. He'd taken the land during the early days of the first Florida boom when all the area from the Atlantic off Florida into the West Indies looked like a land-grabber's paradise, a potential goldmine. He'd never done anything with the land, but they wanted it, so he gave the lease to them. He also gave them some capital along with the island lease, and in a year they'd turned this into real money by shrewd investment in public utilities. Then they bought a rundown highway motel, the same one where the famous Benton photos were taken, and turned it into a very lucrative short-time hotel with bar service, drive-in room carports with private access doors to quarters, wall and ceiling mirrors in dusky pink for those who wished them, and many did. Harry was such an urbane public relations man around the countryside that they were soon swamped with an elite clientele, doing just fine, the island property almost forgotten.

Then the Korean War broke out and Harry had to go, or maybe he wanted to; Marge was never quite sure about this. Anyway, in the Army Harry took advantage of every opportunity as a supply depot sergeant in Seoul where he was stationed. Out of this situation he was able to return home bearing a personal profit of about $50,000 in cold cash.

This hunk was their real starting nut, although in Harry's absence Marge herself hadn't been idle. Marge had acquired a wealthy politician as an admiring client, and although she serviced him only a few times, she managed to engage his permanently loyal patronage, to which Harry could hardly object on his return from the war. For the relationship favored Harry's bright future, not the politician's, since Marge got him to back them in another venture, a staid, deluxe lodge, very private and exclusive, along the Chesapeake shoreline in tidewater Virginia, which rapidly developed into an unqualified success.

When the Maples thought of expanding again, a quick vacation trip to the Bahamas to inspect Ira Benton's island gift convinced them that they ought to do something about Devil Cay, maybe open a small resort, possibly a health spa. Should it fail as a weight-loss factory, there'd be time enough to think about a casino and other attractions. They mortgaged their holdings, moved down, and began to develop it.

They'd gambled well, Marge had thought many times before. Bimini Springs was worth a fair fortune now, business was good though not booming this year due to the inflational recession, for good health and weight loss were always a perennial pair of sales points. Help was cheap if you used the niggers for common labor and whatever skills they could offer, and both of them loved the island. It was a controlled environment that gave them every advantage. What bothered other investors in other parts of the Caribbean and the West Indies—Jamaica, the Virgins, Haiti, the Dominican Republic—just didn't touch them at all. Devil Cay was comparable to a small principality in some remote part of the world with a rarefied atmosphere of its own. But what really counted was cash and the bank balance. And they were plenty solvent; they could take care of their obligations on a monthly basis and still put money aside. It was a delicious feeling to walk around the trim little island and know that it was all yours for as long as you lived—no, all theirs, Marge corrected herself, for where would she be without Harry, and vice versa? Where would he be without her?

Realizing that the shower was no longer running, she popped back into the present, cocked an ear toward the bath, and listened. Aha! Over the hum of the air conditioner she could hear the sunken pool filling, the deepening plash of the water jets as the great square tub became a miniature ocean.

Harry stuck his head around the door. "Sea horse!" he hollered, and Marge rose up on the bed, stripping away her jacket.

"Coming, Neptune!" Marge shrilled at him.

"Anchors aweigh!" Harry chanted as Marge slithered into the huge gold and white bathroom, spread her arms wide, and gripped the rim of the tiled pool with her toes.

"Prepare yourself to receive the goddess of the sea, O Neptune!" she intoned, and stepped gracefully down the tiled steps until she stood thigh-deep in the warm water of the sunken pool, a lascivious smile on her lips.

"Divine seafood mama!" Harry crooned crazily, creeping toward her, doubled over, the waves lapping his chin.

"Correction, I'm Venus on the half-shell," Marge snapped, and dipped her dark crotch into the pool enticingly. "You will dine on me, O Neptune. Get the goddam thing right for a change!"

"Yum-yum!" Harry smacked his lips and rolled his eyes. "Seafood from Venus—" and reached for her solid buttocks, drawing her toward his face.

Suddenly with a demoniacal leer, Marge reached out and clamped Harry's head to her inner thighs, sinking over him into the water, screeching and laughing as they both went under.

A second later they shot above the surface of the yard-deep, aquamarine-tiled pool, locked in each other's arms.

"Hurry, O Neptune, Venus is anxious," Marge hissed in his ear as Harry maneuvered her against the shallow steps, inserted himself, and began to work slowly and deftly on the situation.

"I *am* Venus," Marge intoned, locking her heels around his pounding rump and promptly forgetting everything else in the world, except that they were immortal and she was being carried off to paradise by an expert. . . .

Cindy Brown was in bed in her suite, some hours after she'd fainted in the dining room and Ruth Severn and Dr. Mack had brought her there.

Kevin Mack had just dropped in to see how she was, a gesture she appreciated, for she found him sympathetic and attractive. And he'd arrived alone, no nurse in tow.

"You're going to be O.K.," Kevin said, releasing her pulse. "To coin a paraphrase, Miss Brown, sweet are the abuses of obesity. If you'll pardon my heavy humor. But you didn't come here to abuse yourself, did you? You could do that at home."

Oh God, thought Cindy, weak but agreeable, another goddam lecture. "Yes, I could," she replied. It was pretty stupid of her to build up to a fright and pass out in the dining salon, of all places.

"You mustn't get discouraged about the reduction," Kevin said, suavely professional. "Lots do, and they're usually premature. They don't give themselves a chance."

"But it's so damned depressing, Doctor," Cindy complained. "Up and down scales is the story of my life."

"It is, but you're white, resilient, and healthy. You're not liable to stroke out here or die on us, you know. Families of deceased guests have a passion for lawsuits," he said, smiling, "but in your case we won't worry."

Cindy wasn't certain, but the doctor's smile seemed cynical beneath his composure, which amused her. It was really the very first time she'd glimpsed something of him behind that cool, straight façade.

"Let's talk about obesity—" Kevin pulled up a chair and sat down, bedside.

Cindy nodded, thinking that every time he moved closer to her, she brimmed with flashes. The way he hit her blood pressure was absolutely unaccountable.

"Yes, Doctor," she murmured obediently.

"This is a lecture. . . . Now, it's well-known that Scandinavia, Germany, and the U.S. have the world's highest obesity figures, Asia the lowest. On the surface, this would appear due to a high-diet percentage of dairy products in the West. Not entirely true; caloric intake's a determining factor. Asians not only live on slimmer diets because dairy products are scarce and expensive to import, but they prefer rice and the common vegetables, and they don't overload. While in America and northern Europe, diabetes and coronaries are the prime causes of death. In Asia, where an average normal-weight standard dominates, these diseases are practically unknown. . . ."

"I had no idea," Cindy said dreamily, not paying strict attention. She was fat, she had to lose. What difference did all this mumbo jumbo make?

"During ninety-nine and nine-tenths of man's time on

this planet, he's existed almost entirely on animal flesh, fowl and fish, herbs or roots, and fruits. Research has more or less determined that obesity wasn't always a general problem. But with the advent of refined sugar and grains—called carbohydrates—and fermented or distilled beverages, man's health began to decline. And during the last century the decline's been alarming. Man gets less exercise, he doesn't have to hunt for his food, and refined bread has helped to increase cardiovascular illness enormously. Vitamin E has been removed, and it's a heart-strengthener. . . ."

"Imagine," said Cindy, wondering if Kevin was as well hung as she imagined he was.

"Stuffing yourself's psychological."

"I know—"

"And seriously, you've got to stop it in the future, find another outlet for your nerves, your energy. Just as alcohol provides temporary caesura from tension, food can perform a similar function. Psychic obesity often begins in childhood. . . ."

Cindy could hardly forget her late pubescence, the pounds of chocolate she'd consumed under the sheets late at night, smuggled into the house in her school bag so her mother wouldn't find the giant bars.

"My problem," said Cindy, "was always trying to please my mother, and a lack of interest in myself. My background isolated me. . . ." It had indeed, she thought, for the wealth she'd been made aware of as a small girl was always lurking there, like some demon specter. Her mother would never let her forget that she was independently wealthy, that she had a responsibility to all that money, even as a child.

"So what do we do, Dr. Mack?"

"Psychotherapy isn't the answer, any more than calling your condition a glandular problem. In both physical and mental obesity cases patients sometimes claim they can't help themselves."

"You're not talking about me," said Cindy.

"O.K. That's fine. You're willing to look squarely at the problem. When you're young and fat, the solution's easier than when you're old and fat. And there are two factors to master: eat a well-regulated low-calorie diet daily and practice constant self-denial."

"I've been unsuccessful with both."

"But you're going to change. You don't have a thing glandularly wrong with you. Your thyroid, pituitary, pancreas, and adrenal glands are all functioning normally, according to your medical report. There's no tendency to diabetes, so your obesity's one of three types: compulsive gluttony, glandular malfunction, or plain self-indulgence. I think we'll have to settle for the first."

"The compulsive eater, the stuffer, the crammer."

Kevin grinned at her. "Well," he said, "at least you can call it what it is. . . . All right, tomorrow morning you'll start a new regimen. Skipping food as you've been doing, refusing to exercise, isn't the answer. You've weakened yourself. You're going on a fasting diet. . . ."

"A fasting diet—?"

"It's a very effective method for overcoming intractable obesity."

"But Dr. Mack, that means no intake at all, a no-calorie diet!" Cindy exclaimed. "I'll be miserable."

"On the contrary. It's monotonous and confining, but not miserable. You'll be restricted to your room, and the more time you spend relaxed, the better it'll be. No physical exercise will be required. You can walk around if you like, but no further than outside to the pool once a day, and back."

"Well, at least I'm not going to be a prisoner," said Cindy, relieved. "I get claustrophobic if I'm confined."

"In a way you will be restricted because you're going to be dependent upon a large intake of artifically sweetened liquids, as much as you like. You'll get multivitamin preparations twice daily. And don't worry about a gnawing appetite. You'll lose it fast."

"How's that possible?"

"From an excess of ketones or fat derivatives that form in the body and are transferred to the blood. Appetite loss is directly proportionate to the number of ketones present in your blood. When the ketones diminish in number, your appetite will return. In short, break the fast and the reduced ketone count will bring your appetite back with a vengeance. . . . I trust you'll cooperate and not break the diet, however."

Cindy flushed, thinking of her suitcase of contraband goodies, the several boxes of rich chocolates, the jars of honey, the glazed fruit. "I've—got some items I shouldn't have."

Kevin grinned. "I'll trust you to give them to your maid. We'll plan a seven-day fast at first, and if you're responding favorably, we'll try for two weeks. But if there are any adverse effects, we'll have to stop the treatment immediately. I'll send Miss Cassel in with something to make you sleep."

"I don't need anything."

"She'll bring it, anyway. And concentrate, Miss Brown. Give the weight-loss program your undivided will power, your total determination. . . ."

"Oh I will, Doctor, I will—" She could see that he was about to go, and this depressed her. How could she detain him awhile? "Someone mentioned that you and Miss Severn had both done duty in South Vietnam recently. Is that true?"

"Yes," Kevin replied, "but we don't make any point of it. Miss Severn's worth a hundred ordinary R.N.s you'd find around most hospitals. My own experience was invaluable, mostly in cosmetic surgery."

"What a fascinating field!"

"A worthy one, I think," Kevin said. "Well, I must run along."

He got up and walked toward the door, casually glancing down at the table by the window as he passed. Next to the phone stood a silver-framed photograph of a lovely girl smiling out at the world with enormous self-confidence. Kevin picked up the frame and studied the photograph.

"Some girl," he said admiringly. "Your sister—?"

Cindy felt the flame of a blush even before it appeared in her cheeks. "No," she said, embarrassed, "it's—it's me. . . . Only a few years ago. That's the one souvenir I've got of my greatest slim period; it went on for a year. You see, I can do it."

Still admiring the photo, Kevin said, "You were absolutely beautiful—" then, realizing the implication, he added, "And you will be again, too. Cheer up!"

"Thanks for that much, anyway," Cindy said with a trace of bitterness.

"At least you're alive and healthy," Kevin reminded her. "Be thankful for that. . . ." His smile was impersonal and told her nothing. "Good night, Miss Brown, tomorrow's the big day. . . ." He picked up his bag by the door and left.

Cindy stared at the closed door from her bed, hating herself, her obesity, her whole narrow, pampered life that had brought her here, almost to the end of her patience and endurance, hung up on a man she hardly knew, rejecting her own history in the process. Well, she'd do as he said, she'd triumph over her fat ass, slim down for the future. She'd lose the weight if it took her last breath. But what was the point, really? She didn't have him, she didn't have anybody. "Beautiful girl," he'd said, not even knowing who the girl in the picture was. Her sister indeed!

She'd show him, she'd do it! She lay back on the pillow, clenched her fists and ground her teeth, determined to bring him to heel. . . .

Joan Harrison and Kill Howard sat on the flat rock ledge of Devil Cay's highest moon-drenched cliff point, several feet apart. From their sixty-foot-high northeast prominence, they saw the southern twinkling lights of Bimini Springs and harbor boat house on the small bay, and directly below them the pounding phosphorescent surf, slapping against the sheer face of the cliff. Off to sea on both flanks of the island, tendrils of pale white luminosity glowed along the water—St. Elmo's fire, usually associated with the wakes of ships but often prevalent on pointed reef tips in the tropics, Nature's warning light of danger. . . . Was it a message? Kill wondered.

Instead of a little cooperation, Joan was giving him a frosty lecture, and, being stoned, it didn't set too well.

"Change is brought about by change," Joan pontificated in a stern, preachy voice, arms locked across her breasts, not even looking at him but staring straight down into the sea below them. "Take some heed, man."

"All you militants talk too goddam much," Kill said. "You don't vote, you don't pay no taxes, but you sure as hell're vocal and destructive. Run around shootin' your mouth, trashin' anything you don't like!" He smacked his clenched right fist into his left palm. "I saw enough violence in Nam to last me a lifetime, and I'm sick of it!"

"Yeah, and I suppose you'll just give up on ghettos and discrimination and civil rights? What's wrong with you, man? You got no social conscience—?"

"Shit, woman, I got as much or more'n you have. I'm tryin' to be a law-abidin', tax-payin' citizen."

Joan's brief laugh was guttural and derisive. "You call that lid of grass you brought me *law-abidin'*—a contribution to *humanity*?"

"Better than pills or alcohol—it's something. And I didn't give it to you. You *owe* me for it." He could be bitchy, too, if she wanted to play it that way.

Joan tossed the neat, folded plastic bag of grass at his feet. "Here, take it back! I can live without it if an obligation goes with it. All of us can live without any artificial euphoria."

Kill picked up the package and looked at it thoughtfully in the livid moonlight. "For all your high-soundin' college rhetoric you like to enjoy yourself. Don't bullshit me, woman. You covet your pleasures and your creature comforts and all just as much as anybody. All the black militants I ever met drove better cars than the poor, dumb bastards they were protestin' for," said Kill. "And some of them even had credit cards."

"You'd make a case for yourself outta anything," Joan snarled. "I don't want to hear no more—"

"I'm not through yet," Kill retorted. "What's this jazz about you refusin' to let the girls work more'n forty-four hours a week? Didn't they sign on for forty-four plus four if the extra half-day was required—?"

"Yes, if it's required in an emergency," Joan admitted. "But there's none now. We've got a full complement of workers on all shifts, we're not even fully occupied, and it's just plain white bitchery on management's part to try to invoke it."

"That means you're not gonna let them work, then?"

"Past tense. It's all settled."

"With which one—the Mistah or the Madam?"

"The Madam," Joan said. "And I'm not afraid of him, either. They're both such frauds. But they don't even make you angry, do they?"

Kill shrugged his shoulders, still holding the packet of grass in his hand. "Why should they? I put in my hours and take my pay. Sometimes I dream about other things, but I've had other things, some of the best. Can't focus all my bile on this world. I'm content to be alive. . . . Most of the time that's just about enough."

"I don't dig you at all," Joan said sharply, "not when you rap like that," and scooped up the packet of grass from his open hand, jamming it into the pocket of her dress.

"When you've seen how the rest of the world lives," Kill said, "when you've dug both sides of the political fence and weighed all the arguments, really thought heavy about them, you don't get too chewed up about anything; corruption's universal. You get a laziness, I guess, or whatever it is. All you want is peace and quiet. Especially the peace spelled different. Like a little hunk of you, maybe—"

He suddenly jumped up and lunged for her, and as she attempted to elude him, she fumbled her position on the rock and started to slip toward the cliff edge. Kill caught her in his strong arms and held her tight as they teetered precariously above the boiling surf below them for a frightening instant; then both fell back, locked together, onto the hard, rough rock ledge.

Kill ended up on top of Joan, his arms around her, their bellies pressed together, his mouth against hers. Weak and trembling, unable to resist him, she succumbed absolutely to his exploring kiss. But when it went on much too long, she wasn't ready for it. In his concentration, Kill had relaxed his grip on her. By wriggling sidewise, she struggled free of him, scrambled to her feet, and straightened her dress. As an afterthought she felt in her pocket for the grass.

"It's gone," she said. Kill, sitting up, looked at her. "The grass," she explained. "I guess it fell out of my pocket and over the edge."

"So—?" Kill said, grinning.

"I lost the lid!"

"Never mind. There's more where that came from. You tend to your revolutions, I'll take care of the cannabis." He put out his hand. "Come on, sit down. Get comfortable. . . ."

"No," she said, "gotta go. Got a meetin' with the girls."

"Shit!" said Kill. "Hey, you're not seein' Dickie boy, are you?"

Joan glared at him. "I ought to slap you right in the mouth for that."

"Try it, baby, just try it."

"Wait—!" Facing toward Bimini Springs, Joan had seen someone moving on the rise below, silhouetted against the twinkling lodge lights. It could be a man, it could be anybody. "Somebody's down there," she whispered, and pointed into the darkness.

"There's no one down there," said Kill, used to her diversionary tactics. "Cool it, sit down. . . ."

"If it's Mistah, I'm in real trouble. We're out of bounds for staff. . . ." Only the paying guests had the privilege of going anywhere they liked on Devil Cay, although they rarely took advantage of the opportunity.

"You're goosey tonight, goosey as hell. . . ."

"Really is somebody down there," she hissed in alarm. "Kill, I gotta go. . . ." And off she went, scurrying down the rock's slope, skirting the path that led toward the lights of the lodge by short-cutting through the low undergrowth.

Kill stood up and watched her go, her white dress a blur in the brush, finally losing her in the middle shadows. Then he sat down moodily on the rock ledge where Joan was seated before he kissed her. Still stoned, still horny, he cupped his chin in his palms and stared moodily out to sea, more strung out than ever because it was such a fine night. You can't win 'em all, he rationalized, but wasn't it a helluva night for love nuts!

Part

THREE

The second morning out aboard the *Sarcophagus*, Dan Francovich awoke feeling like a new man. After mailing the letter to Marilyn Thompson, he'd returned to the yacht and fallen into a deep sleep, not waking until dinner, by which time they were cruising through the Bahamas. Mercifully, Thompson left him alone at dinner, and he returned again to his cabin to sleep. There'd been almost no rest the two days before they departed California, and no sleep on the flight. Each time Dan tried to catnap aboard the Lockheed, Thompson buzzed him for something or other—a legal detail on a new drilling contract in the Persian Gulf, a publicity agreement on the new satellite Thompson hoped to sponsor next year, something to do with a recently developed computerized news prompter for commercial television. But now he felt rested, almost rational again, and realized that he and the big man had both been going at a staggering pace for the last few weeks preparing for the exodus.

He was dressing when Thompson banged on his door. Christ, he thought, it's beginning again, and sighed deeply, realizing that his reprieve was only temporary. Thompson, with electronic assistance and Dan Francovich, could work anytime, anywhere.

"Danny boy—"

"I'm coming, Terry—" he said, throwing on a shirt as he went to the door.

"Hurry and open the goddam thing," Thompson shouted through the paneling, "I've got my arms full!"

Francovich opened the door. Thompson stood there hugging twenty pounds of files, obviously the contents of one of the ten special file cases that had followed them aboard the Lockheed and were later transferred to the yacht.

"Here it is," he said, a devilish grin on his lean, gaunt features. "Sift the fucking evidence carefully, boy, and come up with a winner!"

"O.K.—" Francovich smiled wanly. "As soon as I shave and get some coffee. I'm still out of focus."

Thompson's energy was incredible. On sheer maniacal nerve, without pills or stimulants of any sort, not even coffee, he could continue going almost indefinitely, getting no more than three or four hours' sleep a night, sometimes not even that. After Dan had crashed yesterday, Thompson probably drove into Nassau to haggle with the fish vendors on Frederick Street before they sailed at noon. Thompson had explained that each morning small craft came from the out islands loaded with conch and turtle and more ordinary catch to sell in the markets. Thompson's culinary passion was marine food. Francovich could imagine him bouncing around the market like an excited kid, buying a hundred pounds or so of weird-looking stuff for the yacht's reefers before he was finished, then returning to write a ream of memos, make a multitude of ship-to-shore calls, issue various directives to the crew and his other aides who were along for a conference. The *Sarcophagus* was simply a floating office, another workroom, meant to be used incessantly. Thompson, to Francovich's knowledge, had never taken a vacation in his life.

"That's all right," said Thompson, dumping the documents on the unmade bunk. "Get to them when you can. You'll do a good job. . . . See you!"

Francovich stared morosely at the pile of documents, dreading the tedious job ahead of him because it would also be unpleasant. If he knew his boss, and he thought he did, this evidence would destroy Alexander. And Dan's job, a dirty one, was to come up with enough incriminating evidence of fraud and conspiracy to prove Alexander's guilt substantially beyond any doubt. Then, of course, the remainder of the voyage would be concerned with Thompson's new plans for the Bahamas and getting these into proper working perspective.

He scooped up the mound of papers and stacked them neatly on the fold-down desk board by his bunk. He wouldn't even think about them until he'd had his morning coffee and something to eat. Aboard his first luxury yacht, he wasn't going to be able to savor its comfort and beauty, for Thompson would have a million ideas to keep him busy. A dismal exchange for his life's blood, he thought, and remembered that Alexander had occupied this same cabin on many occasions; the parallel was obvious, he mused. If Alexander was now living on borrowed time, it was conceivable that he, too, could join the same club one day—end up in the same unenviable position. Who in hell, what human being, could resist the kind of temptation Thompson might eventually toss his way? Even Dr. Faustus never had it so good. The answer was easy—nobody could resist, not indefinitely. Thompson wanted you to be involved; you worked better, harder, he had often said, when your interests were his interests.

Francovich started to shave. . . . Well, he was relatively poor now, even if he did work for one of the world's richest men, and although his past included the standard cliché set of Western guilts plus a dash of perfidy, his public record was clean. The senator had left him that, at least. But if he continued on with Thompson, special investment opportunities would come his way, he wouldn't have to be poor too much longer. Thompson would show him the way out, offer him a flying carpet. But once he was airborne, sailing high, there was no assurance he'd stay there. Thompson could yank the carpet out from under him any time he felt like it.

But by that time, he thought, eyeing himself cynically in the mirror, he'd be rich. That *seemed* to be what counted; it was also the trap. Here he was unattached and alone; money was a tangible value in times of chaos. Or was it? Was it even important? More to the point: Was it real? Was it what he wanted? He would have to answer these questions when and if Thompson brought him into the inner industrial family. Meanwhile, he would finish shaving, drink his coffee, and go to work. For that was really all Thompson knew and appreciated—work. If Thompson could be called a dying man, he could also be called a driven one.

"If you're taking the Emerald Salad, Alice, I'm taking the yellow and orange one, the Sunset," Phil said at the luncheon table the Bernheims were sharing with the Flemings.

"I'd like them both," Alice said with a greedy grin, wincing beneath her sunburned face.

"Aw, come on," said Rose, also sunburned, "you can't have them both. It's against the rules."

"You're all hunger-crazed," said Phil. "Thank God I've got myself under control!"

"I won't dignify that with a response," Alice retorted. "Personally, Rose, we ought to take the Hearts of Palm."

"Canned," Rose said, and held up a teapot. "Anybody for a cup? Tannic acid dims the appetite."

"I could use a spansule," said Jack.

"I could use a couple," said Phil. "My gut aches like lust."

Their waiter Loyal approached, smiling.

"I'll take the Sunset Salad, Loyal," said Rose.

"And the Anise Delight for me," said Alice.

"Hearts of Palm with vinaigrette," Jack said.

"The Endive Tomato Surprise," Phil ordered, "and a Diet Strawberry. Hey, Loyal, how about sneaking me a stack of rye wafers?"

Loyal rolled his eyes and grinned. "Ah'll try, sir, but Ah'll have to ask Miss Harrison, the diet boss. . . ."

"Don't bother," Phil replied. "She won't budge. Thanks, anyway."

"Coffee, anyone—?" Loyal asked.

"Yeah, three instants," said Jack, and Loyal hurried off.

"Jesus, I'm actually weak-kneed from starvation," Jack grouched. "I don't think I can last out the week."

"Better than ending up a cake of soap like your cousin Solomon," Rose pointed out. "Quit bitching."

"Hey, Jack," Phil said, "you hear the one about the guy who was so dizzy from hunger he ate his mother-in-law?"

"If I got to hear one more of your edible jokes, Phil Bernheim," Alice warned, "I'm catching the next plane to Nassau."

"All you make is promises," Phil replied.

The two women locked glances, obviously in agreement on a predetermined point. "*We* didn't have to come here at all, did we, Alice?" Rose said. "*They're* the real fat ones. *We* just thought it'd be nice to play dutiful wives while they got rid of their gluttonous guts!"

"Right, Rose! *We* are only five-ten pounds overweight. You porkos, both of you, are twenty, twenty-five."

"All right, all right," Phil conceded, "I'll shut up. But I still got nerves from parking my ass around that pool all day."

"You wouldn't go where there's a golf course," Alice said.

"Who's choosing?" Phil asked, and shot her a harsh glare.

"We all ought to walk more," suggested Rose. "We could try the cove for tranquillity. There's a nice pink beach about a quarter of a mile long. Or maybe you boys would miss ogling all that fat stuff climbing in and outta the pool!"

"Over your newspapers!" Alice amplified.

"Which reminds me," Jack said. "*Time* and *Newsweek* didn't come in today."

"Don't expect miracles around here!" said Rose.

"Oh boy," said Phil, "here comes the food. . . ."

Loyal unloaded a tray of plates, set steaming coffees before Alice, Phil, and Jack.

The quartet stared disconsolately at their meager fares, then at one another; all sighed in unison.

"I wish I was back in Miami," Phil grouched, "living like a normal human being. I wish all this was a bad dream."

"It is, friend, it is," Jack assured him.

Kill Howard, standing nearby, overheard them and walked over to their table. "Everything O.K., folks? More coffee, Mr. Bernheim?"

"I haven't touched this one," Phil said tartly. "Thanks, Kilroy, but everything's just great, lovely, beautiful."

"Yeah, stupendous," said Jack.

"Very gorgeous," said Rose, "if we were all bunny rabbits."

"We *got* to be," muttered Alice, wondering how long they were going to stay on in this overweight asylum and play these *meshugenah* games.

As soon as Aggie Bird read the radiogram that Harry delivered personally, she called Dick Carter at the medical station.

"Dick, I've got to see you right away."

Dick read the panic in her voice. "Well, I have an appointment in half an hour. Can't it wait?"

"No, something terrible has happened. I can't tell you on the phone."

"I'll be right over," Dick said, and Aggie started to pace the floor as soon as she hung up. Son of a bitch, she brooded, just when things were going so good. Here she was sober and sensible, feeling better than she had in years, losing a little weight—not a lot, but a few pounds, better than nothing—and now, out of the blue, Wayne was acting up. Jealousy, good God! She'd never expected anything that green and old-fashioned from him. . . . She was still pacing the floor minutes later and digging her nails into her palms when Dick walked right in without knocking.

"What's the trouble?" he said, as Aggie ran to him,

weeping, and buried her face against his chest. Reluctantly, in no mood for histrionics, he encircled her waist with both hands. "What broke you up, Aggie? Your mother die or something?"

Aggie jerked away from him, red-eyed. "Don't try to be funny. She's been dead ten years. It's a cablegram from Wayne. Maple took it off the radio for me, so he knows my business, too. His smirk was a mile wide when he delivered it. We're in for it, Dick. Wayne knows something."

"Let me see it."

Aggie pulled the crumpled radiogram form from her dressing-robe pocket and passed it to him. Dick read:

> FILMING DATE STILL FIRM BUT UNDERSTAND YOU VIOLATING GROUND RULES STOP LOOK FOR ME THERE ANY DAY STOP SHORT VACATION LONG TALK IMPERATIVE STOP AFFECTIONATELY WAYNE

"It's clear enough," Dick said uneasily. "He's planning to fly down and join you."

"It's clearer than that. He's found out something."

"Oh, come on, Aggie, be reasonable. How could Wayne find out that you and I've been—?" He didn't finish the sentence because his stomach flip-flopped.

"He's psychic, I tell you. He's got personal radar."

He knows *me*, Dick reasoned. Wayne was almost diabolically shrewd. "I never saw any evidence of it—" But of course he had. Wayne was just as calculating as he himself was; the extra edge lay in Wayne's ESP or whatever it was.

"Well, if he's not, then some mother's ratted on me!"

"But who could?" Who on the island would find it profitable to sneak Wayne Winslow a message about poor old Aggie's needs being satisfied? Dick speculated. After all, run-down, drunken old floozies were a dime a dozen in show business, they all outlived their times; and even though Aggie was somewhat special, and a good head, maybe Wayne had somebody else in mind for the role since she'd been gone. Or was some weirdo trying to get her into trouble before the filming started? There were only two people who nosed into things around Bimini: Tom Street and Eva Cassel. So, maybe one of them was guilty—but which?

"Dick, what do we *do*? If Wayne walks in and starts an inquisition, you or I'll give it away. . . . Son of a bitch, just when I've grown so fond of you!" she wailed, and threw her arms around him.

"Fonder than you are of Wayne?" It was worth a try even if he couldn't get anywhere; anything was with this unstable creature.

Aggie promptly released him and slumped into a convenient chair.

"Wayne's a good friend," she declared soberly. "He practically picked me up out of my coffin and unkinked me. Without him I wouldn't have *The Bungalow*. I admire him, he's got principles, but he doesn't make me scream for help like you do."

"Sometimes you've got to make choices, Aggie, and decide what you really want for the rest of your life," Dick said quietly, "and which way you're gonna fly for keeps. You still got some time. . . ."

"My trouble is, I've always been a rotten, spoiled, fickle bitch who didn't appreciate the goodies I was getting. I just took them for granted. I've done a lot of heavy thinking here and I know one thing: I'm going to please Wayne and do a great job on the film, the greatest yet. But goddamit, I want you, too. . . ."

"It's your decision, not mine," said Dick, "but you can't have everything."

Aggie studied him as if she were appraising him for the very first time, squinting her eyes. "Yeah, you're a pretty neat stud. You know how to package the merchandise real cool so everybody drools for it."

"I try," Dick conceded, not sure which way she was going.

"What I like about you is you're tough underneath. You've been backed up against the wall like me, Dick, only you keep your own counsel, you don't shit and shout the way I do. . . . You know, you don't even really like me; you love yourself too much for even that."

"I've loved Wayne," Dick said evenly. "Very much."

Aggie's face fractured into shocked surprise. "*Loved* Wayne?" she gasped.

"I still do. There's nothing queer about it. We weren't lovers or anything like that. Like you, I admire him. And like me, I *love* him."

"What the hell went on between you two?"

"Well, we shared an apartment, for one thing, a two-bedroom on Ivar. We knew a lot of people mutually, but we had separate lives. Wayne played it very straight, I kind of hung loose, did some hustling around, stuff like that."

"Stuff like that," scoffed Aggie. "I'll bet!"

"So, I had to make a living. I never liked anything I ever did for bread. I don't like what I'm doing now."

"You sure as shit *act* like you enjoy it!"

"I enjoy making people happy, that much of it, anyway. It's the only unselfish trait I have."

"Unselfish? Mmmmmmh, yeah, I dig, I'll buy that," Aggie replied. "I think the only thing I ever liked about film work was seeing the joy in people's faces at premieres, the excitement of my fans, the sheer naked *love* they'd offer. . . ."

Wayne could be dealt with when and if he arrived, Dick decided. Now to get Aggie off the subject and onto herself; it would calm her down, it always did. Lead her into it gently. If he didn't make his next appointment, so what? This was more important.

"Pictures are a tough business," he said, knowing that Aggie would always jump for this kind of Hollywood bait, no matter how she blasted the fringe culture and her own past.

"Fucking murder," Aggie responded. "Some reporter on *Variety* once asked me if I really liked to make films. Caught me in an expansive mood and I said sure, it was O.K. to invent your life for several months every year, but you couldn't let it take over or the devil got your soul. Christ, was there ever a stink from the studio about that! They were sore as hell. And the local churches damned me; I was accused of being anti-Hollywood. *Me*, imagine! I never took Hollywood that seriously, I was too busy having men and miscarriages. . . ."

Aggie pointed to the divan. "Sit down, Dick, you've got a minute. Don't just stand there in the middle of the room, you look so temporary. There's something I have to say to you."

Dick sat down, wondering what now, she was a strange creature. As messy as anybody could be, yet with that enormous, rampant vitality, that burning sensuality that made you think, once you'd mounted her, you were screwing a love goddess. Hey, that was it! Aggie fucked her audiences, too. Same thing as those Jefferson Airplane cats once said: The platform was their arena, their bed, the audience their broad, dying to get laid. So lay it they did. And it was the same thing with Aggie: she fucked her audiences into *adoration*, and nobody ever called it rape. From the depths of that blubber she was trying to do it to him now.

"I told you everything that happened to me after the premiere of *Kansas Cyclone* was downhill, remember?"

"Sure."

"Everything except meeting you. . . . Now don't look at me like that, I'm serious. I've been in love too often to count, I've had a hundred hot flashes all over the place. I never counted in numbers, I just played the game. But you're unique, Dick. I ooze when I look at you. And you know what? I think it's your total indifference that excites me. You just don't give a fuck, either, the way I haven't, and that's what makes me rise to the prize every time we get together. I know all about the gap in our ages; I'm even willing to play the masochist if it'll make you happy, if that soothes your hostilities any. . . . Oh shit, what I'm leading up to is, I'm thinking seriously of canceling out on *The Bungalow*. . . ."

Dick was shocked. "Jesus, Aggie, you're out of your mind!"

"Maybe, I don't know. But if you'll string along with me, I'll force Wayne to get me out of the contract and we can just coast. What do I care about a so-called big new career? Who's kidding who? It's bullshit. I have enough to live on comfortably. Everybody thinks I'm flat on my ragged ass. Well, I'm not. I could try and settle down with you, baby. What do you say?"

Quick major decisions weren't Dick's specialty; besides, Aggie was leaving too many loopholes. "How'd you spend your time if we made an agreement?" he hedged wearily. "You need to keep busy."

"You mean while living together without the idiocy of marriage?"

"Yeah, that's about it."

"Well, Actors' Academy wants me to coach a new acting class. That's a good outlet for surplus energy. Not a lot of money in it, but it'll keep me off the streets. It'll pay for groceries."

"What about the limelight? You love it."

"Sure, but I've had it. I think deep down I've always fought it. It's a helluva price to pay for that audience love I was talking about. I could be very content with the class and your companionship. I might even learn to live with your grosser qualities, your extradomestic chores—for you'd want them, you can't fool me on that score. They're you."

"And what would I do while you taught your classes?"

"Well, it just so happens that besides the two apartment houses I own there's a block of storefronts, too. You can take one of the units and start up anything you like. Anything to fit the zoning, that is. Beverly Hills isn't such a bad location. But no goddam massage parlor. That's out."

"Aggie, come on. No games. Are you being straight with me? After all, Wayne is—"

"My manager and *your* friend. I know. If I break up with him over *The Bungalow*, I'm probably washed up in the L.A. film industry, or what's left of it, for good. Unless I want to make hard-core pornos, ha, ha!"

Dick grinned. "We could make them together, maybe? They'd sell."

"Oh, Dick!" Aggie squealed and ran to him, knelt and put her head girlishly in his lap.

Some older women, Dick had learned long ago, went crazy during menopause and did irrational, uncharacteristic things. Some young ones went berserk when you cracked their hymens even with their consent and flipped over their first orgasm. So if what Aggie said was true—that he made her explode for the very first time in her life—then her actions were understandable. She really did want him for herself; she seemed willing to compromise herself to get her wish. But if she was doing this for convoluted personal reasons of her own, playing some foxy game and using him as a pawn against Wayne, then everybody was in trouble. He didn't mind the idea of living with her; it might be a gas. He had to admit privately that he was deeply impressed with her fame, more and more as he got to know her and realized that she was really a very ordinary person beyond that—and he liked her wildness, her really crazy passion, more frantic than anyone he'd ever met. Yes, he could see it as a reality, and even though he owed Wayne an enormous debt of gratitude that he could never actually repay, he owed himself the chance at a decent life before he was too old. So, here it was, all set up for him, neat as a pin. Also, she couldn't live forever; she might even leave him something, everything. And if necessary, he'd wear her out to get at it.

"You're really sweet, Aggie," he said, stroking her head, and he meant it, for she could be.

"I do love you, Dick," Aggie crooned, "even if some people think it's a dirty word!"

Cindy Brown lay in bed, relaxed and comfortable. She was thinking about last night and Kevin Mack's lingering attention, marred only by his remark about the silver-framed photo of the "beautiful" girl he thought was her sister.

Sister! she thought, and made herself a solemn vow that she'd stick to the no-calorie fast even if she had a horrible reaction, which didn't seem likely, for so far she wasn't even hungry. Under normal circumstances she'd have been ravenous. So if the water diet proved unpleasant, she'd keep her mouth shut; she was determined to slice off a great chunk of weight fast. *And keep it off!*

But it wasn't going to be easy trying to contain Kevin Mack in the rational role of doctor. The plain fact was that she was absolutely dizzy about him, in a way that had never happened with Poppy or anybody else. Eighteen and on her first serious date before anyone tried to kiss her, she'd imagined the whole charade of flesh touching flesh to be a mighty foolish business. She recalled laughing in the poor kid's face, humiliating him so much that he'd flushed angry red and all but slapped her. Of course, later on Poppy and his touches represented release, freedom, new worlds to conquer, the general answer to boredom. She liked the idea of games, once she realized their potential variety.

Today all looked bright, ordered and sensible, except for that pale cloud of doubt hovering over her that seemed to relate to Eva Cassel's visit last night after the doctor had gone.

"Well, well," Eva had trilled, bustling in with a cloth-covered tray, all smiles and professional starch. "That was a bad moment in the dining salon. Are you feeling better now?"

She chimes like a brass bell, Cindy thought. "I—I guess so. What's that?" She nodded at Eva's tray.

"Oh, just something comfy to make you relax," Eva explained, placing the tray on the bedside table. "Orders from Dr. Mack."

Cindy watched her uncover it, saw a prepared syringe, the phial of alcohol, the cotton swabs.

"I thought I was going to get something orally. I don't like needles."

"Don't be such a baby, dear. It's perfectly painless, you won't mind."

"I'll mind, but what is it?"

Eva smiled. "Can't tell you, dear. Doctor's orders. But you'll be so relaxed in a few moments you won't even recall that I've given you anything. Or care. . . . Now, your right arm, please."

Eva strapped the section of latex tubing around Cindy's

forearm, swabbed a bulging vein at the inner crook of her elbow, inserted the needle expertly, and injected her.

"There now—" Eva removed the needle, dabbed Cindy's arm with an alcohol swab, and closed her arm over the swab. "You'll be just fine. You're under a mild anesthetic, Miss Brown. Something newer and less potent than Sodium Pentothal, a form of barbiturate."

"I don't like injections."

Eva covered the tray. "You'll be just fine in a short time." She rose and turned on the radio, twisted dials, and got a Miami Muzak-type station playing scaled-down Viennese waltzes. "Rest, Miss Brown, relax. . . ."

Through a slight blur Cindy watched Eva glide to various parts of the room, rearranging an urn of begonias, adjusting Venetian blinds, turning off all the lamps except the night light over the head of the bed next to the emergency buzzer. Making me comfortable, Cindy concluded hazily, and smiled at Eva as she perched on the edge of her bed, removed the cotton swab, and took her pulse.

The music moved from Vienna to somewhere else, playing something limp and pallid, vague. As this room is, thought Cindy. I feel giddy, lightheaded, so weightless, a fine white feather floating away. . . .

She saw Eva uncover the tray again, this time drawing the cloth all the way back, revealing a small black box. Eva did something and it lit up, and she felt herself being turned very gently so that she faced the light. The light glowed soft red, flashed quickly on and off, on and off, with a rhythmic beat, almost like music. But no, it wasn't music she heard anymore; it was the audible beat of the metronome-like device synchronized with the flashing light. Roses coming and going, floating.

Ingenious, she thought groggily, delicious, delightful.

Eva's calm, softly modulated voice reached her from a great distance through the shadowy corridors of the drug.

"We're preparing you to enjoy your period of fasting, Miss Brown," Eva purred, "by giving you some basic commands through sleep education. While the body sleeps, the unconscious mind is awake. It never sleeps, it's constantly amenable to control by the power of suggestion. And it's in its most receptive state immediately after you've fallen asleep. Your subconscious mind has absolute control over all functions, sensations, and conditions of your body. . . ."

Eva's voice seemed to fade in and out of Cindy's attention, finally growing fainter and fainter until it was only a small, thin whisper, a rustling of dry leaves. Cindy knew that she was sliding down a long, steep, smooth chute into a pit of velvety darkness, and the sensation was extremely agreeable, welcome, quite beautiful. She sighed deeply.

"In a few moments you will reach that state where your eyes will shut. You will still hear the beat of the metronome, and then it, too, will fade away," Eva's whisper curled around her. "Next you'll enter into such a state of relaxation, of receptivity, that I will be able to give you commands that will make your fasting a perfect event. You will not only feel absolutely splendid during the whole of the first week's fast, you will also enjoy the weight reduction, ounce by ounce, as it occurs. . . ."

Cindy wanted to laugh with joy, to agree eagerly with the soft voice, but she hadn't the strength. With a tranquil expression on her face, she lapsed easily into the first stages of sleep indoctrination, entirely in Eva Cassel's control.

Eva knew a great deal about the art of hypnotism. She had learned about it by working as a hypnotist's assistant in a fairly successful nightclub act that played small cities in the Midwest, some years before she decided to be a medical secretary, later a nurse. She knew every trick of the system and had employed most of these positively to help patients overcome their various problems—obesity among them. Eva always worked with the prior approval of the doctor in charge of her cases. All medically legal, following the rules. But since coming to Bimini Springs, Eva had spread herself. Finding a situation where patients came and went with satisfying regularity, she soon began to exercise a certain secret pleasure above and beyond her normal call of duty, delving into patients' backgrounds while they were under hypnosis. She received an enormous power charge by discovering that old Mrs. X had a private bank account of which her husband was entirely ignorant, about $30,000 worth; that Mr. Y was having a torrid fling with his manicurist and had set her up in an apartment only a few blocks from his residence. Also that Mrs. O was a bigamist, bless her, and that Mr. Q who taught at the local high school was obsessed with boys, always in another town, but not healthy at all for him, considering he was head of a military academy.

Eventually, Eva reasoned, it seemed absolutely foolish not to think about using all this glorious information to her own personal advantage, for money. It didn't, she felt, make her any less professional just because she decided ultimately to remind various patients of their indiscretions after she'd secured their unconscious confidences. So, maintaining a detailed mental card file of her explorations and discoveries—names, dates, addresses, telephone numbers—Eva had for some months now been building up a stack of exceptional case histories, all quite damaging. When enough would be enough, she intended to walk off the job for good and start living. Collecting, that is, on the anxieties of some of those foolish people who'd made such messes of their lives and who kept psychic records of their blameful, unorthodox performances. All for her benefit. For the facts about everyone were all there in her patients' subconscious, in that marvelous cerebral index that was the quintessential memory tape—the subconscious—that always knew and recorded the pure truth.

Eva waited for several minutes until Cindy's breathing became calm and regular, then rose and switched off the radio. Leaning close to Cindy's ear, she spoke in a low, firm voice: "Now, Miss Brown, you're going to tell me the story of your life, from start to finish. I'm going to ask questions, and you're going to supply answers. There will be nothing at all painful to this, you mustn't be ashamed to tell me everything. There is nothing *immoral* in your life. . . ."

Here she paused momentarily, a smile on her smooth face, her eyes very bright. *Immoral*—it always released them, made them babble like babies.

"And when you awaken, you will remember nothing of the circumstances surrounding your life story as you told it to me. All you'll remember is how good it felt to be put to sleep, how wonderful it is to be undergoing Dr. Mack's no-calorie fast. And from now on you'll lose weight rapidly and regularly, Miss Brown. Remember that. You'll be very happy, the doctor will be very happy, and *I* will be happiest of all. . . ."

Eva began to stroke Cindy's soft, round face. A lovely face, she thought, with such a childlike innocence about it. She traced Cindy's delicate jawline with an index finger, then her lips. She slipped her right hand inside Cindy's pajama coat, cupping each of the large firm breasts very gently, pinching the nipples lightly, one after the other, then slowly moved her hand down and across Cindy's convex stomach. When Cindy stirred slightly, emitting a faint moan that sounded like pleasure, Eva quickly withdrew her hand, bent down, and ran her lips over Cindy's mouth, then stood up and smiled at her.

"Now, Miss Brown, we're old friends, and I am your

devoted, affectionate confidante. How old were you when you first masturbated?"

The words touched Cindy's mind; she murmured from the depths of her pillow: "I was fourteen. I was thinking about a movie actor I had a crush on. . . ."

"Yes, yes," said Eva, excited, "go on—" Slowly she pulled Cindy's pajama trousers down to her ankles, sent a flight of fingers racing toward Cindy's shadowy triangle, touching, caressing, finally bending toward it, still smiling, her lips parted.

When Cindy began to whimper, Eva stopped, sat up, pleased with herself. It wasn't always this easy to establish the subtle contact of subliminal sexuality, to create confidence; the rest would come later. What fun she would have on several levels!

"When," asked Eva, "did you first make love with somebody?"

Cindy moved her head from side to side, her eyes closed. It was all so hazy, so mixed up. She kept feeling Kevin Mack's caresses but hearing a different voice, not his, although the joy was there, her loins throbbed with it. Yet nothing was in rational focus, the pale cloud hovered overhead.

"Do you have money?" someone was asking. "Can you get at it easily? Are you married or single? If you don't have a job, what do you do with your life? Are you in hiding?"

She managed to answer them all, then blackness. And that uneasy blackness was all she remembered when she swam back to consciousness—a disembodied voice, a tender sensual feeling. Miss Cassel had given her something to make her sleep, of course, and it was morning, and Miss Cassel was gone. . . .

She was brought out of her reverie by the arrival of the nurse's aide, a black girl named Loris, who was carrying a thermos pitcher.

"Breakfast, Miss Brown," Loris announced gaily. "Honestly, I don't see how you gonna do it. You got the better part of a week ahead of you on *this* stuff." Loris brandished the pitcher aloft. "And it ain't no banquet!"

"Put it down over here, Loris," said Cindy confidently. "I'll manage all right."

"Hmpf!" Loris exchanged the fresh pitcher for the one on the bedside table. "Don't let Dr. Mack or Miss Severn hear you say 'manage' around them! That's the same thing as defeat in their book."

"I was thinking of Miss Cassel," Cindy said, surprised that she had been.

"Miss Cassel's even worse. You gotta overcome, Miss Brown, that's all."

"Well then, I shall," said Cindy. "Thanks for the vote of support, Loris."

"Think nothin' of it," Loris said. "Part of my duty. Besides, at your age you got no earthly reason to be unhappy."

Cindy stared at the pitcher as Loris closed the door. Let Kevin embrace my mind, she mused, for it seemed that he—or someone—had done much more last night; but everything was so vague. That was some shot, all right. Eva Cassel had been sweet and helpful, gentle. But Cindy couldn't shake the impression that Cassel was possibly sinister—the careful make-up, the too-bright smile and perfect teeth, the lithe, slim body that looked feminine but was more pantherish than human. It was the drug, of course, that was all.

She reached for the pitcher. Overcome, she thought. Yes, she'd do it. If not for herself, then for Kevin Mack. The *beautiful* girl in the silver frame is going to be *me* again, she vowed, and poured herself a glass of the livid, raspberry-red concoction, full of ice and saccharin, and drank it down quickly.

The men's quarters for supervisory staff that housed Kevin Mack, Tom Street, and Dick Carter also included Kill Howard. The decision for this integration, as the Maples termed it, was arrived at after a period of heavy private debate. Knowing the trend of the times and recognizing the signs, on Kill's job-site arrival they decided to billet him in the empty room next to Tom Street. This was against their strong personal prejudices, to be sure, but it made the situation look good for them, better than it should have looked. Kill quickly figured out that they were playing him for house nigger, making him token man, and he was right.

"Got to spare ourselves controversy, Marge," Harry said to his wife one night in bed, one night before Kill arrived, the place where they often settled most of their problems, social as well as sexual.

"Absolutely, love," Marge agreed. "Let 'em come into their own gradual-like, that's our motto. . . ."

But today Kill had left a memo with Joan Harrison who gave it to Marge Maple who handled housing. It seemed that in the single-black male bunkhouse Kill's kitchen help were now stacked four to each small, airless room in two sets of makeshift wooden double bunks the staff carpenter had put together with clumsy haste. Kill thought this unnecessary since all medical and nursing supplies were recently stocked at the pharmacy under Tom's supervision, which left two storage rooms at the far end of the supervisory quarters consequently vacant. Kill could see no reason why these rooms shouldn't be turned into dormitories to reduce the crowded four-man occupancy in the bunkhouse. But before he wrote his memo, Kill discussed the proposed possible move with all the whites in his wing. To a man they agreed that the idea was a good one. Then he wrote his note to Marge.

At midafternoon Marge stormed into Kill's room, about an hour after she received the note from Joan.

Kill was lying on his bed, half-asleep, listening to the Stones' latest LP release. Fortunately, he wasn't high; there was no evidence of grass around. But the old bitch could've at least knocked, he thought, regarding her sleepily as she breezed in. He didn't rise to his feet to greet her but merely sat up.

"What's the meaning of this piece of paper, Kilroy Howard?" Marge declared in a loud voice, her cheeks flushed.

Keep your cool, man, Kill cautioned himself. Don't let her get to you and you'll stay on top.

"What piece of paper, ma'am?" He waved toward the empty armchair. "Have a seat, ma'am. Can I get you a soft drink or something stronger?"

Slightly diminished by his hospitality, Marge shook her head negatively and perched on the edge of the armchair.

"Kilroy Howard," she began, "you know this is impossible. We simply can't have the staff people bothered by the kitchen help."

"Bothered? You put *me* in here, ma'am," Kill reminded her. "I'm kitchen help."

"You are *supervisory* kitchen help, Kilroy Howard, and you work *out* of the kitchen, not *in* it."

"Looks like the same side of the bed to me, ma'am. The men who want to move into the empty rooms are all clean, quiet, healthy fellows. They serve you your meals, they mix your salads and wash your dishes. They work hard enough days so's all they want nights is a couple of beers and early to bed. They're no noise or bother. . . . They're not like Miss Harrison's *girls*, ma'am, no needlepoint or lib meetings," he added mischievously, and grinned.

"Kilroy Howard, you are impossible. . . ." Marge had her breath back now, but the room was so chilly her bare arms were getting clammy. She rubbed them briskly and said, "I didn't know you had air conditioning, Kilroy Howard."

"Why not? I wasn't born in the tropics, ma'am. Just the Deep South where they have the four seasons, so I'm not conditioned to heavy humidity. Maybe some folks are and can put up with it, I can't. I bought the A/C myself. . . ."

Marge got his point; he meant that the blacks weren't given air conditioning while the whites were. She tried another gambit.

"You have an education, Kilroy Howard, as Joan does, so you'll understand what I'm going to say."

"Grammar school," Kill said, "just barely. Oh, I got me a high-school-equivalent certificate while I was in Southeast Asia, but I didn't go to school for it; I took some tests. . . . Just grammar school, that's all."

"Anyway—" Marge began in a desperate voice, feeling her control slipping away. Not only was he purposely running circles around her, making everything she said meaningless by watering it down, he was *enticing* her. That was it precisely, enticement! There he lay, all of him, spread out like some big black potentate, hung like God knows what with that bulge, his chest sticking out in that T-shirt, the cool, sharp personal smell of him staining the chilly air. She felt like swooning, but she gritted her teeth instead and continued: "Anyway, Kilroy Howard, the help you want to put in those rooms have to be kept in their place. . . ."

"What *place*, ma'am?"

"Why, subordinate to you, of course!" Marge cried quickly. "You're their boss, their superior!"

"No, you got it wrong, ma'am. I'm their *teacher*. If they knew more than I did, they'd be *my* teacher. It's a give-and-take proposition. I learned in the army that rank doesn't mean a thing unless you got the stuff to back it up."

"Rank is face," said Marge, "and you know that as well as I do."

"That's power talk," said Kill.

"Kilroy Howard, you've got some mighty dangerous thoughts floating around in your head. You've been listening to that Joan Harrison again!"

Kill grinned; she was so predictable. "I listen to the woman in her, not the politician, ma'am. That's what counts. . . . So what do we do, ma'am, about the employees?"

"They stay right where they are," said Marge, "and Mr. Maple backs me up all the way on this decision."

"You're both making a big mistake, ma'am. You might find everybody walkin' off the job one day all of a sudden when the parcel boat shows up on its way to Nassau."

Marge leaped out of the armchair, furious. "Don't you dare threaten *me*, Kilroy Howard! Don't you treat me like some—" She couldn't finish, she was so frustrated with rage.

"Common nigger?" Kill said carefully. "Isn't that what you were thinking?"

"Kilroy Howard, you'll never ever know what I'm thinking," Marge snapped. And he certainly wouldn't, for she would have given her eyeteeth to get on that bed with him and let him mount her. The desire was so strong in her and simultaneously so rudely savage, so against what she felt she ought to be thinking, that she turned and stalked to the door.

"All right," she said, glaring at him, her hand on the doorknob, knowing she'd gone much too far, knowing that she would carry away nothing but misery and self-disgust if she left things like this. "All right, *all right*, Kilroy Howard. You win! I'll let the boys take those rooms, but only six of them, hear, and you'll be entirely responsible for their conduct at all times. Is that understood?"

"Yes, ma'am," Kill said. That and much, much more. Vixen.

"All right, but I don't know how I'll explain my actions to Mr. Maple," she said.

Kill rose slowly to his feet and grinned. "Just tell him you changed your mind, ma'am. No man can argue with that!"

Marge shot him a brief, exposed glance—let him read anything into it he wanted—and banged the door shut as she went out.

She hadn't said good-by, Kill noted, but neither had she summoned the decency to call him anything but Kilroy Howard. He chuckled to himself and lay down again, to continue his interrupted nap. . . .

"This whole thing's a pain in the ass," Kevin grouched to Ruth Severn in his office as the two of them went over the new diet charts, Joan Harrison's parallel menu system, trying to find a way to cut their own work while still giving their patients thorough attention. "There's no need to change any of this, and the Maples know it."

"Griping won't help," Ruth said. "We all eventually reach a saturation point here, I've noticed. Lately Eva's got her mind elsewhere."

Kevin nodded. "True. She listens but doesn't seem to hear. I've seen that numb look flash across her face often lately; it happened at the diet conference. You noticed it. I doubt if she heard anything anyone said."

"What do you think's wrong?" Ruth wondered.

Kevin grinned. "I could say she needs a man around the house, but then you'd just give me one of your funny Ruthie looks."

Ruth put down her pen and studied Kevin. It was time to straighten out a few things.

"You're a pretty funny animal yourself, Kev," she told him, "so don't start with that mysterious female stuff again. We agreed some time ago that we wouldn't open closets and let out any skeletons, family or otherwise."

"Like once I had a very healthy passion for you?"

"Once—" Ruth couldn't conceal her amusement.

Kevin frowned. "Well, what's wrong?" he demanded.

"Your use of the word 'passion'—your terminology. You're so damned Victorian, you really are."

"And you're not too adventurous," Kevin retorted, annoyed. Ruth knew how to get to him.

"That's self-control and prudence," Ruth said. "I remember once I kept you from getting arrested."

"When?"

"Well, you dared me to run up and down the Caravelle Hotel corridors in Saigon stark naked, and I talked you out of it."

Kevin chuckled, remembering. "That was mostly the cognac."

"No, it was before you started catering to the fat and the elderly, Kev, and when you still had a sense of humor. Ages ago."

"We're not getting anywhere, are we, Ruthie?"

"I don't think that's the real problem, Kev. It's still your basic stubbornness."

"How so?

"I was the one who talked you into coming here in the first place, remember? When you got out of the service, you were determined to jump right into your advanced studies until you found out you couldn't manage it financially."

"Sure, I know. And we agreed that maybe the restricted isolation of Bimini might do us both some good."

"That's not exactly accurate. You refused my help. I was willing to work so you could go to school."

"Right, but I'm making headway. I've got several thousand in savings and loan at 5.25 per cent per annum. I've got a contract that gives me room, board, laundry, *and* medical care. It's a way to save money even if it's not really living—"

"I didn't say it was. But who wanted it that way? You're talking about benefits, not emotional hopes and fulfillments."

"Speaking of needs," Kevin began, but Ruth cut him off with her steady gray-eyed gaze, and shook her head.

"The answer's a big fat no, Kev. I'm not interested in something permanent any longer. Not even an arrangement. I see too much around here. I hope it hasn't turned me off of sex permanently, but it's sure as hell put a damper on my libido."

"What's happened to us, Ruthie?" Kevin asked soberly. "We used to be mighty loving and tender. Now all we do is get ass-deep in semantics and start to argue. We could go on like this forever, and we're still sidestepping the central issue. What went wrong?"

"Frankly, I don't know. Two people who once cared ought to be able to analyze it. I can't. I hope I haven't changed that much. I'm still—very fond of you. I admire you, I respect your skill, your integrity as a practitioner. . . ."

"Then what's *wrong* with me?" Kevin demanded. "You used to sleep with me because you liked me. Now you won't even really accept me anymore."

"It's not you, it's *me*—my problem."

"Is it somebody else, somebody here?"

"God no!" Ruth protested sharply. "Certainly not. I guess I'm just bored, like you. This place isn't healthy for anybody except the guests. I think I really ought to go back to something more meaningful, something I can handle that makes some sense."

"Christ, that stupid word! If it's not involvement or the black issue via Joan Harrison, it's doing something significant. All right, why not join Women's Lib?"

"Don't be superficial," Ruth said. "It's not my corner."

"Ruthie, just breathing is a major achievement these days. Holding down a function like Bimini is tantamount to cleaning the Augean stables. Why stick your neck out by going to Peru or some other country and being noble? I thought you had enough in Vietnam!"

"I was talking about not wasting time, Kev. Hours, days, and years. Thirty gets you fifty before you know it. We haven't forever, we're almost both middle-aged."

"You always did have a depressing sense of logic," Kevin pointed out, "but that doesn't mean we can't enjoy each other. Look, tonight's another fine moon, the beach is as great as ever. Why not take a blanket and go down to the cove?"

"No, Kev, I'm sorry, but no."

"And you won't even leave the question of marriage open, Ruthie? We'd make a great team."

"Why, when we can't even define the basic issues? Be realistic."

"I'm trying to, but it's tough to buck your cynicism."

"Mine?" Ruth said, exasperated. "You chase rainbows!"

"It's this goddam island. It's made us strangers."

"No, we've done that to ourselves. . . ." Ruth turned, hearing a noise in the outer office, and caught a fast glimpse of Eva in uniform as she passed the open door. She lowered her voice. "Come on, Kev, let's look official. It's Eva. And if there's one person who likes to gossip better than Tom Street, it's our little Eva."

"What's she done to you?"

"It's what she's tried to do to me a couple of times, what I've had to stop her from doing," Ruth said ambiguously. "But you don't want to hear about that."

"I don't think I have to," he replied, and glimpsed Eva through the partly open door checking the chart boards.

"Eva!" he called out. "Come on in. We want your ideas on the short-cut room service for grounded patients. . . ."

Under her breath Ruth cautioned him, "Now don't you needle her about anything. She's edgy as hell lately, and we're strapped if she quits. Those damned Maples, they're so cheap. We ought to have three regulars, not just her."

A moment later Eva walked in and leaned against the inner door frame, favoring them both with her brightest smile. "Guess what? You'll both die. . . ."

"I haven't the faintest," Ruth said, and blinked at Kevin.

"Well, Mrs. Poor White came shooting out of Kill Howard's room a few minutes ago with murder in her eyes. I think he cut her down to size. I hope so, anyway. Or maybe—"

"Never mind," Kevin said, "we get you. It happens to the best of southern gentry occasionally. Look, Eva, what about curtailing nurses' aide service and still getting patients to think they're being royally serviced?"

Eva made a little moue. "I could use the strobe light—"

"Don't be flippant," Kevin said, "we're serious."

"Then send them all home. Most of them don't deserve half the treatment they're already getting."

"Eva," Kevin said patiently, "I asked you a serious question."

"And I gave you a serious answer. Look, kids, I'm tired. I'm going to take an aspirin and lie down in the nurses' room for ten minutes. O.K.?" And heedless of the reprimanding looks both Kevin and Ruth focused on her, she flounced out.

"Christ, every day it's worse," Kevin said.

"I can't gauge her moods at all anymore, and I know for sure that's all she takes—aspirin. She's too straight for uppers or downers, which is why I'm really worried about her. Kev, you've got to have a talk with the Maples when they're both in expansive moods and demand more staff. No ifs and buts. Threaten them if necessary. . . ."

"Huh, that's almost like talking to you," Kevin said darkly.

"Now don't you be difficult, too!"

Kevin pressed Ruth's arm gently. "Will it make you any mellower toward me if I ask them?" he said.

"No," Ruth answered, "I don't think so, but I know you'll do it for me."

"Yes, that's the trouble," Kevin replied, "and you've always known it!"

Tom Street received a visit from Harry Maple in his pharmacy office, which was most unusual; Harry generally summoned people to his office when there were problems.

Harry plopped down in a chair next to the TV monitor and said abruptly, "It's come to my attention, Tom, that you're a bit too interested in the room action on closed-circuit TV."

"Who would say a thing like that? It's my duty to monitor."

"Yes, but with absolute impartiality, and then forget about it. And when I say forget," Harry waggled a finger at him, "I mean *forget* it, boy. Just erase it from your mind for all time."

"In other words, you're accusing me of snooping?"

"I'm not accusing you of anything, but we keep a clean slate at Bimini. Can't have complaints from guests."

"I'm clean," Tom said, "and I don't overstep my responsibilities. Otherwise Kevin wouldn't let me handle drugs."

"Nobody's mentioned drugs," said Harry. "We know you're careful."

Harry had never been able to pinpoint Tom's sexual drift, and this made him uneasy, causing him to wonder if Tom might not be queer. He'd had a few experiences in his early youth, lay back to a few needs; he could understand if Tom went the route. But what really puzzled him was that there wasn't a shred of evidence about any declared sexuality concerning Tom.

"Sometimes we get hints from colleagues," Harry went on, "and we got to check things out."

"Colleagues?" Tom said angrily. "Who the hell's fabricating stories about me?"

"Did I say anybody was?"

"No, but you—"

"All right. Just be prudent, Tom. Glad you got some righteous indignation in you. Proves you're telling the truth. You know, Marge is a real straightforward woman and won't stand for any drooling over the monitor. She respects individual privacy the way I do, and anyway, who needs a monitor when you got a sweet little cuddly old partner, huh?" Harry smiled and winked broadly.

Yeah, thought Tom, you old fucker! I'll bet you sit down in your office every goddam night just like I do and stroke yourself into action watching that busy little screen. So you can carry something solid in to the little woman, sweet Christ!

Harry rose. "Well, I won't belabor the subject, Tom. But try to be discreet, hear?"

"Of course," Tom said, noncommittally, as Harry strode purposefully from the office.

So, who was snitching on him? Eva Cassel? No, she might bitch him about his interests, but she wasn't concerned with moral issues, she didn't have any. And Ruth Severn? No, Ruth was above it; her interests lay in Kevin. Joan Harrison, boiling over with social injustices? They wouldn't include his preoccupation with the monitor, even if she was contemptuous of most whites. And it couldn't be Kill; he was entirely too cool. All Kill wanted was a toke in comfort. Anita or Dick? Hardly, they'd been around too much. The best guess, the only one, was Harry himself, well aware of his own games and not wanting to let Tom think he was getting away with anything. So, only the two of them knew! The guests, most of them, didn't even pay any attention to the monitoring camera eyes, humping away in happy oblivion. Like that fine five abandoned minutes of climactic action between randy old Avery and bouncy Mrs. McMahon he recorded last night. Who'd have thought those two old farts would scream and scratch like a pair of alley cats? And there was no end to what went on in the guest rooms, if you were vigilant.

Combine work and play, build up a beautiful file, a potential goldmine. The miracle of electronics was more fun than being personally involved, Tom thought, and a good surrogate when you couldn't exactly drop everything and pop off to Mexico City or Tokyo or London. Stay at home, press a button, and presto! there was Cindy Brown reading a novel. Or Mrs. McMahon preening herself at her dressing table as she hummed an old Richard Rodgers tune. Or Jack Fleming trying to talk his wife Rose into an afternoon tumble. Flick a switch, take your choice. Harry was right to be concerned about the monitor, Tom mused, for it brought sex, that most fragile of all merchandise, right into the home—for fun and profit.

Kill Howard was most pleasantly surprised to find Joan Harrison outside his door when he answered the knock.

"I want to talk," she said bluntly.

"O.K., but take off your sword, Joan of Arc. No goddam causes tonight. I'm so damn' weary I don't even want to hear anythin' but sweet talk." He took two beers from the reefer.

"When I said *talk* to you, that's what I meant, Kill. I've noticed some very funny things goin' on around here lately."

"So what else is new and urgent? There's always some bullshit goin'." He opened the beers.

"Tom Street's been actin' odd, secretive—stays late in the pharmacy office, blinds shut tight, front door locked. Never used to. And Carter, that bastard, was at me the other day like a stud boar, right in broad daylight in the supply room. God knows he has his chuckin' hands on that ofay show-biz dame and others enough not to worry me, too. . . ."

"Full moon. . . ."

"That's wanin'," Joan reminded him.

"Here, have one—" Kill handed her a beer, sprawled on his bed. "You oughtta pull in your antennae, girl, before you know too much."

Joan was sitting in the armchair in which Marge had so recently sustained her crisis; Kill speculated as to how he would come out with her tonight. On top, he hoped, but you never knew with her.

"Nothin' to do with moon and tides," Joan told him. "People's stirred up, pussyfootin' all over Devil Cay like that Bernheim, pokin' into things, takin' Polaroid shots. The Brown girl, the one who says she's a secretary when she looks so rich, she got dedication in her eyes all of a sudden for Dr. Mack. . . . And then we come to Evil Cassel who's been givin' off a load of hostility, I can feel it. More she smiles like dentrifice the more she scares me. Ain't natural, that one. The whole place is beginnin' to give me goose bumps."

"You oughtta forget about that voodoo stuff, girl, you too educated for that."

"None of your face, man! I ain't a true believer."

Kill chuckled. "Only thing's supposed to raise your hide is *me*, woman. You got too much imagination. That Women's Lib shit gone to your head. Yeah, I used to see grunts in Nam flip out when they'd hear rockets hit the other side of Saigon. Sometimes pee their pants, too, always thinkin' about danger and dyin'. They called it battle fatigue. You got some of that, girl. . . . Relax, ain't nobody's gonna clean your plow yet. You got a long, lovin' life ahead of you, sugar. Live it. . . ."

"I get your pitch," Joan said coldly, "and I'm not imagining anything. It's all true. Funny things goin' on, believe me."

"You need an injection, woman."

Joan snorted in disgust, put her beer on the table by her chair. "You can wipe that lecherous grin off your face! Seems like everybody's grinnin' all over the place, even *them*. Mistah Charlie's sherlockin', the Madam don't know which end's her face—"

"I know. She came to see me here this afternoon."

Joan jumped up. "To see *you*?"

"Sat right where you sittin', neat as pie, tried to turn everything inside out. All about the double bunks in help's quarters."

"Oh? And what did my hero do about it, huh?"

"Him? He triumphed. The help's movin' in tomorrow, three to a room."

"Well, I hope nobody starts sniffin' around too much," Joan said. "O.K. for you to smoke, you got A/C and closed up. But six of them doin' it right into the wind, that's somethin' else."

"They be cool. I give 'em instructions. They got to go

to the cove and blast when the mood hits 'em. Anyway, nobody's gonna bother 'em here."

"We don't know that," Joan emphasized. "Mistah Wonderful's everywhere. Say, I had a funny dream when I took my after-lunch sleep, about the same time you must've entertained the cream of southern womanhood—"

"About me? High time."

"Not that kind. You got busted for bush, man, right in your own quarters. I couldn't figure who busted you, but it ain't a good omen. Troubled me ever since."

"What's your inference, woman?" She could be so damned straight about grass it always riled him.

"You oughtta keep it somewhere besides around here, Kill. Make a careful stash away from quarters. Stay clean."

"I got a careful stash with Linc. Nobody'll ever find what we key-bricked."

"I hope so. But you shouldn't keep nothin' here. You can't count out somebody official snoopin' round the island lookin' for somethin'. Like your stash."

"Bush ain't a drug, woman, it's a natural plant. I told you a hundred times before."

"The law don't distinguish like you do. Not yet. And until they do—"

"O.K., O.K., don't bug me! I'll think about it. Want to get high?"

Joan shook her head. "Thanks, I'll stick to the brew, if you don't mind."

"What's the matter you so uptight? You got stoned on the rock the other night."

"That was different."

"How?"

Joan paused a moment; a warm smile spread across her strong features. "Well, I didn't expect to have to keep my head straight up there."

"Meaning?"

"If you want to, Kill, just—say the word. . . ."

Kill couldn't believe his ears and sighed sharply, from both relief and surprise. "Girl, I'm almost afraid to speak," he said. "Like if I took one step you'd vanish. Can't risk it."

Joan rose, still smiling. "In that case, best if I move." She switched off the table lamp so that the room lay in semidarkness, only the area light from the outside eaves filtering through the angled Venetian blind's slats.

Kill watched her undress slowly, his heart in his throat, and finally stand nude before him, shapely, dark, her nipples popping out. A sharp, sensual shudder of anticipated joy took him, more eloquent than any formulated thought could be. He blessed her silently for being kind and generous at a time when his need was very great. A wonderful rich moment together with no troubles of any kind intruding. Sure, this was what it was all about, the point to everything.

"Come here, girl," he whispered hoarsely. "Come over here and undress me. . . ."

And Joan glided toward him, warmly obedient, docile, and sat beside him on the bed, reaching for the buttons on his shirt as he ran his hand across her velvety thighs, feeling her move and thrill to his touch.

Real special, he thought, as he sent sensitive exploring fingers between her legs and she leaned down and pressed her soft, hot mouth on his dry, feverish lips. . . .

Two figures stood in the shadows of the bougainvillea arbor just below the main lodge at one end of the tropical garden. Under the arbor's cover, Harry Maple was trying to explain to Anita Pomeroy just why things were the way they were and why they wouldn't change.

Anita wasn't angry; she understood the situation. If anything, she was feeling dull and bored with Bimini Springs, surfeited with the role she was forced to play as Harry's sometime gadget, for the returns were nil. It wasn't as though she loved him and could give him latitude. She required something tangible from a relationship, and there was nothing doing here. And yet she wasn't quite ready to move on. So when she agreed to meet Harry in the arbor for a few minutes, she came determined to play the situation as straight as possible and see what would happen. But of course, Harry always set her off.

"Baby, you know I can't shuck Marge," Harry was saying, and there was no need for him to; Anita already knew this. "We're Siamese twins, Marge and me, joined at the hip. One can't survive without the other."

"That's not the issue, Harry. You want too much from me. You expect me to be at your beck and call whenever you feel playful. You think you act like a lover, but you're really more of a tout. You call the shots, you take the money, half of it, anyway, while I'm the one who earns it. I'll tell you something, Harry, I'm tired of playing bottom woman for any man. You can dress it up any way you like, but you're still a smalltime pimp, and I'm the big, dumb call girl. And eventually this stacks up to my wanting some changes. I mean it, I'm sick of it."

"Aw, baby, come on—"

"It's perfectly O.K. by me what you mount—like that Bird woman, Carter's latest."

"That old tramp—?"

"But you did," Anita reminded him, "and she's no older than you are."

Vain about his physical condition, Harry responded resentfully: "There's one helluva lot of difference between us."

"Which didn't keep you out of her pasture. Harry, it's no-go between us from now on. I'm just not going to put out for you or your clients again unless I want to. I'll do my job the best I can, I'll earn my salary and split tips, but that's all."

"Why the sudden turnabout?" Harry asked suspiciously. "It's part of your job to make everybody happy."

"Through my work, sure. But if I decide some extra attention's warranted, I'll be an outlaw. You know what that is, Harry, you've been there. I'm going to keep my perspective; it's about all I've got left. So if somebody ever does come along who's willing to overlook my faults and offer me a little loving sympathy in the bargain, then I want enough respect left over to be able to respond. I've still got my looks, and my health, and some small part of my sanity. I lost some of it here, but there's still a little left. And if somebody shows me a way out, I'm going to take it. . . ."

"Which means you've already got a party in mind," Harry said, running over his idea of an eligible list. "Well, who?"

Anita merely smiled.

"That Homer guy!" And Anita smiled again, maddeningly silent.

"Avery—that's it!"

"Sorry, Harry, time's up, and you're not even warm. I'm on my way to bed. But remember—the game's over between us. It's gone on too long already."

Harry grabbed her by the shoulders, but she wrenched away. "I meant what I said," she told him. "That's all, Harry," and turned and walked away.

"O.K., O.K.," he said to her retreating back, "if that's the way you're going to play it, look out!" He'd have her off the premises in a week. All he had to do was to drop one hint to Marge that she'd been putting the make on him, and Marge would hammer the coffin lid shut herself. One thing about having a wife like Marge, she was friend and deadly defender in one. Marge would play the dirtiest pool in the world to protect her security; Anita would never know why she was fired.

"Happy dreams, bitch," he muttered as Anita walked off into the shadows.

After leaving Harry, Anita skirted the main building and ran down the long terrace, ducking around corners, sure Harry would follow her. In his feeble brain he was probably figuring that if he could get her into her room he'd get into her pants. That kind of cretinous thinking was his specialty. That was the only way he thought about women. Anita knew. Why she'd ever let him talk her into double duty in the first place, she'd never know. For once done, she was committed. Just because Carter did it with almost everybody was no sign she had to be like Dick.

As she turned another corner she glanced at the first break in the wall, the door to Number Fifteen, now housing one Stanley Conn, newly arrived at Bimini Springs. A pleasant man around forty. Her one straight massage contact with him was the day before. She stopped dead in her tracks. Why not duck into Conn's room and let Harry go tearing by looking for her?

She knocked gently on Conn's door. The light was on, she could see it through the Venetian blinds, and the radio was playing. As far as she knew, Conn was a Chicago salesman down to melt off blubber. He'd come on pleasantly enough, nothing unusual, just a nice, easy manner, no gropes.

She knocked again; this time Conn answered, a bright red kimono draped on his stocky figure. Surprised, pleased, he stood back and held the door wide.

"Hey, Miss Pomeroy!"

Instantly Anita was inside with the door shut behind her, breathless, leaning against it and smiling, hoping Harry was hurrying past right now.

"Nice surprise," Conn said. "What's the occasion?"

"I was just passing and I wondered if I could pick up a copy of your *Wall Street Journal*? I saw some lying on your coffee table when I was here yesterday. I've got a few shares of mutuals. I'd like to see what they're doing."

Stanley Conn beamed at her, his round face pink with pleasure.

"Sure, sure, anything you want. Excuse my attire, I wasn't expecting a guest. Those papers are several days old, but they're all yours. Anything at all. . . ."

Anita advanced toward the divan, uncertain of her next move. It was one thing to walk into a client's room for a professional massage date, maybe linger on for something else and walk away with a tip, but it was quite another to arrive at night, against all rules, declaring open season on yourself.

Ten minutes, that's all she needed. Then she'd go home. Harry wouldn't hang around her door very long, afraid somebody might see him and report him to Marge.

Anita sat down breathlessly on the divan. "I know the way to a man's heart's through his groin, Mr. Conn, but I really did come here for the *Journal*."

"And ran all the way," Stanley observed. "Want a drink? I've got a bottle of vintage bourbon."

"No thanks, I don't drink."

"You don't smoke, either?"

"Nor that. I try to take good care of myself."

"You have," Conn responded warmly. "Good enough for all practical purposes." He took a straight chair from against the library table, turned it around, and sat down with his arms draped across its back.

"Come on, Anita. What's the pitch? What do you want from me?"

Anita picked up a *Journal* from the coffee table, scanned the front page briefly, then put it down. She trained her violet eyes on him.

"What do I want from you, Mr. Conn?" she murmured.

"Yeah. You didn't just drop in here to pass the time of day, not at this hour. Am I being honored for some special reason I ought to know about? Set up or something? I dig the TV eye and the monitoring system, and I sure hate to be a target or a goal post without knowing what the game is."

"No game that involves you," said Anita, "Believe me. If you've got a Raspberry Diet in your fridge, I wouldn't mind one."

Stanley checked the reefer. "That's all there is. Here—" He untabbed the can and handed it to her, draping himself over the chair back again.

"Come on, what's the game?"

"Management and staff. Weighty problems out here."

"I'd imagine your only problem is fighting off the goons. Two weeks of clean living here and some of these old bastards think they're sixteen and sexually solvent again."

"It's not quite that grim."

"It must be pretty bad or you wouldn't have come dashing into Number Fifteen to catch your breath."

"I had a fight with my boss—about my duties."

"O.K.," Conn said, not quite convinced, "but tell me

something, now that we're on the subject. Do you go with the massage package sometimes? You're a mighty tempting attraction."

Anita smiled; this she could handle. "I go with what I like. . . ." She took a sip of her Raspberry. "That's why I'm in trouble. . . . I can't stay, Mr. Conn. I'll go in a few minutes."

"What's with this crazy place, anyway?" Stanley asked. "I came down here because some guy I know lost thirty pounds easy in about three weeks and recommended it highly. Besides, he met a rich widow here for the reduction, and they got married."

"It's Honeymoon Hotel," said Anita. "Didn't you know?"

"Yeah, well, I'm not looking for any rich widow. I'm a normal, lonely guy out for some friendliness. Only I'm not casual or fickle, understand. If I like somebody, they have to beat me pretty hard over the head to make me hate them. When I like them, I want them around all the time. So far—"

"So far, so good," Anita said, glancing at her wrist watch. She'd give that bastard Harry five more minutes, and. . . .

"*So far*," Stanley continued, "I haven't found anybody in my work. I make too much money, more than I can spend. I got no kids to leave it to, either. . . ."

"No wife?"

"Dead."

"I'm sorry."

"You got no right to be. A loyal woman, tiresome as hell toward the end, but a good wife when she wasn't sick."

Obviously he wasn't leading anywhere, thought Anita, so she might as well make a general contribution to the aimless game.

"Men and women are different races, different animals. Marriage ties don't mean much these days. Nobody tries very hard when divorce is so easy."

"Divorce is too *final*," Stanley reflected. "Even more so than death. With death the memories don't die. With divorce they're edited out, the heart withers away. . . ."

My God, a real talker, she thought. Maybe this chubby, bald-headed little guy with the big warm brown eyes was also a poet. As for success, maybe, maybe not. Any jerk could make a claim like that; it didn't impress her. But his sensitivity was something else; he was charming.

"What do you think's wrong with the world today?"

Stanley grinned. "People get polarized. They're committed to intangibles. Materialism's part of the problem, or overpopulation. But the essential issue's loneliness. Back to where I started. Lonely people aren't usually strong enough to reach out and make contact with each other nowadays. Like right now is what I'm trying to say. I'm impressed with you, Anita, and I can't pinpoint it. . . ."

Just as arrogant as they all were, trying to give you *their* values, she thought, and rose, clasping the papers, smiling. "Right now I've really got to go. Thanks for being so kind, Mr. Conn. I'll see you tomorrow."

"Maybe, maybe not," he said. "Like making another appointment for a massage, I don't think so. I'm not sure."

"I like *you*, Mr. Conn, whatever you are," she heard herself saying.

"Oh, I like *you*, too, Anita. But that's not the point. And call me Stanley. That's my name."

"O.K., it's a good start—Stanley."

"It could be," he said reasonably, and let her out. . . .

No one was waiting for her when she returned to her room, and she was relieved. Maybe Harry would simply leave her alone; maybe she'd won. She undressed slowly, thinking of Conn, plain little man with such a warm and easy way, so friendly and genuine. And yes, above all, so lonely. Almost as lonely as she was, she thought mournfully, drifting, looking. . . .

Part
FOUR

For days the *Sarcophagus* had been cruising through the placid, crystal waters of the Bahamas, dropping anchor at night near some island, or whenever and wherever Thompson's whims would dictate. Today was another beautiful and monotonous day.

Sometimes Francovich spent long hours on deck, his tough, muscular body clad only in white duck shorts, shielding his eyes against the dazzling sea glare and watching the low green islands appear and disappear, jagged emerald blurs on the horizon. Thompson never allowed the yacht to come too close to these islands; his phobia for privacy forbade it. At any other time such miraculously limpid water would have been irresistible to Francovich, only a fair swimmer, but not now. His mind was troubled with a million details since Thompson had dumped that monster responsibility on his bunk the first morning out. His task didn't look any the less formidable now than when he'd begun it; and he knew that once he presented the verdict of his findings to Thompson as the ultimate, conclusive evidence of Hank Alexander's betrayal, Alexander was a dead duck. Well, but of course he already was; it was just a matter of legal semantics. And conceivably, Alexander could end up a corpse, although Thompson wasn't, as far as he knew, given to waxing his enemies, only breaking them up—a specialty in which he excelled.

In a hearty mood, Thompson joined him. "Good morning, Danny." His tone was expansive. "Hell of a day, huh?"

"Perfect. How're you feeling?"

"Never better! Nothing like a cruise, Danny boy. You've got to be *on* the sea, not just staring at it from your windows, as I did for three years on the Coast. I stayed away too long. How's everything going with our little project?"

"Great," replied Francovich without much enthusiasm.

"I was hoping you'd say *perfect*, like the day."

"Oh, perfect enough."

"Good. Let's talk about it below. I've asked Carl and Ray and John to join us in the salon in five minutes. Bring your papers. . . ." And so saying, he smiled at Francovich and disappeared below.

A few minutes later Francovich entered the main salon with his documents. Assembled were the three aides—the hear-no-evil, see-no-evil, speak-no-evil monkeys, he always thought of them—who had accompanied them from California on the Lockheed: Carl Winchester, executive vice president of Thompson Manufacturing; John Moore, the senior vice president of that company; and Abel Rose, Thompson's legal chief since Thompson had first inherited the parent organization from his father several decades earlier and immediately started parlaying it into his present prodigious fortune.

Thompson occupied the central black leather lounge by himself, and although his long frame was sprawled informally, almost indolently, across the upholstery, there was nothing indifferent about his focus of attention. His normally pleasant gray gaze was steely and cold; Francovich shivered inwardly. He knew exactly what data Thompson wanted to hear from him and was fully aware that poor old Hank Alexander was already crucified in the minds of the aides, too, no matter what evidence was presented.

Francovich took a seat facing the quartet of judicial expressions, feeling exactly as if he were star witness at a Senate investigation. He'd seen quite a few in his earlier years and was still deeply impressed with their frosty protocol, whatever their content.

"Gentlemen—" he said, and launched into a summary of the early Thompson days of Henry Alexander, when he was chief aide and prime confidant of Terence Thompson. Skillfully he etched in Alexander's several primary accomplishments, including the brilliant maneuver of persuading Thompson to dump his vast block of Global Airlines stock after he lost control of the outfit, although Thompson was later sued by the company for $150 million on grounds of mismanagement and breach of antitrust laws, an interminable case that would probably never be settled in Thompson's lifetime. When Thompson dumped his shares of Global, five years ago, he collected half a billion dollars at $80 per share. Francovich pointed out to the group that the stock had now dropped to $15 per share; but this was the last feather he put into poor Alexander's hat before he pushed him into a coffin and slammed down the lid.

From then on he cited the adverse facts of Alexander's strategies. He stressed the time that Alexander unofficially borrowed a million dollars from Thompson Manufacturing—without interest—to buy into a sure-fire Los Angeles housing development as well as an electronics firm. Later, with more borrowed capital, Alexander set up a number of consulting firms, then hired these firms as security consultants for Thompson Enterprises at fat fees. Alexander's rise—for he made money fast and paid back his loans almost as promptly as Thompson himself had always done—was meteoric and stirred intense envy in business circles, also gaudy rumors of payola. In Las Vegas where Thompson had always had the percipience not to infringe or compete with Howard Hughes' interests, Alexander lined up the town on his own for kickbacks and very nearly got himself wiped out by the Hughes forces.

Graft upon graft, deal upon deal—Francovich named them all, analyzed them explicitly for the quartet, cited their positive and negative characteristics, one by one. Finally he arrived at the immediate situation: Early last year Alexander's relations with Thompson had begun to cool rapidly. The handwritten memos between them became less frequent. Thompson drew his other aides—Carl Winchester, John Moore, Abel Rose—closer to him. And at that point he also brought Dan Francovich into the picture in a strong buffer position as his expert legal investigator, on the recommendation of a Supreme Court judge, one of Thompson's oldest and most trusted friends.

That was it; he'd given them the whole story; there was nothing left to tell after all the facts and figures were stated.

"So, gentlemen, I think Mr. Thompson will agree that you've heard the complete summary," Francovich concluded, "and the case is wrapped up."

A heavy silence filled the salon, a silence of ashes and brimstone, Francovich felt, for surely at this very moment —or some hours earlier, possibly last night—Alexander's preordained fate was working out. Thompson's cohorts had gathered with Alexander at a private conference room of the Century Plaza Hotel in West Los Angeles to discuss the rift between Alexander and Thompson. No direct charges would have been leveled against Hank Alexander, of course, but the ultimatum was a demand for his resignation from the Thompson combine within twenty-four hours.

Francovich could just hear Alexander's anguished cry of panic as his world began to crumble: "Give me a bill of particulars!" he'd shout. "Show me your authority! How do I know you're speaking for Thompson!"

Thompson broke the silence. "Well, boys, that's about it. Oh, I called the governor of California about an hour ago on the ship-to-shore. . . . No trouble at all, got right through. I explained what I wanted to do and why there'd been understandable hysteria at the Big Sur ranch when I was missing from the penthouse. I gave the governor all the necessary details, plus the added onerous duty of calling Alexander and telling him, officially in my name, that he was through. Just to cap the situation. Since John's my old friend, I think he rather relished the chore. . . ." It was rumored that Thompson had financed the governor's last campaign.

The faces of the three aides, Francovich observed, were pale, their expressions withdrawn; no one spoke. Almost as if they, too, had been touched by a similar though perhaps less malignant doom simply by exposure to the facts of Alexander's sordid treachery, or might themselves one day be in positions vulnerable enough to call down Thompson's personal wrath upon their august heads. No doubt about it, Thompson had pulled another unconventional surprise from his bottomless bag of tricks. Winchester, Moore, and Rose had been obliged to make the trip to the Bahamas for one reason—to receive an object lesson on the penalties of bad behavior.

"And I also told the governor," Thompson continued, "that I was alive and well, and not taken by any sinister terminal illness such as Alexander reported to the press. And that I was goddam likely to survive for another twenty years. Without booze and cigarettes, of course. I told him emphatically that I hadn't come down to the Bahamas to die. If I'd wanted to expire anywhere, I'd have gone to any one of the various clinics I support around the country. There's a deluxe room always waiting in each one of them for the day I take a notion to kick off in style. . . ." Thompson turned to Francovich. "Congratulations, Danny, you've done a great job."

It was hardly that, thought Francovich, but smiled his appreciation.

Thompson wheeled on his three senior aides, jabbed an

all-inclusive finger at them. "Now, gentlemen, we're on our way back to Nassau right this minute. And when we get there, you'll find out what I'm going to do next. Then the three of you—Carl, John, Abel—you're flying right back to the Coast on the commercial air. You'll be needed there urgently, unless I miss my guess, to handle Alexander's accusations. But remember, boys, we're a big happy family again, we're on top, and we're going to stay that way. No more plots. . . ."

"Am I going to the Coast, too?" Dan asked, feeling suddenly useless, played out, slightly depressed by the hatchet role of his recent task.

"Hell no! You're staying in Nassau with me," Thompson replied. "You're needed," and threw him an enigmatic grin. "O.K., gentlemen, let's eat! It's going to be crayfish three different ways—grilled, steamed, and sautéed. Brain food, best goddam vittles in the world. . . ."

And on this cue the assemblage rose stiffly to its feet and, without so much as a glance at one another, filed silently after Thompson into the dining salon—Winchester first, Moore second, Rose third—and, naturally, Francovich last, the way he preferred it. At least nobody could stick a knife in *his* back, not yet.

Marge and Harry Maple were at home again, Bimini Springs put away for the night. They'd both had busy days; Marge spent most of hers straightening out the black beauty operator who was newly hired as to why the place was called a springs. This entailed a boring trip to the fresh-water reservoir, an inspection of the power plant and pumping station, and other dull excursions. Phil Berheim followed, snapping everything with his Leica.

Now it was late and Harry was in bed perusing page one of the Miami newspaper that had arrived by afternoon plane, its front spread rich with murder, riots, religious wars, Vietnam, sex, and the internecine power struggle.

"My God!" Harry exclaimed suddenly from behind his newsprint. "What the hell is *he* doing down here?"

"He *who*?" Marge sat deeply preoccupied before her vanity mirror in another one of her vain attempts to stave off time with chemical warfare.

"Terence P. Thompson, America's richest tycoon, that's who! Who else?"

"How would I know *who else* when you disconnect the name from the game?" Marge demanded with shrill logic. "*He's* down here is all you said. . . ." But then the full force of Harry's statement struck her. "Oh sweet Jesus," she moaned, "what do you think that means?"

"That's exactly what *I* said," Harry retorted, "and just what I want to know."

"Why ask *me*?" Marge said, and prepared herself further for the application of her beauty mask with a delicate skin-oil remover.

"Hey, listen, it says here," Harry rattled the newssheet for emphasis, "that somebody, some underling, pressed the sheriff's office to raid Thompson's California ranch. Seems like this understrapper was hollering about foul play, not knowing that Thompson had actually taken a powder. Or split, if you prefer. Seems Thompson's immediate ranch staff either knew nothing about his departure or concealed it from this guy Alexander. Looks like Thompson has his own methods for shucking subordinates. You realize that bastard's got 70,000 employees and we got less than forty?"

"And most of ours are layabouts," Marge observed tartly. "Beats me why anyone with his millions would want to be so secretive."

"For a smart curve you can certainly be dumb at times," Harry said gracelessly. "It's goddam obvious he's a paranoid eccentric, that's why. It's his personal whim to be practically invisible most of the time, and he's sure got the money to make it happen. Boy, he's probably loving the little feud that sprang up between his close staff and his other operations when he sneaked out. . . . Hey, it says here," and he quoted again, " 'Few, if any, of even Thompson's closest employees would publicly second-guess his exact whereabouts or the nature of the doings of their boss at any given time. Other sources verified that Thompson's private four-engined Lockheed jet flew from the California Big Sur Coast to the Bahamas several days ago. . . .' "

"Nassau?"

"Where else down here would they land in a big jet? Seems this Alexander guy, who was real close to him once, has been trying to establish legally that Thompson's no longer mentally or physically capable of handling his own affairs, which are estimated to be worth anywhere from one to three billion dollars. Holy mother!"

"Some plums," said Marge. "You think Thompson's planning to take over the Bahamas?"

"I don't like to think so, honey, but yes, it's occurred to me in the last few minutes."

"Well, if he wants us, he'll have to pay *plenty*," Marge

said, spreading a creamy white mint pack nostrum evenly over her face into a neat mask that left her lips and eyes untouched.

"*If* he wants us, honey, he'll try anything," Harry said quietly. "But I don't think he'll bother with small fry, and that's what we are to him. Hey, here's something else. It says: 'The dispute between Thompson and his aide was settled by the billionaire himself. In a call from aboard his yacht as it cruised the Bahamas, Thompson reputedly told the governor of California, John Murdoch, that he was in excellent health and sound of mind and was quite disturbed about speculation that he had been kidnapped or spirited away. Purportedly, he authorized the firing of his former aide, Alexander, and the governor of California, friends of both men, delivered the coup de grace. . . . Alexander made the statement from his Los Angeles mansion that his ex-boss was suffering from a critical, disabling, and probably terminal illness. . . . From aboard Thompson's luxurious yacht, the *Sarcophagus*, Thompson denied that there was any truth to Alexander's statement and called it grossly inaccurate. . . ."

Marge spun around on her vanity stool and faced Harry, looking uncomfortably like Marcel Marceau. "Of course," she speculated, "Thompson's down here because he owns that huge medical research center in Miami. He wants to be close to it for some special treatment. I'll bet he's seriously ill, all right. That's the real reason he's here, it's not that other intrigue crap. . . ."

Intuition seldom failed her, Marge knew, and she returned to her mirror to test the mint pack's texture lightly with her fingertips. Once completely firm, she'd wash it off and her skin would be fresh, smooth and rosy as a newborn babe's little soft ass.

"You may have a point," Harry conceded. "Hey, here's a graph of his holdings. He's got fifteen corporations and real estate you wouldn't believe. Under *Land* it says 'Undetermined holdings and islands in the Bahamas. . . .' Wonder what that means?"

It was harrowing knowledge, whatever it meant, they both knew, and the implication was quite clear that Thompson could simply move in and take over anything he wished. And if he didn't want their specific cay, he could at the very least put them out of business as competition just for the sheer hell of it, crushing them like bugs under his heel.

"Harry," Marge said querulously, her face muscles twitching beneath the near-rigid mask, "you gotta get in touch with Thompson and tell him to leave us alone. Tell him we're having a rotten season with too many people dieting at home to save money. Tell him we're willing to play along with him any way he wants, even to a percentage, and we're not competitors. We could even turn this island into a real fancy whorehouse, if that's what he wants, and I've heard plenty about the banging he's done with all those titty movie stars. Didn't he know the Bird woman once? Sweetie, you just gotta keep him from busting us wide open!"

"Marge, Marge," Harry said with indulgent affection, "forget the pipe dreams. I couldn't even get through to one of Thompson's chambermaids. That son of a bitch is impregnable."

"Oh bullshit!" Marge said. "You got radio communication, and he's bound to have it on his yacht, that *Sarco*-something-or-other. Where's your balls?"

"The *Sarcophagus*. My balls're in the usual place." He smiled tolerantly at her and shook his head. "Honey, you're a real schemer-dreamer, and sometimes you don't hold water. Anyway, Thompson can't touch us. We got this cay sewed up forever."

"That doesn't ease my mind one bit. I got a nagging fear that some awful catastrophe's going to happen to us."

"Oh hell, woman, you're always in a state about something. Now take off that goddam mask and come to bed. We got better things to do than conjecture about the possible actions of one Terence Thompson, crusty old fart. You can bet your ass we're not his target down here. . . ." He dived back into his paper. "Hey, and here's something else," he said ominously a moment later. "It says that Dan Francovich, one of Thompson's new legal advisers, also issued a statement some hours after Thompson's and corroborated that the old man is merely taking a much-needed rest with no thought of business in mind. . . ."

Marge stared at Harry in the mirror for a long, horrid interval of stony silence before she clutched her throat and emitted a strangled gasp.

"Harry, I just thought of something awful!"

"So did I—"

"That name—Dan Francovich!"

"It rings a bell," Harry said, gone suddenly yellowish. "Christ, that's the prick that put the horns on old man Holt!"

"It's got to be," Marge agreed. "The tall, dark attorney with muscles. He won't forget *our* names, Harry, not if he's checking out the islands for sites. Oh God, he'll get to us legally! Harry, we should've got to *him.* I always told you you bungled that goddam job good. . . ."

"Nothing we can do about it now, honey," he said in a stunned voice, "except wait it out. Come on, take off that thing."

"I'm scared, Harry, I really am."

"Don't think about it. Won't do any good. Come here, you need some calmin'. . . ."

"No!" Marge shouted, and jumped up so violently that she knocked the mint mask bottle to the tile floor where it smashed, spreading a sticky white mess over the tiles. She ignored it and said faintly, "I'm going to take a walk. I need fresh air, I'm going out of my mind."

Harry knew all about her moods of sudden panic and how to deal with them. Usually he allowed Marge to be top dog, but not when she frighted like this. He sprang nimbly from the bed and was beside her in two giant strides. Grasping her firmly at the waist with both hands, he lifted her off her feet, swung her over his head, and flung her down hard across the giant bed.

She bounced high; the force of his action knocked the wind out of her, also her hysterical mood. She lay docilely where she'd fallen, her stiff white mask uncracked, still in place.

"Prepare yourself for entry, woman!" Harry bellowed, and flung off his robe, fully in command of the situation. "We'll do our worryin' when the time comes. Better be fuckin' than fearful anytime. . . ."

"But honey, with my mint mask on—?" asked Marge in a strangely diffident and submissive voice.

"What the hell's that got to do with the other end of you?" Harry growled. "Here I come!"

Irene Tuttle, wife of the well-known war hawk, had not especially enjoyed her stay at Bimini Springs, although the service was adequate; she didn't count it a social success. In the first place, the island was depressingly un-chic by Mrs. Tuttle's standards; she was used to far more glittering resorts.

"Dear Howard," she wrote in her daily dispatch to her Washington-based spouse, "I'm beginning to wonder why you sent me down to this godforsaken spit of no man's land. I am already talking to myself, for there's simply no one of any real distinction around, unless you want to count that perfectly awful Agnes Bird, the actress, who pushes her coarse, vulgar corpulence into the dining salon, behaving like she thought she was as good as Bette Davis, or some beauty queen. I can't find any consolation in the one painfully shy young lady who's here, Cindy Brown. Too fat, of course, though aren't we all, she is always pleasant and well-mannered. And then, there are the Jews, not too many, Howie, but enough to send me to my quarters—a pair of couples, the Bernheims and Flemings, who take over everything, even the dining room. And all those other servile guests too nondescript and dismal and numerous to mention. . . .

"Yes, my dear, I wonder why you chose this place for me? To get me as far away from Washington as you could, even beyond a phone call, but still near enough to summon me home when you think I've cooked enough fatty tissue out of me, or whatever's supposed to come off? Well, whatever, there's at least one person with whom I can communicate quite well, and it's not those revolting owners, the Maples, poor white trash that they are. Her name is Eva Cassel, a perfectly lovely nurse, just as nice as the personable young doctor and his rather severe-acting chief nurse, Miss Severn. Miss Cassel massages me, and much more gently than the big blonde they have here, whose time is always taken up by the male guests, anyway. . . .

"Oh, here comes Miss Cassel. I see her crossing the pool deck, and she's carrying a covered tray. I'll finish writing you when she's gone. . . ."

Eva Cassel entered as Mrs. Tuttle rose from her desk, ready with the vivid smile and the courtesy that Mrs. Tuttle found so beguiling.

"Hello, dear Mrs. Tuttle," Eva cooed. "How about a little neck rub today?"

"Well, my dear, I need one, I really do. But this time you simply must take a little gift. I won't let you do it otherwise."

Eva sighed in mock resignation and rolled her large eyes. "All right, Mrs. Tuttle. If you insist—"

Mrs. Tuttle, already seated and waiting, nodded her head. "Of course I do. I know the best when I see it."

Yes, thought Eva, going to work with skillful fingers on Tuttle's crepe-hung neck, for all the old bag's surface amiability with subordinates—and she'd include me—she's an unrelenting snob. A parvenu, a prude, probably a middle-class racist as well. Instead of ending up like that cabinet member's wife, the one with the big mouth, Mrs. Tuttle had started there and gotten steadily worse ever since.

Eva had a plan; no use *not* trying it.

"You're just not responding properly to your diet and exercise, Mrs. Tuttle," Eva said as she massaged her elderly patient's neck. "I'm quite concerned about you."

"I know, dear, I know," Mrs. Tuttle agreed. "But I've religiously followed the prescribed diet. I walk down to the boathouse once a day and around the harbor and back. I haven't been around the island, but that's a boy's walk, not for senior citizens. And look at the tan I'm getting."

If you like burnished chestnuts wearing pearls, thought Eva. "Simply gorgeous. Your husband'll love it."

"My husband loves only his work, I'm afraid," said Mrs. Tuttle. "He has very little time for me. If I were the jealous kind, I'd say he had a romance going with one of those little snip secretaries of his, but I doubt it. They're all married."

"Are you dipping into the therapeutic pool every day?"

"Of course, Miss Cassel, that's why I'm so tingly all the time. All of it's helped, but I keep having these headaches. You told me I might if I overdid things."

"Don't worry, you've got me. And today there's something special."

"I wondered what was on that tray."

"Something to make you relax completely," said Eva.

"But what is it?" Mrs. Tuttle insisted.

"Well, it's a tiny machine. . . ." Eva stepped to the tray and removed the white cloth. "You'll stare straight into this flashing red light, blank your mind, and we're going to soothe you. You won't think about teas or cocktail parties or Mr. Tuttle's feud with Senators Fulbright and Mansfield. . . ."

Mrs. Tuttle became wary. "My dear, I do not put the faith in tiny little machines that you medical people obviously do. You can forget you brought it. . . ."

Eva controlled her dismay with a smile. "But my dear Mrs. Tuttle, you wanted to get rid of your headaches."

Mrs. Tuttle blinked her watery, mascaraed eyes at Eva. "Yes, of course I do, but hypnotism isn't for me, my dear. . . ."

"But it's only a gadget to relax you, Mrs. Tuttle. Won't you just let me try it?"

Mrs. Tuttle shook her head in a strong negative. "All I want, my dear, is your magic fingers on my nerve-stiff neck and your charming presence for as long as you care to offer it. Other than that, nothing."

Eva, still smiling, returned to the back of Mrs. Tuttle's wattled neck. The old bitch, she brooded, is as wise as an eagle. She knows what a probe is because she knows what humbug her husband's been up to all these years—and she's not going to be pried loose from one single treasured bit of it.

"All right, dear Mrs. Tuttle, we'll continue with the massage. But those headaches may not go away."

"I'm prepared for that," said Mrs. Tuttle, "in which case I'll just have to be a stoic."

"You must do as you wish," Eva replied silkily, and crossed Mrs. Tuttle off her list, as the old lady closed her eyes and tried to decide how she would finish that letter to Howard. After Eva Cassel left, of course, taking that crisp new twenty-dollar bill with her. . . .

"Well, Howie," Mrs. Tuttle wrote three hours later, "I didn't get right back to this letter, thinking about the nurse who was here. For all her smiles and starch, I'm beginning to think she's rather unhealthy in a mental sort of way. I wonder about her. She wanted to *hypnotize me*—can you imagine? With all the things you've told me plus all the powder-room gossip I've heard around the capital, I'm a living stick of dynamite. Why, I could open up a third-world-war front singlehanded in a matter of minutes if I really opened my mouth. And the little vixen thought she could get me to go for that 'tiny little machine' bit—her own transparent way of putting it. Such nerve!

"But all the same, she has marvelously sensitive finger pads. I might ask her to come around tomorrow. . . . And she's *your* type, dear Howie, a really attractive girl. But this place is abysmal, and I'll have words with you about it upon my return, weight reduction notwithstanding. Could it be—and the rumors might be based in fact—that because your great, rich friend T.P.T. is developing a sudden interest in this place, these islands, I mean, you sent me down as sort of an advance agent without even telling me the details? Yes, knowing you as I do, I suspect that could be the case. . . .

"Well, enough of this for now. I want to catch the afternoon mail plane to Nassau. And be sure, my dear, that Pooki and Kooki get their regular walks when Barrett takes her days off. The little babies get so cranky without their daily fresh air, except during blizzards, of course. And remember to wear your Norwegian undershirts, my dear. You know how susceptible you are to winter colds! And also remember that I love you dearly and am devoting my thoughts and my life to you.

Your loving wife
Irene"

Cindy Brown was bored, so bored that she didn't even have enough curiosity left to pick up one of the novels she'd brought with her and start it. Complete isolation allowed for the novels but no newspapers, and so far everything was working out reasonably well. Except for the unutterably dismal situation that was slowly driving her out of her mind, along with the gnawing passion that gave her doubts about her sanity.

A knock on the door brought Kevin Mack to her chaise, calling in on his daily rounds. He took her pulse, asked if she was hungry, and when she said no, gave her a quick professional smile and declared her in excellent condition.

"There's no reason why you can't continue your fasting another week, Miss Brown, then we'll really see some results."

"Results," Cindy sighed, "are all right, but everything's so boring—Kevin. . . ."

Kevin? How had that slipped out? Calling him by his Christian name when he'd always been so perfectly formal with her—Miss Brown this, Miss Brown that. But he didn't look too displeased; he looked amused; he was actually grinning.

"Kevin, eh? That's O.K., Miss Brown. In private. Or *Cindy*, if you wish—"

"I'm afraid I—"

"Informality's a side effect of weight loss, that and euphoria. Don't worry about it. Identity can undergo some very subtle changes."

"I never noticed that the other times I reduced," Cindy said.

"You weren't dieting under controlled conditions."

"Or ever as bored—"

Kevin eyed her with interest. "But why should you be bored? You've got a nice suite, all the attention you need. Or maybe you'd respond to a good spanking. . . ."

She couldn't believe it. Was it a signal? But his eyes were as steady and sober as his manner; no hint there.

"A good spanking," she said, "is what every woman needs now and then."

"Yes, a little chastisement," Kevin agreed, still not cracking. "Miss Brown, you come from a background of leisure and comfort, don't you? This business about your being a secretary. Is it true?"

"Partly. I worked at it earlier this year until something happened that made me decide to leave New York."

"For Florida. Did you like it?"

Cindy shrugged. This conversation was getting nowhere fast. "I'd have liked it better if there'd been some interesting men around, but they're hard to come by these days. . . ." Then, noting that his medical mask was back in place, she added, "I'm sorry, Doctor. It must be all that liquid surging through me. I'm not making good sense."

"Don't be sorry. It's quite all right."

Not making sense? she wondered. "Nothing's right," she declared flatly, "including *us*!" Good God, where had that come from?

Kevin studied her. "Are you sure you feel O.K.?"

Cindy smiled warmly at him and crossed her legs, exceptionally good ones despite the weight in her thighs.

Kevin fidgeted. There was something about the girl that attracted him very much. It had nothing to do with good sense or a clear eye on the future or anything like that. She was smoky, smouldering, promising some wild rides. Probably great in the sack, wow! Sensational. She was already beginning to resemble that sweet creature in the silver frame, the one he'd so stupidly called her sister, managing to look sexy and ethereal at the same time. Give fasting dieters a head start and they were off to the races with all kinds of irregular behavior, Kevin reminded himself, sometimes lightheaded as hell, their juices flowing in all directions. Impetus to the female libido while dimming the male's drive. But, of course, *he* wasn't fasting. He was aware of a token signal in his groin. Well, well!

He smiled warmly and said again, "Miss Brown, are you O.K.?"

"As right as I'll ever be," Cindy stated, "as bored and as young. Why not sit down and chat a few minutes, Kevin? Surely you haven't that much to do around Bimini Springs that you can't spare me a few minutes."

"Well," he said. Clearly she wanted to do more than talk. Sensibly he ought to defer to his own intuition; after all, they were alone together. "Maybe five or ten. You know, I can't see you somehow as a secretary. An artist, maybe."

"I'm flattered." Cindy patted a spot on the chaise longue beside her. Her smile was inviting. "Sit down—"

Once you step over the line—and he hadn't so far at Bimini—it was damned difficult to get back. Be cautious.

"Cindy, I—" He had no idea what she wanted from him. He grinned at her nervously, deciding he should leave.

"Maybe the next ten minutes would be better spent thinking out your boredom, Miss Brown." He glanced at his watch. "I've got a diet conference with Miss Severn and several other calls to make—"

Cindy's smile died. "And you're asking to be excused from fat-lady duty!"

"Not at all. I'm committed."

So was she, fool that she was! "Will I see you soon?"

What kind of a question was that, he wondered.

"My obligation brings me around every day," he said.

"I don't mean during the day. How about a few minutes tonight? I'm concerned with those long, lonely evenings and those endless pitchers of ice water."

"Miss Brown—" He took a firm grip on himself. "Fasting's liable to make patients extremely giddy sometimes. A certain irresponsibility takes over."

"Kevin, I'm not being irresponsible, dammit, I'm trying to get a reaction out of you!"

"You'll just have to rationalize your behavior and live with the condition for another week or so. Then the pressure will go away and you'll return to normal."

"There's no pressure," said Cindy, "and I'm not so sure I want to return to normal, as you put it. . . ." What the hell *was* wrong with her? "All I need is your company," she found herself volunteering.

"My company's required elsewhere, Cindy," he said briskly, but with an amiable grin. "I'll see you later. . . ."

"Just any old time," she countered, underscoring her meaning with a loose smile. "When you get the whim, drop in. . . ."

"Fine, fine," Kevin said, and beat a hasty retreat, puzzled as to what kind of game she was playing. She just couldn't be serious, for if she was, then something very weird had happened to her. He'd given her no reason to treat him as a throb symbol. Maybe he hadn't observed her closely enough. Perhaps the isolation had actually disconnected her temporarily, or the poor thing could have such deep emotional troubles that the fasting had surfaced them and provoked this highly emotional attitude toward him. He'd had plenty of female patients of all ages go on the make, but not this blatantly, and not without any apparent substantial cause. And she seemed like such a shy thing under all that blubber. God, still waters!

Cindy saw Kevin Mack pass by outside her terrace

windows and thought how desirable he was. What was it Eva Cassel had said to her? "The doctor is *extremely* fond of you, Miss Brown. He thinks you're marvelous, really lovely. And you *know* how much you like him. . . ." But no, she thought sharply, Eva Cassel hadn't said that to her, not that she could recall; yet there it was, and why would she remember the words and associate them with Eva Cassel? The doctor was simply a nice, serious young internist, reasonably attractive, obviously dedicated to his job, even though it was a crazy diet one. And she was a young woman with a blasted past, a wasted life—spoiled, pampered, unable to come to terms with either her mother, her husband, or herself—drifting, stagnating, useless. If Kevin Mack couldn't imagine her holding down a secretarial job, then the waste was all too evident and she'd have to start all over again. Push the past back into the dark corridors of mindless indecision, examine nothing, not even her relationship with Poppy. Not now, maybe never. Look for a new interest. . . .

She saw herself as she felt she really was—inarticulate, dumb, foolish, impulsive, no one Dr. Mack or anyone else would ever want. So what the hell difference did anything make? Well, if she wanted to try for Kevin Mack she would first have to concentrate on losing weight. In any case, the reduction was going to be the most important project in her life for the moment, and when that was achieved, maybe she'd examine her other problems.

Sighing with determination, she picked up a novel from the table and scanned the dust jacket. It seemed to be all about a woman who didn't know her own mind, or her husband's—who took a rich, very ancient lover, thinking her husband knew nothing about it. A woman who was greedy enough to want both her husband and her lover but was forced eventually to make a choice between the two.

She opened the book and began to read page one, hopefully. Maybe there was something in it that she might benefit from. Clutch at straws, she told herself. Anything was worth a try at this point. . . . Anything was better than going back to Poppy. But she couldn't put off important decisions forever. Sooner or later she'd have to quit kidding herself and act.

One of Ruth Severn's duties as head nurse was to give periodic lectures on diet principles to which all guests might come if they so wished. Most of them did, for there wasn't that much to do at Bimini Springs to keep them away. The lectures were based on solid fact, Ruth saw to it, yet many of the guests treated them as picnics and paid little attention. This annoyed Ruth very much, but she could do nothing about it. After all, this wasn't a genuine teacher-pupil relationship—it was paying guest and host.

Ruth knew her lecture material so well that she could virtually ignore the audience gathered in the main lounge. She could even allow their faces to merge into one massive blur of features and switch her mind to other things as she talked. The questions and answers at the end of the lecture would bring her back into sharp focus again, but for the moment, she was only obliged to make sounds. They would listen.

"Diet in itself isn't enough, ladies and gentlemen," Ruth began, "as all of you are finding out. You may have thought you knew this lesson well when you tried to get on top of your diet at home. But you obviously didn't or you wouldn't have come to stay with us. . . ."

Here Ruth paused a moment in anticipation of the general laughter that always followed. And it came now, quietly, except for the Bernheims and Flemings, who thought it hilarious.

"On the dark side of diet," Ruth continued, "statistics show us that no more than one or two individuals out of every hundred who achieve a substantial weight loss maintain it for five or more years. . . ."

A general groan of despair issued from Ruth's audience at this point.

"Now we all want to lose weight and keep it off without ever having to count a calorie. [How nice, we think, if it would just vanish!] We'll be happier, more adjusted individuals if we don't have to police ourselves constantly. But to achieve this, we must be intimately acquainted with the whole range and mystique of diet. We must learn to differentiate between *appetite* and *hunger*. . . ."

Ruth surveyed her audience with a pleasant smile as she let this thought sink in. . . . Kevin, Kevin, dear sweet Kevin! He seemed to be receding into the past while he was still very much around; she couldn't understand it. Lately, the thrill that possessed her, right down into her triangle, whenever Eva Cassel switched her ass into the central office was more than traffic could bear. . . .

"And learn our lesson well," she droned on. "We're stimulated to appetite by the memory of attractive foods." Several guests groaned sharply. "Whereas *hunger* needs a more general compensation. Anorexia, loss of appetite, is usually caused by indisposition, organic illness, emotional pressures. On the other hand, the same conditions can produce voracious hunger. So, it's necessary for you to be calm and ordered, thoroughly sane and sensible in the pursuit of your daily life if you want to lose weight and gain control of yourself. . . ."

All those eager, sheeplike countenances out there before her, straining for the vital secret when there wasn't any. You simply got hold of yourself and made up your mind. . . . And yet she couldn't make up her own: She recalled that first time with Kevin; somebody had introduced them at the officers' club. They weren't drinkers, but they'd liked each other immediately, felt a strong mutual attraction, and impulsively started in on stingers, dangerous in quantity under any circumstances, explosive in this case.

"I've got a suite at the Caravelle," Kevin told her after their fourth round, as they watched couples broiling steaks on the rooftop do-it-yourself buffet grill, the lights of Saigon reflected in the pearly night sky above them. In the warm, floral-scented evening Ruth distinguished the heady odor of jasmine wafted up nine floors from the central garden below. The war seemed remote and unreal, even though the distant flash of jungle gunfire occasionally flared up like heat lightning along the skyline beyond the city.

"You've got a *suite* at the Caravelle?" Ruth repeated, impressed. "How'd you manage that?"

"Two buddies who were coming in for the three days with me decided to go on to Bangkok and change their luck, so I kept the suite anyway."

"What'll you do with all that room?"

"Maybe you've got some ideas," Kevin suggested. "We could eat here *if* you like, or go there. I mean the roof restaurant's very good, French. Or we could explore the suite first, Ruth, if that's along your line of thought."

"Tonight my thoughts are your thoughts," Ruth had said with impulsive sincerity. She liked him; he was warm and friendly, tender, considerate. Besides being a doctor whose field work she knew of and admired, he was lighthearted. But most important, he took her seriously enough to woo her a little. Few men bothered. Most brass simply ignored the preliminaries. They assumed you were as horny as they were, and if you didn't want to go to bed with them, there was always someone else who would.

"But they aren't usually, is that it?" Kevin had said.

"No, usually not at all. I keep too busy with the clinic in Cholon. This is the first time I've been out in a long time. And I rarely drink."

"You like your work?"
"I drown myself in it. And you?"
Kevin spoke lightly of the field hospital, of the grim ordeal of splicing and patching that confronted him often for twelve to fourteen hours on end. It was nothing that needed to be discussed in depth with her; she understood what it meant, what it required in the way of professional detachment.
"I do the best I can," he'd said.
"That's all you can do. . . . Let's go. It's been quite a while since I've seen a suite. . . ."
"It's been a long time for me, too," said Kevin, and they'd finished their drinks and gone on.
He was as courtly and considerate in bed as out of it, and expert. He extended Ruth's considerable range of passion, peaked her in several climaxes that almost paralleled his own. They spent the remainder of the night together in essential tenderness. After that she saw him whenever he managed to get in to Saigon for a few days' relief from the bloody horror of his job. And their relationship grew into something she liked to think of as love.
But lately, little remained of the Saigon attachment except her professional respect for Kevin; they could be two entirely different people, even allowing for the differences between Vietnam and Bimini Springs. And the odd, bright face of Eva Cassel kept obtruding itself between them, pushing Kevin's image farther and farther away. And this was a weird, unlikely emotional reaction, Ruth knew, for she really didn't like Eva at all, and hadn't since the day she arrived. Perhaps it was foolish, but Eva impressed her as slightly sinister, evil; and while she'd never touched Eva in any intimate manner, she felt herself progressing almost involuntarily toward something she'd never thought possible before, an irrational, intense feeling for another woman. God, she couldn't call it love, of course, but the emotion was there, the *need*, almost like a hunger. . . .
"There are several causes of appetite," Ruth plunged on. "Some authorities feel that the level of blood sugar predetermines hunger—that's the glucostatic theory. Another opinion claims that we eat for calories or energy units and aren't satisfied until the desired level is stored away. Another supposition maintains that we eat to keep warm, which shouldn't pose any problem in the tropics. . . ." General laughter here, as usual. "The weight watcher who battles hunger should remember that low blood sugar's very common and can cause extreme appetence only

a couple of hours after a heavy meal. Too much insulin rapidly depletes blood sugar. But that's hyperinsulinism, and there aren't any cases among you. It's the opposite of diabetes, fortunately curable, and controlled solely by diet. . . . Now, any questions?"

From the back of the room Stanley Conn raised his hand.

Ruth switched him into focus. "Oh yes, Mr. Conn?"

"What about fasting?"

"What about it? Well, fasting doesn't increase hunger, paradoxically enough. Hunger diminishes dramatically during diet fasting. We're using the technique here right now, as some of you know. If a person's healthy enough to sustain a no-calorie fast without undue strain on his major organs, Dr. Mack recommends it for stubborn obesity cases. But all in all, there aren't any short-term miracles in dieting. What you have to do is *work* at it; you have to cooperate all the time. Diet will materially assist in steady weight loss, of course, but the big effort to maintain that loss must come from you. You've got to learn to shut your mouth and keep it shut between meals. No snacking whatsoever. And you must sincerely desire, above everything else, to say good-by forever to the weight you so agonizingly lose. You must never, never relinquish your control over this desire."

Ruth stepped forward two paces to conclude: "You must also remember, ladies and gentlemen, that a person with a weight problem is the same as an alcoholic with a drinking problem. He or she can *never* let go. So you must all watch the scales and yourselves *forever*!"

Ruth scanned the audience, smiling now. "All right, let's have your general questions. Our next meeting will deal with diet tips, and at that time I'll pass out a printed form that you can all carry with you when you leave us. Hopefully you'll post it in some prominent spot in your home and make this investment at Bimini Springs pay off as long as you live!"

Living, she thought, is what they're really not doing, all these sick and pampered people. They all ought to be forced to read Josue de Castro's *Geography of Hunger*. It might shame them into slimness or continence.

Bimini Springs was beginning to depress her to the point where it would soon start to show. If she couldn't respond to Kevin any more—and it was apparent that she was doing a rotten job of it—then she had to face up to what had gone wrong and the results. It was all so murky, so ill-defined, confused, so hazy. And so frightening. . . .

"Mr. Bernheim," she said, "what's your question?"
"Vitamin pills," Phil said promptly. "Are they safe to use?"
"No medication's safe, Mr. Bernheim, unless your doctor recommends it for you. See him first. Let him judge what kind of supplementary you need."
"See," Alice hissed in his ear, "I told you so! You're not supposed to take Vitamin C without Dr. Elkin's O.K. . . ."

"He's a goddam prick, that's what he is!" Aggie Bird announced out of thin air as Dick pounded away at her flesh through a thickness of housecoat she refused to remove even on the massage table, centered in the living room of her cabana suite.
"Aggie, please don't use the word that way," Dick admonished her. "It's the best part of a man."
"Well, he is," said Aggie, who'd denied Dick her bed and favors since receiving another message from Wayne Winslow reminding her of her obligation to *The Bungalow*. She would allow Dick only the requisite ritual of the daily massage, nothing else—for that was business, she claimed. This refusal, however, didn't intimidate Dick or keep him from reinforcing his conviction that he would eventually get to Aggie again and triumph over all odds—Wayne Winslow specifically. He had decided that if it came to a showdown, his obligation to Wayne not withstanding, he would pitch in with Aggie. But how to keep his sanity meanwhile? If she gave up the potential of *The Bungalow*, she might be hell to live with. What then?
"Who is?" said Dick. "Who's a prick?"
Aggie was always talking in non sequiturs; continuity wasn't her strong point. She would lose a train of thought one moment after she found it, yet oddly enough, her junk recall was fantastic. She could reach down into that old beaded bag of memorabilia and come up with the precise shade and exact cost per yard of the draperies she'd bought for her first house. She could be a tiresome old bag, Dick knew, but with her real estate income! Ho-hum! He guessed he'd hang around for a while.
"Terence Thompson, that's who's a prick, the son of a bitch!"
"You know him?" Dick was finding out she'd met just about everybody. "I read he's in the Bahamas now, up to his usual cloak-and-dagger tricks."
"Tightest bastard I ever knew," said Aggie. "You won't believe this, but he took me out once when I was only a kid. During his Hollywood picture-making period. I was

working in that crazy teenage series then, the ones where they still threw a few pies. I'll bet you didn't know those pies they tossed were actually whipped up from wet plaster and starch, for Christ's sake, so they'd stick to you like glue when they hit your face."

"You were talking about Thompson. . . ."

"Oh yeah. Well, he knew Harlow and Lombard, and then he met me. How I got sandwiched in there between those two blondes I'll never know, but anyway, there I was on the set one day, the only nonbeauty I think he ever dated. . . . Yeah. . . ."

"And?" Dick prodded her buttocks.

"I'm coming to it! Don't be so goddam impatient. . . . So Terry took me out for a drive in his new custom-built sports racer, a hundred miles an hour up the zigzag Coast Highway toward Malibu. I never was a racing freak, scared shitless in the turns. Well, up the coast a ways he said he was hungry. I had some idea we'd drive around awhile and then go to Romanoff's or Chasen's or the Beverly Hills Brown Derby, they were all great in those days. But I didn't think the cheap prick would drive up to a wayside hamburger stand, order a pair and shakes to go, and not have one goddam dime in his pocket! But that's what happened and I paid the bill. And then to compound the fracture, he drove me up to some windy point overlooking the ocean and proceeded to try to prong me while I was still trying to masticate the fucking hamburger. One of his blondes got a diamond pendant out of him worth a hundred grand. All I got was a bunch of gummy eucalyptus leaves stuck to my bare ass, and no thanks from him. He never ever called me again, how about that, and our relationship was supposed to develop into my starring in a picture he was producing! I think it was a remake of Mary Pickford's *Little Annie Rooney*, anyway some goddam tearjerker. . . . He wore the fruitiest suit that day—plaid a foot square. Looked like a Goodwill reject, gravy stains all over it. I'll bet my ass he doesn't dress any better today."

"What does he do with all those millions?"

"Pleasures himself with power, I guess. He always has. He was just imposing his will on me that day at the beach."

"Was he a good lay?"

Aggie screeched. "Is anybody a good lay jackknifed into a racing car with a tree dropping leaves on you? Besides, he was hung like a pencil and no lead to write home with, baby, and *that's the truth.* So help me! Selfish, too, come to think of it. Only concerned with his own pleasure."

"He can afford to be."

"Nobody can afford to be!" said Aggie sharply. "That's the trouble with life today, that's what makes it so pointless. Look, I was crazy to have kids ever since I could menstruate. But do you think one of my husbands cared a shit about children? Hell no, not even one! The three times I had miscarriages they were overjoyed with relief. Can you believe it? And every time I talked adoption they'd carry on like it was self-abuse. Jesus, the male animal's so goddam narcissistic and self-centered it's incredible. If there's one thing emancipated females know about, it's sharing *and* selfishness. All you dogs think about is your stomachs and your dongs."

"You like your sex," Dick pointed out, insinuating himself against her prone thigh. "You like it plenty, as much as any woman I've ever known."

Aggie laughed derisively. "How about the *men* you've known, Dick? *You* like it as much as *they* like it, huh?"

"I'm no authority on that subject," Dick said curtly. "My experience was strictly in the line of duty."

"*Was*, huh? But you've played around! I can always tell when a man has. Wayne has, too. That's why I asked you that question the other day."

"You like it a lot with Wayne?"

"Stop talking nonsense, tend to your business," Aggie said, rolling away from his stiffening crotch. "I'm liable to get carried away."

"When you write your memoirs," Dick told her, "you ought to devote a lot of time to the evaluation of sex."

"Sure, and men, too, the whole trashy lot of them. I got total recall on the subject and plenty to say. You know, I can even remember my first. I was just a cute kid, and Betty and I were supposed to go to a photographer's to model dresses. Well, she got sick, and I went alone, I can't remember why. Anyway, I got into this sweet little dimity frock, long Shirley curls, the works, and this foul old photographer feels me up while he's arranging the poses. Anyway, I'm curious, so I don't scream for help. Then, after the pictures are all finished, he pops into my dressing room while I'm changing and goes down on me, on his knees yet. Then he ups and wet kisses me and, dig this, hands me a stick of Wrigley's Spearmint gum and sends me along home singing. I remember realizing I could use it against him if I wanted to, but I wasn't like that. I enjoyed it. He didn't have to tell me not to tell; I knew enough to keep my mouth shut. And besides the free gum, he'd made me tingle all over for the first time in my life, and I loved it!"

"Wow, you always were horny, weren't you?"

"Sure, and anybody who says they don't enjoy every bit of sex they've ever had is a goddam liar," Aggie declared emphatically. "But some people won't give themselves to the act—or can't. They're crippled and all hung up. They substitute by posing in front of mirrors or using equipment. But that's all self-conscious bullshit. Wayne's a little like that; he's too turned on by the externals. Kind of like a voyeur."

"Sex is important," Dick admitted, "but it's only one aspect of the relationship between two people."

"Ho, ho!" Aggie chortled. "That from you? Tell me more."

"Well, it's not necessarily the ultimate reality, it's only a link. And I'm not trying to be funny."

Aggie sighed. "Jesus, if you're not a comic, you're a philosopher! Well, sex'll have to do until the real thing comes along. . . ."

At this point Dick moved down to her inner thighs, massaging slowly toward her most erogenous zone, all the while pressing himself harder against her hip.

"Hey, Dick," Aggie protested, "knock it off, I say! Quit prodding me. I'm not in the mood for rubbing games, so keep your hands where they belong—and your *genitals*! But especially your hands, those nice, strong, tender, smooth, loving hands of yours."

Dick ignored her request and continued moving in skillfully.

"Oh Dickie, baby," groaned Aggie from the table, suddenly limp and unresisting, "you are *so* fucking marvelous, there's just nobody like you. You got the exclusive on magic fingers."

"I'd like that on tape sometime," Dick said, pleased with himself, "the famous throaty voice and all."

"You bastard!" Aggie screeched, rallying, jerking away from him with a grunt and sitting up. "You'll get it when I'm fucking good and ready to give it, and not until! Time's up for today. . . ."

She rolled off of the massage table onto her feet, taking the Turkish towel with her, and padded heavily toward the shower. Dick was left contemplating an aroused excitement of his own devising, and more involved with her than he really cared to be, for a variety of reasons, foremost among them that he was finding her comfortable and easy to be with and was beginning to depend on her.

Bimini Springs was faced with a medical emergency: One of the guests fell ill with what Kevin Mack diagnosed as acute appendicitis.

"It's serious," Kevin explained to an agitated Harry Maple who was not his usual suave and jaunty self over a crisis. "There could already be an inflammation of the peritoneum."

"What's that?" Harry demanded, almost angrily. "I don't know medical terminology."

"The peritoneum's the transparent serous membrane lining the abdominal cavity; it covers the visceral organs at various points," Kevin told him. "If the appendix bursts, gangrene sets in. It can be fatal in a relatively short time without proper medical attention. In other words, time's involved, and there's a point of no return."

"We're calling in medical flight service from Nassau."

"Even so," Kevin pointed out, "that's a gamble. We don't know how long they'll take to get here. Then there's the return flight time to consider plus whatever obstacles develop at the hospital in Nassau to delay the operation. I could easily perform the surgery right here. We're all set up for it. Much better than taking that long chance."

"But if something happens and you should—" Harry began.

"Mess it up?" Kevin finished for him. "I won't. . . ."

"There's the question of damages; he could sue us. Marge is on to Nassau radio right now. Meantime we'd better ease Cole's discomfort. He's complaining."

"Of course," Kevin said, thinking Harry was a fool. He was the long shot, and Cole could easily die. Well, let Maple do what he wanted; it was his island, his establishment. And fools like Maple often decided the fate of mankind.

Harry dialed the pharmacy.

"Tom, I'm in my office. Kevin needs some Demerol for a patient. . . . Yes, Bob Cole. Will you bring it right over here, and we'll attend to Cole in his room? He's in a lot of pain. Maybe a burst appendix or something, Kevin thinks. . . . Right away, will you? Thanks. . . ."

Harry hung up and mopped his forehead, looking extremely anxious.

"I shouldn't leave Cole alone," said Kevin. "I'll wait for you in his room. You and Tom come along."

"No," said Harry, "I'll go with you," and scribbled a brief note to Tom saying where they would be.

When Tom arrived and found the note, he didn't go immediately to Cole's room. He'd never had an opportunity before to inspect Harry Maple's office this closely. Unlocked files, desk open. Wow! The chance of a lifetime, for the office connected to the Maples' luxurious apartment and was almost never deserted. With Harry at Cole's and Marge at the radio shack, the situation would never be more ideal.

Tom ransacked the top drawer of the customer files first, all neatly indexed. Marge was an excellent worker. In the second drawer sat more customer files, business trade and manufacturer's accounts, work contracts, paid invoices, and so forth. Nothing to interest him. But in the third drawer he found what he was looking for—a large box full of sex paraphernalia behind a stack of monthly financial reports, incredible stuff, all Japanese. Cock supporters with tiny bells on them, jangle as you go; French ticklers with warts and tentacles; a small glass jar of erection salve; a monstrous rubber dildo with plastic straps, the member in gorgeous flesh shades; and finally, a set of extremely succulent girlie books delineating a variety of flagrant sex acts, all too straight for his taste.

In the bottom drawer of the file cabinet Tom made his real kill. He lifted out the black strongbox very carefully, for it was heavy. It was also locked. Momentarily dismayed, he was wondering how he'd open it when he turned the box on one end and discovered a key taped to its underside.

He opened the box and gasped at its contents. Inside was a thick sheaf of neatly printed glossy eight-by-ten black-and-white photos. Some of these pictures concerned people unfamiliar to him. All the participants were nude and in various states of sexual abandon. There were several of Anita and Dick with assorted Bimini Springs guests; none was taken through the closed-circuit TV frozen-frame medium, Tom noted, but obviously made through windows or peepholes with infrared film and a very small, sensitive camera. A certain graininess characterized all the shots but did not blur the graphic details. Blowups.

That evil bastard, Tom thought, mentally smacking his lips. That sly son of a bitch! But then of course Harry was only doing what he himself did; they were both dealing in dynamite, and he had no cause to criticize Harry.

In checking carefully through the photos, Tom realized that most of them were quite old, not from Bimini

Springs. Each was meticulously number-coded, but there was no code-key notebook in the strongbox; so all he had to do now was to find the telltale little code book with the names that matched the photo numbers and he'd be top man around the lodge.

Well, well, so he and Harry had had the same idea all along! No wonder Maple was so edgy about his overt interest in the closed-circuit TV. But where in hell was the code-key notebook? Probably in Harry's safe; he couldn't get into that, of course.

Resisting the impulse to lift a couple of prints, he returned the photos to the strongbox, then locked the box and taped the key back onto its underside and closed the bottom file-cabinet drawer.

Yes, he thought, he'd run onto some really volatile information, but how to get across to Harry the idea that he knew what was in the strongbox without actually admitting that he'd seen it? The ideal gimmick came to him suddenly, a ploy so simple it would do the trick perfectly. He snapped the file-cabinet lock shut, then locked the office as he left to meet Harry and Kevin Mack at Cole's quarters. Later on, if Harry should give any conscious thought to the condition of the office when Tom had walked in, he'd realize that someone besides himself had locked the file cabinet. And if he wasn't quite sure whether or not he'd locked it, there would always be a lingering doubt in his mind. And this was what Tom wanted, to plant the seed, put some fear into him. Heavy with his new secret, Tom walked saucily across the terrace past the pool deck, swinging his medical kit with the Demerol in it.

He nodded and smiled at a gaggle of fat sunbathing ladies.

"A regular angel of mercy," Alice said obscurely from her deck chair as Tom passed in his neat white uniform. "That man Cole's having his appendix."

"*Out*, you mean," said Rose. "Not having. . . . But never mind, he sure does look like some angel, all right. Nice and slim, too—" She glanced irascibly at Phil and Jack, snoring fatly under their straw hats. "And not a gut to his name!"

Kevin had just administered the sedative to Bob Cole, and Tom had already returned to the pharmacy when Marge hurried into the room. Ruth and Kevin were attending the patient; Marge addressed herself to Harry.

"They can't send air service down for at least another

four hours," she explained. "They've had an emergency on Andros, and both planes are involved."

"That settles it," Kevin told them. "We'll have to operate immediately. Ruth can assist me."

"Oh Christ," Harry moaned, frantic, "if anything happens to him he'll sue our asses off!"

"Better a lawsuit on your hands than a corpse," Kevin said with dry contempt. "While we're waiting for medical service to pick him up, he could die on us. No telling when they'll get here."

"That's true," Marge conceded. "They weren't very reassuring."

"Dr. Mack knows what he's doing. Mr. Maple," said Ruth sharply, controlling her fury with Harry but still managing to add her own measure of contempt to Kevin's. Maple was an idiot. "He's taken apart and put together whole field units of patients. You know what M.A.S.H. means, Mr. Maple?"

Harry shot her a sour look. "I saw the film."

"Dr. Mack's worked with M.A.S.H. units."

"Come, come," said Kevin, "we're wasting valuable time. Will you accept the responsibility of delaying Cole's treatment until he can be flown to Nassau, Harry, or do I operate immediately?"

At this point, even though the sedative had already begun to take effect, Cole stirred on his bed and moaned softly.

Harry approached Cole and bent over him, peering into his flushed face. "Mr. Cole, can you hear me?" he asked gravely, and Cole nodded. "You'll have to make a decision—with witnesses. Dr. Mack feels that you have acute appendicitis and wants to operate on you right here and now. From the medical evidence you might have peritonitis. Will you sign a statement relieving us of all responsibility in the event of an operation?"

"Oh Christ!" muttered Kevin under his breath to Ruth, but she squeezed his hand hard and gave him a silencing look.

Groggy, Cole didn't appear to understand for a moment what was being required of him; he turned his face away from Harry and groaned at the wall.

"Mr. Cole," Harry entreated, "this is vital." And at that point Cole opened his eyes and said to the wall, "Yes, yes, I understand. I'll sign. Just do something—"

Marge started for the door. "I'll go to the office and type up a short statement. It won't take a minute. . . ." Out she went and shut the door behind her.

"Where will you operate?" Harry asked nervously.

"In the dispensary, of course," Kevin replied. "It's already set up for table treatment, and the equipment's all there. We'll manage O.K. Don't sweat it, Harry."

"Yes," Ruth agreed, "we'll manage fine. We're competent, Mr. Maple," she felt forced to add, but her irony was wasted on Harry at this point; he was too far gone with worry to notice.

"It'll be a little primitive," Kevin explained, now that he was in control more relaxed, almost genial. "But Cole will be all right. Unless, of course, it's too late already. . . ."

"Oh Christ," Harry croaked, "don't even suggest anything like that! He'd better be all right, Doctor, or it's somebody's ass."

"I didn't create the case, Harry," Kevin eyed him stonily, "and I only answer to myself. It's about time we straightened that out. . . . Here, give me a hand with Cole's stretcher. Ruth, you run along ahead and start setting things up with Eva. Tom'll help, too, if you need him. . . ."

"Yes, Doctor," said Ruth, glad to have the responsibility of something besides wasted human flesh for a change. . . .

Later, when the operation was over and the patient was doing fine, Ruth and Kevin sat in his office, trying to relax over coffee. "No complications," said Kevin. "Easiest ever."

"I haven't seen you come alive like that since you've been here," Ruth said. "You even got *me* worked up. I felt needed for a while. A nice feeling."

"It's the difference between existing and living," Kevin said. "Simple as that. I don't seem to breathe right unless I'm doing responsible work. But now I'm depressed. . . ."

"Why?"

"This—" He waved a hand toward the office, encompassing the entire island in his gesture. "And everything that goes with it. I'm not doing what I ought to be doing."

"You will, Kev, you will."

"The important thing is, Ruthie, I shouldn't be wasting valuable time in waiting."

Ruth was silent for a moment. At length she said gently, "No, Kevin, you shouldn't. You ought to get out of it somehow, and soon."

"What about you?"

"We're not talking about me, Kev."

"Closing me out again?"

"Not at all. You have your interests, I have mine."

"I wish I knew what yours were."

"Yours seem pretty obviously concentrated. She's quite

a charming little thing underneath those remaining layers of fatty tissue. . . ."

Ruth meant Cindy Brown, of course, and Kevin sighed. "Now you're building something. . . ." There was no use talking to her; she'd deflect his every remark. What had changed her so? he wondered.

"No, I'm merely an observer," Ruth declared, "that's all."

"Life could be pleasant for both of us," Kevin said, "if you'd take time out to enjoy it. I think we both ought to start trying before it's too late."

"It looks as though you've made another beginning," Ruth said. "Now, let's go over the daily charts. . . ."

A new guest, José Ortega, sleek and plump, strolled past the pool area late in the day, some hours after Cole's emergency operation.

"Our first Latin customer," Phil Bernheim observed to Jack Fleming.

"Newly arrived this afternoon," Jack replied.

Ortega smiled at the pair as he passed, nodded respectfully to the ladies.

"I understand Cole came out all right," Alice said to Rose.

"So Dr. Mack's a good surgeon as well as a good general practitioner," Rose said.

"Personally, I can do without any of them."

"Right, Alice, so can I. Let's dip in the pool. Maybe it'll settle the rumble in my abdomen."

Jack produced an evil chuckle. "Gut, honey, in your case. Not abdomen. . . ."

Rose stood up, shaking herself into shape, drawing in her stomach. "What you see is what you're stuck with, Jack, so don't knock it!" she said, and belly-flopped into the pool.

Ortega settled across the pool in a deck chair away from the main body of guests, in the shade, for he was dressed in a bright sports shirt and slacks, and given to sweat. A few yards away sat Irene Tuttle, watching him. Between the edge of her copy of *Vogue* and the low brim of her picture hat she studied him covertly, saw him take out his wallet, check through it, and extract what appeared to be a photograph of passport size. He studied it for a minute, then returned it to his wallet, the wallet to his pocket. Mrs. Tuttle wondered if perhaps it was a picture of his wife and family, or some girl friend. She preferred to think of him as a dignified family man, for he looked so distinguished. And since he also bore a strong resemblance to a Central American ambassador she knew in Washington, when he glanced up and smiled at her, leaned toward her in a courteous gesture of what she interpreted as acquiescence, she lowered her copy of *Vogue* and returned his smile graciously.

"How do you do?" he said. "My name is Oretga."

"And I'm Mrs. Howard Tuttle. Isn't it a lovely day?" and she proceeded to answer his general questions about the function of the lodge and its guests after the self-introductions.

"They used to call them 'greasers'," Phil said to Jack, observing the newly formed alliance across the pool. "But they don't do that anymore. Now they call them chicanos. Is that such a salutary improvement?"

Jack agreed it wasn't. "Like changing kike to yid."

"Yeah, right. Chicano is too near chicanery. I wouldn't think they'd like it so much. They still call an Anglo a *gringo* in Mexico."

"I know, because we exploited them. I guess only Castro's Cuba rises above such petty distinctions, now it's got its identity back."

"Oh God," Alice scoffed, "listen to the political experts, will you! Hey, Rose, I'm coming in!" She shed her terry-cloth shift and descended the ladder to join Rose.

"Don't hold your nose when you get to the deepest part," Phil called after her, but she ignored him and paddled toward Rose.

Across the sparkling aquamarine water, Mrs. Tuttle and Ortega had nearly exhausted the generalities; the dowager was now concentrating on the immediate scene.

"Some people just have to make a public display of everything they do," she observed tartly.

"Well, but it's fun to look and appraise, too, Mrs. Tuttle, or we wouldn't be sitting poolside right now. That's the name of the game when you come to a new place to mix with strangers. The same thing happens aboard ship, if you've ever taken a sea voyage."

"In the past my husband Howard and I made many crossings to Europe. We always sailed on the *Normandie*. Today we fly—always first-class, naturally."

"Sailing's nice, but it demands a certain tranquillity from the passenger. Otherwise it's tedious. . . ."

"Mr. Ortega, *this* place is the world's *most* tedious." She studied her charming new acquaintance from beneath her lavender brim and decided she was beginning to like him. Despite his dark skin he was obviously an educated gentleman. "What *do* you do, Mr. Ortega? Are you in government by any chance?"

"No, ma'am," José said, grinning at her indulgently. "All I do is hang around power."

"Hang around power?" Mrs. Tuttle echoed. "That does sound like government, Mr. Ortega."

"It is, and it isn't," Ortega replied enigmatically. "I'm in the investment business, ma'am. And right now I'm taking a little breather, resting up, looking around. . . . And what's your husband's line, Mrs. Tuttle? What's he do?"

Irene Tuttle could not suppress an involuntary gasp of astonishment. "You mean you've never heard of Howard Tuttle from Washington, D.C.?"

"Oh yes, I've heard of him, all right, Mrs. Tuttle," Ortega assured her, suppressing his amusement at her irritation. "I have indeed. But what does he *do*, that's what I want to know?"

Taking him at his word, Mrs. Tuttle began to bend his ear with the public version of her husband's activities.

"I'll bet she's talking about Tuttle," said Phil to Jack.

"She wouldn't know a racist pig from a good Christian," Jack said.

"But *they* would," said Phil, nodding toward their wives splashing around noisily at the far end of the pool.

"Yeah," Jack said gloomily. "What happens when they discover they're as good as we are?"

"Wear our balls, what else?" said Phil.

"Besides that—they already got *them*. My God, what I wouldn't give for an ice-cold beer and a pastrami on rye!"

"Or some herring and sour cream, some chicken livers and schmaltz—"

"Stop it!" Phil protested. "I'll forget why I'm here in another minute!"

Anita was in Stanley Conn's room, giving him her standard massage. Stanley was flat on his stomach, relaxed.

"I've been thinking," Stanley said into the massage table. "We're two lonely people, vulnerable to the world. No real refuges, no escapes. What do you think?"

"I try not to," Anita replied, "most of the time." Even against her avowed intentions she found herself building Stanley up for the special massage: and even though laying a guy was the natural adjunct to her act, she was most reluctant to be so free—or was it generous?—with Stanley Conn. "This damned island makes you think too much," she continued, "look straight into your past. I try not to rationalize anything, but it's not easy."

"Tough early times, huh? You haven't said anything about your life."

"Who needs a dirty soap opera?"

"But you let me ramble on indefinitely about mine."

"A good masseuse is a good listener."

"All you've said is, you come from California."

"Everybody's either from it or going there these days. I come from Hollywood," Anita stated. "And that's not really California. Somebody in the Thirties called it a state of mind, but it's much more than that. It's everything good and bad in our country, all packaged and labeled. In a couple of centuries, when the anthropologists dig us out of the ruins, they're going to have a field day."

"I guess so. . . . But you can take what you want from any place, whatever it is."

"Only people with perception and strength can."

"I got a real nice, ordinary brother lives in Eagle Rock, retired young from a very lucrative hardware business. Bought a whole hilltop, two acres; built several cottages he rents. Just him and his wife in a big, old-fashioned house up there behind a screen of trees. Pretty nice. They don't know anything about Hollywood."

"They're lucky."

"Hey, girl, you sound downright cynical."

"I am," Anita admitted. "I was raised on a casting couch. My mother was an extra in pictures in the days when there was a star system. She never made it as an actress, no discipline, a real dipso—warmhearted and foolish. She was background in a couple of Agnes Bird's early films."

"No kidding? The old actress that's here?"

"Bird would love that. She's not much older than you are. . . . As a kid I found out early that it wasn't the men in my mother's life that counted, it was the life in her men. As she changed them more frequently, they got younger and bouncier. I learned about the facts from her last lover, just before she died of a heart attack over a bottle of gin."

"Jesus!" Stanley said. "You've really had it—"

"Oh, that's just the beginning. Soon after my mother died, I found out that if you wanted to get anywhere in this world, you'd better know how to use sex as a weapon. Does that surprise you, Mr. Conn?"

"No, it just makes me a little sad."

"Why?"

"Because—well, dammit, I feel protective toward you for some stupid reason."

"And I haven't made up my mind about you, either," Anita bantered, working slowly along his thighs.

"Hey, you're getting to me," Stanley said tensely, "if that's what this is all about. Somebody rubbing somebody, of whatever sex, somebody gets to somebody sooner or later. . . ."

Anita laughed; he was nice. "You're either putting me on or you're a hopeless case."

"Both. . . ." He sat up suddenly, pushed her hands away and draped the sheet around him. "That's enough for now, thanks. Sit down, Anita. I got to talk to you."

Anita sat dutifully in a chair, and Stanley swung his sturdy legs over the edge of the massage table, facing her, the towel draped across his loins.

"You hold back when you ought to let go, and vice versa. You hate for anybody to really get to you, don't you?"

She studied his flushed, earnest face, his middle-aged flab, his sincere desire to communicate with her, and was slightly ashamed of her indifference. Well, timidity masking as indifference, she admitted to herself.

"What you're saying is, I'm cynical," she declared.

"How'd you like to go to California?" he asked abruptly. "I really mean it."

"I don't think I'll ever go there again."

"Reasons—?"

"Well, my parents are dead for one thing. My other relatives are living in Portland, Oregon. My friends are gone, scattered around, what few I had. My whole life in L.A. was jinxed; it wasn't any good, believe me. No, I burned all my bridges. When you've done that, you don't go back to a place. . . ."

The memory of the last terrible year in Los Angeles made her shudder inwardly. On pills, dropping acid, turning tricks for Joe, getting herself geared up for the big smack, just a hair away from mainlining. Lucky to have had that blinding fright when Joe was busted and the irresistible inspiration to pick up her wits and walk out, leaving everything—her clothes, car, the hi-fi, everything. Just that final note he would have found in the apartment after she'd bailed him out and fled. Not a very nice person then: greedy, uncaring, totally selfish. Not much better now, after several years, but at least her own woman, responsible only to herself, able to see herself for what she was then, was now, hoped to be. . . . Hoped to be? She heard Stanley's voice from a great distance.

"Afraid of what you might find if you went back?" he

was saying. "If you face it, you're not running away from it."

"It's nothing I can't handle better from this distance," she replied quietly.

"All right, all right. So I was just talking. We both talk a lot; there's no harm in it."

"If you'll lie down, I'll finish the massage," she told him.

Stanley stared at her searchingly for a moment, then shrugged and lay down without another word.

She started to work on him again, and worked in silence for several minutes before he finally spoke.

"That's what you're here for, isn't it? The job?"

"That's right—the job."

"No," said Stanley, "that's only part of everything. The main point is to understand yourself. But you don't want to, do you? You deliberately turn everything off."

"No," Anita said inconclusively, feeling depressed, annoyed that she couldn't penetrate and analyze his behavior while he was able to get to her where she lived. He didn't have to bribe her with the lure of California if he wanted sex, he knew that by now. But why did he have to bring up California at all? She was willing to trust him, almost. Although the poison of those earlier years was still too virulent in her veins, the sham of pretending to feel solicitude and affection for people she disliked, even loathed, was still too distasteful to allow for much trust. She'd worn a mask too long, half of her life or more. Sick to death of it, she was still afraid to cast it aside. If she could only experience just one open, limpid, exultant emotion toward someone, anyone, and if that person could just see what she really was deep down inside, under the big-titted, blonde-with-the-violet-eyes image. Just once. . . .

She went on massaging him, this time not building anywhere, keeping it even and unstated, impersonal.

"No," she said at length, "I guess I don't want to know the whole truth about anything, Mr. Conn. I guess I haven't the courage to hear it or see it."

"Yeah, well, that's a good beginning," Stanley replied. "That's something, that's a start. . . ."

Part
❁ FIVE ❁

"Sometimes you might feel as if you're only getting part of the general picture, Danny," Terence Thompson told Francovich a few days after they returned to Nassau. The billionaire had removed his core of operations from the *Sarcophagus* to the top floor of the brand-new Aquarius Tower, a Thompson-financed operation larger and more luxurious than the Sheraton British-Colonial, and much more expensively rated.

"I get that feeling often," said Francovich, grinning. "In fact, a good deal of the time I'm dizzy from it."

"By now you know it's my style," Thompson replied. "I work in jigsaw puzzles. Everybody has a piece or two, but I'm the only one who sees the whole picture. Keep them mystified. And that makes me the prototype paranoid," he added with pride.

"We all have our hang-ups," Francovich said to conclude the subject. "What's the surprise for today?"

Thompson led him from the main lounge of the penthouse into a smaller living room, part of his suite. Francovich was comfortably located in a large air-conditioned studio with bath and bar kitchen at the opposite end of the sprawling apartment. Tastefully decorated, his unit was all he could ever want in luxury living, but he was more or less a prisoner there; he wasn't free to wander around the penthouse except on the open terrace, and he could never enter Thompson's private domain without first announcing himself by telephone. Another of Thompson's games.

Spread across the oversized conference table was a large, detailed map.

"Sit down." Thompson indicated one of two armchairs placed before the map, its back to the wide glass wall that afforded a breathtaking view of the Bay Street harbor front and the dazzling sea beyond. "Make yourself comfortable, I want you to look at something—"

The enormous map was a superbly delineated cartogram of the one hundred-thousand square miles that composed the Bahama Islands group, reduced to a scale that allowed for the pinpointing of the entire chain. Below the cartogram lay others; some were enlargements of miniscule land masses that understandably showed little development. New Providence and Andros were represented, as well as Grand Bahama, Bimini, Great Abaco, Harbor, and Eleuthera islands—and San Salvador, once called Watling after the pirate, and now considered as Columbus's first landfall in the New World.

"Beautiful, aren't they?" Thompson said, excited as a child, flipping rapidly through the cartograms.

"They certainly are," Francovich agreed. "So you're set on acquiring more property—?"

"Danny boy, that's it. No reason why I should limit myself to California, or the Middle East and the Orient, when all this is just crying for development. California's oversubscribed, the Middle and Far East are thoroughly unstable. This place is pure gold; it's a terrific challenge."

"Seems to me Nassau's pretty well developed already," Francovich observed. "The Aquarius Tower about marks the saturation point."

Thompson waved his remark aside. "Danny, the reports are all in. They're irrefutable. The Bahamas are going to experience a boom in the next few years that'll make their present development look like Stone Age ruins. You see this small chain of islands between Andros and Eleuthera? It starts southeast of Nassau and ends with Great Exuma."

"I remember," said Francovich. "We cruised through them."

"Right! But what you don't know is their strategic geographical features. They're paradise-beautiful, they've got agreeable terrain, and with some astute engineering, they can all have their own fresh-water reservoirs; it's been done on some already. Look, here's Crystal Cay. A group of Miami investors developed this one to the point where they're now selling estates, and it's only three miles long."

"Quite a feat. . . ."

"And this one, Coral Cay, it's being worked now." Thompson paused and looked up, smiling his conspiratorial grin. "You see the potential, don't you? Casinos, private estates, sites for tax-sheltered corporations? The major delay's been fresh water. But with our new techniques that Thompson Manufacturing's developed for salt-water conversion, plus the new reservoir plans, it's a natural, an investor's dream. Money will attract more money." Thompson pointed to a thick folder placed on the telephone table between his chair and Francovich's. "It's all in here, Danny, all laid out down to the smallest detail. It could even be done without the salt-water-conversion scheme if we wanted to get involved in running our own fresh-water barges between the islands, but that isn't necessary. . . . Just think of the possibilities, Danny! Doesn't it make your flesh crawl?"

"I'm thinking," said Francovich, "in terms of hundreds of millions. Terry, do you really feel—?"

Thompson cut him off. "Hell yes, I do! Look, here's one installation already doing a good business: Bimini Springs on Devil Cay. Owned by a couple named Maple. Small, a health spa; class place, family-run. I've thought of taking this one over for my personal use and developing it into a new headquarters."

Maple, Maple. . . . Why did that name sound familiar, thought Francovich, and suddenly his stomach turned over. . . . Harry and Marge Maple! He hadn't thought of them for a long, long time, not since he was associated with Senator Byron Holt. Good God, it couldn't be the same Maples, not those two, but if it was, he'd not only go along with the acquisition, he'd take it away from them if he had to use napalm.

"What chance is there to get leasehold property away from the present operators?" he asked Thompson, and hoped the eagerness and excitement he was feeling didn't show in his voice or manner, or at least appeared to be what Thompson expected from him.

"Every possible one in our favor. I've had a Florida group working on this one for several months. You'll see when you study the report. There was no point in telling you or the boys about it until I had all the evidence in. I just received this last night, haven't slept a wink. Now I want you to get at it, Danny, and let me know right away what you think. You'll be handling major strategy, so your ideas will mean a lot to me."

"I'll do the best I can," said Francovich. "You really came up with something different this time."

"That's the fun of it," Thompson replied, pleased with Francovich's response. "To take the most impossible sort of an idea and make it work, start it going, let it snowball. . . ."

In his room an hour later, Francovich sat down to study the report, but his mind kept wandering back to the Maples and, of course, to Eleanor Holt. . . .

Eleanor Holt was quite a dish. The age disparity between the senator from Alabama and her husband was about the same ratio that existed between, say, Terence Thompson and his estranged wife Marilyn—about thirty-some years.

Eleanor was not as beautiful as Marilyn, and instead of being pale-blonde she was black-haired, fair-skinned, with wide blue eyes that looked right through everything, everybody. At least that was Francovich's impression the first time the senator took him home to dinner at his Georgetown residence and he sat across the perfectly appointed table from his hostess.

"And what's your game, Mr. Francovich?" she'd begun bluntly over the shrimp cocktail. "I know my husband's, but what's yours?"

He wasn't prepared for her candor, but before he could reply, Byron Holt had laughed loudly at his wife's gambit, so Francovich supposed it was all right and said, "The only way a lawyer can make money these days, Mrs. Holt, is to be an authority on something. The day of the generally literate man's gone. By becoming an authority, a man's got a fighting chance to play pilot fish to some big, daring shark. . . . I think Senator Holt's a big, daring shark, ma'am, and after all, you can see that I'm only a little pilot fish. . . . For the present, that is," he added, and grinned warmly at her across the sterling candelabrum, thinking that should do it.

Eleanor Holt took him in for a moment, then continued with her shrimp as the senator launched into some story about the summer lodge they owned in Canada. Eventually she found a wedge during the entrée: "It takes a pretty smart pilot fish to keep from getting swallowed up by the big ones, Mr. Francovich. You think you're nimble enough to keep clear of those lethal teeth?"

Francovich was angry now, but he grinned again, still superficially amiable. "I hope so, ma'am. By the way, what are your favorite games?" He had deliberately pluralized the question.

This Eleanor Holt had appreciated. "Charities, fund luncheons, bridge with Mrs. Vice President once a month. That sort of thing. . . ." She tossed it away lightly, not bothering to follow it up.

Dan Francovich knew her background—rich, spoiled rotten, nearly the same cut as the Bouvier girls, though without their infinite charm; a little too sharp around the edges, unable to tone herself down. The impression came off as strident. He hadn't hoped to make an enemy of her, but the moment alone after dinner with her almost did it, and also put his fears at rest.

They were seated in front of the blazing fire opposite one another; he was drinking Courvoisier, she toyed with a creme de menthe. The senator had just vacated the central position of seniority on the deep middle divan between them to take the library phone for an important call he was expecting from his state capitol office.

As soon as the senator left, Eleanor Holt relaxed visibly and smiled at him.

"I know your type," she said, arch and playful, and kept right on smiling.

"What *is* my type, Mrs. Holt?" Francovich replied evenly. "You've been gunning for me ever since I walked in your front door tonight. Does it bug you that I'm working for the senator?" He knew he ought to tread cautiously; his new job was going to mean a lot of valuable experience he needed, but he was angry, still smouldering from her earlier treatment. "If it's going to continue like this all the way in, I'd just as soon bow out now. I won't starve around Washington. . . ."

Eleanor Holt twisted her emeralds and crossed her legs, slim and beautiful, perfectly shaped to the knees, Francovich observed. He could imagine the rest. Her hair shone like black satin under the soft silk-shaded lamp; the wavering firelight lent a warm glow to her creamy skin. She didn't reply to his inquiry, waiting for him to continue; but he remained silent and held his ground. It was her turn.

At length she said, "I'm sorry. I've got a tricky disposition; sometimes I can't control myself. Byron thinks it's amusing; he's always in possession of the moment. I really didn't mean to explode at you like that; it was bitchy of me. . . ."

"What interests you enough about me to throw me off-balance?" he asked her bluntly. "What do you want to know about me? My background's open enough, and ordinary."

"If I told you, I don't think you'd have a very high opinion of me."

Ah, so she was one of those, he thought. Right off they make a play for you, throwing it at you. Then the minute you snatch at the bait, whammo, they run to daddy or insult you. No thanks, he'd stay as far away from her as he could get—for above all, he was drawn to her sexually.

"I don't think I want to hear it, Mrs. Holt," he replied slowly. "Let's just leave it right where it is. . . ." He heard the senator's footsteps approaching down the hall. "Let's try being friends in spite of everything. You do your job the way you have to, and I'll do mine—"

And so, a frosty-armed truce of sorts existed between them for the next few months. Francovich worked diligently for Byron Holt, learned a great deal about how Washington lobbyists operated, and saw very little of his boss's wife, managing to wriggle out of any dinner commitments that came up at the senator's the few times he was invited. Once Eleanor Holt smiled at him over the rim of a champagne glass at a reception, once again at the senator's office. That was all.

Until summertime. . . . Byron Holt was appointed to an investigating committee and called to the Middle East to analyze the need for further American aid to Iran.

The senator told him at the airport, "I leave her in your trust, Dan. Look after her, see her when you can. She gets lonely." Eleanor wasn't present, having said her good-bys to Holt at home. He hoped he could postpone the obligation indefinitely, but Eleanor called on business matters a couple of times right after Holt's departure, and finally, after some two weeks' negligence—rationalizing it as preoccupation—Francovich decided he'd better call Eleanor and ask her to have lunch with him. A public meeting at the Shoreham Hotel couldn't possibly mean anything more than an exchange of further barbed remarks, he thought.

Eleanor joined him at his table, looking even better than he remembered her from her visit to Senator Holt's office. He remarked upon her clothes, a stunning cool-green wool suit, and her springtime freshness.

"That's the open air," she explained. "I go to a health resort in Virginia sometimes when the weather's right. I keep my weight pretty steady, but a week of rigid dieting under controlled environment and no domestic problems—like having a husband around, no house to run—really works wonders. I've just come back. . . . You look tired, Mr. Francovich. You could do with some relaxation."

Francovich was well aware of his condition, which was nervous and edgy; his fatigue was reflected in the dark circles under his eyes. Lately, from work pressure, he'd had bouts of insomnia. He longed to get away—the Maryland coast, anywhere, for a few days—but he felt an extra added responsibility with the senator gone and couldn't conscientiously take off during his boss's absence.

"Where's this resort?" he said conversationally, mainly out of politeness. At least so far she'd been extremely agreeable and hadn't tried to bait him—not yet.

"Near White Stone, Virginia, in Lancaster County. Did you know there's a place close to it called Tappahannock on the Rappahannock? Well, there is, cross my heart!" she said, and threw back her burnished black head and laughed.

Yes, she was a different person without the senator around, he concluded, and the luncheon went quite amiably. They talked about New York, Broadway, politics, travel, the stock market, inflation, and the polarization of social thought at both ends of the power structure. At length Eleanor returned to the topic of the health resort.

"Seriously," she advised after he'd paid the bill and the waiter had gone, "you ought to look after yourself, Mr. Francovich. Or somebody ought to. When Byron gets back, you must go away somewhere for a couple of weeks. I'll give you the address of the place I like. It's called Soda Springs. . . ." And she wrote it out for him, then and there.

When Senator Holt returned from the Middle East and settled in, Francovich asked for a week off. The senator was so pleased with his performance while away that he gave Francovich the vacation without any comment except to get some rest and enjoy himself. "And where will you go?" he said.

It was on Francovich's tongue to say Soda Springs, but something restrained him, he was never quite sure why.

"Oh, the Maryland shore on the Chesapeake," he lied. He did actually know some people who had a summer cottage out on Point Lookout, and he mentioned that. "Tip of St. Mary's County."

"Good. How can I reach you?"

"There's no phone," Francovich hedged, which was true; and even if he'd planned to visit the Bartletts and they'd had a telephone, he wouldn't have given it to the senator. "I really need the isolation," he told Holt. "What if I call in every couple of days? Would that be all right?"

"Fine," Holt agreed. "Call when you can. I guess it won't matter for a few days if we're not in constant touch. See you a week from Monday, Dan. Have yourself some fun." The senator had winked roundly at him, assuming, Francovich felt, that he was taking some company with him. Female, of course.

Francovich knew the reason that Eleanor Holt had given him the Soda Springs address, so before he packed a bag he called her at home and told her he'd be down in Tidewater Virginia for a week. She evinced casual, friendly interest in the trip and told him to have a good time, to get a good rest.

The first two days at the small, expensive resort were uneventful, pleasant, and spent in solitary idleness. Only a few guests were lodged in the rambling, converted eighteenth-century tavern; and Francovich's hosts, a Deep South couple who had succeeded quite well in ironing out their accents, were Marge and Harry Maple. They were most attentive to his needs, the food was excellent, facilities invigorating, the black servants elderly and congenial. The atmosphere was so relaxed, in fact, that for the first two nights Francovich was in bed and dead to the world before nine o'clock, sleeping until a chorus of churring birds in the garden outside his window awakened him around seven in the morning. He breakfasted in bed, read a Washington paper, sunned himself around the large pool, and generally forgot about the grind he'd been on for many months. Until Eleanor Holt arrived on Wednesday, bag and baggage.

She had artfully reserved the room next to his; both were on the ground floor with outside as well as inside entrances. The weather was warm that first day of her arrival, and they dined out on the terrace with other guests in the evening, then said goodnight after coffee and brandies in the lounge.

Thinking nothing of it, Francovich left the French doors to the terrace open on the garden when he retired, as was his habit. He was startled awake from a deep sleep by two warm arms and a rippling length of burning female flesh in bed with him.

When he realized what had happened—it was Eleanor Holt—his first impulse was to kick her out. But knowing that she would only use such a rebuff against him and admitting to himself that he'd wanted her badly as long as he'd known her, he abandoned himself in response to her considerable passion.

She stayed with him until four o'clock when the first gray light was filtering into the garden, then crept back to her own room.

They had four days and three nights together, and although Francovich found every moment of it exciting with her, he was hounded by second thoughts, thoughts that centered darkly around the senator, whose jealousy was well-known.

He said to Eleanor as they walked down to the bay for their last time together, a Saturday afternoon. "This can't go on back in Washington, you know. It's a fishbowl."

Eleanor had laughed. "Oh, we'll find a way," she said. "We have to. . . ."

They sat on a fallen log and stared at the bay, harsh and glittering in the oblique late-afternoon light. He was extremely uneasy; she was already preoccupied with her return to Washington.

"I'm driving back in an hour," she told him. "I've got to, Dan. He thinks I'm staying with a Baltimore friend. I didn't even call him. And I had to pick an argument to get away. He believes I'm off sulking. I often am."

A very dangerous game, thought Francovich, but that was obviously the way she liked it best.

"We're taking a terrible chance, El. Your life and mine. . . ." She was a great piece of ass, the best, and he hoped she considered him the same. But after all, theirs wasn't a love affair, a genuine emotional commitment; it never could be. Not yet twenty-seven, he was determined to do something with his life; her own devious patterns were already mapped out. All they had between them was chemistry, a deadly explosive ingredient they'd created, a time bomb.

He watched her drive off, feeling depressed and slightly melancholy. A shadow over the past few days that he didn't like at all. He wondered if the time with her would show when he saw Holt again. No, definitely, it couldn't go on; he'd have to be firm about it. Why, he wondered desperately, did he have to follow his libido around? It was a question he couldn't answer. . . .

"Mr. Francovich," Harry Maple said to him Sunday morning. "It's your last day, and you're leaving us this afternoon. Why not go fishing with me? You'll enjoy yourself."

"I'm not a fisherman or a sailor," Francovich said.

"Don't worry, I'm not, either. It's a motor launch, and we won't be going out very far, only a hundred yards or more. And the fish'll jump right into the boat."

So Francovich went with his host. But there was a heavy undertow at that time of day during tide's turn, vicious and swift, and Francovich knew nothing about it. When the boat overturned much farther out than a hundred yards, more like a quarter of a mile, due to a particularly clumsy maneuver of Harry Maple's in getting at the bait box, Francovich was certain for a few panicky moments that he was going to drown. With the tide carrying him out, he struggled and cried out as he watched Harry surface some yards from him, stare at him for a long second, then turn and swim with powerful, easy strokes for the shore. Besides being a poor sailor, Francovich also meant he was a weak swimmer. He discovered that by treading water he could keep afloat although drifting away from the shore. He looked around for the boat, but it was gone. He went under, frantically clawing at air as he came up, and suddenly, seemingly out of nowhere, someone was helping him into a boat, a launch. He hadn't even heard the approaching motor, nor at that time could he figure how long he'd been in the water or how many times he'd gone under. . . .

They brought him to the lodge. The senator was waiting for him in his room, in a pale rage.

"You're a bastard!" Holt said softly but with great force. "I'm sorry you didn't drown like the rat you are!"

Francovich was clutched with a chill, in no condition to deal with the full portent of the situation. "You—" was all he could manage.

"Yes," said Holt, white-lipped and shaking, "these people are my *friends*. We're partners in this business. . . ."

"I see," Francovich murmured, and many, many things were clear to him. Who could say that Eleanor Holt made this kind of thing her way of life or thought of herself as some kind of high priestess who led likely subjects to ritual sacrifice? Who could say that Harry Maple wasn't doing the senator's bidding when that boat overturned? Francovich only knew one thing for certain: His death would merely have looked like a sad and regrettable accident.

"I hope you do see," said Byron Holt. "Come in Monday and get your personal effects. I'll be away in New York. I don't ever want to see you again."

"What about—?"

"Your *career*?" The senator underlined it with a faint sneer.

Francovich nodded mutely, another chill taking him.

"I won't do anything to obstruct your precious career," Holt told him. "But there won't be any Washington doors open for you, not while I'm around."

And that was the last Francovich ever saw of Senator Byron Holt, or of Eleanor Holt, who had played her game well, whatever it was. He cleared out of Washington, D.C., immediately, rather glad to go. It had never been his idea of a fun city. He attached himself some months later in Los Angeles to the offices of a talented attorney who specialized in corporate and probate law. Eventually, by dint of frenzied application, he became something of an authority in the corporate field. Logic was his specialty. What a pity, he thought, whenever anyone mentioned Washington, that he hadn't used his talent for logic where Eleanor or Byron Holt were concerned. . . .

So, the Marge and Harry Maple of Bimini Springs Lodge on Devil Cay were probably the same genial, bullshitting Harry and the same aggressively southern Marge of Soda Springs. Well, there would be a lot of satisfaction in ousting them; they ought to be fairly near retirement by now, and this would be their last pitch for the big money. But Francovich had never battened on retribution, although he had to admit in all honesty to himself that he would do everything he could to get their property if Thompson said the word, and enjoy doing it legally. . . .

Much later, when Francovich had had time to study the report and do some legal research in and around the Nassau courts, Thompson said, "So you think you've found a way, huh?"

"Yes, to get whatever you want down here and below," said Francovich. "Due to a technicality in the colonial charter, the leaseholds that cover all the out islands can be revoked by the simple process of putting them up for bid, if they're over fifty years old. Most proprietors don't technically *own* their land. Naturally, nobody's ever invoked this procedure. A little occasional lobbying in strategic areas has kept the whole subject under wraps for generations. But if the bids were ever to be revised—that is, updated to a new starting price—the asking sum on the open market would amount to about *fifty* times what the present holders or their predecessors paid for them. Times have changed radically in the last century, as you know better than anybody, and values have skyrocketed. I doubt if anybody's capable of coming up with the kind of money that would be needed to renew leaseholds at present adjusted levels. You can break any of them, Terry, and get almost any property—if that's what you really want. . . ."

Thompson slapped his thigh excitedly, delighted with Francovich's findings. "Goddam, I knew you'd come up with something, Danny boy! You're worth your weight in platinum. I don't know what I'd do without you."

"You'd find somebody else, Terry. You know that as well as I do."

"By God, that calls for a drink. What'll it be, Diet Cola or Seven-Up?"

"It doesn't make any difference," Francovich replied. "Whatever you're drinking."

"By the way, we've got top agents lined up who'll physically check out any property we decide on," said Thompson, handing him a Diet Cola. "Several are Florida men who are familiar with the Bahamas; they've been around for a long time. A few are already investigating," he added redundantly, but Francovich had guessed that.

"Got anybody in mind for the development on Devil Cay that's called Bimini Springs?"

Thompson nodded. "Somebody special, with an engineering background. We don't want the owners to know we're snooping until the last minute, so I sent down a spic, a very smooth operator."

"A spic?" Francovich echoed. He knew well enough what Thompson meant.

"Yeah, you know—a foreigner. Name of Joe Ortega."

"A foreign citizen?" He couldn't leave it alone now.

"Hell no, Danny, he was born in the States."

"But you called him a foreigner," Francovich persisted. "I have a Yugoslavian name, and they used to call us bohunks when I was a kid, and I didn't like it much. I guess that makes me a foreigner, too."

"Come on, Danny, that's not what I meant. You're a white man. This one's a Mexican."

"Well, the least we can do then is to call him a chicano," Francovich said mildly, thinking that this was probably the first Meso-American the Maples had ever had on their island. He hoisted the Cola. "Here's to your new venture, Terry. Here's to money—"

"Here's to the personal satisfaction that money can always buy, and to a sense of achievement," Thompson countered. "Unless I miss my guess, you'd like to make those Maples squirm, wouldn't you?"

Francovich stared at him in surprise, dumbfounded.

"How did you know I knew them?" he asked.

Thompson grinned, enormously pleased with himself. "Oh, another of my idiosyncrasies. My passion for exhaustive records on all key people," he explained. "Not just those general personnel files, you understand. I like to know *everything* about a man. It's amazing what comes out when you start digging. I don't blame you with that Holt woman; I've met her. Damned attractive bitch, like that Elizabeth Taylor was before she got too fat. But notoriously flagrant, a real slut. It's a wonder he hasn't shot her. You weren't the first. . . ."

"It's all in the past," Francovich said, "like my wife's death."

"Or my wife's disappearance?" Thompson replied in a tone that indicated the continual depth of his bitterness and frustration. "Don't you enjoy the exhilaration of evening up a score, Danny boy?"

Francovich pondered this for a moment. "No, I don't think so. I'm not built that way." Then he smiled, his dark, sober face lighting up with amiable warmth; he could never underrate Thompson's drive and self-discipline. "But I like doing a good job, Terry, and I like working for you."

"That pleases me," said Thompson. "Well, here's to health *and* money. One's no good without the other. . . ."

Tom Street had been thinking long and hard about the Maples' photo file potential since he'd made his startling discovery, and it took Tom all of twenty-four hours to act upon his new knowledge. When he arrived at a definite decision, he called Harry and asked if he could drop by for a few minutes, there was something he wanted to discuss.

As Tom walked into Harry's office, Harry was seated at his desk, feet up, leaning back in his swivel chair, totally relaxed. He smiled up at Tom automatically.

"Hi there, boy. What can I do for you?" Harry was disposed to geniality because things were looking up for the remainder of the season into Easter. A sheaf of fresh reservations was stacked on the desk, which meant that Bimini Springs would be booked solid in the coming months and might even have to turn away clients. Harry had also enjoyed a pleasant hour under his sun lamp and looked fit and tan. Poor Harry, Tom thought, things were going to be a lot worse for him before they got better.

"I've been pondering the organization," said Tom.

"Well, well, I'm glad to see somebody's got the business at heart besides me and Marge. What's on your mind?"

Go to it, Tom urged himself, wade right in. "Well, it's about a photo file I saw recently, Harry, in a strongbox. . . ."

Harry's sanguine color drained away, he grew white around the mouth. "Photos?" He seemed to be groping for the proper association. "You know something I should know, Tom?" he stalled.

"I think so," Tom replied blithely. "I know you've got a

pile of evidence in that strongbox in the bottom drawer of your file cabinet, that one right over there. . . ."

"So—" murmured Harry, and everything clicked into place, "I *thought* I left that file cabinet unlocked. That's what I told Marge. And I thought it might be you. But why?"

"You mean why did I lock it?"

Harry nodded.

"To alert you, Harry. To give you plenty of time to think and sweat."

"You think I need time for that, eh? Well, well. I'm not God," Harry said impassively, "but I'm a pretty good imitation of same around this place."

"You could get yourself into a lot of trouble with those photos," Tom said.

"There's only your word that they exist. You weren't smart enough to grab a couple."

"I'm smart enough to know how worried you are right now underneath that calm exterior."

Very deliberately Harry rose to his feet. Fully erect, he was a powerfully built man, taller by a head than Tom who was merely of medium height.

"Do I look like a man with worries?" Harry demanded. "Do I have the deportment of a harried, nervous type, Tom? I wouldn't say so. I'd say I was one of the calmest men in the world right now."

He paused, smiled at Tom with insolent tolerance. "Talk about hot water," he said nonchalantly. "Now if my name was Tom Street, I'd take a good long look at myself in a mirror to see how my thinking cap was screwed on. Or better yet, I'd look into that hard-drugs safe every hour on the hour, just so's I could tally up all my precious videotape reels and see if any of the exposed ones are missing. . . . Because they sure are right now, Tom. Marge has 'em. We know all there is to know about getting into our own safes, lad. Got 'em set two ways. . . . And if I'm not mistaken, I think I hear Marge now—"

Tom simply couldn't believe that this was really happening; there was an eerie nightmare quality about the situation. He blinked his eyes at Harry as Marge knocked briefly on the door that connected Harry's office with the apartment and entered carrying a brown paper shopping bag in her arms. Smiling sweetly at Tom, she deposited the bag on Harry's desk top.

"This is what you wanted, isn't it, dear?" she said.

"Yep, that's it, honey. Right on. Your timing's perfect. It's all here in the bag, Tom boy." Harry opened the bag and brought out several cartons of video tape. Tom recognized his personal code marks on the carton covers and began to feel vomitously sick.

"Christ," he muttered, "I can't believe it!"

"Best you do," said Marge in a ladylike tone.

"Ain't nobody gonna help you, Tom," Harry said with awful conviction. "Like I said, I'm God on this island, and you should've thought about that awhile before you did what you did. You went too far, Tom, when you locked the file cabinet. Nosiness I can forgive, arrogance never. Your action didn't alarm me, it put me on my guard. Oh sure, I'm guilty, but it takes a keen scout to find a dim trail, lad, so give credit to an old pathfinder where credit's due."

"What're you going to do?" Tom asked weakly.

"Well now, I'm kind of surprised you asked that, yessir, I really am. I thought you'd know. For one thing I'm going to keep these here tapes, just in case you think you'd like to exercise a large mouth anywhere about Bimini Springs. At a later date, I mean. As for right now, well, I'll expect you to have your work records all nicely cleared up, your suitcases all packed, and be ready to fly out on tomorrow's plane for Nassau. In fact, I'm even bookin' you a complimentary seat. Now, how's that for real friendly cooperation, eh? Oh yes, you can take your video equipment with you—unless you'd like to leave it here, as a favor to me. Or if you think that's too cheeky, then I'll make you a reasonable offer for the works."

"I never thought—" Tom began fuzzily, but Harry cut him off.

"That's your whole trouble, Tom boy—you don't think often enough. Maybe next time when you decide to risk painting yourself into a little old corner you'll do it next to an open door. . . ."

"I've already prepared your formal resignation and your official letter of recommendation," said Marge pleasantly. "All I need is to date them, get your signature on the one, Harry's on the other, and you're all set to go."

"Yessir," said Harry, and clapped his hands together. "We sure wouldn't want to stand in the way of a fine upcoming young pharmacist like you working on other jobs. It's just the reputation of Bimini Springs we're concerned about, and the privacy of our clients. You see, we gotta protect the guests at all times, in every way possible. . . ."

"Yes," Tom murmured faintly, "I see, I see. . . ."

Aggie Bird was seated at the mirrored dressing table in her cabana suite examining the battle scars of her life. When *The Bungalow* was completed, she was going to have a face lift; it was a little late, but it would make her feel the way she wanted, and that's what counted. As she was envisioning the effects of such surgery, someone knocked at her door. Thinking it was Dick Carter, for she had ordered an early-morning massage, she called out gaily, "Come on in!"

The door opened, and Wayne Winslow entered, fresh from Nassau on the morning plane. He closed the door and leaned against it, staring hard at her.

Wayne was nearly Dick Carter's age and in at least as fine physical condition as Dick. He wore a yellow Sy Devore sports shirt that must have cost at least fifty dollars, Aggie noted, and new gray double-knit flares he had never affected in Beverly Hills where his image of conservative young business representative was stiffly maintained by Brooks Brothers. His curly brown hair was casually styled, windblown, but his hazel eyes were formally cold.

"Wayne Winslow!" Aggie fluted, marshaling a smile, rising from the dressing table and floating toward him, her arms outstretched in welcome.

"Aggie Bird," said Wayne. "I was sure one stupid idiot to think I could leave you alone anywhere for a minute," he began. "Look at you! Your hair's a mess, your negligee's torn. You haven't lost any weight that I can see. You're a goddam mess!"

Heedless of his remarks, Aggie was upon him with extravagant hugs and kisses; but he pushed her away, unamused.

"Even a chastity belt wouldn't stop you," he said. "What you need is a pair of double asbestos pants!"

Startled, expecting a different reaction from him despite the warning radiograms—after all, Wayne knew that Dick Carter was working the massage circuit at Bimini when he sent her down—Aggie slowly backed off. Summoning style of her own, she started yelling at him, her usual defense when a quarrel was imminent.

"You can't talk to me like that!" she shouted. "I haven't done anything to be ashamed of."

"That's right, Aggie, you're never ashamed of anything you do. I'll talk to you any way I please, so long as I get to you. I'm your agent, but I'm also your friend—and if it's necessary I'll use physical force to get you in line. . . . Now how do you like that for a greeting?"

"I think it stinks. You haven't the balls to use physical force," Aggie rasped, furious with indignation. "You're a goddam good agent, but you don't have enough *machismo* to lay a little finger on me!"

That was all Wayne needed. He stepped forward and belted Aggie across the mouth with his open hand. The blow sent her reeling backwards onto the divan, shouting curses at him. Moving in, he gave her three more open-handed smacks, then stood back and tried to catch his breath as Aggie began to cry. Whether her tears stemmed from remorse, relief, or love, Wayne didn't know; but then, he reasoned, neither did Aggie.

Wayne did, however, know Aggie and Dick much better than they knew themselves. At one time his friendship with Dick would have needed only Dick's consent to turn it into a serious physical relationship, for it was already jelled as a friendship, with the giving mainly on Wayne's side because Wayne understood that this was the only way it could function. Dick's nature was not a generous one. The two met at a Beverly Hilton cocktail party, a dull promotional affair. Dick was accompanying an older woman Wayne knew casually, the ex-wife of a film producer, wealthy in her own right, quite able to afford to indulge an expensive taste for younger men. Wayne understood Dick's role immediately and that Dick's sole interest in the woman was her money; so did she. Over cocktails, the two men discovered a mutual hobby—surfing. Wayne invited Dick out to his Santa Monica beach house to surf the following weekend.

Later, when Dick's luck was down, Wayne suggested that he move into the beach house for a while. At that time Dick was working irregular shifts at some Hollywood massage parlor that catered to both sexes, and although Wayne never quizzed Dick about his duties, it was fairly evident that Dick was required to service all types of customer needs without discrimination in order to keep his job.

As Dick's life became more hectic, more irregular—sometimes he came in stoned on grass, or spaced out on pills, sometimes drunk, occasionally with a strange girl or not at all—while this was going on, Wayne's career began to boom. He found it necessary to move into Hollywood and take a two-bedroom apartment; Dick went along. It was Wayne's good fortune to fall into a ready-made clientele because of a wealthy gent who liked him. Fat with profits from a procession of popular TV and film actors, he was forced by an acute heart condition to retire suddenly, first passing on several of his lucrative though lesser known clients to Wayne who handled them expertly and was soon doing very well with his own agency.

Later on Dick started fooling around with a freaky, perverse call girl, handsome and expensive, self-inured to the problems she was always creating. Her pimp came looking for Dick one day with a blade, in a very nasty, murderous mood. He found Wayne at home instead of Dick and, having never met Dick, mistook Wayne for him. Wayne received a cutting meant for Dick. Wayne took it well, after the stitches at the hospital, but he insisted that Dick move out; he'd had enough.

It wasn't the end of their friendship, however, but it was the end of Wayne's illusions about Dick; Wayne considered him a loser. Wayne was now definitely on his way up, handling one new client who grossed over $300,000 a year and several others who worked regularly at more modest annual takes. Wayne had little time for Dick, knowing Dick would remain the way he was—irresponsible, charming, lazy, coasting along the easiest route, eventually wearing away his youth and vitality, letting it slip down the drain. But the two men did keep in touch, even when Dick left Los Angeles; and the letter Dick wrote to Wayne from Bimini Springs was decisive in sending Aggie down to the Bahamas for the fat cure. He knew both of them inside out, he knew what might happen when they met, which was why he'd sent the radiograms. In his last communication with Dick he reminded his old friend of the cutting he'd taken in Dick's stead and of the obligation he would expect him to assume—taking special care of Aggie, and not letting her know that the two of them were in communication. Wayne knew there wasn't much Aggie could do on a small island without a bar except lay Dick, and he was certain that despite his request to Dick to go easy, that's what had already happened. . . .

Aggie finally stopped crying and moved to get up, but Wayne restrained her.

"Stay where you are," he commanded. "I've had a long trip and a tough night, and I'm tired. I didn't mean to swat you like that, Aggie, but you're always asking for it."

Aggie slumped back on the divan and dabbed at her red eyes with a crumpled handkerchief. "You don't have to be such a rough bastard," she grumbled. "That wasn't called for."

"I had to get your attention. Now listen to me." He sat

down beside her and took her hand. "I've got something to tell you. *The Bungalow*," he said quietly, "has been canceled."

"Canceled!" Aggie shrieked. "What do you mean?"

"More specifically, *you've* been canceled. They're giving it to Lola Crandall."

"Lola Crandall? Shit, she doesn't need it, she's got Peptone and all those horror movies!"

"Only the voting power of Peptone's preferred stock," Wayne said. "And those horror movies lose money; they're a tax write-off."

"Why that simpering bitch can't act her way out of a public toilet! I don't give a good goddam if she did get an Oscar for *Millicent Jones*. She was *forty-three* at the time, she only got it for longevity, not for talent. I got my special award the first time around, and I was *fourteen* at the time!"

"Second time around," Wayne reminded her.

"Hell, what difference does it make? I got it, didn't I? I've always had what it takes."

"We know what you can and can't do, Aggie. You'd be great in *The Bungalow*, but it's not going to be yours, not now. And knowing how upset you'd be when the news hit the press, I came down to beat the columnists and tell you in person. I also made the trip to see how you're doing and to check out the final possibility of getting the backers to change their minds about you."

"What backers? I thought a bank owned the studio."

"Not any longer. Thompson Enterprises does."

"Terry Thompson?"

"That's right. And he's in Nassau now."

"Yeah, I know. I've got a radio."

"I tried to see him between planes, but the closest I got was the room I rented two floors below his penthouse apartment in the new Aquarius Tower, and a few words on the phone with one of his flunkies. According to the guy, Thompson has a very high regard for your talents."

"Yeah, I'll bet!"

"But there's this approaching critical deal on. One of Thompson's subsidiary companies is merging with a firm owned by Peptone's chairman of the board."

"Who is Lola Crandall's boyfriend. Don't tell me anymore, I know all about that kind of bullshit," Aggie snapped. "Son of a bitch, just when I was getting myself into great shape, ready for the clinches again. . . ."

"Practicing, I know. . . . As I said before, you haven't

lost that much weight since you came down. But you're looking rested."

"I have so lost. It doesn't show in this tent I'm wearing. Dick's pounding it off—and I'm not drinking, either!"

"Dick's always pounding it off," Wayne observed crisply. "But I'm glad you're off the booze. No pills, either? Come on, tell me the truth."

"Honestly. . . . No pills, not one. . . . Hey, you're not especially unhappy about the loss of our contract," Aggie sniffed suspiciously, "and that's not like you. I'm the one who's supposed to rationalize failure—*and* fat."

"Well, we're not going to lose much money. There'll be a substantial settlement in lieu of the claim I threatened to make against Thompson. I got that much satisfaction out of his aide who'd obviously been briefed to let me have my way—up to a point."

"You're getting *money* out of Thompson? Jesus! So what do we do now? Pack up and leave?"

"Tomorrow. Meanwhile I'd like to look around—"

"O.K., I'll start packing." Aggie blinked happily at him. "Jesus, sweetie, I'm glad you're here. But next time we're reunited don't come on so goddam rough. I know the rules are reversed, and you're supposed to be my stern daddy, but please cool it in the future. These are old bones; there's a limit."

"Sometimes you've got to be reminded who has your interests at heart. And another thing, I've already talked to Dick. I had to be a little firm with him, too, to get the whole story. Just firm, no punches. Aggie, you're a terrible, two-timing bitch, but it's not hard to keep one jump ahead of you. . . . You told him you'd had seven husbands. Good thing he can barely read!"

"Oh, *that*! I saw right off he'd believe anything, so I had a little fun with him. . . . I *did* go to bed with all of them."

"You're incorrigible," Wayne told her, "and we're the world's most unlikely team. I often seriously doubt my own sanity when it comes to you. . . ."

And he did, too. He couldn't explain to himself why this old ruin, totally undisciplined under most circumstances, had such a grab on him, and always would. Or why he had deliberately put temptation in her way so he could move in and assert his rights. But what were his rights, really? He liked being a successful agent, he liked representing famous clients; and yet Aggie was almost as historical as Gloria Swanson and not one-tenth as commercially well-preserved, bringing him peanuts. Perhaps the clue was that they supplied roles for one another to play, which occasionally got switched about; and he knew, disgusted as he got, as angry and frustrated over her as he often was, that he'd continue to know and cherish her. Perhaps it was love. If it wasn't, then he didn't know what else to call it.

"Yes," he heard Aggie saying, "and since you made that killing in Unicredit stock, I know you've got more dough than I have, so it's not my enormous wealth you're after. And it's not my fatal beauty, either, that's for goddam sure. . . ."

"I wish I knew what it was," said Wayne soberly. "Then maybe I'd know how to deal with you. . . . Hey, I'm going to my room now and change for a swim. The pool's nice. You can watch me."

"Change or swim?"

"Both in their proper time," said Wayne.

"No surfing here. Dick probably told you."

"He told me too much. The salt-water pool will do fine."

"You'll be the old bags' delight, sweetie. They're all over the place like gaggles of stuffed trout."

"You mean geese."

"So—geese! Go get dressed while I make myself young and beautiful."

"That from you—old enough to be my mother," Wayne said, grinning.

"*You're* the mother, you slimy bastard," Aggie retorted, grinning back at him. "You certainly are!"

Anita met Stanley Conn by prearrangement behind the reservoir when it was dusk. Anita was uneasy about having a rendezvous outside of Stanley's room while Harry Maple was in such a vindictive mood with her, but Stanley had complained about being bored with always talking indoors, so she had agreed.

"I'll get fired if Maple finds out," Anita said as she joined Stanley on the hillside below the reservoir. She hadn't told Stanley anything about her past relationship with Harry. "He takes a dim view of staff making dates with the guests."

"You already told me that," Stanley reminded her, "but I'm glad you came, anyway. How can Maple draw a line between what happens on the massage table and what happens outside?"

"There's a difference."

"Yeah, there is. That's why I wanted to meet you out

here. . . ." Stanley took her hand, and they sauntered down a path toward the gentle shelf of pale-pink beach made tranquil by the protective reef and quiet lagoon. The air was fresh and balmy, the breeze almost cool.

"Yesterday," said Stanley, "you said something about not going back to California because you'd burned all your bridges."

"That's true."

"But you didn't burn me."

"I don't understand—"

"You didn't burn me down. I'm not one of your disaster areas, Anita. Look, I can go to California tomorrow on a new job if I want to. Just before I flew down here I got a fabulous offer to work permanently on the Coast. Division manager of five new hardware sales outlets in the Southern California district. I hate Chicago since my wife died. I've been waiting for a chance to chuck it for good."

"Then you ought to go."

"Not alone."

"Then find somebody," she said rather sharply. She was sick and tired of having guests cry on her broad shoulders instead of a psychiatrist's, and while Stanley Conn was a sweet guy, he was here today and flying out to the Coast maybe tomorrow, which left her just where she always was—alone.

"I'm not talking about just *me*, for God's sake, can't you get that through your pretty head!" Stanley said urgently, stopping on the path and pulling her to him, his face set and serious. "I'm talking about *us*, even if I got to look up to you to say it. Chuck all this crap, Anita, and come with me."

"Us—?" Anita couldn't quite sink this one in. She thought she must be hearing things. No one in a very long time had given her bait like this, long before Bimini Springs, centuries ago.

"That's right—you and me. The two of us together, a pair."

Anita was moved. "You're kidding, Stanley."

"Why the hell should I be kidding you?" Stanley demanded, almost angrily. "Maybe I'm such a little punk I'm not your type, huh?"

Anita put her arm around his shoulders. "No," she protested, "that isn't it. I'm just—not for you. . . ."

"I'll decide that," Stanley told her. "Look, I know the fears you got and how cagey you are, how unsure of yourself. I see all the false starts and fearful steps you take. I have since the moment you walked into my room wanting protection that night and took the *Journals*. . . . Now, here's my proposition with the built-in loophole. I'm a lonely guy, my kids are both married and out of my life. I want that job in Los Angeles, but I'm not going out there alone, I couldn't stand it. You come along with me, quit this goddam rat race and come along, and we'll do the thing like a regular agreement you can break any time. I mean it! You'll get your round-trip fare paid in advance, ticket in your hand, and three months' salary, just what you gross here. Consider yourself my housekeeper or whatever fancy name you want to give it. You don't have to quit outright here—take a leave of absence if you feel more secure that way. You don't have to burn any more bridges, Anita, and while you're out on the Coast, you can look around and see if any of the old ones might still be standing. Maybe you didn't destroy them all. Who knows, you might even find out you've been chasing yourself around in circles and you're not afraid of anything after all."

Anita couldn't trust herself to speak, knowing she would break up. All she could mutter was "Oh, Stan—!" and embrace him with mute enthusiasm, finding him suddenly a person to whom she could react with open tenderness because he had made it possible. . . .

Stanley wasn't the sole audience to Anita's grateful excitement. Harry Maple stood in the shadow of the reservoir pumphouse and watched the two of them, smiling to himself. Now he had just the weapon he needed to fire Anita, for she was in the wrong place at the wrong time with the wrong man. Company rules, his rules, his company. . . .

A few minutes later Harry was with Marge in their apartment office conferring with José Ortega, who had called and requested the appointment.

Ortega was pointing to the documents he'd spread out on Harry's office desk top.

"So you see, Mr. Maple, you don't have a leg to stand on or a window to throw it out of. Read the fine print carefully in these photostats. They're the original leaseholds, the same form as the one you retain for Devil Cay."

The Maples were both very frightened; Harry's reaction was a show of truculence.

"You got one helluva nerve coming down to Bimini Springs and posing as a bona-fide guest and then springing this crap on us!" Harry burst out with no attempt at tact.

Ortega smiled, unruffled; he was used to irate people as

an expert appraiser and investigator. Part of his job was to act as buffer between a client and difficult parties, not always the pleasantest of duties. This time, however, Thompson was paying extremely well for his services, and it wasn't too unpleasant to tell the Maples that their days of greed were coming to an end.

"I *am* a bona-fide guest, Mr. Maple," Ortega reminded Harry. "I made a legitimate reservation, and I'm enjoying the place. . . ." He smiled sleepily. "Nice change of tempo from the States."

"You mean Thompson can actually force us to pay out all that money just to keep what's already ours?" demanded Marge. "Ira Benton rightfully owned this property and deeded it legally to us, Mr. Ortega, and it's ours. How can you or anyone else take it away, I'd like to know?"

"No one's taking it away from you, Mr. Maple. It's a question of what you'll have to pay on the re-evaluated price. This isn't happening just in the Bahamas; it's all through the West Indies, too. And even if you were able to stop our pressing action against re-evaluation of the leasehold, we have another foolproof approach."

"What kind of approach?" Harry asked suspiciously. "Maybe you're afraid to tell us. We might beat you at your own game."

"I'm sure Mr. Thompson wouldn't mind if I explained it," said Ortega. "You see, Ira Benton and several other investors bought their original island leaseholds through a fictitious corporation specifically set up to deal with such transactions. The corporation never physically existed as a legitimate business enterprise."

"So, what's that got to do with us?" Marge said.

"There's an amendment to the colonial charter that definitely provides against fictitious corporations set up to grab land and hold it for continuous private speculation, which is exactly what Sunset Enterprises is, the corporation that got Devil Cay and quite a few other holdings. Ira Benton and the others involved in that initial fraud are all deceased, fortunately for them, so they can't be prosecuted. But as heirs you can be. So, if you won't agree to surrendering the property for the sum Mr. Thompson will eventually offer you, we can force your hand this way. That's it, folks. You don't have any choice."

"Thompson's a rotten bastard," Harry declared. "How'd he get all this information?"

"Part of it came from Crown Advocates, but the final putting together was the work of several experts."

"A guy named Francovich?" said Harry.

"Ah, so you know Mr. Thompson's legal aide?"
"Sort of in a way we do," Marge said.
"So we're going to get screwed out of Bimini after all the time and effort we put into making it a real good-paying proposition. What a crummy deal!"
"Everything's lost," said Marge dispiritedly. "All our hard work."
"No, not lost," Ortega pointed out. "Mr. Thompson isn't going to gouge you."
"You mean he's not the crook everybody says he is?" Harry demanded. "Tell me more. . . ."
"He's a businessman," Ortega replied without blinking an eye. "He's ethical."
"Same goddam animal," Harry snorted. "Well, what's the offer? You're authorized to give us a hint, aren't you?"
José Ortega was allowed to divulge the exchange price if and as he saw fit, but in this case he couldn't resist playing hard to get. The Maples were a pretty crude pair; they obviously objected to the color of his skin, he could sense it in their manner; they resented his presence on *their* island. In fact, he was sure that if they'd known of his Mexican-Indian heritage before he arrived, he'd have been courteously though firmly refused a reservation.
"You'll be generously compensated for your fine development of the plant," he told them. "You see, Mr. Thompson has a very special interest in Devil Cay. He ultimately intends to make it the site of his Caribbean headquarters."
"It's in the Atlantic Ocean," said Marge with intended sarcasm. "Don't call it the Caribbean. We're not even close to the Gulf of Mexico, either."
"I know, I've seen it on the map," Ortega informed her. "Being almost in the exact geographical center of the one hundred thousand square miles that comprise the Bahamas, it's within easy air access of the entire area. Mr. Thompson plans to reinforce the airstrip so that STOL jets can fly in—specifically his new air fleet, probably Lear Jets and something slightly larger. There'll be new buildings, too."
"We're not interested in what Thompson wants to do with Bimini Springs," said Harry dryly. "Get to the point, Ortega, quit stalling. . . ." With no need now for deference, Harry had dropped all pretense of possessing any. "Give us the bad news."
"Well, Mr. Thompson's prepared to offer you $500,000 cash for your leasehold and developments," said Ortega. "This settlement is net, of course, and absolutely clear.

He'll arrange for a Swiss-numbered account if you wish the sum deposited abroad, or if you'd prefer to slot it into a tax-sheltered oil exploration, he owns Intercontinental Petroleum Development. And they have the hottest record of live wells in the Middle East right now. . . ."

"No thank you!" Marge said. "We don't speculate."

"Or if you simply want to retain the money right here in the Bahamas—live in Nassau, for example—that, too, can be arranged. As you probably know, one of the advantages of these islands is the absence of a personal income tax and why so many businesses, including Mr. Thompson's diversified interests, are coming down here. The tax structure offers great benefits—no personal income or business bites, no inheritance or capital gains taxes, along with exemptions of real property, sales or dividend assessment of levies. . . ."

"We know all that," snapped Harry. "Why the hell do you think we came down here in the first place?"

Ortega thought he could parry that question nicely by inferring that if Harry knew so much, why hadn't he looked very carefully into the legal loopholes on leaseholds, fraudulent corporations, et cetera, a long time ago? But he continued without acknowledging Harry's remark: "This tax shelter has proven a powerfully attractive magnet for dollars, rupees, pesos, Tughriks, lira, rials, and pounds—to name a few of the currencies prevalently at work in the Bahamas. What I'm saying is, you could find another business potential somewhere else in the chain if you wanted to, something with a fresh challenge. Or simply lie back anywhere and enjoy yourselves. A half a million dollars goes a long way when you're flat on your back. . . ."

"There was nothing wrong with this island until Thompson decided he wanted it," Marge said vehemently. "Or *somebody* in his organization."

"Our asking price is a million net," said Harry. "And I feel like asking for it in one-dollar bills."

"I'll be glad to convey that information to Mr. Thompson," said Ortega, "but I can assure you here and now that he absolutely won't budge from his original offer. That's a computerized estimate, and for Mr. Thompson the computer's the word of God."

"Jesus Christ!" Harry grouched, certain that Ortega wasn't bluffing. Well anyway, with half a million they could go anywhere, as Ortega said, and live comfortably for the rest of their lives. Some place where there'd be plenty of sex for both of them without their having to rub elbows too often in a conjugal bed. Maybe Mexico—his and hers. Poor countries were the best; everybody poor did it for dollars. . . . Or get a dumb Mexican partner and start a posh lodge on one of the newly fashionable islands like Cozumel off the Yucatan coast. Guatemala was ideal but unstable; Costa Rica was maybe better but undeveloped. . . .

Ortega continued patiently, "I recommend that you give me your affirmative before I leave Bimini Springs tomorrow. Mr. Thompson's offer is very generous. Even if you could pay the re-evaluation price of the leasehold, you'd still only have title to the property for a short time due to that fraudulent corporation factor. Devil Cay's eventual loss would still be hanging over you. Of course, the fraudulent corporation claim will take time to work out, but Mr. Thompson has lots of time," Ortega reminded them, "and all the money in the world to help him prove his point."

"I hope you'll have the decency to get on that Bahama Airways plane tomorrow without wearing that smug smile," said Harry. "We're plenty burned up about the whole matter."

"Does that mean you'll agree to Mr. Thompson's offer?" asked Ortega.

Harry looked at Marge; Marge looked at Harry.

"Probably," Harry replied evasively. "We'll go over all the documents tonight. If they look O.K., then we'll sign the tentative agreement so you can take it with you tomorrow."

"Fine! I suspect Thompson will want you out of here by the end of the winter season, at the time the transaction's legally approved and processed. But in the interim he'll want you to remain on as managers until he takes over."

"He's *so* considerate," said Marge. "We've every intention of staying on as long as we can."

"Agreed," said Harry.

"Wonderful," said Ortega. "Everything's going to be just great. . . ."

He reached into his open briefcase that lay on Harry's desk in front of them, brought out a small Sony TC-40 cassette tape recorder, and clicked off the recording head.

Harry smiled sourly out of respect for Ortega's shrewd maneuver: a live, taped record of their meeting. "Thompson thinks of everything, doesn't he?" Harry observed. "Reaches right out and grabs you by the balls."

"Well, he tries to, Mr. Maple," Ortega replied, and snapped shut his briefcase. "And now, folks, I'll be running along. A pleasant good evening to both of you, and a happy, happy future. . . ."

"Now," said Harry when Ortega had closed the door behind him, "there's a real brown gold-plated motherfucker!"

"Yes," Marge replied, white with fury, "and you certainly proved what a man you are, didn't you? Meek as a bowl of Jell-O, that's what you were. 'Agreed, agreed,' you said! I'm beginning to wonder about you, Harry Maple. You used to have some get-up-and-go, some guts and balls; I could depend on you."

"But for God's sake, Marge, we're dealing with Terence P. Thompson, not just anybody."

"Terence P. Asshole, as far as I'm concerned! We're dealing with ourselves," Marge said in a loud voice, "and it's about time I took *charge* of the situation and taught you a *lesson* tonight!"

Marge had employed the operative words. Harry's normal composure began to melt, slowly trickle away. He stood up with a gleeful bounce and started shucking his clothes. Marge eased away, a Mona Lisa smile on her face, toward the sliding doors of the wall closet. She threw them back in one quick dramatic gesture and reached for the top shelf with one hand while unzipping her sheath dress with the other. In a trice she was standing, all five feet two of her, in nothing at all, and strapping the giant, well-lubricated, rosy, flesh-colored dildo around her hips, cinching the belt tight across her auburn crotch and over her dimpled nates.

"Motherfucker indeed," she rasped, rolling her eyes, reaching to another section of the shelf for the long black snake-whip with the silver tips. "I'll motherfuck you, you poor white-trashin' motherfucker! We gonna have us a little whip-up!" As she strode toward him, brandishing the whip, dildo swinging, Harry leaped nimbly onto the huge bed, whining and groveling on all fours.

"Beg, you bitch dawg!" Marge commanded. "Beg for your meat and pleasure!" she cried, and laid a smart crack of the whip across Harry's bare bronzed buttocks, leaving a thin, red-streaked souvenir on his hide.

"Arf, arf!" Harry barked, and wiggled his behind for more.

Marge laid another lash across him, marking his back a second time, but lightly, and he howled like a starving jackal.

"That's better," she crooned. "Now jump down like a good bitch and let Daddy have some fun. . . ."

Obediently, Harry bounded from the bed to the floor, describing a gymnastic parabola of considerable virtuosity, sidled up to Marge, and licked her feet enthusiastically.

"What's the best kind of time, you bitch?" she demanded hoarsely, cracking the whip in the air above his head but leaving him unscathed.

"Eastern Standard Time," growled Harry, "arf, arf!'

"No, you bitch, the *best* kind of time, I said!" and she cracked the whip again, this time perilously close to his left ear. "Tell Daddy!"

"Pacific Coast Time—?" Harry snarled.

Marge cracked the whip once more, the silver needle-sharp points flicking his buttocks, and shook the helmeted dildo at him.

"Tell me what's the *best* time in the world!" she yelled at him, and leaped on the horizontal plane of his back, tossed her whip aside, and slapped the dildo hard against his spinal column.

On cue, Harry raised up on his knees so that Marge slid along his back as far as the shelf of his jutting buttocks where she perched triumphantly, locked her heels around his waist, and hung on.

"Rahhhhhhkeee Mountain Time!" Harry howled in lubricious joy, bouncing Marge up and down.

"Mountin' time is *right*!" cried Marge, and threw her entire weight forward so that Harry collapsed full-length flat on the floor, toes and fingernails clawing the carpet. Then, kneeling above him, Marge clutched the enormous weapon of her slippery dildo in both hands and aimed deftly for the target.

"Ready or not!" she screamed hoarsely, "here I come! Daddy's on the way!"

Kill Howard knew a graveyard feeling when he got one; all day long the wings of the blackbird had been whirring just above his head.

Getting busted for bush on this scrawny white-folks island wouldn't help his clean record any, and although there wasn't a scrap of tangible evidence he could find to indicate that he was in any possible danger of a bust, his flesh had been crawling with a definitely fuzzy hairiness.

Weird, it was wide open in Nam, anything went; and yet the ex-GIs he knew in the U.S. were always rapping about how great it would be to get back to "the world" again! You could have a Jane in your hand in Nam and a rank walks in and only glares at you. Nothing's said, so you take a deep drag, smile and hold it, the rank turns heel and stomps out. So, what's he gonna do to you? Bust you and the whole goddam army? Yeah, almost too easy over there; he was lucky he never got truly into the wrong line. There were long grim queues of ground-pounders getting behind a lot of wrong scenes. Right on Soul Alley you could buy grass, smack, jam, hash, any kind of grease you wanted. The officers all knew it and overlooked it. They drank, they had their official poison. But all the grunts popped something more imaginative; everybody was behind something. Only thing they didn't have in Nam and had to get from "the world" was LSD, which a buddy's wife sent over on paper strips between the pages of a paperback. Man, that was a mellow party, Kill recalled. Everybody *went*. . . .

But this funny feeling about a bust. . . . There was this new guest, José Ortega, a chicano—sleek, *gordo* type. And not content with settling in right away, resting up for his full course of treatment beginning tomorrow, this cat starts tracking around the island, even sniffing out the reservoir, scribbling away in a little black book, staring at cards in his wallet.

Well shit, he and Linc had a fine, safe stash no narc would ever find. The whole place was getting too eerie, Kill decided, too many creeps and no action. Or a little maybe, when Joan was in the mood, which reminded him she was late tonight. Supposed to drop by after that session with her girls. But, like all pussycats these days, restless, bugged on subjects, impossible to please, put upon. You even pat them anywhere you're patronizing them.

But he really ought to change his personal stash to outside. So where did you put the better part of two keys of mighty high bush were nobody finds it and where it still won't either get rained on or picked apart by inquisitive seagulls? He couldn't get to their big lockup conveniently, not now with all the feet around. He knew what he'd like to do—plant it on the Maples and then make an anonymous phone call to the chicano. *If* he was a snoop. . . .

Door. . . . He dropped the paperback he was reading, shut off the *Pearl* album, and went to answer the knock, admitting Joan in a state of nervous agitation.

"Kill," she said without preamble, "I'm worried," and almost pushed him aside in her singleminded haste to get inside and shut the door.

"Cool it, woman, what's wrong?"

"Snoopers," she hissed. "I swear the whole place's goin' mad, crawlin' with 'em."

"My thought, too. I'm lookin' for a new stash. . . ."

"Kill Howard, you ain't going wanderin' around Bimini with any armful of grass," Joan told him firmly. "So come on now, get it all together and let me have it. Right now, you hear?"

Kill sighed. "Ah, come on, baby. Be reasonable. Ain't nobody gonna bust me this next minute. I got two joints all laid out, thinkin' we gonna toke up and fly away together—"

"No time for that," Joan said sharply. "Look, don't play amorous stud with me, boy. . . ." When Joan grew adamant, her dark eyes glittered; she wasn't playing now. "I mean what I say. Get it out and pack it up and give it to me. . . . I'm waitin', Kill. . . ."

Impossible to get around her. Kill opened his closet door, took down his suitcase, and unlocked and opened it. The key-bricks were carefully wrapped in plastic and firmly tied; he lifted them out, packed them slowly into a cardboard carton.

"Hurry up!" Joan ordered.

"Hey, woman, cool it. I jam along at a real easy pace. I don't worry my chewin' bones the way you do."

Joan grunted. "That'll do, get on with it. Don't you go callin' me no dog bitch. Hand me that stuff, hurry up, man!"

Kill completed the packaging at his own tempo, sealed the carton shut with masking tape. "There," he said at last, "O.K., it's all yours. For the time bein', anyway. I want it back. Hey, you grinnin' like you know somethin' I oughtta be told."

"Well, maybe. I was in this vacant suite, and somebody walked by, a couple. Might not have heard it right, but I think I did. He said to her they's gonna be some conscientious lookin' round in the mornin', and that's all you gotta know for now. Come on, hand me that package. . . ."

"Here." He held it out, let her lift it from his hands. "Where you goin' with it?"

"I ain't tellin' you, Kill. No need for you to know. You ain't got good sense, anyway; you'd go checkin' it out. Now, let me out the door—"

"Hey, woman, I got these two fat stick-joints here—"

"Now's no time for laughin' tobacco. . . ."

Kill tried to kiss her, but she jammed the carton against his chest and pushed him away. "Plenty of time for that foolishness later on," she said.

His hand was on the door. "Shit, guess I'll just have to get high by myself. . . ."

Joan chuckled. "That the *only* way you know how to amuse yourself when you alone?"

He ignored that one and opened the door. "Don't take no chances, sugar. . . ."

Joan shot him a ferocious moue, but her eyes were warm, almost gentle. "Fine piece of caution, comin' from you!" she snapped, and shot out into the night.

Kill stood a moment in the doorway and watched her swing her neat, high buttocks along the terrace, then disappear all too quickly around the corner of the building.

He closed the door, thinking that she knew a lot more than she was ready to tell him and was up to something vengeful; he dug that special look of hers. But what did she know and where would she be going at this hour? Well, maybe she was right; maybe he shouldn't know. A little ignorance never hurt anybody. And trust was a kind of love; he bought hers. For no matter how big her mouth was when she got on his back, her instincts were right, she wouldn't undo him.

He turned the *Pearl* album back on and settled down to enjoy the music and toke up. . . .

A few minutes later there was a knock on Kill's door, a soft, tentative one; he scarcely heard it above the air conditioner and the Boz Scaggs album, but he froze. It certainly wasn't Joan's knock.

Shit, he thought, and went warily to the closed Venetian blinds to check through the slats. Stoned and comfortable, this was no time for brother visits, and if it was anyone else, he could still get rid of that last joint in the toilet. He hoped it was Joan and that she'd changed her mind.

But Tom Street was standing in front of his door; he moved to open it. God, he'd forgotten all about Tom coming over to pick up a lid. Now he didn't have anything for him.

"Hey, man, come on in."

"I—I can't stay," said Tom. "I just dropped by to—"

"Why not, man?" Kill waved Tom into a chair. "You got somethin' more important to do around here?"

Tom smiled and shook his head. "No, not really—" What was more important than getting Kill's good grass and digging a few moments with such a sensationally packaged stud for the last time, one who didn't even know how he shook people up by just moving around?

"Here—" Kill handed Tom the joint. "Toke up, man. Heavy scene around here right now, or so I'm told. I'm coolin' it. You're smokin' all I got for the time bein'."

"What do you mean?"

"Narcs," Kill explained. "But my bush is all stashed in the least likely place anybody would look for it on Devil Cay. I *hope,* I keep tellin' myself. . . ." That is, *if* Joan knew what she was doing, and she probably did, he thought.

"Narcotics agents at Bimini?" Tom exclaimed, aghast. "My God!" Maybe it was just as well he would be leaving.

"What you got to worry about so long as you don't go passing out any hard drugs. . . . Light up, man!"

Tom promptly did as he was told. With grass he never needed a second bidding, for it usually calmed the jump in his guts, made everything nice and dreamy. Grass was never a social party thing for Tom, as it was for many people. He used it for solitary release, for watching the action on closed-circuit TV, or simply for dreaming of making it with guys like Kilroy Howard in a fantasy of masturbation. What he had to settle for when the pressures got too deep even for fantasy was someone like Loyal, the wall-eyed waiter.

"Jesus," Tom said through his first toke, "it's as good as ever."

"It's always good with my brand. Hey, Tom, man, what do you do with all your long, lonely nights? You fuck with any of the guests? Level with me. . . ."

"Never," Tom said truthfully. "Never have, never will."

"Yeah, well, I never heard nothin' about you goin' anywhere to guest rooms and makin' time for yourself."

"I—read a lot," Tom hedged. What would Kill actually think of him if he knew what went on in the office late at night? "I really like books; they're my big escape."

"Book's're a cop-out, man. They're not livin'."

"For me they are," Tom replied. "Sometimes they're more real than people, the characters come alive."

Lying back on his bed, ankles crossed, hands beneath his head, Kill was pondering the possibilities of a situation that seemed almost too good to be true, invited action. Tom had only been high with him once before—that first time he'd turned Tom on gratis, then waited for Tom to ask for some bush before he laid a few free joints on him. Kill always approached dealing very gradually with new customers; you couldn't know at first what lay behind their interests, you took their measure. He'd determined that Tom was safe enough; he was also sure he knew what Tom really wanted. Joan had said no ass tonight, definitely no. But would Tom Street? Kill knew all about Loyal and the furtive, late-night meetings in Tom's room. Loyal blabbed to all the black males while Tom thought he was so cool. A secret knock at Tom's door, lights off, door opens, creep in, get your jollies, creep out. All over in five quick minutes, man, a real capsule sex drama, wow! Kill had always wondered how good Tom was at it. Go easy, try. . . .

"Ever think about other kinds of kicks here at Bimini?" Kill asked, and slowly, meaningfully, stroked the bulge at his crotch.

Tom pretended not to notice the gesture and smoked away voraciously at the joint to cover his interest. Finally he said, "Hey, this is really great stuff. It seems different from the last batch. The buzz isn't the same. . . ."

"Identical, Tom. Hey, come on, man, open up. I know all about your scene."

"What—scene?" For a second Tom looked genuinely alarmed. Had Kill been pussyfooting around the pharmacy late at night? God, he hoped not! He thought he'd covered up that operation pretty cleverly. And the other, the thing with Loyal?

"Your *scene,* babe," Kill said quietly. "Your gay scene. . . ."

Tom pulled another toke from the diminished joint and smiled, but his heart wasn't behind it, Kill observed. "Gay isn't my scene," he said almost inaudibly. "You got me wrong. . . ."

"I'd like to think I got you right, Tom. . . ." Kill stroked his crotch again, then slowly unzipped his fly. He wore no shorts, so his hand met no resistance as he reached inside his lightweight wash-wears and clutched himself, now firmly erect, huge, horny, ready.

He grinned at Tom. "Man, that light's too bright over there on the table. Shut it off, huh?"

Tom dragged furiously on the remainder of the joint, laid it with elaborate care on the rim of an ashtray, then got up and shut off the table lamp, plunging the room into a soft rosy glow from the baseboard nightlight.

Kill left his hand where it was but started moving it slowly up and down. "Hey, Tom, man, sit over here. By me on the bed. . . ."

As Tom came to him, the Scaggs album flicked off. Only the droning of the air conditioner lent rhythm to the room now.

Tom perched on the bed close to Kill, very nervous, a tight smile on his face, the expression a conflicting blend of lust and reluctance, Kill noted. This was almost as good as making it with a bashful chick, thought Kill, and in some ways even better because this cat was so pitifully hung on his phony morality that Kill received an enormous charge of control, of power, which he liked.

Kill pulled his hand from inside his wash-wears. "It's all yours, guy," he whispered, and meant it, and when Tom hesitated, sweat glistening on his forehead, he took Tom's trembling hand and stuck it inside his fly, clamping Tom's fingers tightly around his hard flesh.

"I don't think I should," Tom began, but when Kill arched his back, slipped his pants to his knees, Tom's resistance crumbled. And what the hell difference did it make now? he thought. Better take what's offered.

He slid quickly to the floor and knelt at the side of Kill's bed in an attitude of fervent prayer and, describing slow, rhythmic arabesques with his skillful mouth and practiced tongue, sent Kill steadily up that long undulating incline toward a pounding explosive climax. . . .

On her snoopy late-night rounds, Eva Cassel just happened to be passing the supervisory men's quarters at the moment that Tom Street knelt beside Kill Howard's bed. When Kill had lowered the horizontal slats of his Venetian blinds earlier in the evening, he had failed to note that the bottom slat was caught in the vertical drapery panel's hem, thus hitching it up to reveal a narrow strip of clear window. A strip so narrow that he'd missed it, but enough to give a voyeur a perfect picture of what was going on inside.

Curious as always, Eva saw the strip as she passed, glanced quickly around her to be sure she wasn't being watched, then crouched down and glued her eyes to the window. As her vision adjusted to the dimness within she saw the most provocative scene she'd witnessed in years. There was her beloved Tom Street blatantly performing fellatio on Kill Howard. God, what a juicy item! She could hardly contain her wildly beating heart, her excitement was so great. But as she watched, the scene was suddenly over and Tom had risen to his feet.

Eva ducked away from the window and walked to Kill's door. She reached out boldly and touched the doorknob with her fingers, thinking impulsively that she would knock and surprise them. But as soon as she touched the doorknob she realized that this was crazy; she'd be much wiser to use this knowledge at some later time when it would really pay off. Meanwhile, the only sensible thing to do was leave the area before somebody saw her. So she turned away from the door and walked rapidly down the terrace.

Just as Eva paused with her hand tentatively on Kill's doorknob, Joan walked around the corner of the building on her way back from the women's quarters, saw Eva at Kill's door, and instantly assumed from Eva's smug, victorious smile that she was just leaving Kill's place.

Joan's first impulse was to kill Eva, but the unexpected intensity of her blind anger so overwhelmed her that it froze her in her tracks. All she could do was stand there helpless and watch Eva hurry off in the opposite direction as she shook her fist at Eva and spat out guttural imprecations.

"Dirty, rotten whore-bitch! White slut, she-devil monster!"

It was full half a minute before she caught her breath and realized that she felt no hatred whatsoever for Kill Howard, only for Eva Cassel. Toward Kill she felt a warm protectiveness that was almost motherly, when for all practical purposes she ought to hate him, too. This was an attitude she didn't even want to analyze right now; later would do. But that vicious white whore of an Eva Cassel was doomed, she told herself gravely as she turned back toward her room, not wanting to see Kill now while she was so charged up. Cassel's time was up, and Joan smiled with relish at the thought of the come-uppance that would be meted out to that decadent, vile, conniving white-trash witch. And not a moment too soon. . . .

When it was all over and Tom moved away, using his handkerchief, Kill lay quietly for a minute, trying to catch his breath. Jesus, the cat was sensational!

"Was I—any good?" Tom faltered at last, sitting on the floor, all huddled over, his head downward, shamed, as if he were afraid to look Kill in the eyes, to admit what had actually happened. "I—I don't do this—sort of thing very often. Only once or twice. Not for years, since I was a kid. . . ."

The blatant sad lie, the spoiling of a pleasant scene, suddenly hit Kill as ridiculous, ludicrous.

"Oh man," he chuckled, "you're so far out you'll never get back! I *know* what you do, babe, and what you are. Why try to kid me? Even worse to fool yourself. Why not play it cool and say you loved it? *I* loved it, man, why can't you? There's no labels on anything, man, not anymore." And he continued to chuckle softly to himself, not bothering to reach for the clean towel on the bedside chair or pull up his pants.

Tom sprang to his feet and said abruptly, "I'm going. I'm not going to stick around here and be insulted!"

Kill rolled over lazily on one elbow and stared at Tom, pity in his eyes. "Your poor fucked-up mother, you! You can't even give a little head without playin' a funeral march for yourself. I feel sorry for you, man, I really do. . . ."

"If you ever tell anybody what happened—" Tom started in a threatening voice, and Kill sat up, angry.

"Get out, you little jerk! And don't come back!"

"I'm not about to! And you just remember—" Tom's face was contorted, white; he was actually trembling.

"You're way outta shape, man. Try and straighten up before it's too late. Everybody knows about you. You ain't wearin' no camouflage people can't see right through. Cool it, man, for Chris' sake. Nobody's after your thin white hide. Get some fun outta life—first-hand, man! That's what pleasure's all about. . . ."

But Tom was gone before Kill finished, slamming the door after him. Only that partly smoked joint, now a cold, dead roach on the ashtray rim, testified to his visit.

Kill got up and washed himself at the sink, immeasurably sad and depressed. How bad it was to be so limited, tied only to *that,* he thought, but how truly tragic not even to be able to enjoy even that much openly, honestly, to be released by it when it did happen, not bugged. He was sorry now that he'd made the scene possible, but even sorrier for poor Tom.

Part
❁ SIX ❁

Kevin Mack was visiting Cindy Brown in her room on his daily rounds. Cindy was making good progress in her no-calorie fast; no bad effects, and she'd lost almost twenty pounds; the change was miraculous. This particular day she'd taken special pains with her appearance, fitting herself carefully into a sheer summery magenta dress that contrasted nicely with her light blue eyes and chestnut hair; she'd bought the dress several sizes too small in order to give her the incentive to lose weight at Bimini.

Kevin had just taken her pulse, finding he was more attracted to her than he cared to admit to himself, an attraction Cindy sensed from his reticent though lingering devotion to ritual. Whatever commitment he had to Ruth Severn, Cindy was determined to move in, tingling with an unfamiliar drive she couldn't quite define—for Kevin was the most conventional man she'd ever liked, certainly as far removed from Poppy as possible. The attraction was that Kevin augured a predictable, rewarding future, nothing exciting nor particularly colorful—she'd had all that—but safe and normal.

"You're doing beautifully, Cindy," Kevin said. "We'll terminate the no-calorie fasting tomorrow and start you in on a limited diet. I can't get over your progress—it's remarkable!"

"A little make-up and a new dress helps," Cindy said modestly.

"It's more than superficial. You really look very much like your photograph now." He said this carefully; she knew he was still smarting over the previous slip. "Amazing. I see lots of changes both ways in this business, Cindy, but you're phenomenal."

This was the first time he'd used her given name with ease, Cindy noted. Maybe this was progress, but where would it lead? What did she want? She wished she knew.

"It's important to me, Kevin," she replied. "Like putting myself in order, in good shape to do battle. Decisions. You know. . . ."

"Yes, well, you haven't said very much about yourself."

"I'm just an ordinary person."

"Your medical history says you were born in California, and you're a secretary. But I'd say you haven't worked very long. There's an aura of money in your background; I can feel it."

Was he probing? What was he after? she thought. "Well, a little, there's some money in the family. My problem is that I've never really known what I wanted from life. When I get what I think I want, sometimes I don't want it anymore."

"That's simple human nature. What will you do when you leave here?"

"I don't know," she said honestly, sensing that the conversation was getting out of hand. "What've you got in mind when you finish your contract here? I can't imagine you'll just stay on indefinitely at Bimini."

"No, I intend to finish my advanced studies. I'd planned originally to teach. At least, that's what I hoped to do before I went to Vietnam."

"What changed your mind?"

"The crying need for practitioners in my field. It's cosmetic surgery, restorative work."

"Oh? I had no idea."

"Most people who pass through here think of me as just a routine-type G.P., nothing more. Well, I can do that, too, but working in military field hospitals gave me a more specific outlook. I thought I'd return and acquire the skills I needed, then concentrate on teaching advanced surgical techniques to eager young interns. Ruth got me located here, but the more I began thinking about teaching, the more it seemed like a cop-out."

"Why?"

"I know that's not where the real need is. I have to help maimed and disfigured veterans to return to the world of the living. The casualty list's appalling, Cindy. Thousands are literally crippled, forgotten men. They're back home and hoping to receive specialized long-term treatment that just simply isn't available at present through the government hospitals. Not even private institutions that have the money and the facilities can handle them properly. There aren't nearly enough qualified personnel. It's pitiful. . . ."

Kevin broke off, in moody discomfort, preoccupied.

"I can understand your feelings," Cindy said gently.

"No, I don't think you or anybody can, not unless you've seen what I've seen. I don't mean to sound pretentious, like some dedicated medico on a TV series, but somebody's got to do something. This is every bit as big a need as the returning vets' drug problem, and nobody seems to want to do much besides give it a little lip service."

"And you think you can make a dent in the problem? Isn't that like trying to move mountains?"

Kevin looked at her without really seeing her, seeing beyond her, and said with gravity, "Very few doctors have had the kind of exposure I had in Vietnam. It hooked me. My time here's only interim until I've saved enough to do my studies without financial worry, to get enough together to do what really counts for me in this world. So you see, a fat farm's not exactly my life's work. . . ."

Cindy did see; she saw several possibilities in a rush of empathic emotion toward him. "I'm very impressed," she declared. "What about scholarships? Wouldn't they eliminate this kind of dismal drudgery?"

Kevin shook his head. "Grants are a dime a dozen for just about everything in medicine except my field. Anyway, scholarships don't offer adequate enough funds to attend school without working, and I can't see diluting my interests. I'd rather spend two years here, saving every cent I can; it's my only alternative. . . . This is one of the reasons I'm not too involved—with anybody."

"What about private patrons?" Cindy pursued.

"Well, there are two kinds: Old ladies who expect you to jump through their gilded social hoops, or large, affluent private clinics that bind you to servitude while telling you how promising you are, and eventually you wake up to find out you're an indentured servant and time's passing. I don't need either kind of phony philanthropy. You'd think with all the wealth in this country somebody would have the sensitivity and foresight to try to put back together the broken men they laid on the line. Forgive me if I'm bitter. It all seems so logical to me, and yet nobody else sees it like this. . . ."

"I do," Cindy heard herself saying. "What about getting married and letting your wife work while you study?"

A loaded question, Kevin knew, without being able to

determine what was in Cindy's mind. All kinds of women had put various questions to him since he'd been at Bimini Springs, but this Cindy Brown, whoever and whatever she was, appeared to be about the most sincere of the lot. Perhaps he should explain that while Ruth Severn was one of the world's finest people—practical, sincere, wise—she was really a rather brisk, unemotional creature who didn't need him at all, being quite self-sufficient. And that Ruth had suggested the wife-support bit, too, at one time.

"Well," he replied carefully, "*if* I did have somebody in mind, and *if* I thought I could convince her to live with me and my monomania, I might take the chance. I've never known this kind of arrangement to work out too well. Couples doing this always seem to split up later on. And besides, who's going to understand a surgeon's total dedication to this kind of work?"

"I would," Cindy said, and added impulsively, "Have you thought about me in this context?"

Kevin took her hand and smiled, not too surprised at her statement. "I've thought about you in several situations, to be perfectly honest," he told her. "I'm human, I look around and speculate occasionally. In the last few days I've thought a lot about you. I don't know how things would work out, I don't know you that well, but sure, I've thought about it."

"What if I could help you financially and make it so you wouldn't ever have to worry about money again?"

Kevin studied her soberly. "Who are you, Cindy? You mean just like that you could take care of everything?"

"Yes, I can."

"Well, I don't know. It's too cut and dried. You see, part of the urge to do what I want to do is the challenge. I've explained that. Money isn't the prime consideration."

"I understand that, but I've got more money than I'll ever be able to spend in one lifetime, Kevin. My grandmother left me a lot. My mother's well off in her own right, too. In fact, the whole family's always been rather lousy with it, and it hasn't been put to very good use. These days it's got to be."

"So that's it! You're rich, you follow whims."

"No!" Cindy countered sharply. "That's not it at all." But of course it was, in a way. A rich, fat, self-indulgent spoiled brat who'd almost always had her own way except where her mother had dominated, who'd done nothing with her life and had never faced up to the essential challenges. And right now she was running away from the greatest of them. "I don't advertise the money," she said. "I pretend I don't have much. If you're an on-and-off fattie and show money, people tend to use you. I'm telling you this because I really want to help, Kevin. I believe in you."

"Money," mused Kevin. "No, I couldn't accept support from you or anybody, Cindy. I'm too independent, it wouldn't work."

"But you said if a working wife understood the risks involved and was willing to gamble on a long-term partnership, if she could put up with you—"

"Did I say that?"

"You certainly did! What's the difference if she already has money and doesn't have to work? It's still only a commodity; it ought to be used right. You should be the first to agree with that."

"My situation's different."

"How? Rich girl marries poor but ambitious young surgeon and makes it possible for him to become a boon to mankind. I see nothing complicated or illogical about that."

Kevin was amused at her audacity; he would never have pegged her this aggressive. Or maybe she was playing a game and was only serious about the victory?

"There's just one thing," he said tentatively.

"Yes?"

"You're not allowing me to work out the relationship proposition."

"You mean the formal part? Well, we can play house when the time comes. Meanwhile, how long do you think you'll have to stay on at Bimini Springs?"

"I've some months to complete my contract. I definitely want a clean record here. Meanwhile there's plenty of time to think things over."

"I don't think I need that much time," said Cindy. "I'll get a job in New York."

Kevin suddenly saw the entire conversation as absurd, completely out of hand. He hardly knew this girl, attractive as he found her, and here they were, comparative strangers, planning a world for two on her money! And then there was the obligation to Ruth, a sort of loyalty oath he'd involved himself in. How would he dissolve that commitment, even though Ruth had turned him off in one department? She was still very much his companion in another.

"This is unreal," he told Cindy, "improbable and crazy. People just don't get involved in this kind of dialogue."

Cindy knew a clue when she saw one, no matter how ill-defined it might be. She rose to her feet and put her arms around his neck, pressed herself against him. Kevin responded by encircling her firm waist with his arms, holding her close.

"Why don't we let nature make a few decisions?" Cindy suggested, kissing him on the neck, then on the lips, melting against him with a slight shudder, feeling his excitement against her belly.

Finally Kevin held her at arm's length; his face was flushed.

"Hey," he said thickly, "this is company time."

"So?"

"I've got rounds to make, and you've got to take your nap right now."

Cindy giggled. "Where's Miss Cassel? Isn't she around today?"

"No," he said. "I thought for once I wouldn't need her protection, but you see what happens when I ignore medical etiquette."

"Who gives a damn about medical etiquette?" Cindy said, wondering at her own temerity, still stirred by Kevin's embrace. "Etiquette's for people who can't make up their own private rules."

She drew his face toward hers. "A little honest affection's not going to ruin your reputation, Kevin. You don't relax enough, that's your trouble."

As she kissed him, she wondered what she'd do about her own reputation when she worked out a corporate existence with this serious young doctor and all hell broke loose. Well, for one thing her life would alter drastically; she wouldn't have much privacy for a while. But for the moment she wasn't even going to think about the trouble she'd spark when she began to press her decision. It was something she had to do.

"Now I've really got to go," Kevin said, breaking away, breathing with difficulty. "Forgive me, Cindy—"

"You're forgiven," said Cindy, "but you'll have to take a rain check."

"O.K.," he agreed, not doubting what she meant.

Tom Street was involved in the abhorrent job of cleaning out his office preparatory to vacating it permanently. Rallying from the interview with the Maples had cost him a sleepless night, and he knew what he had to do with the VTR—take it with him. To hell with leaving it for Harry

Maple so he could make blue movies! And even if Harry did keep his exposed video tapes, at least for the time being he would have no way to run them, not until he bought his own equipment.

What he really ought to do, Tom thought, was contact Anita Pomeroy and Dick Carter and hold a serious conference with them, get them to threaten Harry about the photo file. But knowing their mentality, he realized that they'd long ago prepared themselves for the shock of this kind of public exposure. It was a job risk they took, insurance that allowed them to accept their measly tips for tricking with patients. They'd be indifferent to any argument he might present.

Tom could congratulate himself on one thing, anyway; he was lucky to be leaving this sordid hole. The final humiliation was last night, that moment with Kill that he didn't even want to think about. What Kill had told him wasn't true; he wasn't that way, not really; it was simply a weakness he'd never been able to overcome and that occasionally took possession of him. Keeping on the move had helped, but the thing was still there. Maybe that was why he'd always preferred the overseas construction world since his introduction to it in the early 1950s. Its motley, disorganized atmosphere suited him perfectly, gave him a chameleon-like security. But here the place was too much like the States; he preferred more exotic climes. And Bimini would get along just fine without him. There was no substitute for the wild, sandy wastes of Saudi Arabia or the hashed-out weekends at Marrakesh. The Maples would find some other sucker glad enough to take his place. He could hardly wait to get on that afternoon plane. . . .

Eva Cassel poked her head around the partition and smiled at Tom as he sat in the midst of piled-up personal effects.

"Tom, heard the news?"

He thought she was making snide reference to his dismissal.

"Don't be so fucking bitchy!" he growled.

"Nothing bitchy about the good word, love," chirped Eva. "Maybe we're talking about different scoops—?"

"I'm talking about getting canned, fired, let out—that's what I'm talking about."

Eva was stunned. "Fired? My God, that *is* news!" Tom could see that she was neither too displeased nor too inclined toward sympathy. "Peeping Tom, is that it?" she pursued.

"You really are something special. You aren't even sorry."

Eva shrugged her shoulders. "Darling, I'm sorry enough, but you won't starve, as light on your toes as you are. While the news I'm bringing affects a lot of people, not just one. And some of them are going to find it tough to get work elsewhere."

Tom scowled at her. "I can do without the cryptic suspense."

"Well, the Maples lost the leasehold on this island. Old Hairless Harry and Menopause Marge are going to be out on their pompous southern asses! Isn't that divine news? I, for one, am ecstatic. Couldn't happen to a nicer couple. I can always find another job. . . ."

She wasn't just a bitch, Tom thought, she was an unfeeling monster. She really savored the distress of others, battened on it.

"What happened to the lease?" he asked, and Eva launched into an outline of the information she'd received partly from her private sources and partly from Marge that morning.

"So," she concluded, "what I think I'll do is find me a nice rich old dowager, or maybe a nice rich young lady—or just a nice, comfortably off fat young lady."

"You can't get your jollies unless you're a meddling cunt, can you?" Tom snarled at her. "There's only one party around here that fits that description: Cindy Brown. Got your poison hooks in her, too? Jesus, you stop at nothing!"

Eva kept her smile fixed brightly in place and concentrated on a vague point through Tom's wide window. "Dear, me," she purred softly, "I was only exercising my fancy."

"Yeah, sure." Tom leaned back in his chair, crossed his arms, and grinned at her. "I always thought you had tendencies. Now you tell me because I'm leaving."

"Everybody knows about you, too, darling. But let's just say I'm adaptable on an AC/DC level. I'm not inflexible—like you obviously are."

"I wouldn't demean myself by answering a charge from you, Eva."

"For all I know, there may be lots of charges you wouldn't care to answer to."

"Yes, and you might even be a witch. It's conceivable."

This genuinely amused her, and she laughed. "I'm just

about anything that suits me at the moment. Where'll you go from here, love?"

"Maybe foreign again, if there's work. Otherwise, I've got a friend who owns a chain of pharmacies in California. . . ."

"Why does everybody want to go to California with all those earthquakes and political trouble? Why not big, open Montana? It's so safe and empty."

"California's got a lot more going for it than Montana."

"Oh yes, I forgot. You're a voyeur."

"Yeah," Tom replied, keeping his temper, "and like I said a minute ago, you're not very nice."

"I've been told that I'm lovely."

"Lots of people don't have good sense. . . . I guess you'll hang around here and try to break up what looks like a going thing between the doc and your fairy princess."

"Oh, it's not that simple, love."

"You did all right with Severn."

"You'd do better," Eva said icily, "by minding your own business. . . ."

"From now on, baby, that's my new project. Little old Tom exclusively. Now, if you don't mind, fuck off. I'm packing. . . ."

"You know what you are, Tom? You're insignificant and vulgar. And you don't belong here or anywhere. You're a pariah, a zero balance, and besides, you're a closet queen! That's my little truth for today. See you!"

Tilting her nose high in the air, Eva stalked out of Tom's office, leaving him to wonder again how such an attractive and vivacious woman as Eva could be so utterly vicious and vitriolic, so driven and warped and plain goddam evil. He knew the devious means she used for kicks and just hoped she hadn't pepared Cindy Brown for a fall. She got to many of the guests, as well as the staff, all in the guise of merciful angel, the therapeutic companion. Anyone could look at Severn and see where Eva had tried to score. Well, hell, it wasn't his problem, nothing here was anymore. Sooner or later they'd find out about her at Bimini Springs or wherever else she went. She was her own self-contained bad-luck package, and someday it would all be measured back to her in a lethal dosage. . . .

In the shower, Aggie Bird thought wistfully of Dick Carter and his body. Whatever other lies they'd exchanged, nothing could dilute the plain truth that Dick was the best lay she'd ever had. All that stuff about paradise for the first time—well, that wasn't very honest, but then, Aggie knew that the best moments of her life had nothing to do with honesty. And she was determined to evaluate this moment with Dick for what it was. Could orgasm, she wondered, be better than security and guidance, or was it the same damned thing?

"What the hell am I cut out for?" she demanded aloud of herself in the steamy shower. "What do I want from life?"

As she toweled herself dry, she tried to analyze her question. It wasn't any longer the need for motherhood, she knew that. Or sexual fidelity, and God knows she'd proved that! So why, when it came right down to it, why was she on this planet? To bring joy into the humdrum lives of her audiences? Bullshit! That was only an excuse for her ego trip; it didn't help her to face reality. Sure, she thought, I'm one of those disasters that's happened to America. It's cock-crunchers like me who've brought us to Women's Lib. But it wasn't too late, she knew, to start behaving like a decent human being, calm down, straighten up, live right. . . .

Born Aggie Vogel, in Germantown, New York. Street days, poor neighborhood, carpenter father always out of work. Mother pressed for a dry cleaner. Six brothers who all left, one by one, as soon as they could earn a living. Good old Betty wasn't a sister, just a pal, for there were times when she confused her studio biography with the facts. . . .

"Hurry up, Aggie!" Wayne shouted, banging on the bathroom door and bringing her sharply out of her reverie. "We'll miss the plane!"

"Oh shut up!" Aggie shouted back. "I'm ruminating."

The truth was, she had little discipline except in her work, and to get from her private life to her work was and always had been one big hassle. There were always so many casualties and wreckage strewn along the route to impede her progress. But on the screen, in the finished product, she was regally serene, in total command, the epitome of order and intelligence.

And that Wayne. . . . In other times, other frames of reference, she would gladly have told Wayne and all the studs in her life to go fuck themselves with whatever was handy at the moment. But her point of view was mellowing. The climacteric had claimed her and was gone; and while it had been a rotten, hysterical period, she'd survived it. Or could she—without the film? The glory of being finally able to reveal her fully mature talent vanished with the loss of *The Bungalow*. Yet she'd learned something from the bad news: Losing what she wanted most didn't necessarily mean anguish. Last night she'd slept with a sense of genuine relief. Why was that?

She realized now that she'd been so irritable and highstrung, so craving of the raw, casual passion Dick Carter delivered because she was substituting the sedative of compulsive sex for the sedative of compulsive eating. Switching surrogates, so to speak. Toss in Harry Maple, too. Once only. Yes, the prospect of a fairly predictable future, at least for a while, had its beguiling attractions. Let Wayne take over; full of surprises, he would guide her. No more bitching at directors, no more petty jealousies toward younger actresses, no more brawls with executives. And no more booze, no more pills, uppers or downers. She'd had just enough of a respite from all of her excesses, just enough of a release in sex, to discover what every woman in menopause needs most of all—the need to be herself. Wherever it lay hidden. . . . But how did she juggle both elements in balance—Dick *and* Wayne?

She emerged from the bathroom in a silk robe Wayne had given her last Christmas, looking almost radiant.

"I was just thinking," she said, going to her closet, "screw those suffragettes! I'm going to start living as a feminine *woman*. I don't need that kind of support."

"Don't be vague," said Wayne, "and nobody calls them suffragettes, Aggie, for God's sake. It's about time you cleaned out your big mouth, you know. I hope I'm not going to have trouble with you because of *The Bungalow*, am I?"

"No, sweetie, you're not," said Aggie decisively from the closet. "You'll think of something else to calm me down."

"That's good because eighty-year-old matriarchs don't talk dirty."

"Well, shit," said Aggie indignantly, "I'm no eighty-year-old whatsis, that's for sure!"

"Just an old, nine-lived pussycat, huh?"

"I resent that!" zipping herself into a blue dress.

"Try it for size sometime. It might fit."

Aggie was about to deliver herself of an invective when there was a knock on the suite door. Dick Carter entered at Wayne's command, embarrassed at seeing them together.

"I—I didn't mean to butt in," he apologized.

"Don't sweat it," Wayne said. "You're just in time."

"I only came to say good-by," Dick muttered.

"To Aggie or both of us?" Wayne's smile hovered somewhere between superiority and amiability.

"To Aggie. I didn't know you were here."

"I'm here to stay, Dick."

"Yeah, I know."

"As long as you know," said Wayne.

"You're both leaving for the Coast this morning?"

Aggie said, "The film sort of fell through, Dick. But we're going, anyway."

"*The Bungalow*—?" Dick was appalled; he wondered if he'd heard correctly.

"That's right, a dead issue," Wayne replied. "It went to somebody else, but we'll survive.... What will you do? Stay on at this morgue?"

"I don't have any better offers," Dick said.

"Maybe it's just a question of getting three people to agree on a single issue," Wayne observed.

"What do you mean by that?" asked Dick. "I don't understand."

Wayne shook his head. "Sometimes, Richard, that's your greatest charm. At other times it's a pain in the ass. I know, I've been stuck for it once already. But I'm willing to forget that gamy little episode. Forever. You're off *that* hook."

Dick grinned his relief. "Thanks."

"Careful. Don't count your blessings yet. There's an obligation involved."

"I'm adaptable."

"That you are. O.K. then, think about this one: We're going to be out on the Coast for a long time, unless I miss my guess. I haven't even told Aggie the details yet; I wanted it to be her homecoming surprise. But it won't hurt to tell her now. A new TV series starts filming in two months. Aggie's been prime choice all along, but the film commitment canceled out that possibility. Now that she's free, the series is still hers. I preferred *The Bungalow*, but never mind, this is great exposure. As I was saying to her just before you walked in, she'll have to change her style a bit. Matriarchs don't run around telling everybody to go fuck themselves."

"Oh Wayne!" Aggie cried, "I can't believe it!"

"Better all three of us do," said Wayne. "Now here's my suggestion. I think I understand you two better than you yourselves do. It's my business to sell clients to a sensitive market, but to do it I've got to know how to deal with them and all that that implies. It's especially my business to know what Aggie Bird likes and what Dick Carter can offer. Let's face it, Dickie boy, you don't have any future here; it's triple O. All you've got is an inglorious past. How'd you like to have me set you up in your own body shop in Los Angeles, maybe along Santa Monica near La Cienega?"

"Don't play with me," Dick said to cover his surprise.

"I'm serious. I need you, Aggie needs you. We want you around."

"What's the catch? I'm not going to be let off that old hook after all, is that it?"

Wayne grinned. "This is a different kind of hook. Let's not kid ourselves. You've got a commodity Aggie really digs—"

"Hey, wait a minute!" Aggie protested. "Quit talking about it like that!"

"I'm not a commodity," Dick retorted stiffly, "I'm a human being."

"There's always room for debate," Wayne pointed out wryly, "but for the time being we'll let your interpretation stand. You'll have a chance to prove it. So, I know what Aggie digs, and there's no reason why she can't have her nerves soothed now and then. As for me, well, you've always known how I felt where you're concerned. I don't have to put tags on things, do I?"

"Not with me," Dick answered.

"Jesus!" exclaimed Aggie. "I'm right in the middle of something weird!"

Wayne ignored her. "O.K., Dick. We should be able to work out a nice cozy little arrangement convenient for everybody. You keep us happy in whatever way works out best for the three of us; in return we keep you happy. There won't be any written contract on this giddy group, but I don't think we'll need one. And, sooner or later, if we all decide that the trio ought to be a duet, or maybe even a quartet, or that everybody does a single, we'll talk about that arrangement, too."

"You've sure turned into one cold-blooded machine," Dick said, a grudging admiration in his voice, but not sure he liked the whole idea of an arrangement.

"Oh, come on, Dickie boy, be realistic. I'm fighting fire with fire; I'm being absolutely practical. We all have definite needs, we've got to be protected in the pursuit of these needs, and we'll probably find out that this is the best possible setup that three civilized people can make for themselves in a world where the so-called ideal values don't work any too well these days. . . . You can start packing right now, Dick, if you want to. And tell the Maples you're coming with us this afternoon; there's no point in dragging it out."

"My God, just like that?" Dick was stunned by the abruptness of Wayne's unexpected offer. He could hardly believe it after the scuffle they'd had yesterday. "How can I just pack and go? Anyway, I don't even have a plane reservation."

"Don't think about it," Wayne advised him. "Go pack. Do it! I'll take care of the plane reservation."

"I don't know," Dick said hesitantly.

"You can and you will—*if* you want to join us. And I think you do, man, I really think you do."

"Yeah, I guess I do," Dick admitted. "Why not?"

"That's right. Why not?"

Aggie stared at Wayne with prideful awe as the thought crossed her mind that perhaps he'd stage-managed the entire situation from the very beginning, long before she'd even heard of Bimini Springs, knowing exactly how things would work out.

"You're a real genius," she told Wayne. "You're fabulous, sweetie. And you're also—like I said yesterday—a real slimy bastard. Calculating and conniving, too!"

Wayne smiled. "Well, now that we all know *what* we are, maybe we'll try to find out *who* one of these days. Meanwhile, let's get moving. . . ."

When Eva Cassel returned to her room from the pharmacy, she found Joan Harrison waiting on the terrace by her door. Joan was not in a friendly mood.

"I want to talk to you, Eva Cassel," Joan said without preamble.

Eva smiled sweetly and unlocked her door. "Please come in. What can I do for you?"

Once inside, Joan slammed the door and leaned against it.

"What were you doing in Kill Howard's room?" she demanded.

Eva appraised Joan silently for a moment. Joan was beyond anger; she emanated a cold, numb fury.

"Goodness gracious," Eva said, "you'd better sit down and tell me what's troubling you."

"I don't need your hypocritical hospitality," Joan snarled. "You know damn' well what I'm talking about.

You were at Kill Howard's last night. I walked around the corner just as you were leaving with that shit-eatin' grin on your face, you bitch! And don't you give me any phony double talk—I saw you with my own eyes!"

Eva smiled faintly, for she knew she had the upper hand here and had no intention of losing it.

"But what a fantastic story," she murmured. "To imagine that I'd be interested in Kill Howard."

"You're liable to be interested in anything that will stir up a hornet's nest of trouble. I know how you see yourself," Joan said. "Better than black flesh or anybody. As some powerful white goddess who's gotta have everything, who's gonna make it with a black man for the *experience*, so's she can feel superior!"

"Really, Joan, you're too much."

"Listen, and listen good. What's done is done and can't be undone. But I'm telling you this for your own good, Eva. You've had it around here, woman. Your days are *numbered*."

"What do you mean?" Eva said, feeling suddenly chilled.

"You tampered with *my* property, see, and nobody ever gets away with that!"

"*Your* property? Kill Howard is your property?" Eva teased, smiling. "The Bahama sunshine's cooked your brains."

"No, it's the other way around," Joan said, moving away from the door and approaching Eva with such a fierce expression on her face that Eva stepped backward involuntarily, her hands fluttering to her face.

"You're the one whose brains are cooked," Joan hissed in her face. "You're a foul freak, Eva Cassel, and I'm not just some house nigger with a whitey accent you play with, see? And Kill's not just some load of stud, either. We're decent blacks all the way through, and we know about people like you. I had my honky education, but I've seen plenty of *macumba* in my time, and I know your kind. You go around pretending to be so goody-goody, one of those love-thy-neighbor nurse types, when all the time you're plotting how you can screw your clients, how you can make innocent people pay for their miserable weaknesses! Oh yes, I know your kind!"

Things were going too far, thought Eva, and she said, "Joan, I've never been inside Kill Howard's room. I don't even know what you're talking about. And besides, I don't have to listen to this kind of garbage from you or anybody."

Eva moved to reach around Joan for the door, to open it and induce Joan to leave, but Joan wrenched her fingers from the doorknob, slid in front of her, and blocked her exit.

"No you don't, you bitch," Joan raged. "You don't run from me! And going to the Maples won't do you any good, either." She made claws of her fingers. "Somebody ought to throttle you, that's what!"

"Joan, I warn you. This is an outrage to my person. You have no right to behave like this," Eva said, edging into a position that put her buttocks broadside to her bed.

"I got every right," Joan declared, "because you're a witch, that's what you are—a foul, evil-breathing witch. You think because I'm black I'm stupid. Well, I'm a lot keener than you are; I got your number the first second I laid eyes on you. You're just like that honky bastard from Georgia who tried to down-talk Jim Brown on that TV talk show last year. You think you can act any goddam way you please and get by with it."

Eva was pale with fury. "I won't listen to any more of your crap," she cried, gripped now by a genuine fear that Joan might suddenly decide to use extreme physical force on her; she was younger and stronger. But she had an ace card, so she smiled and played it: "I wasn't in Kill Howard's room *or* his bed last night, but I know someone who was. Yes, that's what I saw through a chink in the blinds. That's what amused me."

"I don't believe you!"

"Would you believe it was Tom Street, down on his knees making strange love to Kill Howard, your *precious* Kill Howard?" Eva taunted, enjoying her moment.

"You're lying," Joan screeched. "It's a foul-mouthed lie!"

"It happens to be the truth, the absolute truth," Eva said. "Now, get out! Go on, I said, get out!"

But Joan glared at her and held her ground.

"Where my ancestors come from in Dahomey they know all about people like you. The Djougous believe some folk got the power to injure others without visible means. It's a substance inside some people's bodies they're born with. A man gets it from his father's blood, a woman from her mother's. And the only way to tell if somebody has this terrible substance is to slice them open after death and look inside for it! So, anybody can be a witch and spread evil, and who's to know till they're dead!"

"That's ridiculous. Medical science says—"

Joan laughed derisively. "What I'm talking about's got nothing to do with medical science, only what's true and what isn't."

"I never had anything to do with Kill Howard, or his filthy dealings in marijuana."

Joan's eyes narrowed; she studied Eva.

"Marijuana?" she said. "What do you know about that?"

"Well, for one thing I smelled it when I passed his room. I know he smokes it. And I suspect he's been dealing in it, he and Linc Bailey."

"You're a liar!" Joan said harshly.

"No, I don't think so. If anything, you're lying."

"You're a terrible creature—" Joan said, moving closer.

"Don't you touch me!"

"I ought to kill you, but that would make me just like you. Evil is as evil does. So I'll let the forces of good take care of you, Eva Cassel, and believe me they will."

Joan made one quick lunge toward Eva, and Eva scuttled backward against the wall of her room, then sank to the head of her bed, cowering fearfully against the mounded pillows.

"If you don't go right now, I'll—"

"You will see," Joan chanted in a hoarse singsong voice, pointing at the huddled figure. "You will see, *you will see*—"

Then she turned on her heel and abruptly left the room. A click of the lock and Eva was alone. . . .

Eva lay for a brief moment curled defensively on her pillows, trying to sort out the scene that had just occurred. Of course she was innocent of Joan's ridiculous charges, but Joan's angry passion was something else. Eva had a strong faith in signs and vibrations, and she was convinced that Joan meant what she said—something bad would happen to her. In a way she was glad that Joan had confronted her with her jealousy, for the showdown had given her the needed impetus to cut loose here and fulfill her commitment in Nassau. Now she would not just make a trip up there, she would go for good. Running was the only sensible thing to do. Run fast, run to stable safety. A pity she couldn't use what she had on Tom Street, but her personal well-being was more important right now.

At last she summoned strength to rise. She paced the

room aimlessly for a while, dizzy and frantic, kneading her palms with her fingers, ordering her pounding heart to quiet down. And gradually she regained her composure. When she was breathing normally again, she decided to pack at once and make the next plane out. Bimini was finished. Joan as an enemy was no trifling matter. But all the same, the witch label was idiotic. Witches might exist in Joan Harrison's funky black world—not in hers. Eva drew magic circles around herself by gaining power through secret knowledge that she would one day use. But she was no witch.

She yanked down her suitcases from the top shelf of the closet, surprised that her vanity seemed so heavy. She opened it and was puzzled to find a sealed cardboard carton inside. She grabbed scissors, quickly slit the masking tape, raised the carton lid, and gasped at the plastic-packaged, raw, murky-green bricks of marijuana that lay nestled inside.

Oh God, she could practically fry for a stash like this if she were caught. How did it get there? she wondered. What to do about it? She couldn't possibly flush all that bulk down the john in the next few minutes; it would take hours. And although she was reluctant to carry the stuff with her to Nassau, she was also aware of the brisk market there. Bricks were valuable. And she hadn't the time to dispose of it anywhere on the island, particularly in broad daylight. The only solution was to carry it with her. All right, she smiled to herself, thinking how surprised a certain British subject would be. Yet on the other hand, she mused soberly, this could be a warning. A shadow flitted across her mind, and she thought, maybe somebody's trying to tell me something. But the shadow passed as quickly as it had come. Never mind, this was no time to get cowardly. The important thing was to crowd onto that plane and leave the island. Today, this afternoon. . . .

She lifted the phone as she debated what she would say to Kevin Mack, to Ruth Severn, to the Maples. Well, it didn't matter that much. She was leaving, and that was that.

"Kevin," she purred into the phone when he answered. "I don't know exactly how to say this, but something very serious has come up. You see, I got a letter yesterday from my sister in Miami. She has cancer, and they're making more tests to see whether or not it's metastasized yet. I've been miserable all night thinking about her, and I've decided I have to go to her right now. Today. . . . So,

I'm leaving. . . . Now I hope this doesn't handicap you too much, but I'm powerless to do anything else except go."

"You ought to know you can't mix business and pleasure," Harry lectured Anita in his office. "A good employee knows when to separate personal feelings from his work. And you don't. When help gets to the point where they blur the lines, then—"

"Boiled down," said Anita, "I'm fired."

"That's about it. You can wait out the season to Easter if you want to, but we're going to start looking for your replacement right away."

"I don't understand you, Harry. You start out by romancing the help, then you get jealous when they do their jobs or go a bit beyond regulations, but you can do anything you want to, anytime. You make your own rules."

Harry looked smug. "In my empire, I'm the king."

"You're also a selfish bastard!"

"You can leave now, today, if you want to."

"I'll leave when I'm damned good and ready," Anita said spiritedly; she was fed up with him. "I could split this island wide open if I wanted to. You and Marge don't know the meaning of the word ethical. You're just lucky I'm not the vindictive type."

Harry sighed and shook his head. "This seems to be my season for getting threats. Drop it, Anita, I got pictures."

"Pictures?"

"Of you servicing some of our more enthusiastic clients. Photos of you, photos of Dick. Two star performers. I like to keep tabs on my people."

"Why, you dirty— What've you got?"

"Eight-by-ten black-and-white glossies. Spectacular, too. And I just added some very interesting color video tapes to my collection. Fabulous kinetic art, courtesy of one of our trusted staff—who's now an ex-employee, I might add."

That would be Tom Street, of course. So that's what Tom was doing with those machines in the pharmacy back office, she thought, all hooked up to the monitoring system. Wow! The idea was funny, or would be if it weren't so degrading. Some collection! But it was better that Harry had her in living color than Tom. Unless pushed into a very tight corner, Harry hadn't the nerve to use them except for one-hand solo readings, while Tom would have employed them to maximum benefit.

"O.K.," she said, "but they don't mean anything, Harry. They're just the rotten part of Bimini Springs, what you and others represent—and that's got nothing to do with me, not anymore."

She turned and walked out of Harry Maple's office and straight into Stanley Conn, who appeared to be waiting for her.

"Stanley!" Anita cried, and collapsed in his arms and began sobbing.

"There, there, baby. . . . I know. You got fired. So you don't have to burn any bridges here, it's all been done for you."

"I'm so—damned *humiliated*," she said, unable to tell him about the photos and the video tape. Maybe at some later time when she had herself under control, but not now.

"So's the whole world, at least once every day," Stanley consoled her. "And I'm the kind of nut I say I am. I don't ask any questions. We're off to L.A. like I said. . . ." He put his arm around her protectively and started walking her along the terrace. "With me you're not tied down to any work contract and don't forget it. You gotta keep that foremost in your mind. It'll give you room to move around in, find out who you are again. . . . I *like* you, Anita Pomeroy, remember it. Friendship comes first—otherwise what's the point in anything?"

"The point is," said Anita, still blubbery, "that I've never in my whole life before ever had anybody who liked me for myself. It's always been my big boobs or my violet eyes, my blonde hair and sexy mouth. Gadgets, ornaments, that's all they ever saw. Everybody always took inventory and never cared about how I felt."

"Not me!" Stanley assured her. "I see the total picture, and like I just said, first and foremost you're my friend. I relish the extras, sure, but like *you* said, that's all they are—ornaments, trimming. You'd be the same sweet, good kid if you were homely as hell."

Anita couldn't help laughing. "God, I'm glad I'm not!"

"I'm glad, too, baby. I like you the way you are—so start packing. My time's up today; I already told them I was leaving. You can diet me when we get out to the Coast. We've had it here. . . ."

"Kevin, what's the matter with you? You're all nerves today," Ruth Severn told the doctor in her office. "You're trying to bring yourself to tell me something—frowning and fidgeting, chewing away on your lower lip. When you get like that, I know something's bothering you. Now tell Ruthie—"

"A personal matter," Kevin said uneasily. He'd walked into Ruth's office with the express intent of declaring that Cindy Brown liked him a lot, using it as a wedge to analyze his involvement with Ruth, if any, and to straighten things out between them once and for all time, if possible.

"What could be so dire and portentous that you're embarrassed by it? Come on, open up."

"Well, for one thing, Cassel's just quit."

Quit?" Ruth looked surprised, but calmly asked, "What lie did she give you?"

"Something about her dying sister in Miami, terminal carcinoma."

"Oh God, she would! But that isn't what you came to tell me."

"No, I just sent a radiogram for Cassel's replacement," Kevin explained. "It's about us, Ruthie."

"What made you wait so long? We've both known for some time now that we're simply firm friends and working buddies. I respect you as a person and a professional, and I hope you feel the same way about me."

"You know I do. We've been through all that."

"Then what's bothering you? That thing we had in Nam, those lovely few times together? They were two different people, Kev. It was mutual therapy strictly from need. A little sanity in all that horrible madness. You're the one who insisted on turning it into a sustained image of romantic love. But romance and reality aren't always compatible attitudes. And besides, something happened here that's made me do a lot of thinking."

"Might I know what it is?"

"In due time I suppose I'll tell you."

"So, you've had the whole thing between us rationalized right out of existence for quite a while?"

"I think I have," Ruth said, and her smile was warm and agreeable. "Look, I'm not especially hung up about being female, or about your masculinity. I don't entertain the fashionable attitudes, it's not in me. And as for sex—hetero sex, that is—well, I've had the other kind, and I'm not repelled by it. I'm realistic, whereas you're romantic. And after all, the mechanics of sex are pretty stupid, aren't they? I mean, a protuberance is inserted into an aperture, there's a lot of squirming around, and two people achieve heightened and separate good feelings for a few seconds. That's about it, and it's not aesthetic, Kev, it's simply basic, like eating. And there's no stigma or obligation attached to enjoying it. Friendships can continue independently of it. If two people need each other for whatever purpose, they'll find a way to get together. You worry too much about mystiques, values. . . ."

"Ruth, I—"

"You're part Victorian, Kev. What you need is someone as romantic as you are, yes you do. Then, if you get hurt, she gets hurt; you can have fun hurting each other. Like that Cindy Brown you've been so attentive to. She's coming out of her chrysalis and she's a beauty. I saw you stare across at her in the dining room this morning. I don't need to hear what you think about her, Kev. I saw, I know. . . ."

"And you're not—angry?"

"I asked you to work down here because you wouldn't let me help you with your advanced studies. Saving your own money had to be your way. Now perhaps this Cindy, who looks and acts rich, she doesn't fool me she's a secretary—perhaps she's convinced you where I failed."

"I think I'm in love with her, Ruthie."

"And you've decided to give up your advanced studies and marry her?" Ruth chided him gently.

Kevin's reaction was pure shock. "My God, no, Ruthie! I'll just get to them sooner than I anticipated. Cindy says she has more money than she'll ever need. She wants to start putting me through university right away, and with this organization falling apart by the minute, it's the logical move, but—"

Ruth said sincerely, "That's marvelous. So what's your hesitation? It's the best of all possible worlds—particularly if you love her."

"But taking money from a woman—"

"Scruples!" Ruth said in consternation. "You're a fool sometimes, Kev. If you weren't such a damned good doctor, I'd give you a long lecture on values. But your professional drive will carry you through fine without my advice."

"What should I do?"

"You're asking *me*? Why, let her help you, of course. What else?"

"You really think so?"

"Kev, I wouldn't say so if I didn't. Is marriage the ultimate goal? And how soon?"

"Well, it probably wouldn't be for six months or so, until after I finish up here."

"Why?"

"I don't want to break my contract, but still—"

"Kev, my God, do it now! Don't wait. Share a place, go to school, work out your problems, and see what happens. It's as simple as that. I don't see why it has to be such a big deal."

"I'm concerned about you."

Ruth smiled. "That I'd go to pieces from the news? Then you haven't been observing me very closely these past few weeks, my dear. I'll go work foreign somewhere. I'm fed up with the States and general conditions, anyway, and especially places like this—they're only extensions of the Stateside malaise. I've also been thinking about going back to Vietnam. Or do a tour of duty on the S.S. *Hope*. Or maybe even learning Spanish and going to work in Peru; they still need lots of nurses down there."

"You mean you wouldn't stay on here after I left?"

"It's a living death. I want to be needed somewhere. As it is, I'm only an appendage to you, Kev, and with you gone, it'd be a nightmare. Bolstering up middle-aged wills and crippled egos and fighting devious staff members on my own? And particularly our venal bosses, the Maples! No thanks, Kev, when you go, I go!"

"But why Vietnam again?"

"It was only an idea. And really a lot more gratifying for me than being attached to any one individual. I'm not a female breeder, I don't need to sink my claws into the earth and settle down. And I'm not a fem-libbing Amazon, either. I'm just a plain, practical creature who wants to reach people through my work."

"I had no idea you felt so strongly about social things."

"You never asked, Kev, but that's the way it is."

"Then I guess I needn't have worried."

"About you and Cindy?"

"About us."

"About anything, Kev. I want what's best for both of us, my dear, and I'm not trying to be noble, believe me. When you go, I'll pick up and go my way, too. . . ."

"If that's how you want it."

"Ah well," said Ruth, "that's the way it is. . . ."

How could he be sure, Kevin wondered, that Ruth wasn't simply being self-sacrificing, faking a permissiveness she didn't truly feel? No way, no way at all, for Ruth was strong and controlled, she knew how to order her emotions so that nobody could read them if she so chose. But one thing he knew for sure; he felt suddenly empty, drained of comfortable habit and support. He would miss Ruth's dependable loyalty. So now he was free to start making plans with Cindy, to find out what he had to know about her. And yet, Ruth would always be larger-than-life to him, she was so real and direct. She could deal head-on with almost any situation, while he often floated through various stages of indecision before finally reaching a confrontation with the facts. He would miss her enormously when they parted, for she had given him shape and balance, and he wondered gravely if he was doing the wise thing in letting her go. . . .

Shortly before lunch, Phil Bernheim walked into Harry Maple's office and declared himself, presenting official identification that revealed him as a narcotics officer on the the make for a bust.

"Somebody on this island's been dealing in heroin," Phil explained to Harry. "This is a point of entry for the Bahamas, and eventually the U.S. We don't know how it gets here, not even with our extensive connections out of Miami, nor how it leaves. But I'm here to check out sources, make arrests, if necessary, and in any event, to look around as I see fit and to search anyone I consider suspicious among guests and staff."

"Am I under suspicion?" was Harry's first statement.

"Not momentarily," Phil told him, "but you'll have to accompany me while I look around."

"Mmmmh," Harry mused, "I like that 'looking around' jazz."

Bernheim's declaration of identity explained a lot about his recent actions but also threw Harry into a mild state of shock, which he managed to conceal from Bernheim. Drugs scared him shitless; his idea of a bush head equated with fiends and demons. Since pot was excessively repulsive to him, heroin was inconceivable. "But the staff's clean, always has been," he said to Phil. "We pick and choose only the best."

"I'll be the judge of that," Phil announced crisply. "Let's go."

"I hope you don't suspect me and my wife."

"Not your climate, Mr. Maple," Phil said dryly. "And I'm not interested in Mack, Severn, or Cassel, at least not in their quarters. I've already gone through them. Got a negative there."

"I thought you would," Harry said, relieved. "What about Joan Harrison?"

Phil's expression was cryptic. "We've had our eye on her."

"That's pretty underhanded," Harry retorted, but what he really meant was that they'd sure be sweating it out if anything happened to her. Joan was essential to the success of their operation; she was their mediator with the blacks, even if she did sometimes stir things up.

"Ha, ha! Underhanded. Listen, Mr. Maple, the way organized crime fights and the way we gotta respond, nothing's underhanded. Drug dealing's no fairy tale. *They* make the rotten rules, not us."

"You like your work?" Harry said, genuinely curious.

"When I'm behind a desk with my ass on a chair, yes. Like I usually am. I'm no action type."

"I can see that," Harry said.

Phil glared at him, but let it go. "We'll check out the hard-drugs safe with Street first, then look at your inventory and treatment charts. All routine," he explained. "I'm not going to bust the goddam lodge. Cool down."

"I should hope not," Harry retorted. "What about Pomeroy and Carter? They're part of medical."

"I'm satisfied they're not involved in drug traffic. We won't discuss that other matter. You see, I have accurate surveillance on your staff."

"By whom?" Harry demanded. "We don't want any spies around here. I'll bet you bribed one of the maids."

"That's *my* business, Mr. Maple. Come on, let's go. You got lots of people pulling out today. Don't want to miss anybody."

Harry dabbed at his brow with a monogrammed silk handkerchief. "Yes, I know," he said glumly, "I know. . . ."

A few minutes later Phil Bernheim entered Kilroy Howard's room with Harry Maple's passkey, but without Harry, who had bowed out of room searches.

"Beneath my dignity," was Harry's excuse as he disappeared on lodge business.

Phil smiled over this as he closed Howard's door behind him. He'd studied guest/staff behavior carefully since the first day of his arrival, fortunate in having Alice and the loud though pleasant Flemings as company—and camouflage. Why the organization had sent him out here when it was really a younger man's job could only be his own bad luck. Or Alice's big mouth with the organization wives, talking about island vacations, et cetera. Well, anyway, foursomed with the Flemings, Phil had studied the layout carefully, and although there were some strange people at Bimini Springs and some stealthy sexual hanky-panky, there was nothing to concern him officially. The reports he kept sending back daily to Nassau and Miami were negative, all too negative. With his retirement imminent, he was expected to come up with something big—either an arrest or a substantial lead. And the search of Howard's room was the last formal gesture he could make, except to funnel guests through the airstrip waiting station.

This spade was sure a natural for everything, thought Phil as he worked his diligent way through Kill's closet, item by item. While a hundred yards away Kill was setting up food courses in the lodge kitchen, blissfully unaware of Phil's inspection.

Phil finished the closet and came out and sat on the bed, perspiring despite the air conditioning, taking time to study Howard's artwork tacked to the walls. Those weird posters: Old Man Leary, stoned in Africa, the Rolling Stones in concert with that Jagger weirdo; Clearance Creedwater group or something like that; Joplin, dead, and Hendrix, too, the whole heavy gang of perverts. Jesus! But the room was immaculate, freshly painted, airy and neat as a pin, frosty from the air conditioner. Hey, better look into that, he thought, going over to the machine that churned away in the window. With time done in Saigon, a local shack job in that funky black ghetto, Soul Alley, Howard was apt to be a cool one. No questionable record from the service, all clean. Yeah, but Howard had known some pretty unsavory macks in Georgia, too, Phil recalled before he came down here. A natural for drugs.

Well, nothing in the air conditioner, nothing under the bed, nothing stashed in the hems of the draperies or in the hollow bedposts. Shit, nothing anywhere! It was hard to believe. Something had straightened this cat out, Phil knew, because there ought to be, according to all rules, at least a small stash of pot somewhere around, an ounce or two. It figured. What had happened?

Maybe the guy'd reformed, he thought. But who ever saw one of *them* reform? No chance. Well, never mind, if he came up with zero on the total search, they couldn't break him back at headquarters, he had seniority over the whole gang; and next time they'd have enough sense to send a younger man. Anyway, he was fed up with the whole schmeer.

He turned slowly in a complete circle, checking out the room again to see if he'd missed anything, anything at all. No, he hadn't. With Howard it would have to be a waiting game. Very strange, and unfortunate; his report would be negative.

The local informant hadn't done him any good. Of course, he couldn't tell Harry Maple that their operative wasn't a maid at all, but Joan Harrison, a woman with an honest, straightforward record who'd agreed to work for them quite a while back because she'd lost a younger brother to an overdose of skag in the States and knew what it was all about. All this some time before Howard came down, of course. At the beginning she'd been real great about checking and reporting to the Miami office, but recently she seemed to have fallen apart, gone all nerves, and apparently just about the time Phil arrived. He wondered why again for the dozenth time. But after all, he couldn't do much more than speculate. She was far too keen and observant for him to try tagging *her* around all day, and if he'd started hounding her nights, somebody would have seen and reported him to the Maples, and Joan would soon enough know about it and cease to be of any use at all to them. Besides, Alice wouldn't let him out of the room alone nights, once she decided to retire. She didn't trust him with the maids, and she was right. Nothing like a schwartze piece now and then to spice up the menu.

Phil sighed and consulted his watch. Nothing here. The girls and Fleming would be packed now and waiting to join him in the dining salon for one last rotten meal. Rotten was only the word for it. The one bright prospect on his horizon was the happy anticipation of all the lox, bagels, cream cheese, and pastrami he could glut down back in Miami as soon as he got home. And the glorious comfort of his swivel chair behind that big desk in the private cubicle, *his* office, *his* world. Well, he'd make a last showcase inspection at the airstrip after lunch and conclude his official visit, goddammit, and that was that. Might as well move his ass.

He walked to the door, cracked it six inches, monitored the terrace for clearance, then slipped out into the boiling sunshine, feeling as he always felt after a search, guilty as hell; nothing like fine-combing a pad to bring you down. . . . Rotten food, rotten lodge, rotten business, rotten life. A wonder he didn't have jumping ulcers. He simply wasn't cut out for this field-action bit, never had been. His best work was done with a pencil and a dictating machine. And as for the weight loss, what a laugh, that was no vacation. Sheer drudgery. The sooner he put it all back on, the happier he'd be. At his age, why worry about a waistline? Screw Alice's Dr. Feldman, what did he know?

Happier just thinking about the mounds of rich kosher food he would soon be consuming in blessed Miami, Phil strolled casually toward the dining salon to join Alice and the Flemings, empty-handed. . . .

Dick Carter packed slowly, depressed as he always was when he traded a moment of relative certainty in his life for the unknown and unpredictable. Through the window, as he laid out some shirts, he saw Eva Cassel across the garden giving orders to the black porter about her luggage that he was piling onto a cart.

Eva Cassel leaving? Wasn't it kind of sudden? Maybe she got herself fired. Christ, everybody was splitting from the island like rats from a derelict. Was there a lesson here he'd missed? Maybe, but he couldn't care less. It would serve the Maples right if the goddam place fell apart; couldn't happen to a nicer couple. And as for that hysterical bitch Marge, she'd find some other willing stud to play her sly verbal games with, some cat with a real long strong tongue for argument. Marge was an expert at talking *around* sex—a lousy, cold-fish lay that could flash-freeze your cock. What she loved best was to screw you to a cross so she could beat you unconscious with her fluting southern vocabulary. Words were her favorite sport.

Too bad, thought Dick, that a beautiful spot like Devil Cay, all pink beaches and lush tropical green, couldn't be stripped of its thin coating of civilization and allowed to go wild again. Wouldn't that be something? Just birds and sea and sky! Dick sat down on the bed and saw himself dreamily in such a heaven, richly weathered by nature, striding bare-assed across the island. Fishing with a crude spear, living on island mangoes, bananas, coconuts, the fruits of paradise, all plentiful for the picking. But of course it couldn't ever happen, and he was even further depressed by this thought. . . . So he might as well finish packing and prepare himself for the limbo of Los Angeles, letting himself be led again as always, the pattern of his life.

"Shit!" he said aloud in frustration, cursing his weakness, his availability. Heavy with the somber reality of his pedestrian life, which was far from the dream, he sighed and returned to his packing.

Linc Bailey collected Eva Cassel's luggage an hour before plane time.

"Just these three," Eva told him, pointing to her locked blue bags by the door. "And be sure you deliver them to the waiting station at the airstrip."

Linc grinned at Eva as brightly as she smiled at him and said unctuously, "Yes'm, that's exactly what Ah'll do. . . ."

When Linc had loaded the cases onto his cart, he poked his head in the door and spied the yellow vanity case on the bed and came inside to get it. Eva was at the mirror fiddling with her hair and whirled around as he headed for the case.

"No," she said sharply, "not that one. I'm carrying it."

The vanity contained the grass bricks that she'd damned well better carry herself if she wanted to get off the island with the rest of her intact, and this was vital. Since she'd discovered the grass, it had been locked in her large case with the security combination that would defy anyone's entry; they'd have to ruin the case to get into it. Now it was repacked in her vanity. And because she trusted no one, it would be carried by hand, never out of sight.

"Seems as lots of folks is goin' today," Linc said conversationally at the door, waiting politely for his tip.

Eva extracted a crisp dollar bill from her purse and smiled as if she'd made it herself. "Oh?" she said. "I wonder why?"

"Radio says they's a big storm brewin', ma'am, a real *huracan.* 'N' they says it gits big enough, they gonna name it Brenda."

"Oh yes, they begin them alphabetically each year, don't they, and this would be the second in the area. . . ." She handed her dollar bill to Linc, who thanked her, doffed his cap, and whistled out to his cart, pushing it down the terrace to the main building.

Eva checked the room again to make certain she'd left nothing, picked up her purse and the vanity case, and closed the door on her life at Bimini Springs.

A few moments later she knocked purposefully on Harry Maple's office door to tell him she was through.

"Come in!" Harry called out.

She opened the door and saw that the tile floor was awash with suds; Laura, one of the black maids, was mopping up. "Cleanin'," Laura said succinctly, glaring at her, and went on working.

Reluctant to carry the vanity case inside and set it down on the wet floor, Eva deposited it just outside the door—it would be O.K. there for a minute—and advanced across the slippery tiles toward Harry's desk.

Harry noted that she was wearing a bright silk print dress and high heels. No uniform.

"What's the occasion?" he asked. "You're dressed up fit to kill."

"I'm leaving, Harry. Quitting, walking out—anything you want to call it."

The maid dawdled at her mop pail, one ear to their conversation.

Harry said, "That's enough, Laura. Take five. You can finish later. And close the door as you leave. . . ."

Laura slopped down her mop, glowered at Eva, and slammed the office door behind her.

"Niggers," Harry muttered. "Now, Eva, what's this all about?"

"I said I was leaving, that's all."

"But you can't," Harry said. "Everybody's just walking off the job, for God's sake. We need you, now that Tom's going."

"You were wise there, Harry, but not even Tom's departure is enough to make me stay. This is a very unhealthy place for a health resort; I'm getting out while I still can. Besides, Linc said something about a storm coming up."

"Yes, there's a report out."

"Well, they terrify me."

Harry shrugged. "Storms are always brewing out in the Atlantic. A general alert doesn't necessarily mean one's coming our way. There's nothing to worry about." He assumed his genial mask of warm persuasiveness. "Come on, Eva, stick around, huh? Your cheery smile's the happiest thing at Bimini Springs. Marge and I'll miss it, so will the guests."

"Don't con me, Harry Maple. I'm going. I've got five days' pay coming on my next paycheck. You keep it. I want out."

Harry's geniality vanished. "We could make it mighty tough for you on a recommendation, walking off the job like this," he declared.

"I wouldn't recommend that approach with me, Harry Maple," Eva said in a quiet, icy voice. "I know enough about this place and both of you to put the torch to it!"

Harry sighed. "This is sure not my lucky day. Well, I suppose if you have to, you have to. . . ."

"I have to," said Eva flatly. "There's a forwarding address in my file, but you won't need it. I won't be receiving any mail after I've gone. Say good-by to Marge for me. . . ."

"We'll miss you," said Harry. "I wish there was something I could do to make you stay on."

"You've already done too much," Eva told him, smiling brightly, and teetered across the damp floor on her high heels. At the door she turned to him: "Harry, why don't you give up the idea of a fat farm and turn Devil Cay into one big, alfresco bordello? A fun fair with sex games for everybody? You'd make a fortune. . . . And besides, you're halfway there!"

"Good-by, Eva," Harry said coldly. "And thanks for the suggestion."

Outside, Eva picked up the vanity case and walked briskly off through the garden toward the airstrip, a short and pleasant walk along jasmine-scented paths, elated to be going. When you overplayed your hand, you simply got out. It had happened before. No use sticking around to let somebody put their marks on you, which is what would happen if she stayed on at Bimini Springs.

As Eva emerged from the garden at the edge of the asphalt airstrip, she saw the waiting station crowded with passengers and smiled with inward satisfaction. She'd done an excellent job of calling as many guests as possible that morning and suggesting sweetly and sincerely that they'd be safer leaving the island since the threat of a potentially perilous hurricane was in the air. And it looked like most of the guests had heeded her warning. Telling them was the type of obligation she really enjoyed performing.

Irene Tuttle was among the crowd, floating about in diaphanous lavender voile beneath a large picture hat. Aggie Bird slouched against a wall in the shade, wearing orange slacks too tight for her cumbersome ass, and a floppy yellow frilled blouse; she clung to the arm of that young Winslow who'd flown in the previous day. Dick Carter was with them, looking exceptionally meek, Eva noted. And in a wheel chair piloted by Ruth Severn sat Bob Cole, the appendectomy. Only Tom Street was totally detached from the babbling group over which Phil Bernheim appeared to be holding official court.

As Eva neared the assemblage, she realized with a shivery start that Bernheim was very seriously and conscientiously checking and inspecting all luggage, clearing each piece separately to go aboard the plane that was due down in approximately twenty minutes or so.

Next to Tom Street's mound of sealed cartons Eva identified her three blue cases and shifted the yellow vanity uneasily in her hand. It might have been her vivid imagination, but somehow the vanity seemed appreciably lighter to her; and as she considered this she panicked, remembering the grass that she had momentarily forgotten. Oh dear God, it was too late now to do anything as obvious as dumping it; she'd simply have to brazen it out with Bernheim and pray for the miracle that would cause him to ignore it.

Tom saluted her insolently as she approached, grinning slyly as though he harbored a heavy secret. Kinky, closet-queen bastard, Eva thought, and ignored him.

Phil Bernheim, bent over an open suitcase, glanced up at her and pointed to her luggage on the tarmac.

"Miss Cassel, are those three pieces yours?"

Eva said they were and could feel the vanity-case handle burning her hand. She hoped she didn't look as wildly tense and frightened as she felt.

"Will they open without keys?" Phil asked.

"Oh, they're already open, Mr. Bernheim," Eva said casually. "Why would they be locked?"

Phil shrugged his shoulders, thinking what a weirdo she was. "Routine," he mumbled. "With rough handling or turbulence, they could pop open in flight. Some people lock them as a precaution."

"I'm not worried," said Eva. "I've nothing valuable or incriminating in there."

Play it close and cool, she warned herself, watching Phil turn the bags flat, open and go through them rapidly, expertly. Then it was all over, she was sweating profusely, and the black porters were snapping them shut again and carrying them to the cleared luggage area.

"O.K., Miss Cassel, that's it," Phil said, "except for that overnight thing you're carrying."

"This?" she faltered, thinking here it comes, they've got me. She fancied that everyone was watching her; she felt Irene Tuttle's cool, appraising glance, Tom's scrutiny, sensed that a silence had fallen upon the crowd, that all had turned to see what would happen next. She began to feel faint, very faint and weak, nauseated; the sun beat down savagely on her bare head. Her sweating increased.

Eva smiled weakly. "It's just a plain overnight vanity case," she told Phil with desperate gaiety.

Phil regarded her with a stony glance.

"Nevertheless we'll have to check it, Miss Cassel," he said, and she thought she read a sense of triumph in his eyes.

Eva hesitated for the merest fraction of a second, then inhaled sharply, smiled at Phil, and handed him the yellow vanity.

Phil set it on the tarmac and snapped it open.

Standing over him with screaming nerves, dying a million deaths, Eva stared down into the parrot-green moiré-lined depths and thought she must surely be going mad—for instead of bricks of grass, all the case contained was a small nosegay of bright flowers, fresh from the lodge gardens. Nothing else!

Still smiling, she murmured in response to Phil's quizzical look, "You see, Mr. Bernheim, this case belonged to our former housekeeper. She loved flowers. She left it with me and I'm carrying it up to her in—"

Eva began to black out, felt herself falling into a deep, black and bottomless abyss, helpless to prevent the long slow slide to darkness. Phil Bernheim caught her just as she crumpled forward toward the tarmac.

"Must be this goddam heat," Jack Fleming observed.

"Who knows?" said Phil. "Gimme a hand!"

Clutching Wayne, Aggie said, "For Christ's sake, nurses aren't supposed to faint!"

Wayne laughed. "Actresses aren't supposed to turn in bad performances, either, but they do."

"Ha! You can stuff that one for Thanksgiving, sweetie!" Aggie chortled, and squeezed his arm.

Dick Carter studied the pair of them. One thing you could say for the immediate future, he decided, there'd certainly be a lot of goddam laughs in this new scene, not saying what kind though. And that was O.K., as long as none of them were on him.

Anita and Stanley, holding hands in the deep shade of the waiting station, ignored the general commotion of departure and missed Eva's performance.

"You think a few days in Chicago'll bore you?" Stanley asked Anita solicitously.

"Honey, a few days anywhere after this menagerie will

be sheer heaven," Anita replied sincerely. "Don't worry about me. Paradise was never like this, thank God. . . ."

Exactly right, thought Ruth Severn, overhearing them, grateful that Eva Cassel was going. Maybe now she could analyze herself objectively. Eva's departure was like a great weight lifted from her troubled mind; she could already feel the fresh salt air of the island cleansing her. Impulsively, she reached down and patted Bob Cole on the shoulder. "Are you comfortable there, Mr. Cole?" she asked.

"With a nurse like you and a surgeon like Dr. Mack, I'm just fine," said Bob Cole, and smiled at her with something akin to worship.

Joan stood some distance from the scene in the shade of the palmetto windbreak, shading her eyes, watching Eva Cassel straighten her dress and regain her usual metallic composure, as if nothing at all extraordinary had happened. Did Eva, Joan wondered, know what *had been* in that vanity case? Was that why she'd practically fainted, then looked so relieved when it turned out to be empty? But why was it empty? Where had Kill's key-bricks gone? She was mystified and slightly alarmed, realizing she'd probably never find out now. Anway, she was glad she'd protected Kill, and too damn' bad she hadn't succeeded in fixing Eva's wagon, for she wouldn't have another chance. However, there was always the law of averages and her deep, abiding conviction that evil is as evil does. It caught up with everybody who tampered with people's lives, sooner or later. . . .

"Got to admit I did it," Joan confessed to Kill on the front steps of the Bailey cottage a few minutes after the Nassau plane departed.

"Woman, you got plenty of guts, I'm proud of you. She could have caught you."

"I knew she was on duty with Cole. No trouble there. What bugs me is she got away clean. Ripped off or somethin' before she could get busted by Bernheim. I thought I had it all figured. That he'd search her room and find it first, or if she found it first, she'd try to make off with it. But it zonks me the way that evil bitch is protected in everythin' she does."

"You too much, girl," Kill chuckled. "Goddam, you sure are! Here you run off with my precious two-brick stash and drop it in Cassel's pad. I think all this liberation shit's gone to your head."

"What'd you expect I'd do to protect people I like?" Joan demanded. "I ain't in love with dope like you are, but, anyway, what else could I do? Climb up to them eerie caves in the dead of night and find a nice safe stash there for your bricks? You crazy? No tellin' what'd chase me around—dead men's bones or somethin'."

"All right, all right. I'm appreciative. Didn't say I wasn't. But what happened to the keys?" Kill said, genuinely puzzled. "They didn't walk off by themselves. They still on Devil Cay somewhere. But who *took* 'em?"

Joan shrugged her shoulders. "Don't look at me sidewise like that, Kill Howard. I only done my duty as I seen it. I ain't no detective, man!"

"You'd make a good one."

"I was doin' you a special favor, man. In case you missed it, your room was fine-toothed this noon by that ofay narc Bernheim."

"I know, I hear. And I got eyes."

"I'm sorry about the smokes, man."

"Don't get strung out." Kill patted her on the shoulder. "Linc and me's got inexhaustible sources. But I'm still curious where the bricks went to."

Linc strolled out onto the porch at that moment, having overheard the last of their conversation, looking wise.

"Well, whomever took it's gonna smoke it," Linc volunteered. "That's the plain truth."

"It's a mighty uneasy mystery," Kill said. "Kinda gives me the crawls. And I ain't restin' easy till it's revealed."

"Mebbe I better tell you, then," Linc said, and both Joan and Kill glanced at him sharply.

"Tell what?" said Kill.

"When I went to fetch Cassel's luggage, I noted she was mighty nervous about somethin'. And all the time I was there she kept lookin' and lookin' at a small round bag she had. I'll never know why," he said, looking sheepish at this point, "but I had this urge to look inside it. So, when she stopped to see Mistah Wondahful, I popped the lid, right there by the daisies and marigolds. And what do you suppose I found, mmmmmh—?"

"I know what you found," Joan said. "You found the key-bricks."

"Goddam!" Kill exclaimed to Joan. "So that's where you put them!"

"Where'd you think?" Joan said. "But I wish she'd of got caught. She's an evil woman with a vile tongue. Sometime I'll tell you the things she said."

"About *me?*" Kill inquired casually without flicking an eyelid.

"About who else? Anyway, that's all over and done with," Joan said with relief. "The white bitch is gone forever."

Linc chuckled. "Wonder what she thought when she found them posies in the bottom of her bag instead of the grass, huh?"

"You did that?" Kill said.

"Why sure, man. My little farewell joke. No need to let her and her friends find out what we really got down here. Now we can relax and enjoy our own. Place is bound to get better and better."

"Better by the minute," Kill agreed, and grinned at Joan.

"Don't leer at me, Kill Howard," Joan said. "I don't settle into paradise as fast as you do. Several things're still pokin' through my mind."

"You get them settled, woman, maybe you'll quit fussin' so everything's gonna work out."

"Too early to tell yet," Joan said airily, and went inside to talk to Lulu, Linc Bailey's wife.

The Maples were in a state of understandable panic. With part of the staff already gone, more employees, the greater lot, were planning to board the mail boat on its way back to Nasasu in a very short time. The Maples were too numbed to do much more than groan about their misfortune.

"Rats," Marge stewed, pouring a large straight Scotch for herself at their suite bar, "they're all selfish goddam rats."

"Don't even mention rodents," Harry said, flopping across the bed. "That's the worst kind of luck, making trouble jokes."

"I'm not joking," Marge fumed, "I'm making a comparison. What's so funny about bad luck? This isn't a slapstick comedy."

"That part I'm not so sure of." Harry stared morosely at the ceiling, thinking that if the storm's capricious nature brought it their way, he might soon be staring at the empty sky instead of a roof over his head—tomorrow or the next day. "All we're gonna be left with is some white staff and nigger help."

"You mean *black* help," Marge said sarcastically.

"I mean what I said."

"Harry, what do we do?" Marge fretted. "I'm worried."
"Tighten our assholes if the storm blows this way, sit it out. Nothing else we can do, honey."
Harry reached for the radio on the night table and turned it on. It sputtered and crackled as he twirled dials, and a disembodied voice floated through the room. It spoke of increased barometric pressure drops and the ominous presence of a large counterclockwise atmospheric disturbance already formed and lying some distance east of the Bahamas. Named Brenda, it was beginning to move, slowly and inexorably, at about twelve miles an hour, in a general westerly path toward the tip of Florida.
"Don't mean a goddam thing," Harry said, switching off the radio. "It could turn for us anytime."
"Oh God, I just hope the doctor stays," said Marge. "We may need him."
"He wasn't on the flight manifest, but he can always decide on the mail boat. Tom Street and Eva Cassel went."
"Good riddance on both counts," said Marge. "He made me nervous, he'd look right through you; and she wasn't wearing that moronic happy smile for nothing. She did a lot of manipulating with the guests."
"Mmmmmmh," said Harry. "Anita Pomeroy was also on the flight, with that guy Conn," he added, monitoring Marge for her reaction.
"That bitch!" Marge muttered. "Big blonde moron, I could kill her!" She walked to the bed and leaned over Harry, arms akimbo, waving her Scotch at him. "You think I don't know about you and her, huh? Well, I know *everything*. I make it my business to know, just like you do."
"Don't whip a dead horse, Marge," Harry warned her. "You might stir up a powerful stink."
"I'd like to stir *you*!" Marge snarled, red in the face.
Harry yawned and said nonchalantly, "That's one thing we haven't tried yet, honey. Hey, almost forgot. That *beautiful* Dick Carter also made the flight. Out with Agnes Bird and her manager."
"So?" said Marge.
"You think I don't keep track of your shenanigans, sweetie, you're off your feed."
"Oh, go get nuzzled by a sea urchin, Harry Maple," Marge growled, and walked away. "So we're having a private encounter session, so what? I've been loyal to you in the only way that counts, and you know it."

"Sometimes you try too hard."

"Aha, maybe we both do, love," Marge replied.

"O.K., O.K. Let's call a truce until the storm warning's over."

"We've got to, Harry. What if it turns into something awful and heads straight for us? We've been really lucky all these years, they've all missed us."

Harry sat up and smiled at her. "We got each other," he reminded her.

"Oh sure," Marge smirked wryly, "and that ought to be more than enough to carry us through."

"If we get organized."

"We will, we got to. And tonight, when all's snug against the storm it'll be Rose Marie and the Mountie," Marge purred.

"Oh Christ," Harry muttered at the ceiling, "not again! Let's make water sports. You know I can't sing "Indian Love Call" for shit in falsetto."

"I don't care," said Marge, belching a mist of Scotch in his direction, "you look absolutely gorgeous in all those beads and feathers!"

Part SEVEN

As the Bahama Airways plane gained altitude and soared out over the open sea toward Nassau, passengers saw to starboard the far-off bank of marching weather. Fleet, leaden clouds scudded counterclockwise along the horizon; the sea had lost its normal crystalline blue-green brilliance and had turned gray and frothy. The plane leaped and bumped through the turbulent air, and at one particularly rough moment, Mrs. Tuttle shrieked in alarm and grasped the hand nearest hers—Eva Cassel's.

"Oh dear," quavered Mrs. Tuttle, "that was a really scary one! With all the flying Howard and I've done, I simply never get used to planes."

Eva smiled. "I've been in rougher. Weren't we lucky to get away from Bimini Springs? I wouldn't want to be on that island when a hurricane hits."

"Do you think it will? They're so unreliable."

"Like people," Eva said, and thought how surprisingly hostile Irene Tuttle had been to the strobe light, really reared up and gave off sparks. No way of gaining her confidence. But maybe there were other approaches where Mrs. Tuttle would lead the way. "Hurricanes veer, you know, and low land masses are extremely vulnerable," Eva continued.

"Yes, I'm glad I didn't stay a minute longer," Mrs. Tuttle declared firmly, "and apparently some of your staff got the same idea, from the looks of the group aboard. Are you stopping in Nassau for a breather, my dear?"

"In a way, yes, you could call it that. I'm visiting friends for a few days, then on to New York."

"How nice! A vacation?"

"Sort of. I didn't get Christmas and New Year's off," Eva lied, "but the Maples are such good people they've made me take the time."

"Are they?" said Mrs. Tuttle, unconvinced. "Personally, I thought the place was dreadful, I detested it. It's a lovely island, but that food, and the services were simply lax, all except for you medical people, of course. And come to think of it, there's something rather sinister about Devil Cay itself, don't you think? I wonder what that agent Bernheim was looking for at the airstrip?"

"I haven't the faintest," Eva replied.

"Well, it must have been something very important or he wouldn't have gone through us like a dose of salts. I resent that kind of strongarm treatment—and so would Howard. He'd be raving."

Tell the old sow nothing, thought Eva, just smile at her. "Yes, I suppose it was something important."

"And you didn't seem to feel too well there for a moment, my dear. You practically fainted."

"Oh, I'd rushed about so madly getting ready to go at a moment's notice" Eva explained, "that I was worn out. The Maples are always short of help.... It's difficult to get qualified people out there, you know." *Out there*, she mused. Devil Cay was already receding, a thing of the past.

"You know something, my headache's gone," Mrs. Tuttle declared. "I think I left it at Bimini Springs."

"How nice! Mrs. Tuttle, may I ask you something?"

Irene Tuttle braced herself in her seat. Against the plane's choppy action or Eva Cassel's coming remark, she wasn't quite sure. "Of course, my dear, fire away."

"Well, I may not stay too long at Bimini Springs on my return. I find the tropical climate debilitating. You have your headaches, I get depressed. So, I was thinking, do you happen to know anyone of quality, senior citizens preferred, who would need a reliable companion-nurse? I'm best with elderly ladies," Eva said, "but I would settle for a gentleman...."

The nerve, the absolute nerve of this creature, thought Irene Tuttle.

Mrs. Tuttle laughed slickly. "Oh, but you don't need my commendation to secure another job, Miss Cassel. I'm sure the Maples will give you glowing credentials whenever you leave Bimini Springs, not to mention Dr. Mack and Miss Severn."

"They will, they will, Mrs. Tuttle, but the personal

touch in making new contacts is extremely important. Isn't there anyone you know who might appreciate my services?"

"No one," said Mrs. Tuttle, sweetly adamant. "But you *are* a fine worker, Miss Cassel, and anyone who submits to your massages is going to feel refreshed and elevated."

"You're so kind," said Eva, wishing she'd taken a seat somewhere else on the plane. The old bag was a drag; she would never open up. As big a politician as her husband.

Mrs. Tuttle patted Eva's hand impulsively. "And you're such a dear, sweet person, Miss Cassel. You give me the courage to be serene."

"Why, it's the very least I can do for someone as nice as you," said Eva, without a trace of the rancor and frustration that seethed through her mind. Instead she smiled serenely, hands folded in her lap, head against the seat back, closed her eyes, and terminated the relationship with Irene Tuttle. . . .

In a window seat, Anita Pomeroy lay her blonde head on Stanley Conn's shoulder and went promptly to sleep once the plane leveled off, her face calm. Stanley considered this an excellent omen for the future and stared happily past her head and out the window at the nasty weather, thinking cheerfully about their possible future.

Behind them, Tom Street scowled at the storm and wondered if he'd have to stay overnight in Nassau or if he could manage a fast transfer flight to New Orleans. N.O. was as good a temporary set-down as anywhere; he had friends there, it was a far cry from Devil Cay. He didn't envy Kevin and Ruth, such duty-bound types, electing to stay on the island, or anyone else who hung on. They could all be washed away and drowned. And he didn't worry about his future. Something would turn up, it always had. He liked to leave his fate to chance, play life like Russian roulette. He'd make out, he wasn't dead yet. . . .

"You just ruined our lovely vacation," Alice jawed at Phil in their forward seat. "And your search was a bomb."

"You two girls didn't make it all that lovely," Phil replied sincerely. "I never saw two such yentas in all my life."

"Well, don't blame Rose!" Alice burst out. "She took her cue from me, I took mine from you. She's a nice girl. A Mata Hari I'm not, as you know, and I loathe playing Yiddisher mamas about as much as you relish your role of papa. You know what you are?" Alice ranted. "Well, I'll tell you—you're an inverted sadist!"

Phil grunted and muttered to the overhead luggage rack, "Now she calls me a queer!"

"And you're impossible besides!" Alice continued. "This is the last time I do a masquerade with you. I hope you retire soon so we can both relax. It'll be a change."

"Maybe they'll retire *me* after this one, and quick." Phil had never had the nerve to tell Alice that his full early retirement now hinged on the successful outcome of this mission. Otherwise, he'd have to sit out his full service and lose the bonus pension as well. There was just one more chance—Nassau and some quick thinking. He wasn't beaten yet.

"As far as I'm concerned, it can't come a moment too soon," said Alice. "Why do they always pick on you for these schlimazel assignments?"

"Who knows?"

"Probably because you're the biggest schnook in the Miami office, and you'll go anywhere."

"Now don't start that, you wanted to come here, you jumped at the idea. Anyway, I concede the argument. Let's knock it off." When Alice got like this, he might as well give her total points. "But consider that I'm also less suspicious-looking than most operatives, agewise and all, and when we're a team, nobody ever guesses what I am. Add to that you two girls mouthing it up over pinochle all the time, we're about the worst!"

"Hey, Rose." Alice leaned forward and tapped Rose on the shoulder in the seat ahead. "Did you happen to hear what this husband of mine just said?"

"All I know is I'm getting real queasy," Rose complained, her face paper-white.

"I said, Phil thinks he gets these assignments because we're such a colossal pair of squares, who'd guess what he's looking for!"

Jack Fleming swiveled around and grinned admiringly at Phil. "Oh boy, you can say that again! You sure had me fooled, Phil, your disguise is perfect."

"Thanks," Phil replied grudgingly. "I'm not sure I like that."

"No, you're perfect, by God! Especially when you started talking about yard goods and your shop."

"Got a brother in the textile business," Phil said, "and I listen when he kvetches."

"So that explains it. What I really wondered was, during

all our schmooze, why does he come down here where there's no kosher food when it's all he talks about! Obviously it's the passion of your life."

"Well, now you know why. And I'm going back empty-handed, first time in my career. Not even a scrap of information any fink couldn't turn in. That's not the action they expect. I'm supposed to bring home the bacon, if you'll pardon the goyism. Hope to God this is my last challenge. I've run out of glick."

"It probably will be," Alice said, "which means we'll never get to California on company time."

"How many times do I have to tell you California's not my territory?" Phil said patiently. "You got some real weird one-track ideas, Alice, about touring America free at your convenience."

"Well, I figure if they keep schlemiels like you on the payroll, they got to be dizzy enough to hand you the cornucopia sometime."

Rose groaned. "Don't talk about getting dizzy, I'm already sick—"

Jack shoved an emergency paper air bag under Rose's chin as the plane dipped sharply and several female passengers shrieked in fear. "Aim for the target, honey," he urged her.

"Now don't *you* get sick, too," Phil told Alice.

Alice snorted. "How much sicker can I get from just looking at you? My hero!"

"Next time if there is one, I'm going alone," Phil resolved firmly.

"Make that a promise and stick to it," said Alice, as the plane flew bumpily on toward Nassau. . . .

At Terence Thompson's Nassau headquarters in the Aquarius Tower, Dan Francovich and Thompson were monitoring the weather reports coming in on the hurricane named Brenda.

Thompson had the best possible tracking equipment he could buy as an adjunct to local TV and radio coverage. The penthouse living room was hooked up with a specially designed weather teletype circuit service that brought in all significant weather bureau forecasts from city and airport offices along the U.S. Gulf of Mexico and the southernmost Atlantic seaboard regularly every few minutes. A second teletype circuit served all other city and airport offices along the northerly Atlantic coast from New Jersey to Portland, Maine. In addition to the circuits, Thompson also had installed a private custom-built TV monitor in one corner of the living room that received a series of still photos from a closed-circuit TV satellite tracking system. So he was not only covered locally and along the American coastline from Texas to Canada by all this equipment, he was also able to view the disturbance called Brenda from space.

Both men were especially engrossed by reports emanating from two of the Atlantic hurricane centers, Miami and San Juan, Puerto Rico, these being the closest to Brenda. Once the disturbance had exceeded 74 miles an hour, it became an official hurricane, and being the second of the season in the area, it had been christened Brenda automatically from the prepared list for the year.

Brenda had already proved herself dangerously erratic during her short lifetime, rapidly changing course at least four or five times already, making normal advance storm warnings of twenty-four hours useless. It was anybody's guess whether she would blow right across the spine of the Bahamas as she moved westward and southward or wear herself out somewhere in the vast Atlantic or head north toward the Carolinas, building vicious energy en route.

Beyond the penthouse windows the sky was deceptively clear. ATS satellite had first spotted Brenda long before her signature was recognized by the falling barometer. Now visible from the glass walls of the penthouse were long, high swells rolling in on the New Providence Island beaches, breaking with a thunderous sound that could be heard up in the lofty tower suite that was some distance from the sea.

As the hours passed, the sky turned gray, the weather became increasingly oppressive and sultry; winds were variable, wave action more rolling, with occasional dead calms.

Thompson saw Brenda's weather as an omen.

"Maybe I'm not meant to invest out here," he said to Francovich. Into his fourth Coke of the late afternoon, he was stripped down to a sleazy T-shirt and beltless Levis, his incipient gut jutting out over the top of his jeans. He hadn't shaved that day; his chin looked frosty. "Maybe I'm being told by the Almighty to get the hell out while the getting's good," he speculated. "This is a risky damn' part of the world, so close to Cuba and Haiti and all."

"So's drilling for oil in the Middle East," Francovich reminded him, "but you play that game in depth every day."

"I suppose you're right. The Reds could walk in anytime and take over. Or, more realistically, the bloody Arabs could nationalize me and my rigs today or tomorrow, and spit in my face. I'd be powerless to do anything about it, except cry."

Thompson studied Francovich's impassive features carefully. "Danny boy, do you think my wanting to expand down here is wrong?"

"What do you mean by 'wrong'?" Francovich countered. He knew exactly what the big man meant; Thompson's conscience always got to him when he was about to implement an action that would either dislocate or annihilate any resisting force that stood in his path, such as the small businessman.

"Well, I mean, I create jobs where there aren't whenever I take over something. I bolster sagging economies."

Yes, he was a study in social cancer, all right, thought Francovich wryly. "No," he replied, "seen in that light, there's nothing wrong with moving in. Why're you asking me all of a sudden?"

"I was reading that book of Eldridge Cleaver's about the Black Panther movement and he said there are several kinds of social sickness. One's homosexuality, the other's baby-rape, and the third's wanting to become head of General Motors. . . . Now, for Christ's sake, that makes me the sickest of all, according to him, doesn't it? Because I'd like to become head man of the universe. But not rule people," Thompson confessed, "only control the purse strings, make the economy bend to my judgment."

"Cleaver's an extremist," said Francovich. "I think you have to examine his militant viewpoint in the light of his personal experience." It wasn't the answer Thompson wanted to hear, he knew, but it was the best he could do. "I think I'll get some fresh air." He excused himself and slipped out onto the terrace for a moment to stare at the red-orange sunset, all flame and tortured thunderheads.

During the past few days he'd had more exposure to Thompson than in all the previous months put together—the *Sarcophagus* cruise, and now the confinement of the Aquarius Tower penthouse—and he wasn't at all sure about his reaction to it. Very soon now he would have to make a decision, probably after the weather crisis had resolved itself.

Would he continue on with Thompson? This was the thought that was beginning to plague him to the point where he found it difficult to sleep. Did he really want the kind of gross materialism that could eventually make him a multimillionaire as Hank Alexander had become before he was thrown out of the empire? And if he did, then he knew what to expect: riches and a generally demoralizing dependency on object values.

Dan was still young enough to shape the future to his wishes, still essentially flexible, but it was a vital obligation to know where you were at all times, whatever your actions, to know how to deal with both worlds—call them hip and straight—if you liked those terms. Call them anything. In his association with Thompson, Dan was seeking a frame of reference that would ultimately weigh in determining a self-disciplined life-style. A balanced viewpoint was vital if he wanted to be of even modest value to his age. Exposure to Thompson would be a significant tool in his work, but the price for this exposure was high.

During his wakeful nights he'd come up with the idea that he might like to teach law at some small college. Possibly live on his own farm close to the college, ideally getting back to values that most people were in danger of losing or had already lost. Or was this too sweepingly idealistic, too naïve? But then, he couldn't remain in the clutch of a power syndrome forever; it would ultimately claim his spirit if not his soul. It may already have come for Thompson's, he thought, who, for all his homespun façade, was a highly sophisticated mandarin, a dedicated wizard of sorts, exuding an overpowering stench of money that was almost putrescent. The Midas touch had a built-in fatality factor, a pay-as-you-go clause. Once Dan had learned all he could about what vast amounts of wealth meant in the abstract and how they could be manipulated for good or evil, then he was determined to break away. Another six months, a year? He didn't know now. But this would be his weapon for life. Yet, while he fashioned this cudgel, there existed the constant temptation to reach out and use the power so close to him for selfish reasons. This must be assiduously guarded against, resisting Thompson's bribes when they came, for he knew he was as vulnerable as the next man—as Alexander had been. His character could stand just so much beguilement before it capitulated. So, if he remained on, he would have to strike a delicate balance between the need and the temptation, restrain his head, keep his cool.

Dan stared at the fiery, portentous sunset, then turned and walked along the wraparound terrace to the southeast that faced the islands over which Brenda was now gathering her central strength—a huge, misshappen doughnut of a monster generating enough energy every second of her existence to equal ten Hiroshima bombs. One hour of Brenda's energy equaled all the electric power the U.S. could generate in a year. Awesome thought!

Dan shook his head, smiling to himself at his marshaling of statistics. Yes, he was even beginning to think like Thompson, in the negotiable terms of a computer. Even the terrible force of this giantess of nature could be reduced to Thompson's TV screens and teletape, to the dry, comparative facts Thompson would convert into the rhetoric of personal power. The big man, he decided, knew no other language, had probably never felt a truly warm, personal emotion in all his life. Or was that a side of Thompson he would never see? Was Marilyn Thompson that single exception? He rather hoped so; it was easier to forgive Thompson most of his excesses if he had at least loved and cherished one human being during his long, busy career instead of lavishing all his heart on a prime core of power.

Dan thought briefly about the letter he'd dared to send Marilyn Thompson through her mother. It might bring them together; it might fall on deaf ears. Anyway, he felt that his underhandedness in sending it was fully justified; it would prove something. Maybe they both weren't real, maybe Thompson enjoyed the role of martyr, or Marilyn liked being the pampered child, or perhaps even nearer the truth—Thompson refused to accept his own mortality and the gravity of his illness.

But there were graver issues than this, lessons to be cited. Such as the fact that Thompson wouldn't even look at a hurricane named Brenda as some willful, magnificent natural phenomenon, but only as a business factor determining his future course of action. And Brenda, Dan knew as he watched her ominous bulk gathering on the distant horizon, was liable to be an extremely difficult girl, capricious, full of terrible surprises.

The Nassau mail and cargo boat docked in the small southern harbor shelter of Devil Cay on its return voyage to New Providence from the southeastern islands. It was able to absorb all the black help who wished to flee the possible approaching holocaust, as well as José Ortega and other remaining guests who couldn't make the afternoon plane and had since changed their minds about remaining on the island.

The voyage to Nassau would take the boat the rest of the day, possibly several hours into the night; and it was liable to be a rough one. Yet at least everyone felt they'd be sailing away from the worst of the storm—or so the mail-boat captain assured them—and that the weather should, with some luck, remain more or less constant during their voyage to Nassau, though stormy and rough.

From the slight rise of the terrace at Bimini Springs, protected by the bulk of the main building, Cindy Brown and Kevin watched the mail boat pass through the choppy reef channel and head out into the gray and turbulent sea, bound for New Providence Island. There would be quite a few seasick passengers, Kevin knew, but they'd have a safer refuge at Nassau against total disaster—if it came, and he hoped it wouldn't.

"You should be aboard that boat," Kevin told Cindy as they headed for his office after the small ship had disappeared across the gray horizon.

"I prefer to stay here with you," Cindy replied. "I'm not afraid."

"You're sure you're all right?"

"Just fine."

"You seem nervous and preoccupied over something, Cindy. Having second thoughts about us?"

"No, not about us."

"I hope not. By staying on, you've put yourself entirely into my hands and made me responsible for your safety."

"For my future." Cindy smiled and took his arm. "That's the way I want it to be. What about the others who're staying?"

"Well, Ruth would naturally hang on. She never runs away from anything. She's always where she's needed."

Cindy considered this for a moment as they walked. "An admirable trait that implies worlds of self-control. I wish I could be like that."

"You put yourself down too much," Kevin told her. "You and Ruth are entirely different people with very different motivations. You're not being fair to yourself by making that kind of comparison. For example, take Ruth's background. She was on hand in central Saigon a couple of Christmases ago when that officer's billet was bombed, the one where the VCs drove a truck of explosives into the courtyard and it tore out several lower floors of the building. Ruth was on the roof garden at the time. She didn't panic; she rushed downstairs and took care of the wounded and saved some lives."

"I remember reading about the bombing. It was horrible."

"But Ruth was as calm as always. She's even been known to pass out coffee and tranquilizers during Saigon's heaviest rocket bombardments. She can take just about anything in her stride."

"Yes," said Cindy impatiently, not wanting to hear more. "Ruth's an admirable person."

Kevin studied her profile carefully. A moody creature, he'd already discovered, possessive and jealous. He supposed it all went back to her early background of wealth and indulgence.

"What's bothering you? Is it Ruth?"

"Of course not." Cindy replied so brusquely that Kevin wondered if she was perhaps straining to brush aside her growing fear of the storm's threat, for she had admitted to being worried about the approaching hurricane.

They entered Kevin's private office, closing the door against the rising wind, shutting out its burgeoning power, yet even the closed room still breathed with the storm's accelerating pulse.

"Let's see." Kevin was at his desk. "Who's staying on?" He ran over a lodge list.

"Well, Joan Harrison's still here, and the headwaiter, Kilroy Howard," Cindy said.

"Yes, and the Baileys, the gardener and his wife."

"Oh, and don't forget the lord and lady of the manor, our dear Maples." Cindy's tone indicated quite clearly what she thought of them.

Kevin's phone rang; an agitated Harry Maple was on the line.

"Doc, I think we got some real worries," Harry said. "Brenda seems to be bearing down on us."

"Yes, it looks that way, all right."

"O.K., so we'll prepare for her. Let's all meet in the main lounge in half an hour and decide what we'll do. This one could be a bitch."

"O.K., see you then." Kevin hung up and turned to Cindy. "Harry's planning his own reception for Brenda."

"And I suppose Marge will be looking her immaculate best?"

"Not a hair out of place, even in a hurricane," Kevin said, wondering what was really bothering Cindy, for it wasn't the Maples. . . .

But neither Marge nor Harry appeared their usual snappy, well-turned-out selves when the group met in the main lounge less than half an hour later. The Maples were dressed for combat in matching rainsuits.

"The crisis is serious," Harry explained when all were quiet. "Brenda's no joke. We're going to have to knock out the generators soon, which means we won't have power. We've got some food ready, and I suggest you eat as much now as you can. This'll be the last hot meal until this thing blows over."

"What if it don't blow over, Mr. Maple?" Linc Bailey asked.

"Well, Linc, if it hits us real hard, we won't know the difference after a point, will we? We're on pretty low ground here."

"There's always the caves," Kill suggested, and all heads swiveled toward him.

"Yeah, that's right," Linc agreed. "The caves are high and dry."

"Thank you, gentlemen," Harry said with intended irony. "I'm very familiar with caves. I was just about to say that they may just be the safest place on the island if things get real serious. We both have a good point, Kilroy."

The caves lay beneath the cliff crest where Kill had made his rendezvous with Joan. They consisted of two long passageways roughly seven feet each in diameter—natural tunnels, symmetrical enough to have been driven manually through the porous volcanic rock instead of erosion-carved.

Harry explained the caves to the group: "The two passageways on the landward side that face toward Bimini Springs Lodge have separate entrances. They form the lower branching arms of a giant Y some one hundred and fifty feet long. The confluence of the Y is the highest point in the passageways and leads into an upper pocket cave with a vaulted ceiling. It's stuffy in there, but easily capable of sheltering us all, should this be required."

"Even if the storm gets really rough?" Ruth Severn asked.

"Well, if monster waves start battering the rocky point from the seaside, we'd have to expect some flooding of the seaward passageway," Harry pointed out. "But the wave action would rush up, through and down the branching passageways of the Y, and then flow out through the landside cave entrances toward the island's center, thus providing a gravity drain. We might all get soaked a few times, but we wouldn't be in any great danger, not unless the eve of the storm passes directly overhead."

"What then?" said Ruth.

"In that case the wave action would reverse itself under wind pressure and drive sea water clear over and across the island and up through the two landward forks of the Y—"

"Which means?" said Kevin. Harry was so damned slow and pompous about everything.

"That we'd better start praying," Harry told him, and glanced at Marge, not so serene beneath her composed features.

Kill stood up. "O.K., then, what're we waiting for? Everybody ought to eat what they can, and we'll pack food and water up to the caves right away while it's still light enough to see. You want to eat now, men, or come with me?" Kill addressed only the black males. To a man they agreed to go with him at once.

"Aren't the caves a little premature?" Kevin asked Harry, not wanting to see the group unnecessarily alarmed at this point. Tension would mount high enough later on if they were hard-hit.

Surprisingly enough, Harry was pleased with Kill's initiative, completely amenable to his packing up the supplies. "No," he replied, "I think Howard's right. The sooner we face up to it, the better. This looks like a bad one."

Joan rose briskly. "Come on, ladies." She addressed Lulu Bailey and the two other black women who had stayed on, one a maid, the other a kitchen helper. "Let's get us organized on blankets and wet gear for everybody."

"I'll see about lanterns and securin' the power plant," Linc volunteered. "We can batten it down careful enough so's it'll operate again once this thing blows by."

"Fine, fine," said Harry, "and the rest of us'll do what we can to protect the lodge buildings and equipment."

"What about the office machines and records?" Marge said.

"I'm going to lash them down with tarpaulin, especially the big file cabinet."

"Should've been in the tower room all along," Marge reminded him. "Like I'm always telling you."

"Oh, it'll be O.K. unless—"

Marge shivered. "I don't even want to think about *that* prospect."

Nor did Harry; a disastrous storm would finish them off. "Never mind, honey." He gave her a love pat on the shoulder. "We won't worry about anything. Brenda's a gamble, but no worse than being forced out."

Marge looked as though she might cry at any moment. Embarrassed, Kevin turned to Ruth and Cindy. "Let's see about organizing some medical supplies. . . ."

"That bastard Thompson," Marge grouched when they were all alone.

"Calm yourself, honey. We'll come to that crisis when it happens. Meanwhile, let's do our chores. Might as well get set to meet Brenda eye-on. Got to be ready for the caves even if we don't have to go up there. . . ."

"Those dreadful caves! If Brenda does pass over, I plan to fly right up into her eye and sail all the way to New England with her," Marge said, desperately trying for humor. "Anyway, I read somewhere that birds do it. Or else maybe—" and she stopped.

"Else maybe what—?"

"I'll just go *down* on my knees and *pray* to God, asking Him to spare us."

"Don't be sacrilegious, honey," Harry cautioned gravely, and gave her an affectionate pat on the nates. "Save that kind of action for the right time of night!"

Toward late afternoon the storm grew worse; the wind churned the sea into a boiling fury of angry waves and driving spray. Shortly before midnight the Maples decided that the safest place on the island was the caves. The phone system had already water-logged out, so Harry and Marge personally rounded up the group in the main lounge once again.

Kevin checked heads as the last group members filed in. "Everyone's accounted for," he told Harry. "When do we go?" He was leaving the final authority to the Maples, for after all, it was their island, their lodge; they were the ones who had the most to gain or lose from the effects of Brenda.

"We'll go now," said Harry, just as a particularly vicious gust of wind smashed several poolside deck chairs against the windowed wall of the lounge and sent shards of flying plate glass in all directions, narrowly missing the group. "Spare those electric torches when you can, folks. We won't touch the lanterns yet," Harry advised, "not until we're settled in the cave. No use wasting light; we don't know how long we'll be all cooped up together in there."

Nor how frightened we'll be, thought Cindy, but it was

better than facing the other alternative, the decision she dreaded more than the hurricane.

Kevin and Ruth had stocked the cave with an assortment of medical supplies earlier; and Joan and Kill had taken up enough food to last four days. The main lodge buildings had been made as secure as possible.

Rain gear was handed out; there were no jokes as the group dressed in silence against the storm's savage howl. Many carried small valuables; Harry's treasure was an expensive short-wave radio that he cradled beneath his rainsuit in a thick waterproof bag.

"This baby works miracles," he told Kevin. "You can get anything on it. Should come in mighty handy."

If it works inside the cave, it'll be a miracle, thought Kevin, knowing what confinement and dampness had done to the sturdiest radio equipment in Vietnam. But he made no comment; Harry had enough on his mind at present without another worry.

Finally all were dressed and ready to move.

"O.K., group," Harry called out, then opened the main lounge door and stepped into the roaring darkness.

Cindy Brown hadn't fully realized the enormity of the storm's power until she was out in it. The crowns of the languid, graceful palm grove behind the main lodge building were cracking like whips in the frenzied gale; several tall trees had snapped off near their bases. Debris lay everywhere; the roar of the sea was monstrous—a seething, raging mass surrounding them on all sides.

They moved slowly through the stygian darkness, their puny electric torch beams lighting the wind-driven spray that whipped across them in zigzag white sheets. It was difficult for many of the group to remain upright against the wind. The crash of waves racing inland over the lowest flanks of the island sounded perilously close to Cindy, almost at her feet, and the air reeked of seaweed and brine. It was easy enough to imagine that the sea was devouring the land, she thought, and clung fiercely to Kevin's sturdy arm as they moved toward the center of the island through soggy scrub and low pines, climbing over broken branches, slipping and sliding as they went.

Bent over double against the wind, they ascended very gradually toward the rocky rise at the northeastern flank of the island. The wind seemed to increase substantially as they proceeded, rising higher and higher until it became an eerie, keening shriek above the freight-train roar of the sea.

Joan held up the collar of her rain gear to protect her face from the icy sting of the driving spray. The Baileys and the other blacks following her started to sing a weird, moaning chant, half tribal, half spiritual, that was lost in the chaos of the storm. Probably some island supplication against nature's cruelty, Kevin decided, and probably as good a catharsis as any pallid radio report could give them at the moment.

"I'm scared," Marge shouted, leaning on Harry as they struggled along.

"That makes two of us, honey," he shouted back. "I don't exactly feel like John Wayne. We'll be all right when we reach the cave. It's not far now. . . ."

Once in the shelter of the lower Y-branch of the cave, they were at least out of the bludgeoning wind and the merciless assault of driving rain and sea water. The group struggled up to the confluence of the Y where the two rough passageways joined to form the single, slightly inclined descending cliffside channel.

The women grouped into the upper pocket chamber above the confluence, damp and muggy but away from possible flooding. The men stationed themselves at the lower level of the Y, with access to all three passageways and a few feet below the pocket chamber.

Kill trimmed the kerosene lanterns while Harry spent several minutes crouched near the lower landside cave exit trying to bring in a coherent short-wave radio report on the storm. All he got came through as gibberish over the pop and crackle of interference and the steady roar of the storm. Inside the cave he could get no radio response at all. He returned to the men, cursing roundly.

"Goddam thing's let me down," he grumbled to Kevin, wet and disgruntled.

"It's not important," Kevin said. "We're doing the best we can, and we're safe in here. I hate to think of the people on other islands who have to stick this out at sea level. . . ."

Gradually everyone settled down to the new environment. The black maid and kitchen helper were stretched out asleep in a few minutes, as were Linc and Lulu. Kill and Joan made themselves as comfortable as possible near the confluence of the passageways.

"This is the best place to be," Kill said, "not crowded into that stuffy chamber. If the waves start poundin' up over the cliff and shoot through, we can still scramble for higher ground."

Joan snuggled against him. "I keep thinkin' about that vile Cassel creature, all safe and sound and out of it, in some neat Nassau hotel, the bitch!"

"Don't think about nothin'," Kill said. "Relax, girl. Try to get some sleep. . . ."

Ruth and Cindy, wrapped in blankets, dozed side by side near Kevin. They were all lucky, Kevin reflected. Even the mail boat could be in trouble on its rugged return trip to Nassau—*if* it got there. And the poor island, Devil Cay, might not make it, either. By this time the sea would be swishing and gurgling angrily under lodge doors, windows would crash inward against the tattoo of the savage gale, and God knows what would happen to the smaller wooden buildings once the insidious rollers started running in from the flat harbor beach. Although most of Devil Cay was limestone and brick-solid, Kevin knew that the wide pink beaches might very well disappear in a storm of this magnitude, gouged out by its monstrous fury. Complete devastation possibly, which probability the Maples were taking rather well, he decided. Marge wedged against Harry's chest, her mouth slack in exhausted sleep; Harry's chin dropped on his collarbone, snoring. Lulu and the other blacks were arranged in a dim pile of blankets and rain gear. Joan and Kill looked so peaceful, close together.

Kevin studied Cindy, asleep next to Ruth, wanting to awaken her and talk, to hold her. But this was impossible with Ruth close by. And anyway, he was beginning to wonder about Cindy. Since yesterday afternoon she'd become extremely moody, withdrawn, only responding to him when he made a special point of commanding her attention. And his questions were unable to probe what was on her mind. Maybe it was unwise to consider the break from Bimini, to let this rich, unstable, outrageously spoiled creature support him, to be governed by her whims. While Cindy could make life easy for him in one sense, would she complicate his life unpleasantly, he speculated, and claim his independence? Well, whatever, the final decision still needed much thought. Specifically, he would have to know Cindy far better than he did now, even though the physical attraction was definitely there. And the money.

He leaned his head against the cave walls, tense and uncomfortable on his self-appointed vigil. It was somewhat like waiting for a field barrage you knew was imminent in minutes or hours, only in this case it was the peak of the expanding storm instead of shell fire. Gusts of wind boomed like cannon through the rock overhead, then died down suddenly, to be replaced by the permanent lower-keyed roar of driven wind and sea.

At intervals huge waves crashed against the cliff, making it shudder beneath each fresh wave's impact. Kevin could almost see the rough rock walls vibrate like jelly at each new assault. All of the refugees were about as safe and dry as possible, he thought gratefully, determined to stay awake until dawn, although this was a useless watch; there was nothing he could do against the storm's force. Then, very gradually, the monotonous, repetitive rhythm of the storm lulled him into a light doze, his head fell forward, heavy with fatigue. He slept. . . .

Joan stirred against Kill, opened her eyes, and looked up into his.

"You O.K.?" he asked, and groped for her hand, gripped it hard.

"I'm all right. How you doin'?"

"O.K., if you O.K. . . ."

"Funny fool," Joan said gently. "Strange man—"

"No, the strange one is you, girl. Always so fightin' mad and burned up about everythin'. Been all through *myself* a hundred times in this life, and I ain't strange at all. Just a plain human bein' inside out."

"Can't honestly say I know myself all that well," Joan admitted. "I try, but sometimes the issues get blurred."

"You'll settle in one day soon."

"But will you?" Joan said, and sat up. "Like putting roots down somewhere—?"

"Maybe, who knows? Still lookin' for my private gig. Fought enough in other folks' wars. About time I dug my own game, huh?"

"Ha, so you do follow me on some of my thoughts?"

"Some of them, sure. The bad folks gotta go, any color. Like Eva Cassel and some others we know. Walkin' over people's seen its day."

"Tell me—" Joan glanced toward the Maples. "I know."

"But my thinkin' ain't political, not like yours."

"You can be cured of that!" Joan said, elated, and moved closer to him just as a giant wave smashed against the cliff and set the rock around them to quivering.

"Man, that was a big mothah!" Kill murmured.

Joan drew even closer to him. "I'm scared, Kill. Tell me a bedtime story or somethin'—"

"Might come out more like a nightmare," he warned her.

"Just take my mind off that thing out there."

"O.K.," he said, wondering if he should. "Once there was this grunt, infantryman. Didn't like combat but got assigned to it, anyway, nothin' he could do, he was black. Had a chance to get transferred outta the field and into the big city once, take a fine job with officers' mess 'cause he knew how to handle it, havin' done restaurant business before the army. But this grunt's C.O. was a honky son of a bitch who wouldn't let him loose. Didn't need him, but wouldn't let him go. White grunts came and went, but this black one stayed put. . . . Hey, you know what a fragmentation grenade is?"

"I know what a grenade is," said Joan.

"Well, a fragmentation grenade's the deadliest kind. On impact it drives shrapnel slivers into anything within its range. Don't even issue 'em to troops no more, but they did when this black grunt was in the field. So, he knew another black grunt who also couldn't get transferred out because of the C.O. . . . And they talked it over. . . . Nobody knew who done it. Or if they knowed, nobody told nobody what they thought. Real pop sport in Nam, gettin' to ornery brass that way. Goes to prove that necessity works to liberate. Sure, the C.O. got liberated. And now you tell me, does that make the grunt who finally got transferred to the big city a bad one?"

Joan was silent for a moment, sifting the truth from the nightmare. "Don't know exactly what I'd do in the same situation. Hard to judge. Other night up above here on the rock when you got rough with me, I was mad. I wasn't in the mood. I thought about pushin' you over."

"I sure know that."

"You tussled, and we almost went over together—and then you sorta saved me. . . . I guess we dyin' all through our lifetimes," Joan said, "but sometimes we can't stand it no longer. We gotta break through. Life and order got no meanin' in the ordinary way. So, if I could've pushed you over, I guess I would have. And if you had to zap somebody to change your luck, you had to. Maybe that was the start of lookin' for your own private game. . . ."

"O.K.," said Kill, grateful for her words. "But I wasn't bein' rough the other night, it was love."

Joan laughed. "Yeah, love. Well, sometimes I want that, too, man, you know. But I don't like bein' treated as an object, not by brothers and sisters, or lovers. I get that treatment all the time from honkies. I wasn't gonna take it from you."

"All the same you're a nice object," Kill teased. "Nassau girls got pride. . . ."

"Wasn't always a Nassau city girl," Joan confessed. "Born a country girl on Andros Island. Didn't I ever tell you?"

"No," Kill said, thinking that she was constantly full of surprises. "You always rappin' about 'Over the Hill' in Nassau and how you gonna wake everybody there up one day. I thought it was your birthplace."

"Andros-born, but I got plans for the whole Bahamas. You'd like Andros, a big wild place with waterways and tidal creeks and no real rivers—estuaries, sort of. Two, three big islands all stuck together like one. Some parts never been explored, it's so low and swampy. There's some fine forests, too, flamingo all over the place. And you don't know what mouth-waterin' means till you had some home-baked breadfruit loaf and lime pie. Out in the Tongue's some of the world's best deep-sea game. Pot Cay's where I dream of livin' sometimes. Maybe build me a nice, airy castle of rock and just sit out my life there. . . ."

Kill regarded her dreamy, transfixed expression as she spoke. Underneath that urgent commitment lay contradictions he didn't understand too well, but she really was a simple country girl.

"Hell, woman," he told her, "I could settle there myself with a name like Pot Cay wrapped around me. We could build us that castle for two, start a resort of our own. Blacks only, no honkies allowed on the property. . . ."

Joan giggled. "Why not? Andros only got about twelve thousand folk there today since 1780—all pretty primitive types. Comin' from Andros you could believe in Chickcharnies, little dwarfs that live in high-top pine. And there's the luscas, half-dragon and half-octopus, livin' in caves. They snatch and eat you if you pass too close by. . . ."

"Now I know why you wouldn't come down in the cave with me the other night."

"I don't subscribe to such things," Joan snapped. "I only said the people from Andros believe in a lot of queer things. I'm here in the cave now, am I not?"

"You sure are."

"I believe in myself, my own power to live," Joan said stoutly.

"My money goes there, too, girl," Kill said, and embraced her as the cave shuddered once again from a giant wave, much larger than the last one.

Joan settled against Kill's chest, shutting out the storm's terror as best she could. "I'm tryin' to believe in you, too, Kill, but you a gypsy. . . . Maybe one day we can go to Andros if there's anything left after this blow. I've not been back since I was sixteen."

"We'll go to Pot Cay," Kill said, tracing the line of her jaw with his index finger. "We'll walk all over it. Together."

"Maybe," said Joan, and closed her eyes.

A few minutes later they were asleep again, sharing each other's warmth. . . .

Thompson and Francovich continued to monitor the weather reports on Brenda as they came in. They dined on lobster thermidor from TV trays in the vast living room so as not to miss any fresh news and were attended by Thompson's two husky male nurse aides who had accompanied them from the Coast.

Until he had overheard the conversation aboard the *Sarcophagus* the previous week, Francovich had always labeled Thompson's use of male nurses as personal servants a form of hypochondria. Now that he knew about the big man's specific illness, the aides seemed a logical appendage, although they were rather sullen and mute for the most part and did their bidding with a certain unstated arrogance. Which Thompson seemed to ignore, oddly enough, thought Francovich. And there could be only one explanation for this; the aides also acted as Thompson's personal bodyguards, packed weapons when they moved with him, thus saving the big man two salaries. So once again, Thompson won the game; there was no argument that his shrewdness with money continued to buy the power he cherished.

Toward midnight, gusty winds of high velocity whipped around Aquarius Tower and pressed against the thick plate-glass windows of the penthouse. A waning moon still shone dimly through a gauzy blanket of racing clouds.

Before Thompson turned in, yawning and bleary-eyed, he said casually, "By the way, Danny, I got a message that Joe Ortega's on his way back from Bimini Springs."

Thompson's "spic," of course, the chicano.

"How's he traveling?" asked Francovich. "No planes are up in this weather."

"He took the mail boat. He ought to be here by morning. The boat's giving the storm a wide berth and sailing the westerly route around New Providence."

"I was wondering about him," said Francovich. "That's a relief."

"I hope it is," Thompson replied ambiguously. "It'll depend on what kind of action he got for me. Well, goodnight, Danny boy. Don't let Brenda keep you up all night; she's not all that great."

"Goodnight, Terry."

There, thought Francovich, that was part of the problem. Thompson always thought of people as pawns to do his bidding, impersonal factors spewing out solved problems like computers, and never as vulnerable individuals who might possibly be motivated largely by their hang-ups. Did Thompson really have a heart, a true core of warmth and understanding and love that he'd never shown, or was he cold business all the way through? Packed with ticker tape, marketing reports, mergers, patents pending, contracts?—all the nuts and bolts and wheels that made high finance go? Well, he would probably never find out, Francovich felt, and at this point he wasn't at all sure he cared one way or the other, feeling directionless, played out. Abruptly he decided to follow Thompson to bed and let the storm take care of itself.

Aggie Bird was drunk in her suite at the Aquarius Tower. It was past midnight, and she'd been drinking steadily since her arrival from Bimini Springs with Wayne and Dick that afternoon. As the storm gathered outside, Aggie decided that the only antidote to losing the role in *The Bungalow* was a bottle—several of them, if necessary—and she'd ordered accordingly from room service.

Wayne Winslow had taken their three-bedroom suite for two nights, figuring that by the third morning they'd be able to fly to Miami in relatively calm weather, the storm having passed on by then. Neither Dick nor Wayne had had anything stronger than Coke, and as Aggie became more inebriated, more loose-mouthed and abusive, Dick had simply yawned, claimed fatigue, and retired to his room, leaving Wayne and Aggie to keep the night watch.

Aggie was into her second bottle of cognac, a very fine old one, worth a fortune at room-service prices. And the more she drank, the more she reflected with anguish on the loss of her *Bungalow* role, and the madder she got. Instead of directing her wrath toward Thompson, she was concentrating on Wayne, and Wayne was trying to ignore her, first reading a book, then staring at TV, hopefully holding the idea that Aggie ignored was an Aggie subdued. It didn't work out that way.

Aggie sprawled on a divan across the room from Wayne. To replenish her glass she had only to reach for the bottle on the coffee table and pour. She could see Wayne's composed profile watching storm statistics and dull weather reports on TV.

"Fuckin' medium," she growled. "Mass shit, that's what it is. Just as empty as McLuhan says. . . ."

"Oh, it's better than that," Wayne said, his eyes still on the screen. "You'll get used to the idea that you're bringing entertainment into millions of homes that you'd never reach otherwise."

"So who said I wanted to reach them in the first place? Besides, my old movies show up on TV."

"Well, you certainly snapped up the idea of the series fast enough when *The Bungalow* fell through."

"A drowning person snatches at anything," said Aggie flatly. "Now I'm having second thoughts. The synopsis you showed me isn't worth the paper it's written on. It's the worst pile of turds I've ever seen. And you want *me* to give the world a spoon so's it can eat shit! Sometimes, Wayne, I think you're a cold-blooded shark."

"I've got just as good teeth, Aggie, and I try to look out for you."

Aggie rolled herself into a sitting position. Her face was flushed and mottled, her hair disarrayed; the dress she wore was wrinkled, spotted with souvenirs of the soup that Wayne had forced her to ingest earlier.

"You selfish snot!" Aggie shouted, rising. "You've never had a single thought in your life that didn't concern your own personal well-being! You think I've been around movies for close to thirty-five years without some of it getting through to me? I've known a lot of bastards in my time and very few fine ones, and I know exactly how tough and cold and chiseling people are when the big stakes are involved. Even some of the good apples turn rotten under pressure. They say a stiff prick's got no conscience. Well, neither has the lust for power; it's devastating. And you know all about *that*—"

Wayne got out of his chair to switch off the TV. His eyes glittered coldly as he sat down again. "Are you all finished?" he inquired, and there was no tolerance in his voice.

"I'll never be *finished,*" Aggie retorted. "That's exactly what I'm talking about."

"No," he said slowly, "what you're talking about is plain stupidity. You're presenile, Aggie, but nobody's ever had the courage to tell you before. So I'm telling you now. All the booze and pills have gone to your brain. You're washed up, old girl, you've had it. I'm just carrying you along for old time's sake because I'm fond of you. You were my idol once, like you were for millions of others. And it hurts when idols fade or turn up with clay feet. That's why I fought so damned hard for *The Bungalow*—to keep an illusion going; you, Aggie Bird—and when I lost, right here in this hotel the other night, I think I was just lucky to have that TV series to fall back on. . . ."

"Oh shit, you make me sick with your slimy con!"

"For Christ's sake, Aggie, be realistic. A lot of fine actors are eating crow these days. Jane Withers does plumbing commercials, Henry Fonda snaps instant pictures. Jimmy Stewart's on a TV series, so's Rock Hudson and Shirley MacLaine. That's where the action is; they're lucky to be in business at all in times like these. Some, like old Patsy Kelly, made eighty movies and was plenty lucky to get into a Broadway show. Most people didn't know she was still alive. Fifi Dorsay, too. Listen, there's only one Duke Wayne who goes on forever. Even Crawford and Davis aren't working too much these days. So be reasonable, Aggie, face facts. The star system's dead, and you're too damned old and has-been to try to resurrect it. Try to settle for what you can get. And if you don't want it, if you think you're too proud to play a flighty matriarch in a domestic situation series, then O.K., walk out, that's your privilege. Turn it down. But when you do that, Aggie, that's the end of my responsibility and probably the end of your career."

Aggie glared at him with undisguised hostility.

"You really got a fuckin' nerve!" she burst out. "Think back to the time when I chose you from a line of snot-nosed kids to play my little boy in a walk-on. And you didn't have the talent to make it beyond that in pictures. Sure, you went to an acting academy, you made second leads in the Los Angeles little-theater circuit, but you never made it to the screen again, did you, huh? You got a keen eye and ear and nose for business, Wayne, you're a nine-day wonder, all right, I got to hand it to you. But you're a bust in the mouth for real talent, baby—and that's what you've always wanted most, isn't it, that talent! You never had it, and you never will. The best you can do is sell what somebody else has, which makes you some kind of a pimp, doesn't it? Well, doesn't it?"

"Aggie, you're going to regret this outburst in the morning," Wayne declared, "as you always do. You'll have a brutal hangover, you'll feel like death, and you'll be sorry you showed me your big mouth. I've got patience, old girl—God knows I need it in my business—but I exhaust it eventually. . . . Now look, TV's the medium that'll persist whether movies go from Russ Meyer and *Gimme Shelter!* to much, much worse. Every day the general audience for films gets younger and smaller. I'm thirty, Aggie, I can see both sides. I know what's happening, and I'm in there working. The big money, while it's around, is in TV. There isn't a star today who can command a million dollars a picture, except maybe the Duke, and he's unique, an all-time monolith, a natural wonder."

"I don't care, I want *The Bungalow*!" Aggie screeched with renewed fury, and snatched up the bottle of cognac, swigging from it on swaying feet.

Wayne shook his head dolefully. "You're a pitiful spectacle, Aggie. I think Dick had the right idea. I'm going to bed, too."

Aggie banged the bottle down on the coffee table. "And that's another thing," she raged. "You're a sneak! At least Dick openly plays the field. He admits it, he's honest. . . ."

"Aggie, Aggie," Wayne said with carefully controlled anger, "you're going too far."

"Oh yeah, whatever you do is O.K., is that it? Anything you say or do, that's just dandy. But if I want to do anying, it's a no-no all the way down the line!"

"What do you want to do, Aggie, besides make an ass out of yourself?"

"Go upstairs to his penthouse and kick that fucking Thompson in the cubes if I have to so I'll get *The Bungalow* back! I might even throttle him while I'm at it!"

Wayne sighed wearily; he'd had enough. "Don't be a fool, Aggie. Simmer down. Drink yourself unconscious right here if you feel you have to, but don't do anything as dangerously stupid as that. Anyway, I doubt if you could gain entry to Thompson's apartment. It's guarded."

"I'm not a fool," Aggie slurred drunkenly, "I'm a goddam good actress. Hell, I even got my footprints in Grauman's Chinese courtyard. I'm one of the all-time

Hollywood greats, and I want the chance to prove it again! *And* I won't shut up until it happens—"

Wayne stood up. "In that case I'm not going to stick around and listen to a talk marathon while you're waiting. Goodnight, Aggie. And for Christ's sake, go to bed. You're a revolting mess."

"You're worse than that!" Aggie shouted after him as he moved down the hall toward his room. "You're a goddam sexual hypocrite!" But Wayne chose to ignore her, and went into his room and closed the door behind him.

Nothing had to be futile, Aggie thought; there was a way out. She glared with affection and defiance at the cognac, wishing for miracles. She reached out uncertainly for the bottle to uncork it and take another drink, then hesitated. No, she'd had enough. That wasn't where the answer lay. And suddenly it dawned on her; she knew what she had to do. Now was the time—now or never. She lifted the telephone and asked for the operator.

Kevin and Ruth awakened simultaneously in the cave's pocket chamber. Ruth lay with her head pillowed against the tarpaulin-covered medical kit.

"It hasn't worked out the way we planned," Kevin said, almost contritely.

"You made the plans," Ruth replied, "I didn't," and her words were barely audible above the storm's tattoo. "It's all right, Kevin. Cindy's O.K. for you. You oughtn't to be so concerned about other's feelings when you've got your own to service. It's amazing you're a doctor at all with your hypersensitivity to people. You empathize too much."

"Is that another way of saying I'm weak and inconsistent?" Kevin said. "I chose medicine because I like to get involved. Maybe empathy's just a synonym for guilt."

"Well, don't sweat it. Take what you can and things'll take care of themselves. Maybe if we were more alike—but there's no point in going into that. Goodnight, Kev. . . ." Ruth smiled at him, turned her back, and settled down with her raincoat across her shoulders.

Remarkable woman, thought Kevin. Not a beauty, no feminine graces or special sensuality, but a wonderful, practical warmth emanated from her. Almost opulent compared to Cindy. And how was he going to handle the Cindy problem? His weariness settled over him gently; he blinked, regarding Cindy's quiet form thoughtfully, then leaned against the damp rock wall, hoping he could stay at least half-awake and not doze off again. There seemed to be no appreciable change in the storm's tempo, so maybe they were going to be all right after all. . . .

Sometime later Harry Maple woke in the flickering lantern light, and as he moved, Marge stirred next to him.

"You O.K., honey?" he asked, his lips against her cheek. "You comfortable?"

"I'm awake."

"I ought to sneak down to the office and make sure that everything's still protected."

"No!" said Marge sharply. "You stay right here! It's dangerous outside, and besides it's too dark to find your way." She put her arms around his neck and held him tight. "Stay—"

"But the photos and everything—"

Marge put her hand on his mouth to silence him and shook her head in a violent negative. "You aren't going anywhere, Harry Maple. Now settle down!" And finally he subsided into a light sleep, with Marge curled against him. . . .

"I'm Aggie Bird, and I'm going in there and talk to him!" Aggie shouted at the white-coated aide as she stood in the elevator foyer of Terence Thompson's plush penthouse apartment.

"You can't, Miss Bird."

"Goddamit, I know he's inside or you wouldn't have told me on the phone I couldn't see him!"

The husky male nurse was unimpressed by this fat, middle-aged harridan with the reeking breath and bloated features. Behind him lay the sacrosanct quarters of the big man, and he knew his responsibility—to admit no one at any time without his boss's clearance. And it was hands down against admitting this party, he knew; it would mean his job.

"I'm sorry, Miss Bird," the aide said with cold courtesy, "there's nothing I can do. Mr. Thompson left strict orders not to be disturbed by anybody."

"I'm not just anybody, you jerk!" Aggie bellowed. "I'm Aggie Bird, the actress!"

"Ma'am, if you were the President's lady the answer would still be the same," he replied, jangling a set of keys impatiently in one hand. He had come out into the foyer to try to reason with Aggie so she wouldn't create a disturbance and had locked the main door to the penthouse apartment behind him. But he hadn't calmed her down, and she was wasting his time.

"Why, you lousy snip!" Aggie screeched, and moved in like lightning, jamming her solid knee into the aide's groin. As he crumpled groaning to the floor, doubled over with pain, Aggie snatched his keys and let herself into the penthouse.

Once inside, she closed the door and leaned against it to catch her breath, winded from her encounter. Jesus, she was drunker than she'd thought she was downstairs. Taking matters into her own hands because Wayne was just too pussyfoot was one thing, but she'd have to act fast before that male nurse came after her. Now, where was that Thompson son of a bitch? It looked like a big apartment.

She staggered down a thickly carpeted corridor past vivid oil paintings splashed against white walls to a larger area with a spectacular triple glass-walled view of the storm raging over Nassau beyond. She found herself in the main lounge of the apartment and glanced at the bank of machines in one corner, TVs and tape monitors. At a huge table in another corner of the spacious lounge sat Terence Thompson, in sloppy pants and crumpled T-shirt, poring over a pile of papers and maps at a large study table.

Aggie paused and blinked. No photographs of Thompson had reached the public in several years; she found the change in him shocking. She had always remembered him as extremely youthful from their first meeting, with a shock of curly brown hair falling over his high forehead, a truly abrasive square jauntiness about him, a corny vocabulary, and a nervous, persuasive manner to match. But that was the past. He sure as hell wasn't the Casanova now that he'd been in his prime when rumor had it he claimed a record of mounting more than 300 chicks. Gaunt and withered, dried-out, with a slight stoop and graying features, he didn't look as though he could service his own wife—*if* she returned to him, which seemed unlikely.

Aggie advanced toward the study table and paused uncertainly a few yards from the figure bent over it.

"Terry Thompson?" she said above the shriek of the storm, her voice strident enough to carry easily across the room.

Thompson glanced up, startled, then leaned back suddenly in his chair. Before him stood one of the crones from *Macbeth*, or almost, and the creature was calling him by his first name.

"Who the hell are you?" he demanded, rising to his feet. "How'd you get in here?"

The creature tottered closer. Now he saw that she was quite drunk, her dress disheveled, her make-up smeared.

"I'm Agnes Bird. Aggie.... You know, the actress. What's the matter? Don't you remember me?"

Aggie Bird. Of course, but way, way back to the time when he was having such unbridled fun and all of Southern California was his for the taking. Golden days. The corporation was booming, all the girls flocked to date him. That fabulous time when anything he touched sprang to miraculous life and he had enough bravado and *machismo* for the whole goddam country. She'd been a tiny thing, then, great tits, nice firm ass, crazy legs; petite was what they called her. The face was heart-shaped then, piquant, framed by a dark cap of curls, and when she'd smiled on the screen, audiences would lean forward and bask in her warmth. He recalled their meeting at a Malibu party given by some director—Hawthorne Finlayson, that was it. A case of mutual admiration, he seemed to remember, their juices bubbling. He'd offered to drive her home because she'd come with her agent who was called away on urgent business; his kid had had a bike accident or something like that. She'd lived just down the beach; she was going to walk home, but he didn't have to talk very fast to get her into his new custom-built racer. She'd asked him in for a drink. They talked, she put on some music, a few of her songs and some dance music. They had a couple of drinks and started dancing and things got a little warm between them. Then, the first thing he knew he was in bed with her slithering around, banging her. And next, right after he climaxed, she started screaming rape and scored his back with her long red fingernails—as if she'd suddenly waked up to what they were doing after practically dragging him by his cock into the bedroom.... Angry, humiliated, his back a mass of stinging welts, he'd dressed and run, and that was all there was to it. He'd seen a couple of her films since, but he'd never seen her again face to face until this moment. And he hadn't even thought about her until her agent started making rude noises about that role she wanted in the film. Tonight he'd refused her call, and from all indications this meeting wasn't going to be especially propitious. The old bitch looked piss-ass.

"Aggie Bird," Thompson declared. "You called earlier from a downstairs suite. I'm busy, Miss Bird. Who let you in?"

Aggie giggled and flopped into a chair near him, brushing back a limp strand of hair from her eyes. "I guess I went too far," she confessed. "I put the knee to your male nurse, grabbed his keys, and let myself in. I'm pretty good at self-defense."

Thompson scowled angrily. "You got one helluva nerve," he told her, and pressed a concealed call button attached to the underside of the table.

"Yeah, I have, haven't I?" Aggie was immensely pleased with herself. "But you're locked up tighter than the goddam mint around here. You gotta fucking nerve, too."

"Me?" Thompson glared at her. "Why?"

"Maybe you don't remember Malibu and ancient times? We met at a party Hawthorne Finlayson gave."

"I recall enough."

"I thought you would if you tried," Aggie said, and at that moment Thompson's second aide appeared.

"Sir?" He glanced with surprise from Thompson to Aggie.

"Check the foyer, Bert," Thompson told him. "I think Jim's lying out there on the carpet. This—Miss Bird here got a little rough with him a minute ago and took his keys."

The aide glanced at her impassively. "Right, sir, I'll check immediately," he replied, and left.

"About that Malibu thing," Aggie resumed with her little girl smile, ignoring Thompson's smouldering anger and the situation she had created, "I was all set to walk home, but you said you wanted to show me your new sports car, and you'd drive me. So we went to my place. Where you made your first move—a very definite commitment about a part for me in a very big picture you were involved in as producer. I didn't suggest doing the part, you did. And then one little thing led to another, which is always O.K. with me under most circumstances when that's the only central issue. But just as you bounced off the goddam ceiling and got your nuts, yelling 'Here I come!' so loud the neighbors could hear you—in that same breath you told me that somebody else already had the role. . . ."

"Now look here." Thompson shook a furious finger at her. "What's that got to do with you busting into my apartment at this time of—?"

Aggie pounded her fist on the table and shouted, "Goddam you, let me finish!" She was starting to feel the rough, sobering edge of her cognac. "I went along with you and your big name and your parlor-sized cock—just about as far as I could. I didn't ask for that role, Terry Thompson, like I said. I didn't even know about it until you mentioned it. It was your original idea I should work for you. And what still pisses me off plenty to this day whenever I think about it is that you *used* me under false pretenses, you double-fucked me. If you'd said, 'Listen, Aggie honey, I'm horny, I need a little, let's roll'—O.K., that's my kind of language, I'd've understood you just fine. Or maybe you're so bullheaded you can't figure out simple basic things like that about women and you have to make everything devious and complicated, is that it? Tell me something, is making money the only thing you know how to do right, Mr. Thompson?"

Thompson fixed her with a look so malevolent it would have annihilated anyone who worked for him, but Aggie wasn't in the least intimidated.

"Come on, Terry, tell me."

"I won't dignify your stupidity with an answer," he replied stiffly. "How does all this crap relate to your present visit? I've got important work to do here, and you're wasting my valuable time, Miss Bird."

"Yeah, you'd put a price on anything, wouldn't you? Don't worry, sweetie, I won't take very much of your precious time. Relax, sit back. Let me say what I came to say and I'll leave quietly."

Thompson hesitated a second, then slumped deep into his chair, chewing on his lower lip, glaring silently at her.

"I don't know what you want out of life, Terry Thompson," Aggie said in low, throaty tones that barely reached him, thus demanding his full attention, "I don't understand men like you, I never did. I guess it's the power sickness. Don't you ever stop to think about the human element when you make a move? Aren't you ever concerned with anything besides the corporate bulk of a transaction? I don't think you are. Which brings me right to my point. I was chosen not so long ago for a very coveted role in a film called *The Bungalow*. When I saw it on Broadway, I'd have bought it for myself if I could have, and when it was offered to me, I jumped at the chance. I guess I don't have to explain the details, do I?"

Thompson shook his head silently.

"All right! So I got the role on talent, not for my lovely face or pretty ass," Aggie pursued. "And then yesterday my agent flies in to Bimini Springs from Hollywood with the sad news that I'd lost the part to Lola Crandall, of all people. Because Thompson Enterprises is planning a critical merger with one of the subsidiary companies of Peptone which is owned by Lola's current boyfriend who's Peptone's chairman of the board. Complicated, but I got the message right off, I'm good at getting behind the scenes. And for your information, it was a blow in the guts. I honestly felt like cutting your goddam throat. That cock-cruncher Lola Crandall couldn't act her way into a detergent commercial, Terry Thompson, and you know it as well as I do. So what kind of a game are you playing—good business? I don't think so; for sure as hell, if you put Lola into that picture, you're going to lose your bankroll. She's a living death warrant. And what you'll gain from Peptone spin-offs you're sure to lose twice over on *The Bungalow* with that bitch in it. While *I* could quadruple your investment in the film."

Thompson was deeply amused at her reasoning and allowed her the ghost of a grin. "Other than those hysterical reasons, what makes you feel you ought to have the part?"

"Oh hell, what kind of a stupid question is that?" Aggie demanded. "My superior ability plus the commitment you once Indian-gave me in my own bed, Terry Thompson. Unless of course you've become so goddam warped and callous you can't get your kicks any other way except giving and taking away whenever it suits your whim. Goddam it, you owe me the picture!"

Now Thompson grinned widely. Perhaps it was the Indian-giver label that struck a responsive chord, he wasn't sure. Anyway, the old bag was right, he had to admit privately, he did spend a large share of his time giving and retrieving favors; that was one of the reasons Marilyn had run off. At the time of their marriage he'd promised her she'd be able to do as she liked—take trips anywhere when she felt like it, have private tutors, entertain guests at the ranch as it pleased her. But he hadn't allowed any of these promises to become realities. Special guards hounded her wherever she went, even up to Kim Novak's, a special friend of hers; she could never go anywhere on her own. He claimed that tutors snooped, he wouldn't allow her to study at a university; and the only guests who found their way to the ranch were his special business associates, and her mother a few times—though he never spoke to the woman.

"So, I owe it to you," Thompson said, repeating Aggie's phrase. "And you think it's that simple, huh?"

"I don't think anything's simple anymore," she responded seriously, "I'm too damned old for that. But I do believe that a few decent acts between people are still possible, like consideration and honoring your obligations. What the hell is this world coming to if you or I can't do something for somebody only because it makes them feel good, keeps them alive—and not for any ulterior motive?"

Yes, he thought, the old girl is desperate, with his exact look of need in her eyes, in the sag of her jaw. The merger with Harker could be approached easily from another angle; Francovich or the three monkeys would think of something for him. And fortunately, due to the storm, he hadn't yet sent word to Harker that Lola Crandall would be the new star of *The Bungalow*. Only Aggie Bird's agent had been informed of the change.

"All right," he conceded, "all right. The part's yours again. I'll see to the necessary arrangements. . . . So you're trying for a comeback, is that it?"

"Comeback, shit!" Aggie growled, "I've never been *away*! I want *The Bungalow* to define my status as the senior female member of a dying industry. The film will do it, don't worry, because I'll do it to the film. And you'll make more goddam money than *The Devil Has Wings* made. Which incidentally was the picture you *didn't* give me a long, long time ago. . . ."

Thompson stood up, weary with her.

"O.K., Miss Bird. Tell your agent to get in touch with me in the morning. I'll talk to him."

Aggie had forgotten how tall he was, how sort of hunched over, like a bird of prey. Scruffy was the word, she thought, and no graceful aging here; he was all lumps and bumps and exhaustion. Maybe he was ill, or simply a frantic, lonely old man. Too damned bad that he hadn't found somebody who could tolerate him. She was better off than he was, with all his money and power, for she knew that with her inner resources she could rise above anyone—Wayne, Dick, anybody. But Thompson looked helpless, almost forlorn. His strength might be his genius for finance, but in any other area he was Samson minus the long hair.

"I hope I can trust you," said Aggie.

"Don't challenge me!" Thompson barked at her. "I might change my mind."

Aggie smiled at him, the old radiance infusing her features momentarily with warmth.

"Thanks a lot, Terry. I'll go now. . . ."

"And for Christ's sake, woman, do something about your appearance, you're a fright."

Aggie lifted her sagging bosom and shot out her chin.

"Listen here—!"

"I've read *The Bungalow,* and I know you're supposed to be a wild-haired old broad, but you don't have to look type-cast."

Aggie smoothed her wrinkled dress, fluttered a hand to her hair. "I've still got some weight to lose," she admitted, "a balance to reach. Don't you worry about me, Terry, I'll do you proud. I'll be all right. . . . And thanks, thanks a lot. I—I respect you for everything."

"Will you please go," said Thompson.

"I'm going, I'm going," she said, starting for the corridor, then paused, fixing him with a backward glance. "And while we're on the subject, you get yourself together, too, Terry. It's late, sweetie, and we haven't got much time. . . ."

Long afterward Kevin wasn't sure whether the screams and the cannon-like crash came simultaneously or whether the high, shrill sounds were a prelude to the blitz of a wave that hit the cliff. Anyway, the wave's shuddering aftermath caused the rock beneath him to tremble sickeningly, almost to lurch, and Kevin jumped up in the wavering lantern light, startled, rubbing sleep from his eyes.

Most of the group had also been awakened by the violent concussion. Ruth and Cindy were upright, looking around dazedly. Joan and Kill were getting to their feet, and the two Baileys beyond them were sitting up with the other blacks. Kevin looked for the Maples, saw only Marge standing in the center of the Y confluence waving her arms about crazily. Her mouth was wide open, her head thrown back, and a demented scream tore from her throat. Harry was nowhere in sight.

Kevin scrambled across the bodies, grabbed and shook her. "Where's Harry?" he shouted, but Marge wasn't even vaguely aware of his question and continued screaming. Kevin slapped her across the cheek; she staggered backward, shook her head, then slowly began to focus on him, her expression pure, frenzied fright.

"Harry's gone," she sobbed.

"Where?" Not out in the storm, Kevin hoped, but where else would he go?

"To the lodge," Marge amplified, confirming his worst

suspicions, then collapsed against him and began to cry. "He wanted his photo file," she blubbered into his shoulder, "and some other important papers he'd signed. He went while I was asleep."

"Oh no!" groaned Kevin. Outdoors was sheer suicide. One big wave like the last one could easily sweep a person right out to sea.

"Dead, dead," Marge chanted, pushing away from him. "Killed, I know it!"

Kevin turned to Ruth. "Get something from the kit," he ordered, and Ruth jumped to obey. The kind of hysteria that Marge was presently engendering was infectious; in a few minutes, if she weren't sedated, Kevin knew it could spread to all of them.

He turned back to Marge, but she wasn't there. He glanced toward the lower branch of the Y and saw her stumbling down through the passageway toward the howling darkness beyond.

He ran after her, and just as she disappeared into the driving horror of wind and rain, a second huge bomb of a wave struck savagely against the cliff face, smashing into it like a battering ram, its liquid force cascading up and over the crest of the rock and rushing down the landward slope with enormous force, sweeping everything before it. Marge was engulfed by the wave before he could reach the mouth of the cave.

Kevin stopped just short of the opening as a foamy surge of backwater swept violently up through the passageway, soaking him waist-deep in chill brine. Damn, there was nothing he could do except stagger back up the inclined passageway, wet and dripping. Fortunately the wave's force had sent it up and over the rock. Had the huge volume of water been driven straight down through the upper tunnel entrance, he might have joined Marge in certain death. And he reminded himself that sooner or later one of the big ones could easily sweep through the Y stem's upper entrance along the confluence and down out through the lower arms. Then, of course, the only refuge would be the upper corner of pocket chamber—and maybe not even that, for they could drown in there just as easily, too, if the volume of water grew great enough. Nevertheless he'd better move the group.

Herding them all together, he placed everyone as high up into the pocket chamber as possible—most of them had been sprawled dangerously close to the confluence. And his hunch was right; for they were no sooner settled in their new location than another giant wave hit the cliff, sending a torrent of cold salt water gushing and surging through the lower passageway, depositing swirls of foam almost at their feet. Kevin wasn't personally frightened, but he shuddered to think what might have happened had there been no proper shelter. Now there was nothing they could do except cross their fingers and hope and pray, waiting out the big periodic waves, one by one, as they hit with the noise and power of a head-on train collision, huddled damp and miserable and cramped in their stuffy quarters, shivering and not a little frightened. . . .

At last, after what seemed like weeks—it was only a matter of a couple of hours—a thin gray finger of light crept up the passageway to the confluence below the chamber. The sea sounded much calmer; the waves seemed to have passed their zenith force. Brenda's energy center was hopefully moving away from Devil Cay.

"Let's go out now," Kill said to Kevin, impatient to check the hillside as the morning light grew stronger. "Let's look and see what she did, Doc."

Kevin restrained him. "It's died down so fast we can't be sure we're not going through the eye of the storm. Better wait awhile."

"Doctor, we're not in the eye," Joan said. "I've been through too many of them. I know the signs. It's definitely moving away."

"Let's wait another half hour, anyway."

"Hey, how about my trying the Maples' radio?" Kill suggested. "I could fiddle around the cave entrance and maybe pick up some news."

"Go ahead," said Kevin, and Kill began to look around for it. But in the move to the upper cave chamber, Harry's radio had somehow been forgotten by all of them. Now it was gone, swept out and down the cliffside, probably by that one first giant wave that nearly flooded them out.

"O.K., so what do we do now?" Kill asked impatiently.

"Wait," said Kevin. "We stay right here and wait. . . ."

"And among the priceless little gems I turned up with my invaluable monitoring system," said Eva Cassel, "was Terence P. Thompson's wife. . . ."

"My God, how fantastic!" exclaimed Nancy Gilmore. "You get to the source of everything!"

"I try to explore all possibilities," Eva said complacently, and allowed Nancy to fondle her again in the darkness of Nancy's Nassau bedroom.

Eva had said her good-bys to Mrs. Tuttle and the Bimini gang at the airport and hired a taxi to bring her into town to Nancy's place. With Nancy she knew she always had a refuge or even a permanent home, if she so desired. Nancy was ten years older, entirely interested in women, a former nursing colleague who'd come into an inheritance and set herself up in a small Nassau boutique. Nancy was inordinately fond of Eva, willing to accept all favors when Eva was in a generous mood. But Nancy had reservations about Eva's character and had never felt that Eva's genuine talent for inducing the hypnotic state in patients was properly used. A perverse, murky streak in Eva's nature had restrained Nancy, lonely as she sometimes was, from insisting that Eva settle down with her, share her life, although she always found Eva exciting, full of surprises, an original. It was more a matter of tolerance for Eva than deep affection, Nancy thought now, as the two of them lay entwined naked in Nancy's huge bed with the frilly canopy. Nancy wasn't even too pleased that Eva was grounded here indefinitely by the approaching hurricane, for she had arrived in a bitchy, agitated mood, unusual for her, and no telling what she might be up to this time.

"Marilyn Thompson's her name," Nancy said. "But didn't she disappear a year or so ago?"

"With money that isn't difficult," Eva replied. "I'd always wondered why such a rich young woman would marry *him*."

"And did you find out?"

"Enough. It seems she didn't know any better, being utterly unsophisticated. Her mother'd kept her cloistered, considered her too good for the eligible suitors. Well, she happened to meet Thompson absolutely by accident one weekend on the Pebble Beach Golf Course—early, when they were the only ones teeing off. Her mother was asleep in the hotel. Little did she know! Anyway, the attraction was instantaneous. Thompson had flown up from his Big Sur ranch to play; his own nine-hole affair was being installed. I guess Thompson was the daddy-o she'd always wanted—and she was his daughter image. Anyway, the magnetism was there; they started seeing each other."

"And sex wasn't important?" asked Nancy.

"Oh yes! He taught her a lot of naughty games right off, then married her and locked her away from everything she'd ever hoped to enjoy in a marriage. So finally she ran away. She's been living around the country incognito ever since, moving here and there at will, gaining weight and losing it. She's a screwed-up woman, but I did my best for her, trying to set her up with Dr. Mack."

"Your medical director? But she's still married."

"Ho, ho!" Eva chuckled. "I've never had a taste for men like Thompson; they're selfish, ego-bound brutes. And she's too sweet a thing to spend her life running from that ogre. Ruth Severn *thinks* she likes Mack, but she won't push anything, she's so nauseatingly self-sacrificing. And besides, I liked Ruth myself: I wanted a little response from her. And the relationship with Kevin was simply an obstacle."

Nancy had never heard Eva talk this boldly before, and for the first time she began to feel a slight revulsion toward Eva, even doubts about allowing her to make a visit and what they were doing in bed together. "You're a meddler," she said to Eva sternly.

"One makes plans," said Eva slyly. "Oh, eventually I gave up on Ruth, too strait-laced and strong-willed. But it was those damned blacks who finally drove me off the island. One did, anyway."

"I can't imagine anyone ever intimidating you," said Nancy, and Eva laughed.

"Well, when someone threatens you with extinction and running's the only way to save your skin, you go."

"I guess you do," said Nancy, not wanting to hear more, sensing that this wasn't by any means the whole reason Eva was here. If you wanted to read Eva correctly, there were usually about three levels of motivation to work through. So far, Nancy had only pierced the single superficial cover. Eva had changed a lot since her last trip up, Nancy decided. High-strung, jumpy, inconsistent, almost paranoically aware of others' attitudes and movements. Nancy had no idea what caused this, but she knew it wasn't healthy. Eva had grown too thin, with dark circles beneath her eyes; she was wound up as tight as the mechanism would go. Another turn of the main spring and she'd fly apart.

"You really ought to stay away from sensitive areas," Nancy's euphemism for meddling in others' lives, "and not take dangerous chances. You push yourself too much, Eva."

Eva jumped out of bed and stood in a shaft of light that angled into the bedroom from the half-open hall door. Her small, tightly boyish figure was strangely touching, thought Nancy, as she lay and studied her; she should have been an artist's model or a dancer. What a waste of intelligence and talent. If she would just settle into something instead of forever picking up and leaving jobs because she got too involved with people in the wrong ways. There was no real warmth in Eva, all angles and intrigues. Driven, that was it.

Eva stretched, then walked over and turned on the rose-shaded boudoir lamp on Nancy's dressing table.

"Nan, dear," she said, sitting down at the table and grooming her hair with Nancy's silver-backed brush, "I never take chances, I make plans. When I called Thompson's apartment while you were showering, I talked to an aide of his. . . ."

"You didn't expect to get through to Thompson, did you?"

"I thought I might. After all, it isn't everybody who can prove where Marilyn Thompson is."

"And what do you expect to get for your trouble?"

"Why money, of course, darling. Didn't you know?"

"Another form of blackmail?" said Nancy, and Eva slammed down the brush and stared at her friend in the mirror.

"I may just go to the Aquarius Tower right now in person and demand an interview with Thompson."

Nancy sat up in bed. "You're out of your mind! You can't go traipsing around Nassau in a hurricane like this! You'll not only get soaked to the skin, but there's flying debris everywhere. You're liable to get yourself killed."

Eva swung around on the boudoir bench and faced her friend.

"Nancy, dear, you're a lovely lay, you're a sweet person, but you haven't the guts of a jellyfish. Don't you know that little Eva's indestructible? I'll take a taxi."

"You won't get one to come out here for you."

"Then I'll walk into town."

"You'll get lost, Eva."

Eva sighed. "Nancy, Nancy, you're so full of chicken soup. . . ." She walked from the dressing table to her open suitcases by the wall closet, chose a pair of lacy briefs, and climbed into them, then lifted a brassiere from an open suitcase, slipped into it, and clipped it fast.

"Since when," observed Nancy, "have you taken to wearing padded bras?"

Eva laughed. "I want to give that old bastard Thompson

his money's worth, dear. . . ." She chose a light, filmy minidress in pale lavender and began buttoning herself into it.

"Now I'm going to call a taxi, Nancy, while you dress. Then we'll have a quick drink together and I'm on my way to the Aquarius Tower. . . ." And she went out, leaving Nancy alone.

Ominous was the word for Eva, Nancy decided. The metallic smile seemed enameled in place, indicating strained self-control. Nancy knew that Eva was quite capable of anything if she set her mind to it. She recalled vividly that night fire in hospital records when they were both employed by the Pennsylvania sanitarium where they had first met. No one had ever found out how it started, but the fire smouldered so long that when it finally burst into flame it took the entire office in a short, raging inferno of noise and smoke. Nancy always suspected that Eva was responsible for the fire; she had easy access to the area. But then others did, too, of course. The fire destroyed all staff personnel records at a time when the sanitarium was reviewing qualifications and setting up a new classifications system for employees. Nancy had often wondered if perhaps something in Eva's past wasn't too clearly spelled out in her personnel record, that she was afraid that a critical review might bring it to light. Well, whatever Eva had done, her tensions were greater now, not less, and Nancy knew she was stuck with Eva for the storm's duration. Deeply annoyed with herself for allowing Eva to manipulate her this way, she admitted that she'd never been too sensible where her heart was concerned. And no matter what else Eva was, she was often sweet and desirable. There had even been a time when Nancy wanted to share her life with Eva. But no longer. . . .

"The line's dead," Eva announced, handing Nancy a drink as she walked into the living room. "Not even a buzz. Actually, Nan, I wouldn't get lost if I walked."

"I won't hear of it!"

"I know exactly how to get downtown and exactly where I am any time of the day or night."

Nancy could have voiced doubts about this statement, but she wasn't going to fight Eva; it took too much energy.

"I just don't think it's advisable to go out at this hour, Eva. If anything happened to you, there'd be no one around to help."

"Nan, I've got valuable information. I know Thompson

will pay good money to find out where his wife is. If I can only get past his damned henchmen and talk with him. And I will, once I'm in the Aquarius Tower, don't you worry."

"How can I help from worrying?" She knew Eva would go; there was no stopping her once she'd decided on something.

Eva finished her drink. "I can take care of myself. I'm going now, Nan."

"Eva, please."

"What's really the matter, dear? You think I'm afraid?"

"No, I don't think you're afraid, that's just the trouble. You've got some kind of death wish, Eva. As if you're compelled to ask for trouble, for some person or force to track you down. Everything you've been doing lately—well, it's not very appetizing. And it's dangerous besides."

"Darling, I'm not like you. I see people for what they are, and they're mostly rotten. Funny you've never learned that in all the time you've barnstormed around."

"I've learned one thing," Nancy said stoutly. "If you're good with people, they'll generally return a rough equivalent. But if you're mean, you get your share of the bad. I'm too old to involve myself uncomfortably in anything, Eva. I've got this house and my business and some good friends in Nassau. I like my life here, give or take a few hurricanes. And with Thompson coming in, things should get even better. He'll spend millions to promote new tourism. Everybody's going to benefit. Why can't you leave well enough alone? Settle down here, find a job, start a new life? You frighten me, there's too much destruction in you."

"I have the power to make things come my way," Eva declared, "and I'm not going to waste it. I'm seeing Thompson tonight if I have to climb up the side of that building, and nothing you say will make me change my mind."

"Nobody ever sees him," said Nancy.

"Believe me," Eva assured her quietly, "I will." She put on her raincoat, slipped into lightweight plastic galoshes, and picked up her alligator bag. She'd been risking it to carry the stuff out, admittedly, but that stupid Bernheim had stopped short of the real treasure, the kilo cache of snowy white powder neatly sewn into her brassiere. The precious heroin had been carried from Mexico via Nassau to Bimini, marked eventually for the States, dropped with Eva by a colleague during a recent week's stay at Bimini, and Eva was to drop it in Nassau when the time was ripe. The colleague had suspected surveillance and had gone on before Bernheim's arrival. Well, she'd made it to Nassau, and now she must deliver the shipment to the Aquarius Tower, collect her commission, then try to see Thompson. It would be impossible to pry money from Thompson, of course, but Nancy was so dumb about these things. She'd make her delivery and forget about that, too. Why be bothered about the substance and what happened to its users? Eva could easily enough rationalize the significance of smack or anything else in her life.

"Thompson will make it well worth my while. . . ." Eva embraced Nancy. "So, my dear, I'm on my way."

"Eva—"

"Darling, you're beginning to sound like a broken record. Don't worry. I'll call if I can, and don't wait up for me."

Nancy bolted the door behind her, thinking that Eva must be crazy.

Eva thought so, too, once she had walked a few yards into the storm; it was an enormous rampaging monster. But as long as she stayed in the protective barrier of buildings, she could move along reasonably well. There would be some perilous corners, about fifteen of them, and she'd have to race across them somehow, but she wasn't worried. She'd soon have her commission, and she would at least try to call Thompson. But even without any reward from Thompson, she wasn't doing so badly. She had about $30,000 put away, she could pick and choose her next job, making sure it was a long-term jackpot. And after that she'd coast. . . .

She crossed the first corner easily, leaning against the stinging gale, ducking small debris that whipped through the air, most of it too high to be dangerous. God, she thought, Nancy was such a timorous thing, she'd never come out into a storm like this. But this was actually the safest time to consummate her delivery. Nobody'd be around looking for what she carried at a time like this.

She was approaching the second open corner when a palm tree trunk sailed low overhead, snapping the high-tension power lines just above her in a brilliant, cascading shower of sparks. Trying to duck the lashing lines, she stumbled toward the protective cover of a porch, but too late. The snaking live lines caught her across the waist as she ran, wrapping themselves around her. She screamed once, her scream lost in the hurricane's roar, and that was all. Her alligator bag sailed into the storm, one of her shoes flew off as the power lines thrashed her about; her raincoat and dress were torn, and her brassiere ripped open, the white powder dissolving in the torrent of rain. But all this meant nothing to Eva Cassel, for she lay face down and stone-dead on the wet pavement, already electrocuted. . . .

Not much later Phil Bernheim was being escorted in a Land Rover across storm-ridden Nassau. The ride was by courtesy of the local constabulary to whom Phil had presented his credentials, explaining the gravity of his mission. Eva Cassel's airport cabbie, whose number Phil had taken, quite cordially offered him the address to which Eva was driven after Phil officially identified himself. The cabbie gave it with pleasure; she had neglected to tip him.

Although unfit out for man or narc in such wretched weather, Phil ventured forth despite Alice's pleas not to.

"Who wants to be a widow in Nassau?" was her reasoning, and there was some sense in it.

But a job was a job, as Phil pointed out to Alice and his constable driver, and a score was a score. His peers had already taken Eva's Aquarius Tower contact into custody, and Phil was confident that he'd find Eva Cassel at Nancy Gilmore's house, for where else would she go in such a storm? The Nassau authorities were holding a British subject, part of the ring that had lately been operating through the Bahamas, Puerto Rico, and Jamaica, and who was very free with Eva's name, among others, under pressure.

"Tonight's the night," Phil said as they scuttled across town, dry behind their storm flaps in the Land Rover. "Otherwise I can consider my ass overhauled back in Miami."

"How can you set a goal, sir?" the driver asked. "I don't understand."

"Well, we get into so much trouble over pot busts," Phil explained, "we gotta even it out with a smack drive once in a while."

"You're a strange people," said the constable, and swerved suddenly from their straight course, skidding into a side street on two wheels and narrowly missing an open storm drain.

"Jesus," Phil shouted, "what the hell was *that* for?"

"Can't go that way, sir. Power line's come down in the

road," his driver replied, and reached for the radio mike to report it.

"Yeah, that could electrocute some poor careless son of a bitch if anybody besides us is crazy enough to be out in a thing like this." Phil patted his service revolver affectionately. "Don't get impatient, honey," he said under his breath, "we'll be there in a minute."

Dan Francovich slept fitfully and had a dream about his dead wife, Marty.

Marty was all the reason he'd ever needed to live—when she was alive. Her fatal accident was an unavoidable yet utterly senseless tragedy. While on her way to meet his commuter train one afternoon, a van skidded across an icy road directly into Marty's lane of traffic. There was nowhere she could go but into it. The truck hit her head-on, and she died instantly in the crash.

The night before the accident they were talking in bed about honesty. Some of their best conversations happened in bed, Dan recalled, because everything had seemed to fit there, flesh and fantasy, and made such good sense. In this instance their talk concerned Dan's persistently obstinate refusal to take enough money from Marty's father to set himself up in a private law practice. Even though the loan would have had no interest attached to it, being "within the family," as her father phrased it.

"I'll never understand your reasons for rejecting Dad's offer," Marty told him from the depths of his embrace. "It'll give you the precious freedom you want so much."

"It goes deeper than that," Dan told her. "I just don't want to assume an obligation from someone whose motives I don't admire."

"Oh dear, we're into that again," Marty said in mock anguish, and nipped at his neck. "I admit he's pretty sneaky in business, but he isn't rotten. He doesn't gouge people, and he hasn't ruined anybody that I know of."

"That makes it even worse," Dan had replied. "He's not detectable. Like a subtle dose of poisonous effluent running into a pure stream—you drink a little, O.K., you survive. You drink a lot of it over a long period of time, and you're dead. He's a killing influence, Marty. I'd rather go about getting my practice set up in my own way, thanks just the same. . . ."

"It'll take years," Marty reminded him, pinching him on the stomach.

"Then that's the way it has to be," Dan said, and fitted

himself neatly on top of her. "Come on, love, let's think about something else for a change, something a lot nicer."

"That's all you ever think about," Marty said, "and I hope you never stop."

They were so happy, so friendly and tranquil and perfect with each other—all those sweet years they were together. And once in a while he dreamed about her, not every night any more as he had in years past, just occasionally. Like now, remembering her in one of her jubilant moods, picnicking on a hillside meadow, lying together in May flowers, heads together, eyes on the blue bowl of sky over them, soft breeze, Marty singing to the radio on the blanket, her toes against his. And then, as always, he came back and he was alone. . . .

Only tonight he was awakened several times by the wind as the night grew into early morning. He'd left his corridor door wide open, and once he thought he saw a large woman in a vivid print dress pass along the corridor, but he dismissed this as his imagination. Thompson surely wasn't entertaining any wild-haired creature like that; he must have dreamed up the harpy. Thompson wouldn't even let a female maid inside the penthouse to change linen and dust; his aides did all the menial chores.

About three o'clock in the morning, Dan got up to close the sliding-glass terrace doors he'd left slightly ajar; the storm was blowing in too strongly. Once up, he found it difficult to think about going back to sleep. In robe and slippers he wandered into the living room to get something to read. He found Thompson still hunched over the conference table, the Bahama property reports spread out on top of a pile of cartograms, obviously unable to sleep, too.

"What the hell are you doing up at this hour?" Thompson asked him.

"Brenda woke me—"

"It's pretty bad, isn't it?" Thompson grouched, rubbing a hand across the thick gray stubble on his chin. "She's driving straight across the middle chain now. I'm glad I sent the *Sarcophagus* to Corpus Christi for the overhaul." He shoved the reports aside and pointed to the master cartogram that lay on top of the map pile. "It'll smash the cays all to pieces. There won't be a goddam thing left to buy!"

"Except the bits and pieces," Francovich said, "and they'll go cheap."

Thompson had no concern for the wretched victims

stuck on those vulnerable islands, Dan noted. Some were probably drowned, most of them flooded out of their sea-level dwellings and their livelihoods. The big man was a self-centered, insensitive egomaniac where human values were involved. People were simply so many dice to be tossed on a table to serve the luck of his game, nothing more, with Thompson calling the numbers. What drove him so? Surely he'd gotten worse since Marilyn had gone.

"You're working—"

"Not really. Just reviewing some facts. I want to get this thing together while I still can," said Thompson, with a haggard, almost trapped expression in his eyes, one Francovich had never seen there before.

"You've got all the time in the world, Terry," he said, knowing this was what Thompson wanted to hear.

"Time!" Thompson snarled angrily, as though he loathed the sound of the word. "There's never enough time for anything!" And Francovich was reminded of the conversation he'd overheard on the *Sarcophagus*, wondering if Marilyn Thompson had ever received his letter.

Never enough time to change the pattern of one's life, thought Dan, to adjust to the imbalance, to right the wrongs? Is that what his boss meant, wanted? Probably he'd never find out, for he suspected he was now about as close to Thompson as he'd ever be allowed to get. A stranger in the house of the master—not an enviable position, or a warm one, or one that he could take indefinitely. He wondered what Marty would have thought of him now, how she would chide him about his vaunted honesty. As a matter of fact, just how did he rationalize working for Thompson, who made his own rules about fair play?

One of the burly aides in white ward suit entered the living room. Dan wondered if they slept in shifts.

"Mr. Ortega's arrived, sir," the aide said respectfully.

"Christ, at this hour?" Thompson said.

"He'd like to see you as soon as possible."

"Well, don't just stand there," Thompson said impatiently. "Send him in. . . ."

The aide nodded and disappeared.

"I'd better go," said Dan. Wiser to volunteer now than to be asked to later.

"No, stay, Danny. This concerns us both."

José Ortega walked in, moving easily across the long room toward them. He was smiling diffidently, an attitude that Thompson preferred to one of total self-confidence from subordinates, and Francovich was reminded of their recent conversation about spics and foreigners.

"Joe, for God's sake, I was really worried about you!" Thompson said genially, pumping Ortega's hand.

Francovich had never heard Thompson make such an affable remark to an employee and wondered cynically what ulterior design lay behind the amiability.

"We had a pretty rough voyage," Ortega admitted. "The mail boats are sturdy enough, but I wouldn't want to repeat the trip." His eyes flicked over the apparatus in the living room that was monitoring the course of Brenda. "There won't be too much left of Devil Cay by now. The storm's passing almost directly over it."

"I know, I've been studying the reports. Did you get the information we needed? Most of the data for the other areas came in yesterday. I'm putting it all together right now."

Ortega grinned at Thompson, shot an oblique glance at Francovich. "That and more," he said. "Mr. Thompson, could I see you in private for a moment? Excuse me, Mr. Francovich, it's urgent. . . ."

"Anything you have to say—" Thompson began, then changed his mind. "All right, all right. We'll go to my suite. You stay here, Danny. . . ."

Secrets upon secrets, thought Francovich, watching them go, wondering what Ortega could have learned that was of such vital importance even Thompson could read its urgency in the man's eyes.

Weary, the dream about Marty and the sunlit meadow still vivid in his mind, Francovich slumped into a deep leather chair next to the automatic coffee service and poured himself a steaming cupful. When the storm passed, he'd have to have a long, serious talk with Thompson. His life had to change drastically very soon. He had to get some meaning into it, some direction. He was drifting. Otherwise he'd be as lost and lonely as this man who held the power of a dozen regents in his hands yet was tragically incapable of enjoying any of it. . . .

"So that's about it," said José Ortega, and shut off the Sony TC-40 tape recorder on which Thompson had just heard the Bimini Springs conference tape with Marge and Harry Maple.

"You did a great job," Thompson congratulated him, "absolutely excellent. And you really think the island's worth taking over from those people?"

"Yes, if it's survived the hurricane. It's just what you're looking for—mostly flat except for some prominent rocky cliffs at one point."

"Well, let's hope there's more left to it than just the cliffs. The airstrip's what sold me on it in the first place. Very few small islands anywhere have that kind of landing facility. And the isolation's attractive, too."

Ortega agreed. "And don't forget the reservoir, although it's probably full of salt water right now. The central buildings could be turned into offices, but you'll want to build a new central complex. Once you've seen it I know you'll agree with me."

"Fine, fine," Thompson said, pleased. "I was hoping for good news. We can thank the U.S. Air Force for laying down that coral and asphalt training strip during the 1940s—before the present leaseholders made their development. All reports emphasize its value, but I wanted your judgment."

"As I said, it's in fine condition—or was. Any place else you chose, any small island, you'd have to lay your own airstrip, Mr. Thompson, and then use small prop jobs or STOLS, conventionally geared."

"My thought, too," said Thompson. "A pointless expenditure. Now keep this to yourself, Joe, but I'm thinking in terms of three or four Volpar Turboliners."

Ortega was impressed. "That's around a million and quarter U.S. dollars."

"I know, and with a seventeen-passenger coach load each. The airstrip's close to 4,000 feet long, isn't it?"

"That's right."

"Well, the Volpars will land easily on about 3,500 feet of strip; they can take off in about 3,000 feet. Or maybe I'll get some 22-seat Swearingen Metros. They're about $500,000 each, and four of them will wipe out the old-fashioned prop-job competition in the out islands. We'll bring in our aircraft as subsidiaries of my American interests, bypassing the usual red tape. Even Bahama Airways won't stand a chance."

Ortega smiled and thought, nobody does where Thompson was concerned; he did as he pleased. "Yes," he said, "Devil Cay should service your requirements perfectly."

"I'd like you to prepare me a formal report, Joe, just a few pages."

"I intended to start from my notes in the morning."

"Good! And if you have any second thoughts, I'd like to know them. Remember, the agreement's not firm unless we want it to be—that's the way we set it up. We can always cancel out if we're ultimately dissatisfied."

"I don't think you'll want to unless the storm's been pretty vicious. Heavy wave action could make a shambles of the flat parts, but that's a problem anywhere in these islands."

"Good God," Thompson said abruptly, shocked at his own negligence, "I almost forgot to ask you about the picture—"

Ortega smiled and reached for his wallet. "I was leaving that until the last." He extracted the small photo that Mrs. Tuttle had seen him studying at Bimini Springs, and handed it to Thompson. "I'm sure you'll want this back."

"Well, go on!" Thompson said impatiently.

"She's there, sir. I'm certain of it."

"You mean *now*—in this storm? Christ, Joe, you're not serious!"

Ortega was apologetic. "I had no orders to interfere with Mrs. Thompson or to identify myself to her, sir. You merely told me to report my findings to you when I returned."

"You idiot," Thompson exploded, "you should have radioed me at once!"

"Sir, when the weather became threatening, I finished taking the general pictures you wanted and cleared out. That's how I missed the plane, and I almost missed the mail boat, too."

"What you're saying is, she's still at Bimini Springs."

"Well, not necessarily, sir. She could have taken the afternoon plane without my knowledge," Ortega said, frightened now, certain that Mrs. Thompson was still on Devil Cay.

"If she took that plane, she's here in Nassau," Thompson declared, "and Christ knows where! She couldn't leave New Providence in this weather. Everything's grounded."

"You could get the passenger list from Bahama Airways when they open for business in a couple of hours, sir, and find out."

Thompson's anger broke. "You stupid son of a bitch!" he bellowed. "You could have done something for her! There's no radio contact now with any of the out islands and won't be indefinitely. God knows if there are even any of them left."

"I'm very sorry, Mr. Thompson, but I was following your explicit instructions." Ortega was tempted to add that a Thompson employee's creative interpretation of the big man's orders was never tolerated.

"You're *sorry*!" Thompson barked. "Is that all you can say? You're finished, you dumb spic! *Finished,* do you hear me?"

José Ortega rose slowly to his feet. "I don't have to take that kind of abuse from you or anybody, sir," he murmured with quiet dignity.

Thompson stepped forward and delivered him a stinging, open-handed blow across the face, then turned and strode from the room.

The photo lay on the floor where Thompson had dropped it. Marilyn Thompson was quite a pretty woman in the picture, though fleshy; but José Ortega didn't envy her, didn't blame her for running, not one bit.

He pressed his palm to his smarting cheek; Thompson had connected hard. For his age, Ortega thought, the old bastard packs a mean wallop. Obviously Thompson's rage only concerned his personal pride. He hadn't even asked how Mrs. Thompson looked, how she was or what name she was using. A corny name too—Cindy Brown.

Ortega picked up his suitcase, heading for his room on a lower floor of the Aquarius Tower. By noon Thompson would probably have someone on the phone to him, apologizing, telling him to forget the incident. Ortega needed the job; he'd like to forget it. But he also had to deal with his own pride. And maybe it was about time he did something constructive instead of being leg man for a hard-nosed white-racist tycoon who called men spics, who had almost everything else in the world except compassionate self-control, the most valuable asset of all.

When Kevin considered it safe to emerge from the cave, dawn had come. In the previous hour the wind had died down considerably; the waves that still smashed against the cliff were spacing themselves farther and farther apart, definitely diminished in strength.

Kevin took Kill with him to reconnoiter. Emerging into the gray blustery morning, the view below took their breath away. An incredible chaos of devastation had transformed the idyllic green island into a mashed and pounded piece of garbage.

The boathouse and pier were gone—the launch, too, of course, plucked by the waves and sent spinning out into the Atlantic. All outlying wooden structures had disappeared. The bright graceful gardens that had been Linc

Bailey's pride and joy, and the greenhouse, were nowhere in sight, wiped out as efficiently as though the blade of a giant bulldozer had scraped them from the rocky isle.

Built of steel, concrete, and tile, the main lodge was at least intact, but had sustained heavy damage. The roof of one wing was stripped off. Myriad windows were punched out, heavy doors unhinged, ripped away. A brutally twisted palm trunk had fallen across and bisected the male supervisors' quarters, and the Baileys' cottage was gone. Only the substantial steel and concrete block generator house and its radio shack annex with the sealed equipment looked relatively untouched down on the flats. Kill noted this with some relief, for in the locked generator house was the watertight fuel drum with his and Linc's entire stash of several key-bricks of homegrown bush.

"Man, I can't believe it!" Kill said. "Been on a troop transport in a typhoon, but nothing like this land thing."

"It's frightening," Kevin agreed. "Maybe it's a blessing the Maples aren't alive to see all their hard work wiped out. They couldn't take it."

Kill grunted. Fuck the Maples, he could feel no sympathy for them; they got it right. "Aerial's gone, but the radio shack looks O.K. from here. That's mighty tight-sealed equipment. If I can get that auxiliary power supply to working, maybe we can contact Nassau."

"That's great. I didn't know you could handle radio equipment, Kill."

"I was once in the Signal Corps, way back. Manually dextrous, that's me, Doc. All I know is just what any handyman ought to. Well, I'm on my way...." He grinned at Kevin and moved off down the littered slope toward the generator and radio shack, whistling, as Linc Bailey emerged from the cave.

"*Hurracan,*" Linc muttered darkly, "I'm going on down, Doc. . . ." And he hurried to catch up with Kill.

Cindy, Ruth, and Joan appeared, and together all three women, awed, stared silently at the savage devastation stretching across the island, as Kevin returned to the cave.

"Total war," said Joan.

"Like the final bomb struck," Cindy agreed.

Yet even in total war a few unlikely objects would remain curiously unscathed, thought Ruth, whereas Brenda had trashed everything in her path. The reconstruction would be expensive, possibly prohibitive in price. Except for the airstrip, which, apart from scattered debris, appeared to be intact. The waves had merely rushed across its flat surface and gone on.

"As a child in Andros," said Joan, "they used to tell us a hurricane could've always been worse, could've taken your fingerprints with it. And if your house blew away, then you said a prayer and started building a new one. Bahamian urban renewal. Well, I'm going to check below with Kill," Joan told them, and took off.

"We should all be grateful that we're alive," said Ruth.

"I know I am," Cindy replied.

Ruth turned to her, unsmiling but pleasant. "It won't be long now, dear. Be patient. . . ."

Cindy glanced at her sharply. "You're angry—"

"Not angry," said Ruth honestly. "Confused maybe, and thinking that all things eventually pass. Even hurricanes. No, I'm very much my own woman, Cindy. Psychiatrists call it being well-armored. The new thought puts it down, but it's a good way to be; you learn to adjust to the disappointments. Now, how about helping me collect that medical gear inside and getting our refugees moving?"

Cindy knew then what she must do. "Anything to help," she said quietly. With the passing of the storm she had regained her sanity, she could focus once again on the past, as well as the present. The future was something else, of course.

"You're a good person, Ruth," she said warmly. "You're compassionate and mature."

"That's not always the best way to be," Ruth replied. "It takes too much out of you. Being realistic and seeing clearly, you don't miss much, but it's a lot more painful than just having a good time. Come, Cindy, let's get a move on. . . ."

In the relatively windless protection of the radio shack, Kill gave one last twist to his hastily improvised joint, a scooped-out, tailormade filtertip packed with fine sticky bush from the fuel-drum supply. Undamaged by the storm, the bush was as fine as the day he and Linc had stashed it lovingly away. Moments earlier he'd rolled the first joint for Linc, who was now off poking through the shambles of his greenhouse, poor cat. Only he and Joan shared the shack.

Kill struck a match, flamed the joint, and inhaled deeply, then passed it to Joan, who turned away from it in ill-concealed disgust.

"What's the matter with you?" Kill said.

"You don't think of nothin' but *that,* man!" Joan exploded. "You're crazy!"

Kill exhaled and chuckled noisily, inhaled again, held it and talked over his toke. "Oh, I can think of one or two other things. Mainly like enjoying myself."

"You could try getting through to Nassau for us," Joan said icily, "and tell them we're still alive out here. That's *important*!"

"You a real nervous woman, baby. Why'n't you cool it?"

Joan's black eyes flashed; she balled her fists on her hips and aimed her chin at him.

"Cool it, cool it!" she barked. "You always wanting me to cool it! Never get involved, always be patient, lie down, let people kick me, use me any way they want, shit on me!"

"Hey, now," Kill protested, exhaling.

"Not since I come to know you have I seen one time when you'd stand up to something."

Kill took another long toke and began to fiddle with the radio; it had survived beautifully in its heavy watertight steel case sealed into layers of thick plastic. Maybe he could get it operational after all. Better to try that than talk to this hysterical woman; he'd never know what she wanted.

"Baby," he said quietly, "I ain't *bad*."

"No, I guess you ain't. And stop callin' me 'baby'! I ain't your baby or nobody else's, either. I'm *me,* Joan Harrison, me, myself, and that's the way I stay. We ain't never gonna see eye to eye, Kill. Never!"

"Why is that?"

"Forget what I said up there in the cave last night about Andros and us tryin' to make a life there. We ain't for each other, Kilroy Howard, and never was."

"Go ahead, tell me more. You got my ear."

"I want to see some real changes in my world, all kind of improvements that mean growth and progress toward a better future. That bush ain't the answer, or anything stronger."

"Who said about anything stronger?"

"I know all about what bush leads to. My brother went to smack. And it took him. So I can't help fightin' back." It was on her lips to tell him everything, how she'd been recruited to inform but had instead protected him. But her actions had been so illogical, so disloyal on both sides, how could she? He would loathe her.

Kill put down his half-smoked joint. No use going on with it; she'd ruined his high. He thought he saw where she was heading, and she was right; it would never, never work between them. "You fight too hard," he said.

"I got to, to make things better."

"Better world," Kill scoffed. "That's real rich, when everything's fallin' apart all around you! What you expect to gain by puttin' yourself on the line?"

"I don't know," Joan replied honestly, thinking of the negative reports she'd consistently turned in to Bernheim.

Kill had a flash that she was concealing something he didn't want to hear defined in words, that she knew a lot more about the island's surveillance than she had told him.

"I think I can guess why you took my stash and moved it when you did," he said.

"Don't guess, Kill. I thought maybe I could protect you," Joan admitted, close to tears. "Change you, maybe."

"Change *me*?"

"You don't want anything that makes you *work*! You want it all hangin' from trees so's you can reach right out and pick yourself a pleasure."

"That's right," Kill said, regarding her coldly, wondering how he'd ever even tried to make things work with her. "This is my world, the way I am. I want to be left to it. And you can't get that through your thick black head, can you, girl? You got to have big principles, open yourself up so life can barrel-ass down on you, use you and destroy you. Well, that ain't gonna be my way. You got plenty of learnin', but you ain't got good sense. You're foolish. . . ."

Joan thought of her ugly commitment to the Nassau organization that was connected to the Miami organization, of her regular reports on the Maple spread, her vulnerability because of her kid brother. Then Phil Bernheim had come to the island and she'd found that she couldn't set up Kill and Linc for a bust; it wasn't in her. She'd lied to Bernheim to protect Kill, but she had also lied to Kill. And now she hated herself for the whole nasty business, and Kill was beginning to distrust her; he'd already guessed at her involvement.

"I believe," she said firmly, "in myself. And I want to live so's when I die I won't have any regrets."

"That's where we're different. I got no regrets now and never did. And it all comes to the same thing in the end, woman. We die."

"I'm walkin' right out that door now, Kill. It's the end for us, you hear me?"

"Maybe there never was a beginnin'—"

"I don't know nothin' about all that bush, or nothin' about *you*. You go your way, I go mine."

Kill grinned tolerantly at her. "Fine. Always did aim to go my own way, baby. Thought you knew that."

"I know it now," Joan said bitterly, tears on her cheeks, and stalked out of the shack.

So who's the weak one, Kill speculated, and shook his head sadly over the radio console. Just go ahead and try to tune in Nassau, he ordered himself. Mighty sweet bush in Nassau, or anywhere in the world. Reach right out and pluck it, it's growin' on every tree. . . . He wasn't going to worry about anything, either living or dying. Joan Harrison was really a great, good, and confused woman, but not his kind. Never again was he going to lift his hand or voice in protest; there were so many other safer, easier ways to hack it. Slide along, man, coast, space out the future and enjoy, *enjoy*. Love was being left alone to live as you wished with no regrets or commitments. And that was going to be his life from now on, for always. . . .

Even before Brenda began to change course, moving off to the north to spend herself in the Atlantic, Thompson was making arrangements from the Aquarius Tower for a special charter plane to pick up all storm refugees from Devil Cay and bring them to Nassau. His reconnaissance had already advised him that the airstrip at Bimini was being cleared of debris by several survivors and was otherwise in good enough condition to land. Food, clothing, and medical supplies had been dropped; radio contact would soon be re-established.

Francovich sat with Thompson in the penthouse living room as Thompson laid out future plans for the Bahamas.

"When the *Sarcophagus* comes back from Corpus Christi," Thompson said, "we'll take it out and see exactly what's left of the islands. We'll make an on-the-spot evaluation."

The storm had given Francovich all the time he needed in which to formulate his decision. He must make his declaration now, and it wasn't going to be easy.

"Terry," he began tentatively, "I'll go on the survey, but that's the last trip I'll make with you."

"What's that?"

"My final duty, Terry. Then I'm cutting out on my own. I have to, if I'm to survive."

Thompson stared at him in shocked disbelief. "Aw, come on, Danny."

"No, Terry, it's true. And no hard feelings. I must leave, that's all. I'll finish my work on the Bahama projects, I'll see everything through, then I'm leaving."

"But why!" demanded Thompson, banging his fist on the conference table. "Haven't I treated you fair and square?"

"Of course you have, Terry," Francovich declared, "but I've been doing a lot of soul-searching lately. What happened to Hank Alexander is never going to happen to me."

"Jesus Christ, how could it? You're genuine. Alexander was a phony prick."

"He didn't start out that way, or you wouldn't have hired him. I'm afraid if I stick around too long, Terry, I'll end up like him. Not a carbon copy, but *changed.* I don't want to take that chance. Frankly, it's too shattering a concept."

Thompson sighed deeply, his expression morose. "You've decided that power corrupts."

"In a way."

"Dammit it to hell," Thompson growled, "I'm no chicken. I don't adjust to people easily anymore, Danny, and I hate to lose a valuable man like you. They're practically extinct as a species."

"We're hanging on trees, Terry. I'm no prize."

"You are, Danny, you're pure gold. I'm at ease with you, we have fun together."

I am a court jester, thought Francovich, a judicial juggler, but remained silent.

"Those jokers, the three monkeys—Winchester, Moore, and Rose—they're vaudeville stooges compared to you. And my other aides are all creeps, zombies, ciphers that do my bidding. Dammit, don't you realize that you're the only real flesh-and-blood man with any guts on my whole staff? You have depth and dimension, Danny boy, and what's more, you won't even let *me* bulldoze you. I admire that kind of character."

Never during their brief relationship had Thompson ever been this persuasively personal with him. Dan had received compliments on the quality of his work, but that was to be expected when a job was well done. He suspected Thompson now of conscious flattery, intentional exhortation.

"But don't you see," he pointed out, "if I hung around indefinitely, I'd eventually become a clayfoot and finally worthless? You know that, Terry, as well as I do. You build people up, you inflate them for your own private reasons, drain them, and then discard them. A few fight back dirty, like Hank Alexander, in the way you've taught them, fire with fire. I could just as easily be another loser, Terry, and it wouldn't take years."

"I don't see any chance of that myself," said Thompson stubbornly, "but I can't hold you with threats, Danny boy, only with promises. And maybe they aren't all that attractive to you. Maybe you're not challenged enough to appreciate them. So, what'll you do if you go?"

"Well, I've always wanted to live somewhere in the Northwest," Francovich said, "around Puget Sound. I like the green and cold and rain, things like that. I might try it up there for a while, live on my savings, see how things go. Maybe buy a farm, teach somewhere, I'm not sure yet. And if I'm pushed, then maybe a private law practice."

"That could be a mistake," Thompson pointed out gently. "You could discover that you're not built for that kind of life anymore. Then what?"

"I'll work it out. The only mistake would be to overstay my welcome in your outfit. That would be suicide."

Thompson got up and strode over to the glass wall and stared down at Nassau and Paradise Island across the harbor.

"I'm always trying to build empires," he said, his back to Francovich, "and nothing I've ever done has satisfied me. I always go too far. I expect too much from projects and people. And now maybe it's too late to hope for perfection."

He turned toward Francovich, his expression enigmatic. "Danny boy, I have to hand it to you. You're going to do what you have to do, and to hell with everybody. Even T. P. Thompson can't stop you. Well, I admire you for making your stand. Not many would have the guts to chuck everything for so little."

So little? Francovich grinned, for it was so like Thompson to praise him and then cancel it all out.

"That's where we're different," he told his boss. "What about you and Mrs. Thompson?" What he really meant was, the old man needed her badly now.

Thompson's face clouded. "Oh, yes—that. . . ." He shrugged his shoulders, trying to shuck an immense, invisible mantle of weariness. "Nothing, absolute zero. . . .

When Marilyn first left me, it became a point of honor to find her and bring her back. You see, Danny boy, I went about her all wrong from the beginning. I think she loved me once, I really do, or she wouldn't have married me. But I did a great job of killing it; I never gave her a chance. I tried to make her trade her world for mine; I wouldn't even listen to her signals. And yet when she took off, I was crazy mad. And I wasn't concerned with her feelings even then. What I couldn't stand was the thought of what people were saying—laughing at me, a crusty old, worn-out bastard of a billionaire who couldn't even keep a young wife happy with all the money in the world. My first marriage bombed, too, but at that time I was young and merely relieved. She was a nasty bitch. Not Marilyn. She's a good person, with perception and some talent. She always wanted to be an artist, a painter. Not a great mind, but she's loving; she wanted security from me and I never gave her any. So when I wouldn't let her do what she wanted—go to school, entertain at the ranch, travel—she picked up and ran. She's as stubborn as I am. Oh, I knew why she'd gone, but I didn't want to admit that it was mostly my fault she got fed up. She didn't even leave me a farewell note! I've tried every means to trace her, but her mother always saw to it there weren't any leads; she hates me. Marilyn's been gone for some time. And now that I know where she is, it all doesn't matter anymore, I don't even blame her for going."

"You found her?" Francovich said, surprised.

"Ortega located her. She's been taking a fat cure at that Bimini Springs place. Getting ready for something, God knows what. I got pretty sharp with Ortega for not bundling her on a plane and bringing her back. She's been there all through the hurricane."

"She'll be all right," Francovich assured him. "Maybe she'll—"

"Come back? No, she'll find somebody else, if she hasn't already. And maybe I will, too, when I get around to it. If there's still time, which is the one thing money can't buy." Thompson shook his head gloomily. "Or love," he added.

Francovich wondered if he should mention the letter he had written—now was the moment, if ever. "Terry, you've got all kinds of time. You're in good condition for a man your age. You don't abuse yourself."

"The abuse is past, all right, but so's the time. I wasn't going to tell you this, Danny boy, because I was expecting you to stick around. And this isn't a pitch to try to change your mind, but, anyway, my last medical report was not too good."

"I know," said Francovich. "I overheard that conversation you had with Dr. Becker the morning we sailed on the *Sarcophagus*."

Thompson didn't say anything for a moment, staring at him. Then he sighed and said, "So you know everything, then?"

"It's more than just knowing, Terry, I wrote a letter."

"A letter? Who to?"

"Your wife, in care of her mother. The letter you should have written."

Thompson's expression was frozen fury. "You dared to play God in my life!" he barked.

"You should have told her yourself," Francovich said calmly.

"You had no right to meddle in things that don't concern you!"

"As your representative this concerned me. It ought to concern your wife, too."

"I don't want your pity, and I don't want hers, goddamit!" Thompson shouted. "We all have to face it alone. Nobody's going to get lugubrious over me before the fact." He walked away from the window and slumped into a chair. "What's happened between me and Marilyn has nothing to do with you. Even if I've told you about it."

"That's where you're wrong, Terry, and that's one of the reasons I don't feel I should stay on with you. You build too many walls, you won't let anybody into the sacred preserves except on your terms. I respect your ability and the way you've organized your industrial talents, Terry, but you're blind as hell about some things, some very important things."

The two men were silent for some moments; only the murmuring remnants of the storm filled the room, filtered through the sealed glass walls.

Finally Thompson spoke, his tone mild, almost plaintive. "All the same, Danny, I wish you were staying."

"No, Terry, I don't think I can. If I kept on, we both know what could happen; I'd have to make choices, too, as you've done. I'd only compromise myself eventually. Maybe I'm an idealistic fool to think like this, but right now I prize my integrity more than anything else in the world. Since my wife died, this seems to be about all I have in life. It's one of the last free avenues of statement still open to a man in this universe. God knows I don't have a very clear idea of what I do want out of life, but I know for sure that it isn't a high, cold place sealed off from the rest of the world, living for myself—the kind of life that you lead, Terry, and others who've made the same choice. . . ."

Thompson's smile was thin and melancholy. "You don't give me very good odds, Danny, but you're all right, you're O.K. You really are. . . ."

"The odds aren't very good for any of us right now," Francovich replied, "but at least you've made your statement. Mine's ahead. . . ."

"I'm hungry," Thompson announced with abrupt irrelevance, and rang for an aide.

Once Kevin had cleared the cave, the refugees descended to survey storm damage and see what they could salvage from the general devastation.

Ruth and Kevin headed immediately for the clinic and treatment rooms, Cindy with them.

Ruth was well aware of Cindy's emotional tension, not precisely sure of its cause but deciding that it at least partially stemmed from Cindy's interest in Kevin, partially from the storm's terror. But whatever caused it, Ruth felt that she should diplomatically remove herself from the scene—not as a noble gesture but merely to give Cindy a chance to sort out her anxieties with Kevin if she wished to. Undefinable pressures were quite evident in Cindy's strained features.

Ruth wiped her hands on a damp clinic towel and told them briskly that she was going to look at her quarters. "I can't do anything more around here right now," she announced. "I'll be back later."

"But we haven't even begun," said Kevin.

"You and Cindy poke around. I want to check out the kitchen and see if somebody's working on a meal."

"While you're at it," said Kevin, crouched over a sodden box of medicine, "see how Kill's doing with that radio. I hope he'll get through soon."

"That's no real problem since we don't have any casualties, only missing persons. A plane ought to be dropping supplies soon, and once we've removed the airstrip debris, they'll be able to land. Small craft ought to be sailing from Nassau to the out islands tonight, I imagine, or tomorrow morning at the latest. We'll survive," Ruth declared, and left.

"She's enormously capable," Cindy declared. "I wish I could be that organized and determined. I respect inner drive and the ability to stick with something."

"A very practical, considerate woman," Kevin said, "with a nice, quiet sense of humor, and never bitchy. The perfect working colleague. I don't know anybody else with her stamina and control."

Cindy sat on a damp chair and surveyed the clinic's mess disconsolately as Kevin continued checking through the supplies. The letter from Dan Francovich lay in her pocket, a leaden weight. So far she had been unable to bring herself to discuss it with Kevin, although she knew this was inevitable.

"I'm just the opposite of necessary and practical," said Cindy, and shivered. "I'm useless, that's what I am."

Kevin glanced up sharply at her. "You're cold. I'll give you my jacket."

"No, don't," Cindy protested. "That's not it. It's something I should have told you before the storm. A letter—"

"What letter?"

"Maybe I should go back to the beginning, to a time in Pebble Beach when I met him on a raw misty morning. We were the only two people at the first green, more like the only two on earth."

"I don't follow you."

"He didn't earn it, he inherited the base of it from his father and grandfather and the thing grew like a runaway cancer. It's so vast, Kevin, so frighteningly prodigious, I don't think anyone knows exactly how much there is at any given moment. I don't think he could ever count it, and that's the way he wants it."

Kevin looked at her in exasperation. "What in the hell are you chattering about, Cindy?"

Cindy drew the much-handled letter from her pocket. "I got this the day before yesterday in the afternoon mail. It was forwarded from Beverly Hills by my mother. A man wrote it because he thought I ought to know what it contains. Read it, Kevin. It says everything better than I could."

Kevin took the letter and sat down and read it through slowly. When he finished, he looked out the window toward the radio shack, watched Joan Harrison emerge and head with long, purposeful strides toward the lodge kitchen. He said nothing for some moments, and finally when he turned and looked at Cindy, his expression was calm. She thought she read a certain relief in it.

"You should have told me right off that you were married," he pointed out. "How did you imagine we'd ever be able to work things out with a problem like this still pending?"

"I—I don't know," Cindy replied. "I guess I thought I was in love with you, that was a start—and you didn't exactly reject me."

"No, I didn't," Kevin said softly, "but that's all different now. The circumstances are changed."

"They are?"

"Yes, you're Marilyn Mix Thompson, wife of the billionaire industrialist, world benefactor, King Midas, plus all the other things people call him. And you're not plain Cindy Brown, a wealthy, troubled girl who had a brief crush on a doctor. You played with me," Kevin said bitterly, and he wasn't smiling.

Cindy hadn't expected this. "No, I didn't," she remonstrated indignantly. "I was deeply drawn to you. I don't quite know why now, but I was."

"But you were lying to me."

"Cindy Brown's a real name—it was my grandmother's."

"No, about your position."

"I'm not going back to him. We've been finished for a long time, and it wasn't my doing, either."

"You have to go back to him, it's your responsibility."

"And be a prisoner again? No thank you. He's out of my system and has been long enough for me to know we don't belong together, not on any basis."

"Look, Marilyn Thompson, don't start to rationalize your obligations. He's still your husband."

"It's only a formality if you've stopped working at it," Cindy retorted. "I wasn't lying when I said I'd put you through school, Kevin. If anybody ever needed the kind of help I can give, you do, and I can do it painlessly. I have the money. And even if we can't make it together, it's still all over with Terry. I'll have to sit down with him one day and talk the thing out—I've been putting that off too long, running from it—but it was finished between us long before you and I met. I think knowing you helped me to put the terminal seal on the project and made me realize I have to be free.

"I'm impulsive about a lot things, but I'm not as superficial or flighty as some people might think. Money gets in the way of honest judgment sometimes, Kevin, and a lot of people just won't give me an even break. But with you, it was odd, as if somebody had cast a spell over me. I felt this enormously powerful attraction for you that I can't explain. And some of it's still there, but it's different now. It's more a fondness, an affection, something I'd like to feel for Terence P. Thompson."

"Cindy, Cindy." Kevin shook his head at her. "You are a very complex creature."

"I've been wrong, but for what it's worth, there it is. Please try to understand. Since I left Terry, you've been my one indulgence. And I'm deeply grateful for the experience."

"Running from Thompson, not your weight?"

"I came down here to get enough courage to come out of hiding and ask him outright for the divorce. Now there's this medical complication."

"SLE. . . . Cryptogenic cirrhosis of the liver. As the letter explains, it's eventually terminal. He could die in the next few months or live another twenty years. Your friend Francovich got the information together right."

"I don't know Francovich," said Cindy. "He's become Terry's newest personal aide since I left."

"I admire him for having the courage to write and tell you about systemic lupus erythematosus."

"It sounds pretty horrible."

"It's easier to live with than some forms of cancer."

"Poor Terry," Cindy murmured, close to tears.

"Cindy," Kevin said sharply, "you've got to decide what you're going to do. You have obligations."

"I'm aware of them," Cindy replied evenly. "Poppy wanted children, and my argument was that he was too old to enjoy them. He thought with a couple of children I'd be too absorbed to wander off to other interests. Oh, I wish I could wipe out the past in one fast stroke and start all over again."

"You can't, and that's the reason you've been running."

"It's idiotic, isn't it, how we try to make things fit when they don't—or can't? Like coming here to lose weight, hoping to shed the guilt, too. Well, a restructured life might not include Terry, but I know one thing, if he wants me back he's got to take care of you!"

"Of me?"

"Yes, provide a base for your continuing education, and later on maybe a research seat for you when you're ready to take it on. With no strings attached."

"I'll get along. Don't worry about me."

"I intend to," Cindy told him. "It's the least I can do

for you. You really ought to be with Ruth. I've come between you."

"No, Cindy, it's not that cut and dried."

"I wonder if I'll ever grow up and get over my self-preoccupation? You know, when it gets to you what a fool you've been most of your life, and how out of joint with yourself, rationalizing your actions to suit the indulgences, you get a damned big jolt. That letter threw me quite a responsibility, and it's obvious now that I've got to do something about it. Well, if Terry and I ever work things out, we can always adopt a family. Or better still, provide the basics for raising a few thousand children across the world. If there's any justification for his money—mine, too—it's using it wisely for others' welfare."

Kevin nodded gravely. "An altruism that might help to bring the times into focus for both of you."

"You're really a very decent person, Kevin. A bit stiff and noble, but there's nothing wrong with that. It's as rare as it is refreshing. If there were more people like you—"

"Or like you," Kevin said, and kissed her gently, knowing that she would do the requisite, make the gesture of seeing Thompson again, now that she was in the grip of ascending emotions.

"No!" she cried shrilly, breaking away and running out of the building, forgetting the letter in her haste and leaving Kevin to think what a pompous creature he sometimes was—Ruth was right—and why he couldn't graciously accept the golden egg at the rainbow's end when it was literally handed to him. And the fact also remained that he did love Cindy; they could have worked out something. The letter hadn't made any difference about that; it had only determined him to send her away because that was the way it had to be.

On her return to Kevin's office after what she considered a decent interval of absence, Ruth saw Cindy Brown running up toward the lip of the rocky cliff in the general direction of the caves. Something in Cindy's distraught manner alerted her, and for a second Ruth was tempted to go after her, thinking she might be in a self-destructive mood. But Ruth decided that she was merely projecting her personal attitudes into a situation that involved only Kevin and Cindy and excluded her.

Or did it? So many odd things had been going on around Bimini Springs for so long that nothing could be judged in a normal frame of reference. For instance, her unaccountable attraction to Eva Cassel, who wasn't her idea of woman of the year, and her docile surrender to Kevin's interest in Cindy. Was her relief genuine? She guessed it was. Kevin's behavior had surprised her, but it had also taught her something. She knew pretty well what was in her own mind now and that she was going to have to plan her life so that work was prime and all else was secondary. She could do it, she had the discipline. Oh, not that work was all she wanted from life, but who gets much more, she thought. If it came, it came. . . . She wouldn't sweat it.

A few minutes later she walked into the gutted office and found Kevin brooding over a broken autoclave.

"What's wrong with Cindy?" Ruth asked. "I saw her dashing up toward the caves."

"You're not going to believe this," Kevin replied, "but we were playing truth games, and Cindy Brown turns out to be none other than Marilyn Mix Thompson, missing wife of T. P. Thompson."

"Terence Thompson, the billionaire?"

"The same."

"My God!" Ruth plunked herself on the edge of a desk. "Come to think of it, she always did seem a little too special—or is the word *privileged*?—to be plain ordinary little Cindy Brown, chubby secretary."

"How about that?" Kevin forced a smile. "And when the whole story came out, I had to tie up the package and hand it to her." He told Ruth about Thompson's illness. "Marital loyalty, all that stuff."

"Well, well, a real soap opera!" Ruth exclaimed.

"And I sounded like a prig, I guess, but there wasn't much else I could do."

"Being Kevin Mack, no. Sounds like the plot to some creaky old Viennese operetta."

"It's depressingly lifelike," Kevin replied, "because it's inconsistent and illogical. She'll have to work something out with him, but that's her problem. . . . How do you feel about things, Ruthie?"

Ruth stared at him long and hard for a moment, thoughtfully, her lips pursed.

"I think I'll just let that one lie," she said at last. "At least for the time being. Kill's got the radio crackling away. He ought to be making contact with Nassau any time now. He's quite a fixer."

"And I'm a bungler. . . . Well, we'll be in touch with the outer world again. I guess Cindy—or Marilyn—will want to talk with Nassau right away. Thompson should be there, or he was before Brenda hit."

"Brenda did a great little promotional job all around, didn't she?"

"I'm afraid she did," Kevin responded with a sigh, understanding her inference. "By the way, our Mrs. Thompson wants to get the old man to set up a fellowship for me."

"You'd take it?"

Kevin shrugged. "Why not? I know where I've got to be, Ruthie. Making myself useful wherever I'm needed."

"Well, that makes good sense. With the Maples gone, this place is already finished. I'm going to start thinking about Africa."

"Couldn't we think about ourselves, working and being together somewhere?"

"Oh come on, Kevin! I'm not the same person you met in Saigon. I've been through some drastic changes since then. I guess I've got Eva Cassel to thank for a few. She at least made me aware of my potential."

"Oh, but you—" Kevin said, and stopped, not knowing how to complete the thought.

"I've a new perspective on you, too, Kev. You and I couldn't make it together under any conditions, not on the Saigon premise. Allowing for our hang-ups, however, we stand a good chance of becoming complete individuals. *If* we learn to settle for what's there and not live in our fantasies. I'm trying. Maybe you will, too."

"I was thinking along similar lines when you walked in the door," Kevin said. Whatever they might come to mean to each other, they at least now had the basis for a solid, dynamic friendship, one that could endure a lifetime.

Ruth studied him carefully, thinking that he was really a nice, well-meaning soul, a bit unimaginative but good-hearted, and a warm smile spread slowly across her round, pleasant face.

"You know, I think you actually mean that," she said, "Now, let's get busy and start tidying up around here. There's plenty of work to do."

"We've been thinking it over, and we've come to the conclusion it was Eva Cassel who caused it all," a voice said behind them.

"Except for Brenda," another voice added.

Ruth and Kevin whirled toward the open door of the office, unable to believe their ears. In the doorway stood Marge and Harry Maple, groomed, complacent, radiating their familiar and suspect professional geniality. As if the storm had never happened, as if Kevin hadn't seen Marge disappear after Harry into that giant wave.

"We *know* that's who it was," Marge insisted, talking in her usual italics. "We've been piecing it together ever since we *found* each other again."

"Good God!" Kevin exclaimed. "We thought you were both dead!"

"You were supposed to be," Ruth said, stunned.

"Now, now, Ruthie." Harry's smile was wide and indulgent. "Is that a nice thing to say about your employers?"

"Former employers," said Marge. "We don't have a window to throw it out of, only a shambles."

"But we've got a buyer for the basic plant," Harry reminded her, "even if he's changed his mind by now." Harry turned to Kevin. "That's Terence P. Thompson, as you've probably heard."

"I've heard too much about him already," Kevin replied.

"Well, we signed the papers with that Mexican who was here before Brenda. He works for Thompson."

"We're not interested in Thompson," Ruth said, and was almost tempted to tell the Maples about Marilyn.

Harry laughed. "Hey, that goes for us, too. And maybe not even this place. It could blow away again next week. Storm season's just beginning."

"Next time it might take *us* along," Marge declared.

"How did you both manage to survive those waves?" Kevin said.

"For me it was easy," Harry explained with the complacence born of success. "I just coasted downhill on a big one, skidded right along on my ass. Washed me plumb up to the main building. And before the next one came along I had plenty of time to scramble through our apartment and up that flight of stairs to the cupola loft where we store our old records. That's a sturdy tower."

"We built it with emergencies like Brenda in mind," said Marge. "About the same thing happened to me. When I got crazy with grief, thinking Harry was gone, I just took off. I ended up half-drowned by the swimming pool."

Harry slipped his arm around Marge and squeezed her affectionately; she looked up into his eyes, totally adoring.

"Honey," he purred, "you don't let go of me easy, do you? Not even thirty feet above the pool, in our loft, with the sound of waves stroking away." He sighed, wet his lips. "Why, that storm didn't even matter. . . . So, how's everybody else who stayed on?"

"Fine, just fine," said Kevin. "A little damp, but O.K. Kill Howard's at the radio shack trying to activate the equipment."

"Hmphf!" said Marge. "He's *always* fooling around with something!"

"You know, Howard and Joan are two mighty fine folks," Harry said magnanimously. "Valuable assets to our operation."

"Maybe they'll stay on," Ruth suggested, poker-faced.

"What's to stay for?" Marge said plaintively, and without warning dissolved into tears against Harry's shoulder.

Harry tried soothing her with a hug. "Now, now, honeysuckle, we always find a way out."

"But it's most all washed away!" Marge bawled, seemingly inconsolable.

"You'll start somewhere else," said Kevin. "You've both got long lifelines."

"With the money we'll get from Bimini Springs," Harry told him. "Thompson made us an agreement for the basic property, and that's what he's gonna get if we have to spend the rest of our lives suin' him for it."

"Right, Harry," Marge agreed. "But there'll never be another fat farm like this one."

"Never," said Harry. "It's the passing of an era."

Ruth and Kevin acknowledged this parcel of wisdom with a grave silence, for there certainly wouldn't be another. How could anyone ever put it together the same way twice?

"You've got to stay with me now, Danny boy," Thompson told Francovich after a two-way radio conversation with his wife Marilyn from the Aquarius Tower penthouse. "The plane picks her up in a couple of hours. She'll be here by evening."

"You won't need me anymore, Terry, not since Mrs. Thompson's agreed to come back."

"Ha! You don't know Marilyn. She only agreed to the initial meeting because you're here. She says none of it would have happened if it weren't for your letter."

"I wasn't trying to play God," Francovich said, annoyed at being placed in a position he found uncomfortable. "It's much wiser if I pack up and go."

"You haven't finished the Bahama property papers yet."

"There's nothing special about them that Ortega and the others can't handle."

"Don't you want to be in on the kill?" Thompson asked and grinned mischievously.

"The kill? What're you talking about?"

"The moment when we give those Bimini Springs people their due. The Maples—you haven't forgotten who they are?"

"I remember them, all right, and you've got a written agreement with them. It was legally witnessed by Ortega who's a notary public, among other things. What're you driving at?"

"A written agreement I mean to break," said Thompson. "I'm not giving those crooks anything for that pile of debris. I'll find another location for my headquarters, and it may not even be in the Bahamas."

"You have a commitment, Terry," Francovich reiterated. "If you don't want to make Devil Cay your personal headquarters, it could still be used as a central air station for your proposed Caribbean Airlines system. By leveling what's left of the lodge area you could add another two thousand feet to the present airstrip, then build hurricane hangars and make other requisite supportive improvements. Or maybe you'd like to do what you've talked about doing for a long time?"

"What's that?"

"Develop your own private weather-forecasting station on Devil Cay and function in the South Atlantic like Grand Cayman does in the Caribbean. Give the U.S. Weather Bureau a little healthy competition besides performing a vital new service."

Thompson shook his head in admiration. "Boy, you beat everything! Those crooks nearly did you in once, and now you go all out to protect their interests!"

"Is that what I'm doing? I thought it was simple honesty, Terry. Or isn't that the best policy, not being the most lucrative?"

Thompson's first reaction was indignation, but he reined it in. Whatever he might feel toward Dan Francovich, he had no right to express it in anger, not at this time. Nothing he himself had done to try to lure Marilyn back had had the effect of Dan's simple letter, written over and beyond the call of his responsibilities, of course, but also in full consciousness that he might easily lose his job for his pains. This was the kind of a man he couldn't afford to lose; he'd be a fool to alienate Dan because of his usual bullish temper. After all, what was a quarter of a million dollars, the initial sum involved in the Bimini Springs deal? Franchovich had already proven himself worth much, much more, and if Dan were to remain in the industrial family, what was one quixotic gesture more or less?

"O.K., O.K., Danny boy, you win! I'll honor the Maple agreement just to please you."

"No, it's not to please me, Terry. I thoroughly detest them. It's for you. Let's start to weigh the scales on the other side for a change. Remember, you were the one who was talking about time."

"Against my better judgment, goddamit!" he growled. "Then you'll stay?"

"Against whatever. Yes, I'll stay for a while. And by the way, isn't it about time you stopped calling me 'boy'? I think I've outgrown the title by now."

Thompson felt he had won; he could afford to be magnanimous.

"You're right," he agreed affably, enjoying his own unctuousness. "Marilyn will think it mighty funny if I'm treating you like a kid, although I've sure treated her like one sometimes."

"Mrs. Thompson may think a lot of the things that go on around here are pretty funny," said Francovich wryly. "Now, let's talk about a welcome-home party. I've got a few ideas that might please your wife."

"Goddam, you ought to get married again," Thompson said. "You'd make a damned good husband and father."

Dan smiled thinly at the big man and said, "First things first, Terry. Got to get you straightened out before we start thinking about me. And that's going to take a lot of doing."

Thompson clapped him on the shoulder. "I won't say you aren't difficult sometimes, Danny, but I like you. Yessir, I couldn't like you much better if you were my own son."

"All I'm trying to be is your own conscience," said Francovich. "And that's as good a place to start as any."